Copyright

All ri

The characters and events portrayed in... ...ny similarity to real persons, living or dead, is coincidental and not intended by the author.

Cover photo by: Alina Cardiae

THE GLOUCESTER BOYS

by

Pete Nice

Contents

PROLOGUE THE PRIVATE MEMBERS CLUB
CHAPTER 1 CYCLE OF ABUSE
CHAPTER 2 THE OFFICE OF RECORDS
CHAPTER 3 FRIENDS WITH BENEFITS
CHAPTER 4 PREPARATION
CHAPTER 5 THE STEPFATHER
CHAPTER 6 THE GODFATHER
CHAPTER 7 EDUCATING RITA
CHAPTER 8 TOP BOYS
CHAPTER 9 THE SCHOOL ASSEMBLY
CHAPTER 10 SARAH'S SECRET
CHAPTER 11 LANDS OF HOPE AND GLORY
CHAPTER 12 EVERYBODY LOVES RAYMOND
CHAPTER 13 STEPPERS
CHAPTER 14 TROJAN HORSE
CHAPTER 15 TARGET PRACTICE
CHAPTER 16 WHITE HORSES
CHAPTER 17 THE GREENWICH PENNINSULAR
CHAPTER 18 SEND FOR THE ZULUS
CHAPTER 19 PUBLIC DISORDER
CHAPTER 20 MISSING PERSONS
CHAPTER 21 PROTECT THE MONARCHY
CHAPTER 22 RATED EIGHTEEN
CHAPTER 23 RISKY BUSINESS
CHAPTER 24 GREEN LANES
CHAPTER 25 WHITEHORSE REUNION
CHAPTER 26 POLLARDS HILL
CHAPTER 27 THE NEWPORT ALLIANCE
CHAPTER 28 TEMPLE'S TEMPTATION
CHAPTER 29 TOTAL ECLIPSE OF THE HEART
CHAPTER 30 A GAME OF MONOPOLY
CHAPTER 31 THE ROYAL GARDEN
CHAPTER 32 THE SOCIAL GATHERING

CHAPTER 33 STIFF LITTLE FINGERS
CHAPTER 34 FOR AULD LANG SYNE
CHAPTER 35 GOLDERS GREEN AND GLOUCESTER
CHAPTER 36 JULIET CHARLIE FOXTROT ROMEO
CHAPTER 37 NOMURA INTERNATIONAL
CHAPTER 38 THE VANITY
CHAPTER 39 PENTHOUSE PASSION
CHAPTER 40 THE MORNING AFTER
CHAPTER 41 THE HANGOVER
CHAPTER 42 THE BILL HAVE EYES
CHAPTER 43 RED ALERT
CHAPTER 44 WHAT HEART'S DESIRE
EPILOGUE

Acknowledgements

Georgia Verapen, Stella Hall, Sharon Betts, Tina Gray. Sharon Cronk-jell, Kellianne Hogg, Ashley Spence. Ade Adeniyi, Rudi Arts, Jenny Temple. Barley Jarman Gillam Terry 'The Face' Ellis. Sharon Payne, Kelly Rose. Nikki Marie 'Bowlsey' Bowles. Tania Mothersole. Susie Akehurst, Raquel Van- der-Voort, Paul Caslaw. Lisa Wisby, Marcia Watson, Donna Charrett, Michelle Andrews. Julie Richards. Julie Pietrasik, Lady Eve. Carl MC Flux Thomas, Nikki Lambert, Mary Joseph, Terrasa Dower. Jo Brookes, Dave Davski. Julie Macey, Anthea Attard. Tracey Stewart. Danny Rhodes and Robbie Bloomfield.

Special Thanks

Chief editor Killa, for proofing and historical fact checking.

SWORDSMAN

Definition - South London terminology. A player participated in orgies and female debauchery.

This book is dedicated
to all the original
Whitehorse Estate boys & girls
and my iconic anti-heroes.

PROLOGUE

THE PRIVATE MEMBERS CLUB

The busy atmosphere of the Royal Mayfair was filled with music and jovial laughter. Friday night was always busiest for this exclusive private member establishment, even more so as it was New Year's Eve 1967. The partying was already at its peak and everyone attending felt at ease amongst the cigar and cigarette aroma, the back drop of red and black velvet overlooked by sparkling chandeliers, shining light dimly onto long red draped curtains. Leather Chesterfield sofas flanked the neat rows of tables and chairs that filled most of the floorspace. The scantily dressed showgirls of varying sizes of voluptuousness, paraded in frills and diamanté's, holding infectious smiles, weaving amongst all the seated men that boasted of outrageous wealth with diamond pinkies, gleaming cufflinks and ostentatious dress watches.

Meanwhile, the upstairs housed the offices and penthouse, formerly used as living quarters, the new proprietors were conceding it, to facilitate at a premium, the space available for private hire.

"Look at you." She beamed. "I'm so proud of you darling."

"Not bad eh Ang?" Sid boasted with pride, leaning back into the luxurious leather chair, in his Gieves and Hawkes tux, immaculate shirt and black tie. His Cartier cuff links sparkled the final touches of finesse. Lester was over with him and sparked the heavy gold lighter for him to bellow heavy cigar smoke towards the ceiling.

"You are looking at the guvnor of the Royal Mayfair." Lester announced purposefully with his Jamaican twang, his deep eyes cutting hollow into her. She stared back at him unappreciatively at his snide remark, after all, she had known Sid and Pete and their father since the brothers were young boys and she was the young tom boy that ran errands, including driving for them, carrying fake i.d to fool any traffic stop and the usual police spot checks on the illegal shebeens that she worked for them, when she should have been tucked up ready for school in the morning. All of them raised on the tough streets of Woolwich, South East London.

"Well I'm not about to start bowing or curtseying to my Siddy. Am I now?" She replied back cheekily and kissed Sid on the cheek as she approached him in the chair. Lester frowned jealously and sparked up a cigarette of his own.

The knock on the door drew all their attention to the recently retired owner, Francis Kidbrook or 'Franny' to his friends and to Sid and Peter's late father. The club was the most exclusive in town, both him and Bertie Bryan had owned and entertained in for the last two decades. The local gangsters harassing most of the West end owners out of town, nobody came to Franny and Bert's club because they were respected by everyone.

They had many famous clientele attend over the years, from politics to the big screen, who graced the seats and tables downstairs. From Gary Cooper to Kirk Douglas. The Duke of Gloucester, Lord Boothby to one or two of the Hollywood movie moguls, to the most ruthless and unsavoury members of the underworld. It was even rumoured that Etta James was discovered, and Kennedy first acquainted with Marilyn Monroe at the Mayfair. John Wayne has also made several cameo appearances over the time.

Their father's and Franny's legacy were handed down as directed, but also due to the conflict of interest. Franny had a more deviant clientele from the exclusive society, who would pay him eye watering rewards. A far cry than the usual knocking shop, that required a bunker style operation and be a million miles away from west end eyes.

"Look at him. If only your old man could see yah right

now." Franny radiated proud, he produced an expensive silk handkerchief and wiped what seemed like forced tears from his eyes.

"When is Pete due out?" He quickly disguised false sorrow by a swift change of subject. He sat down opposite Sid looking proudly at him.

"Not long for Pete now."

"You two need to keep this place at the highest echelons, you'll know when the vultures come knocking." Franny worried.

"Well, like I said he'll be back after the new year, Friday we hope. The witness has been taken care of, so prosecution will have to let him go."

"Well, that is a relief, make sure he stays out of the limelight, that goes for you and all Sid. Some of the people downstairs will take liberties with the girls, but you can't keep getting heavy handed with them all." Sid held his hands up to gesture an apology again. Reflecting on the incidents, including the manhandling of the Viscount Riddlesdown, jumped up ponce, who had mistreated Rita with one of his usual drunken tirades.

"Terrible business, dat sudden loss of memory." Lester announced unsubtly. Digressing back to the prosecution witness with a clear case of mistaken identity, swore blind that it was Pete that shot the aide to the Viscount in the leg who unfortunately slowly bled to death through a femoral artery wound, on a bench in Hyde Park. Rumour spread that he was nailed down in a somewhat symbolic execution.

Franny looked up at him suspiciously. Angela had the same look, she had heard all the rumours about him, in contrast to the sweet man that captured her heart. He blew a sarcastic kiss towards her that tingled her spine, unassured to whether it was his sexy smile or the chilling thought of him throwing people from four story buildings and slashing people with razor blades. His enforcer role earned him the nickname Animal.

"We'll keep everyone in check from now on, Mr Kidbrook."

"Just make sure you do." He tutored.

"So, what was the thing you wanted us to look into." Sid quickly switched topic.

"Yes. That's where I was going. Our Royal Highness wants to know if there is any chance of the dark… sorry coloured lady accompanying him next week."

Sid, Angela and Lester all looked around at each other. It wasn't often permission was requested for a booking such as this.

"Rita?" Angela butted in with astonishment, to which Lester threw her another stern look.

"No." Sid insisted, after slowly realising how inappropriate the request was. "She does the concessions, cigarettes, matches. She's not a brass."

Franny looked back at Angela who had a no-nonsense serious frown on her face.

"I can take her and drop her back?" Lester suggested. This was almost a test to Sid's authority, there was rarely any occasion or task that Lester would feel to object to, he was of little resistance to ethics when it came to earning a potential bonus. Sid threw him an angry stare for even hinting that he was open to negotiate. But Sid would stand firm on this, regardless.

"It's only for dinner, to boost his ego a little bit. He doesn't want to cause an outrage by breeding darkies. No offence." He offered insensitively.

Lester shrugged unperturbed, he'd been called a lot worst, even by so called friends, being the only black associate on the firm, he wasn't too sensitive to the prejudices. Sid was looking up at Angela and back towards Franny with a non-negotiable look.

"You'll have to grow a thick skin in this business. No is like a slap in the face to our clients so just be warned." He finally surrendered.

"Over my dead body Sid, she's just a…" She was silenced suddenly as Lester grabbed her forcibly towards the door.

"There's no need for that Lester." Sid protested as the door was slammed shut.

"What the fuck is up with this lunatic?"

Franny stared towards him almost in apology, for the enforcer that Sid would have to inherit.

"I won't miss that black maniac that's for certain." He chuckled. Sid didn't see the funny side as Franny gave him an education on the best way to temper, with as little engagement with him as possible.

Outside, Lester shoved Angela hard into the wall, the shock stunned her as she began to quake nervously as he squeezed her arm almost locking it behind her back.

"Who de raas said you can interfere in our business?" He shouted angrily.

"Fucking let go of me." She reacted angrily, kicking out with her legs.

He held her off patiently while she vented unwomanly at him, until he had enough of the playing around and struck her swiftly across her face.

"Go downstairs and do what you paid fe do." He ordered.

She looked up at him pitifully from the floor. She helped herself up staring in disgust, stroking against the sting that radiated from her jaw.

"That's right gwarn." He bellowed towards her, his face was so up close, his breath blew at her hair like a storm, staring at her as if challenging for another word to earn another strike, before he returned with his eyes still trained on her back inside the office.

Franny was now around the other side of the table with Sid embracing him affectionately.

"You do this place proud young Sidney. This is your time now." He said proudly wiping his eyes again with his hanky as he became overwhelmed by emotion. He saluted him with his drink before necking the golden-brown malt swiftly.

"Right I shall do my last tour amongst the guests. Any time you want to consult me. Just call." He turned to leave, Lester held the door opened for him and nodded his own farewell.

Sid was in deeply troubled thoughts but saluted him in time with his glass as Franny disappeared out of the door."

"Where's Angela?" He stormed at the tall dread.

"She garn downstairs boss." He replied.

"Is she alright?" He paused to light another cigarette.

"Yeh mon." He shrugged.

"I do wish you would stop roughing her up like that. What the fuck is the matter with you?"

"She shouldn't be here interfering."

"Yeah? Well neither should you. My brother'll be calling me in a minute." He stormed, hinting towards the door.

Lester looked at him vexed, being second in command at least warranted more respect than this. Sid gestured him again to the door as he reluctantly obeyed and left slamming it insolently.

"Fucking animal." Sid cursed to himself, he sighed deeply and stood up and peered out through the window to the bright illuminated busy street, pondering with deep thought. He was so conflicted but would at least entertain for her to make up her own mind if she wanted to go to dinner with the future king. The thought sat jealously in his mind until the phone began to ring. He greeted his brother who was currently sitting ironically at her majesty's pleasure in The Scrubs, fingered for a murder but soon he would be free. The discussions lead to the same topic about the man that had assisted his brother getting his liberty back.

"He's part of the furniture." Pete sighed.

"We have better people like Boycie and the Naden's, solid as you like, we don't need him."

"Lester knows the landscape I guess."

"But can we trust him? What's the deal with him?"

"Never trust him." Pete advised. "He gets the girls in line, spots the talent and he's not adverse to a bit of heavy lifting."

"Fuck knows how dad tolerated him."

"As a favour I guess. Or he lost a bet." Pete laughed.

"My money is on him losing a bet."

"Well it couldn't have been that white smile of his and what was this I heard from Angie, that he tried to throttle one of the customers a few weeks back?"

His brother's queries triggering a host of comedy but Sid held back the laughter, with Franny's words still ringing in his ears about the incident.

"Yeah, it took a few of the lads to hold him back. He didn't take kindly about that MP snapping his fingers trying to order him about." Sid surrendered.

Although it was an incident that needed a few egg shells tip toed around to smooth the water, Sid still couldn't help finding the funny side, picturing Lester frothing at the mouth and almost choking the member of parliament with his own tie...

"In all fairness, I don't think he took too kindly to his Rivers of blood speech on the tele."

"Oh, I didn't realise it was that fucking wrong'un. Fair play." Pete joined in with the laughter. Although they would have to rein that behaviour in, whatever the customer's views.

"It evens out some of that rough treatment on some of the girls, the nonce. I suppose that was one positive." Sid hypothesised.

"That Lester is a ticking time bomb that's for certain." Pete warned.

"There's no way he's from Jamaica, I was led to believe that they were all docile from smoking all that pot." Sid laughed.

The humour was a timely relief, Pete was using his phone privileges to keep up to date on all the workings of the club and the people whose palms needed greasing but there was still the topic of the shy sweet girl, that they had taken under their wing, who had become regrettably, from Sid's point of view, the object of desire for one of the most powerful men in Britain. This sat on his mind as he sought guidance from his elder brother, but Pete saw this opportunity only for what it was.

Angela was downstairs at the bar with a martini, she had already downed two Campari and sodas out of anger. The third drink had her somewhat simmering about this fiancé of hers, she began to wonder, whether the taboo of being with such a man was worth the constant mistreatment. Her mind often forgave him due to the pressures of being around all the bigotry. Always, despite all the good he did, he seemed to be looked down on and never given praise or the pat on the back that she knew that he yearned. And yet, despite all the caring and encouraging words she would bolster his ego with, she's the one that he always took it out on.

Her mind diverted away from the bastard that was Lester Morgan when she caught the glimpse of her smile through the crowd. She looked sweetly towards Rita, smiling her warm smile, making her way over to her, her radiance always heartened her so much.

"Angela." She said Joyfully. "It's so busy tonight, I'm so rushed off my feet." She immediately hugged her affectionately with such pride for how she saw so much fun from concessions. Her bubbly character encapsulated everyone, she was so trusting of the downright lecherous eyes from some of these archaic nobles and the outright vicious nature of some of the underworld clientele that she served.

Angela began to mother over her loose strap, that was slightly falling off of her shoulder and smartened up her hat at a perfect tilt.

"Have a break Rita. They can wait."

"These people, oh my gosh Angela. I love this place." She chuckled as the respite for her tired feet was short lived, just as she was about to sit down to join her for a drink. Angela grabbed her by the hand and kissed it. Rita leant awkwardly over her teller's tray, to hug her back for getting her this fun gig.

"I'm thinking of running away one day Rita, to get away from all this, wanna come with me?"

"Oh Angela. Why would you want to leave this wonderful place? We can't leave Sid, he needs us so much. And what about your Lester?" She chuckled at the crazy idea.

Angela looked into her lovely green eyes that burned with so much childlike innocence, impatience and ambition. There's no way she could go anywhere and leave her to the west end dangers after previously rescuing her once already.

"You are right, my little sweet. There would be absolute carnage if we left. This place would fall apart." She sighed. "But listen to me carefully Rita, if I'm ever not around, don't you ever let anyone force you to do anything that you don't want to do. Do you hear me? No One." She emphasized sternly with a sad teary look in her eye.

"Not a chance, with you and Sid looking out for me. Come on its nearly midnight. Time to celebrate." She raised her voice excitedly with a huge smile.

"I love you. You beautiful heart you." She sighed to herself. She pushed her Martini away and stood up to face Rita, swaying her hips as the young woman named Lulu on the stage, entertained the crowd with her sumptuous harmonic notes. Angela studied her silently, Rita quickly waved her goodbye when she was summoned by another potential customer, beckoning for the coveted Regals and Consulates.

She turned sharply away from the bar as she saw Lester approaching, she wasn't in the mood to hear his usual apologies, especially knowing that he was not objective to pimping her beloved Rita, just because an inappropriate royal wanted companionship, for one evening or even for a lifetime. She was uncomfortable with that. Rita was an innocent girl, but she was beautiful and she hoped that Sid's affection for her would do the right thing, she exited hastily towards the door.

Her hair blew in the breeze after the smartly dressed concierge opened the large glass door for her and bode her a goodnight. Stood in just her eye-catching low-cut cream satin Mary Quant, complementing her long legs and naked feet, were the matching high heels that strapped smartly on to her ankles, she hugged herself against the chill, with a waiting patience and caught his eyes.

Sammy, caught unawares as he glanced at his watch, with quickened pace, he cut short his conversations with the other young drivers of the line of Daimlers and limousine's. Standing by her designated vehicle, looking almost apologetic, he stood aside with the car door ajar.

"Are you not waiting around for midnight with the others?" He queried looking back towards the club to see if any of his other employers was leaving as well.

"Take me away from here please Sammy. I'm not in the mood to party."

Closing the door behind her, he rushed around the front of the white Daimler to the driver's seat and started the four-litre sovereign, then carefully edged his way out into the traffic.

"Where to Angie." Sammy looked back at her, wanting some kind of direction instead of a blind tour of London Town.

"Just drive around, head back across the river. Anywhere."

He purred the gleaming car away into the night. He kept his eyes onto the road but couldn't help looking back at her in deep thought. Usually the life and soul, he began to wonder what was playing on her mind, admiring her stunning looks sat so elegantly into the deluxe leather as he gazed at her through the mirror inquisitively.

He tried to strike up the usual conversation with her about any of their plans for him. Sammy was only with the Mayfair firm for a few weeks. Francis Kidbrook was his mother's boyfriend over the years, although he had a string of the present and ex-call girls, for many an out of hours call out for sex, away from his own wife and kids. He had also been looked after by the Bryans.

The previous year an embarrassing incident had occurred

when the young and unruly Sammy Wilshere, stole a black taxi and crashed into a dignitary's parked car in Knightsbridge, to stop him ending up in a borstal for the charge of armed robbery, Franny had to use his influential powers, with previous TDA on his record Sammy was facing a harsh sentence.

Driving for the Mayfair organisation and running errands for Mr Kidbrook and the Bryans gave him the opportunity to direct some focus, but also, so they could all keep eyes on him, from his rampant urges to steal cars and keep him out of prison. He continued looking back at her lovelorn, the street lights shadowed and then illuminated her face which strikingly reminded him of Maureen O'Hara by her sparkling eyes, like the earrings that dangled inside her hair while she daydreamed forlorn at the scenery outside.

"You alright Angie?" He asked again when it appeared that her mind was distracted.

"I'm so sorry Sammy, could you please just drive." She said with an apologetic smile.

CHAPTER 1

CYCLE OF ABUSE

This South London borders of Surrey showed little signs of the depressing decay of the 1970's, a time of discontent, industrial action, the I.R.A and racism. Leading into the end of 1976, in comparison to nearby inner-city towns, politicians spoke of an upturn to recovery putting a positive spin that it would not be decades away before the borough would begin to thrive again.

From the outside, the flats of the Whitehorse estate in comparison to the concrete jungle in neighbouring boroughs were not so much of an eyesore. The 1950's-built properties were a good-looking brighter urban expansion projects, the flagship four adjacent blocks especially, all named after different type of trees, Birch house, Maple house, Oak and Willow.

Proud occupants housed within a post code that bordered Croydon, Thornton heath and Selhurst, if they were asked, many answered arrogantly of hailing from The Whitehorse. Not that they differed in any way from residents anywhere else in the borough, it was just another regular closed knit community, the occupants experienced the usual woes as everybody else, some more than others, screaming and shouting of warring families and the regular echo of domestic abuse reverberated comparatively behind closed doors.

"Leave my mummy alone." He screamed angrily, beating his small fist onto his back, he grabbed onto the thick matted hair with all his might but could not protect the blows still landing onto her face, she screamed in pain when his knuckles battered into her cheek bones and belly with that crazy violent glint in his eyes. Her clothes were bloodied as her nose dripped and blouse flung open flapping against his violence. Tables and chairs fell around them in the melee, a vase thrown towards him had deflected onto the wall leaving shards imbedded into the shagpile.

He clung like a rodeo on his back, gripping to him while pounding with all that his small fists could muster. Lester with an almighty shrug sent the boy airborne and colliding onto a side cabinet, contents crashed around him in chaos, including a heavy Hooper Struve soda syphon that missed his head by a fraction. A picture frame of the couple smartly dressed at a party with their friends fell onto him, the same pair in a different world of embrace, as he continued to pound her face with no compassion towards the woman he continually declares his undying love to.

Like clockwork this occurred, for as long as he was old enough to remember, a pattern of raised voices cursing, 'bastard, bitch, cunt, at each other, where the 6-year-old became increasingly distraught. On most occasions the bedroom wardrobe's dark and hollow solace would absorb away most of the sound, also his hands clasped tightly to his ears to drown the noise and eyes clamped shut made him immune.

Why did she always fight with him, why must she respond to him and never back down. She was so brave to stand and take it with excuses that it was all her fault. When the calm fell upon the household was the only time he would reappear, only her voice could coax him out from his hiding, regularly he beat upon her, regularly her bruised face and slamming of the front door as he left, concluded both their ordeals.

What could set it off had no pattern, a wrong flavouring of soup or a joke taken the wrong way to one of her friends down the telephone. The boy often never spoke when he was around, just in case anything he said would provoke another bout of violence. The silence sometimes irked him to hurt her some more.

Today, little Raymond had had enough, this was a combination of hitting one of his bullies in the school playground that day. Violence had begun to spill into another place most children should feel safe. Teachers, alarmed by the ferocity had called for him to be removed permanently, which contributed to today's argument.

It was the ripped and bloodied new parka coat that had triggered the bulky dreadlocked man, that the young boy had already stopped relating to as his father, to rage upon the feisty blonde again. Yesterday they were in love, he could never understand them laughing and drinking and falling asleep in each other's arms, to hitting seven bells out of each other, how does her love towards the child contrast so much, compared with the love of his parents, that escalated consistently as this.

The youngster, heartened after realising what his own fist could do, found the bravery to try and help her for once. The screams and shouts rattled against the scarred walls. Direct and indirect neighbours banged and stamped on their carpets and poked at ceilings from adjacent floors, shouting in vain again, for him to leave her alone, which disguised the heavy pounding of the front door. The rescue party had arrived in full force from the Gloucester, following a phone call from a neighbour. The close-knit community triggering alerts to the real maintainers of law and order. Two large men finally barged into the room as the boy laid giddy on the floor, powerless to rescue his mother.

"Come here, you bastard." One hissed, grabbing Lester by the hair and throwing him against the wall, with a swift uppercut to his belly.

"This is the last time you put your fucking hands on her. Get this degenerate out of my sight."

Two younger lads entered and manhandled him. Lester defiantly struck at one with his forehead, which surprisingly gained him no advantage except for a retaliated knee into his groin area, which made his own knees buckle.

"What do you want us to do with him?" Said Sammy, as four more men entered, crowding the already congested room.

"Every fucking day yous two." Pete Bryan shouted like a mediator of warring clans. "Count yourself lucky, my brother has a kinder heart than mine otherwise he'd be carved up and thrown into the Thames." His face already etched at the disappointment he felt about the overruling.

"I'm the degenerate? That skaghead bitch spent all me money." Lester lashed out his feeble excuse, once he began to catch his breath back.

"And last week was because she asked you for a few bob to get the boy a winter coat for school. You're pathetic. You can't be here anymore, we can't have you around. That's it. End of story." He cemented his will, directed towards them both before she could protest.

The boy angrily but wearily stumbled to his feet and with a weakened aggression began to pound again, just above Lester's waistline until he was held back.

"Come to mummy baby, you can't attack your father like that. Do you hear me?" Angie began to hug him unable to calm the aggressive look on his face glowering towards her abuser.

The men all looked around pitifully at her, with more rage at this brute who had just lashed out and missed with a violent kick towards the child in retaliation.

"He's got some fight in him the kid. Maybe he can take his place on the firm." One of the other large men named Tommy Akehurst chuckled. Pete glared up angrily towards him, not entertaining any of the humour, although the spirit of the kid he couldn't ignore.

"Get him the fuck out of here." He repeated.

"Shall we take him to the Naden's?" Tommy suggested.

"No! Just fucking get him off the manor."

The men frog marched Lester roughly who was still trying to protest his innocence, with no one entertaining anything that he had to say, which led to a desperate departure down the hallway and the stairs, banging him purposely into the wall and railing.

"Fuck you and that dirty stinking bitch. Fuck all of you! I'm Lester bloodclaart Morgan. I'll be back fe kill all you."

"Yeah-Yeah! You're all fucking mouth Animal." Pete screamed back at him from the top of the stairs as he watched them escort him down.

"More like insect." Sammy chuckled as they walked back inside the flat.

"Take the kid wiv yah, get him something to eat, I want to have a word."

"Come on boy." Sammy reached out, with slight force to prize him away from her grasp.

"It's ok my baby, go. Sammy will look after yah."

He followed Sammy without any further hesitation, almost happy towards the prospect of a new environment.

After remaining mainly silent while the gang of men from the pub invaded her living room, she began to tidy the chairs around the table once they had all left. Pete watched in pity towards her as she then stared back at him, embarrassed.

"How many times Angie. The man is an absolute headcase, keeps doing this to you."

"A boy needs his father around and I have just got to learn to keep my big mouth shut."

"Jesus. You keep doing this, sticking up for that no good…"

"Pete, I know yous all care but its none of your business."

"None of my business? look at the state of you." He held her face up to examine the cuts and bruises on her. She shied away from him and continued trying to tidy the place.

"Leave the fucking furniture." He bellowed. Slamming one of the chairs to the carpet. "He's not coming back here, he's a fucking embarrassment and you, you are no better doing all this filth, especially around the boy. You need help." He examined the blotchiness of her skin and the reddening at the fold of her arms, the 24-year-old was a far cry from her stunning attractiveness, with the last five years taking its toll.

"He's all right, isn't he?" She questioned rhetorically. "I've never done anything around him."

"Mother of the fucking year? I heard what he done up the school." Pete raged again unsympathetically. "Anyway, we're keeping him with us until you sort yourself out."

"Who the fuck do yous think you are? I'm his mother, he stays with me. He has to stay with me." She repeated and began to wail hysterically beating onto his chest. It was a hopeless desperate gasp as the prospects began to hit home.

"Angie." He paused drawing in a long sympathetic sigh. "I know who he is." His eyes on her simmered with more pity, it was a disaster to see her this way, he has to make things better for her and removing the toxic boyfriend was stage one.

She was interrupted before any of the feelings that pitted inside her could respond. Sid walked in and hung his head in shame as he examined the room. He gestured to his brother towards the door who at the same time, subtly expressed relief as he walked out of the front door. Sid retrieved the picture frame from the floor, viewing it nostalgically, but changed his mind mid thought on whether this was the right moment to reflect on more happier times. He walked up and hugged her as she continued to cry, squeezing her tightly to him and shed a silent tear with her.

"Let's make no mistake here darling, the only reason that man is still walking this earth is because of you. Time and again you find an excuse for him. But this finishes tonight. That poor little kid needs you. You need to keep yourself together especially for that boy. Be a good mother for him, he can't be all around this, it isn't fair." He demanded showing disgust towards the debris around the flat.

"You might as well kill us both then. Stick a knife in my heart..." She thumped a fist onto her chest angrily. "Because I struggle to be alive. Thinking about her burning to death in a ditch screaming and dying alone."

"Is that what this is all about?"

"I looked her in the eyes Sid, that I would do everything to protect her and that baby. We were supposed to protect them, you and me."

"Angela, we done everything we could. Switching cars using..." He paused feeling choked. "We thought of everything to throw them off. It's not your fault. My decisions let her down. We all let her down."

"Every time I look at him..."

"I know my love, I know." He drew her even tighter as they both wept together. "All we need for you to do is to love him like he's yours. We have to do it for Rita if nothing else."

"Every day, I keep hoping that I'll pick up that phone one day and it's her. I let her down Sid. I let that lovely soul down and it hurts me every single day I'm alive. I miss her so much." Angie wiped her tears, unable to hold the emotion. Hyperventilating against the battle with guilt and secrecy. She winced at the touch of her tender bruises, her head began to pound severely as Sid became aware of her plight, her body became wilted, which forced him to support her onto the sofa. Then on to the floor and onto her back. He looked deep into her empty eyes, slightly panicked. Her laboured breathing bore signs that she was in deep trouble. He immediately grabbed for the phone and dialled.

"Angie, stay with me girl. Help is on the way... Yes Flat 10, Oak house, Whitehorse estate..." He declared to the emergency operator. "Yes, she is still breathing but very laboured."

He continued responding to questions into the phone. He hung up and called into the pub next, to get a few bodies back round to assist him.

Within a few desperate moments, help arrived in the stature of a small boy, similar in age to the youngster that had already left with Sammy.

"Angie if you can hear me love, Little Boycie is going to stay with you until help arrives." He whispered calmly. Then turned to face the kid still panting from his frantic bike ride from the other side of the estate.

"When the Ambulance people turn up or the Old Bill,

what you gonna tell 'em?"

"I heard screaming, a lot of crashing about and a black fella run out."

"Good boy, and she's your auntie Angie."

"Me auntie Angie, got yah."

"Ride with her and later, Sammy or Tommy will come and get you from the hospital."

"Ok Sid. Don't worry I know the apple."

"You're a good lad. Good stock just like your father. We'll take care of you later." He pointed towards the paraphernalia on the floor, the kid positioned himself on his knees looking over her.

Sid left the flat hurriedly, after whispering some more encouragement to her. He sat down on the floor and began to stroke her long blonde hair, turning on the water works just as the paramedics showed up.

CHAPTER 2

THE OFFICE OF RECORDS

"Do you have the date of birth please?"

"Between August and early December 1969, or thereabouts."

The clerk at the civil registration office flicked through the box of index cards removing the most relevant from the search.

"You'll have your work cut-out Detective, follow me." She began to walk in front of him as he followed the clerk from behind her desk.

"The needle in the haystack." He sighed.

"For Keyne and the variants of, you'll have all this section, J to L in aisle number eight. On the right, births and deaths, you are free to have a look and take as long as you like. Mark down the card number of interests, if you need anything for copying, we will Xerox for you to collect at a later date. Here." Pointing onto the reference card, looking down from her glasses at the detective as he stooped down and searched his way back up.

"How many records are we looking at?"

"Keyne is not a common name but we have maybe over two hundred entries of Keyne's, between 1938 and 1957. Then all the way to present day, then there are Keane's and Keen."

"Well it's not as though I have anything else to do today." He sighed again, grabbing the first box, he began the task.

She stood beside him for a while as he scraped a stool along the floor to sit down.

"That will be all." He dismissed.

She gave a sarcastic smile and turned swiftly to toddle away. He watched her in her tight skirt as she took elegant strides back to her position at the front desk. He began by taking out his notebook, pen and twenty Regals, removing one from the box to light it up.

This task was a teach you a lesson punishment and he knew it, he had always been, speak first, action later and may have questioned too much into the closed case. The untimely death of one Miss Rita Keyne. He discerned quietly, the belief of his superiors that a child might have been and should have been amongst the wreckage from whatever unfortunate accident befell the source of this investigation. The post-mortem recorded no pregnancy but the details of the two bodies recovered from the mangled and burned out wreckage, gave little or next to nothing that could settle the nerves of the people pressuring his superiors for the answers. He had also questioned this phantom pregnancy or which of the highest level of the establishment or government official they were trying to protect.

The timeline was sketchy at best. Initially a possible abandonment was deduced, therefore all would indicate that there must be at least, a birth certificate.

The mother's death had been a forgone conclusion over seven years ago. His beliefs all along, that they knew more about her than they had led all previous lines of enquiries to trust. The then owners of the West End club were deemed untouchable for decades, until it became an everyman and woman for themselves scenario. The protection backtracked enough for them to ditch what was once the most famous closed community adult entertainment venue, post war. They made no statement or comments from the whole furore, the unprecedented fallout, even to this day the whistle blower never came to the fore. Seeing that the reports involved many from the upper classes, privileged and degenerate from high society, even within the establishment, including his met superiors. The less that came out, satisfied the fears for the majority.

The accusations and counter accusations were awash

with scandal. Nonetheless, his discretion through that embarrassment was handled very well, his bosses had commended him and for all its worth, that it was kept out of the mainstream rag with censorship on the largest scale to date.

It took him thirteen cigarettes to smoke fill the tall ceilinged room and fourteen boxes of records before he had realised, he had lost track of the day, as the clerk returned.

"It's 3:30. I'll be leaving soon, will there be anything else you require?"

"Nah love I have around fifty or so, give or take."

"Is it possible for you to return tomorrow?"

"Listen up treacle, there are reasons to believe, that this is a matter of national security and I will not be leaving until I have what I came for." He said in a dull authoritative tone, indicating with his note pad. She placed her coat and bag down on one of the work benches and stared towards him with a stern look.

"Then let me help. Then I can get home to feed my family." She huffed.

He sat in silence, continuing to match birth certificates to his notes, record after record brought no satisfactory result so far but he battled on.

"How many children do you have….?"

"Doreen." She stated. "I have two boys,13 and 17."

"You look very youthful, for a mother of teenagers."

He continued his work as she pulled records out to assist him.

"Thank you. I think." She replied jovially.

"I can always lock up afterwards you don't have to stick around, keeping your husband and family waiting."

"Hmm. Husband?" She dismissed. "He…ran off with a home wrecking tart named Edith eleven years ago and the boys can fend for themselves." She pulled one of his cigarettes from his pack and flicked at the lighter

"Do you mind?"

"No. Go right ahead." He shook his head, gazing curiously towards her as she blew the smoke out in front of her, her strong perfume charmingly blended over the tobacco scent.

"Have you never considered, why, with such a threat to national security. Such a task would not draw one hundred pen pushers to search for what you seek?" She scathed.

"A hundred pen pushers or just Me? I unfortunately drew the short straw."

"Your bosses must love you." She chuckled.

"Or I felt the wrong collar." He laughed back.

"So, what exactly will this search entail?"

He passed her his notepad for her to look at the details. Registered Keyne/aliases? Mixed/Black, sex unknown/1968 -1969- Father unknown...

"Over the whole of Great Britain. For an unaccounted fetus?" He interrupted. "Birth certificates there's around one hundred or more. I have broken down to 'father unknown' but there's one hell of a lot."

"Do you have children yourself inspector?"

"A daughter, 21 last month. She had a surprise birthday party, invited all of her family except me."

"I'm sorry to hear that." She sympathised.

"She bought me some cake."

"That's nice of her."

"Anyway..." He evaded. "We are looking for a sprog of mixed or black heritage, born either 1968 or 1969."

"That narrows it down I suppose."

"Well according to academics, we are close to one hundred thousand in the UK alone and the bosses are giving me a right old pain in the Gregory, over all this."

"That many, who would have thought eh?" She sounded aghast, knowing at first hand, the taboo.

"Yep, many of our English roses have been lured by the darkies. I'll never understand it." He purported with a bigoted smirk to himself.

The awkward silence had him finally looking towards her

again as she stubbed the cigarette into the ashtray. She placed two of the records in front of him.

"These." She gruffly proclaimed and picked up her coat and handbag and turned to him again. "Do see yourself out."

He continued to look down towards the records she had identified as best matched. 16-year-old Margaretta Keyne-Abu. Deceased 4th November 1969 with no next of kin detailed, she paired with three entries of birth, one from the registration district of Bexley, 11th October 1969, Andrew Keane, Mother Brenda, Father unknown. The information deflated him as abruptly as Doreen's departure, as her shadowed reflection through the corrugated glass walked down the hallway towards the exit, signalling another dead end.

CHAPTER 3

FRIENDS WITH BENEFITS

On the leafy suburbs of South London, school had finished a little while ago and after throwing down books and ditching uniforms, it was straight back out, for the pre-teatime window for many inner-city children. Football matches were in full flow down the side streets and in the parks, Choppers and Grifters versus five speed Racers, competing to finish first in races around the block. Playing knock down ginger and penny up the wall, territorial rivalries and bonded friendships were forged forever. Some eating crisps and drinking Coca-Cola from glass bottles outside pubs, waiting for their respective parents/parent.

Friday after school was the start of the weekend, so no rushing home for your tea. Heaven was having a quid to buy a portion of chips with crackling on the house and a bottle of Cresta to wash it down.

Raymond and Christine descended on Windmill Park to kill the last hours of the day. The swing rocked from side to side unevenly, as he kicked out on the down movement, the grey winds swept his eyes that became teary in the early autumn gust when he came down rapidly in full pelt momentum.

"Please can we get out of here? I'm so fucking bored. Let's go to the Whitgift." She demanded.

"Blimey. The language on it." He laughed.

"Sorry mum!" She retorted sarcastically.

"Ten minutes. He'll be here, you want your four quid back don't you?"

"Yeah but don't bash him up for it."

"What about your bike that he nicked? It was defo him, the thieving prick."

"Hark at him. Mr Policeman? You can't prove it was him, please let's just go."

"Just because you kissed him, stop trying to protect him."

"That's not the reason, it's because you are always getting into fights over me, please don't."

"For you Christine…" He continued swinging higher and higher as the chain's swooshed back and forth. "…. I'll just give him a slap."

"Yeah, I don't believe you. When you get angry you're like a wild dog."

"Not anymore. My uncles got hold of me, said I have to knock it on the head."

"Well you should listen to them."

"Look. I'll just ask him for the money, nicely." On the last upswing he leapt from between the chains landing with a 'perfect ten' controlled thump onto the grass.

"Is that all?"

"Yeah.That's all." He turned to Christine to see if she was impressed with the commonly known leap of death, then worried at the expression on her face. Frozen by the sudden appearance from the rear of the park, when the group of boys came into view.

"I heard you were looking for me?" Said the lead skinhead, his eyes revealing slight hatred towards Ray who looked him up and down with a confident and assured glare.

The tall acne faced boy wore a black Harrington jacket, white Fred Perry polo, tight skinny jeans and long black steel toe capped boots with white laces, he looked older than him, maybe thirteen years old but his other three mates looked to be the same age. In fact, he knew one of them, Todd, who used to live on the estate but moved away last summer or maybe earlier.

After his mother had died, his father left him most days to fend for himself then, due to his father serving life in prison after a planned arson went awry that killed six Pakistani's in a rented building. Following his incarceration, he was three and a half years into his term, when he died from a blood clot on the brain. Todd moved into his grandmother's house on the Pawsons road, which saw him hanging about with the Selhurst Skins gang as this little crew were known by. First, after being bullied by them, to then accepting him when he battled with them on a daily basis, taking the fight to them every day for a fortnight. He also went to the same school.

"Where's her fucking readies shithead?" Ray answered heatedly and stepped closer with fists clenched ready. He nodded acknowledgment to Todd who looked conflicted.

The smirk on the skinhead's face opposed Ray's staring menacingly back towards him, unmoved.

"He remind you of anyone?" John hinted back at Steve with reference to Todd.

"Let's just go Ray, let him keep it." Christine interjected, still worried about an escalation.

"Yeah! I'll leave it as long as he returns the bike and coughs up four quid for my inconvenience."

The park bellowed with laughter from the main skinhead and his mates. Todd remained straight-faced looking at Ray, looking cool and calm, even though he was outnumbered four to one.

"So, you are a hard nut are you, chocolate drop?"

"He uses big words and all this one, who's a clever little spade?" Malcolm, the second skinhead added, presenting his face up close.

"I'm half-caste." Ray announced proudly. "And how can yous talk that shit to me, calling me a spade and chocolate drop when your mate is and all. Are you gonna stand for that? Chocolate drop?" Ray turned to Todd, who paused with concerns with the debate in his head.

He wasn't like them, the sheer fact they talked NF even when he was with them, made up his mind. He winked back at him with a huge devious grin.

"Come to think about it, they call me a lot of names, don't yah? Especially you Malc." Todd threw a left hook into his crown and bundled him to the ground.

"Get him off me." Malc's distress call was muffled as Todd held him in a headlock, with a volley of punches with his spare hand.

"You fucking nigger loving traitor." Steve hissed, angered by Todd's turn of allegiance. He was the third skinhead of the trio, who had previously remained silent. He was dressed in a stylish black Fred Perry T Shirt with red braces, trying to land kicks into Todd's ribs as he continued to wrestle with Malc on the damp grass. Todd paused on Malc, with a swift punch into Steve, which caught him square in the groin.

"Money!" Ray grinned, with more menace towards John as he withdrew a rounders bat.

"Ray! For fuck sake." Christine cried in surprise at the concealed weapon.

John was distracted by Todd turning Judas and caught the bat right across the bridge of his nose.

"Have that!"

"RAY!" Christine screamed again, louder, masking John's, as the volume from the skirmish began to echo inside the park.

He was even more surprised by the searing pain. John was howling for his mercy as Ray laid into him with intent. Steve, short of breath by Todd's accurate punch, looked around worried, towards John being beaten by the bat and Todd's relentless bullying of Malc, pinned to the grass being punched, slapped and poked in the eye. Steve weighed up his next move.

Unexpectedly and even with the numbers in his favour, Steve cowardly turned on his heels and took off through the park, with the intention to get reinforcements. Ray ignored the fleeing individual, deducing that he would have fifteen – ten minutes at worst before any help would arrive. He continued unabated striking John on the kneecaps and arms repeatedly.

Christine squeamishly was unable to look away from the ferocity of his attack, which seemed to have escalate with him in increments throughout the last summer. Each blow she witnessed disabled any form of resistance and more worryingly, the way Ray's face was descript with sheer enjoyment, each blow almost tickling him in response.

"Argh...Take the fuckin money." John bellowed in submission, his hands trembled as he struggled writhing on the floor, trying to get into his pocket, then reaching the fistful out towards Ray. He counted seven one-pound notes and threw three back at John as he continued to writhe in pain.

"Bleeding hell Todd. Have you finished feeling him up? Kick him in the goolies."

Todd wrestled himself loose and kicked Malc in-between his legs.

"From now on I'm gonna stick with my own." He boasted, smiling intensely at Ray who had turned to Christine.

"I'll meet you back at the flats a bit later. Here." He commanded placing the money into her hand, she forced the notes back into his pocket with an awestruck glint in her eye.

"Keep it, I can't take it." She rejected.

"He'll be alright." He tried to convince her, but she had already begun her walk home. She looked back at his wolf whistle as she walked away, staring and grinning towards her departure, she waved back at him with a smile.

Todd continued goading his former mates, boasting and looking down at John. He collected the three pounds that Ray had tossed back at him.

"Come on." Ray beckoned. "Before more of your bonehead mates come back."

They jogged confidently together towards the gates at the opposite side to the park, across the main road through the North side of the Windmill estate until they were outside the Gloucester public house. The pub was a large building that situated prominently across a four-road junction and was owned by Ray's uncle Sid and uncle Pete. The Bryan brothers and their associates headquartered their pub and many other business ventures, including cigarette and contraceptive vending machines, that they supplied to their three other public houses, The Mail coach, The Propeller and the Victoria cross, along with eighty percent of the pubs and clubs across London and other main cities across the UK.

"Was you seriously going to take us all on?" Todd questioned.

"Were you seriously hanging about with them boneheads, Chocolate drop? You do know they are NF?"

"Yeah! Well, British Movement."

"Same bloody thing ain't it?"

"John's usually alright really, Malc and all, sometimes. They just always get carried away in the heat of battles. They were always good for a tear up down the Palace." Todd explained.

"It didn't look like it today." Ray dismissed.

"Plus. Malc's related to that Theresa Downey, he said she was a slag and puts it about a bit."

Ray stared towards him with a slight look of disgust, then began to laugh.

"She drinks at the pub sometimes and she let me feel her tits behind the bin shed once." He smiled at his childish white lie, he usually did to impress his peers. Like most boys his age, they had never explored any part of the girls that most of them often boasted on. Ray led him into the pub and looked towards everyone sheepishly.

Pete and Sid Bryan were both huge menacingly brutish looking men. Sid was a year younger of the two as they approached their mid-forties. He wore trendy horn-rimmed glasses with his hair always smart and smoothly brylcreemed, he always wore shirt and trousers with shoes most weekdays when he conducted business in the pub. On other days and most weekends, he would be in a black polo shirt with jeans and always had an air of leadership that commanded respect, by all his friends and associates that were gathered in or around the pub. Pete's long scar always distinguished himself apart from his brother, he also had an eye for detail, although more casually dressed in smart jumpers and draped in tom. He used to wear a fist full of sovereign rings that would make a trademark imprint, if you were given a bashing from either of them, the sovereign imprints, usually confirmed that it was Pete who had dished out the punishment. They were both equally quick tempered.

"Is it ok if I take my mate up?" Ray asked politely

"Who's this and where've you been?"

"This is me mate Todd from school, we were over the Windmill with Christine uncle Sid." Ray replied easing himself around the bar trying to avoid his gaze.

"Well, why'd you take me bat and leave the ball behind. Div." Sid chuckled. "Sly little git this one I tell yah."

"The bat." Sammy was now stood in front of him blocking his path with his hand out as some of the other drinkers looked on inquisitively.

Ray's look of innocence staring up at Sammy, didn't flinch as all eyes were now peering towards the insolent schoolboy. He hesitated a little while longer before finally unzipping his coat and removed the object from the inside pocket.

"Get upstairs." Sid ordered as the other drinkers began to laugh. "Little fucker stealing me bat."

Todd looked back towards all the menacing faces in the bar. He recognised many that knew of his father, who had on many occasions sold hot property to some of the individuals who acknowledged him with a wink.

"Don't worry about them mate, come on." Said Ray as they both climbed the stairs. Ray threw his coat down onto the neatly made bed and knelt down to retrieve from under it, a medium sized cardboard box and placed the money that he took from John inside with the other loose notes.

"Fuckin hell Ray! have you been robbing banks or summink?"

"Nah just bits and pieces, helping out my uncles mainly. I'm saving up."

"For what? You're too young to buy a motor."

"Saving up to help me mother. So we can pay for a place of our own."

"What's wrong with living here. At the pub? It's big enough." Todd stood up still aghast. "How much you got there anyway?"

"You ask a lot of questions."

"Well I'm just wondering, not a lot of boys our age has that amount of readies."

"Yeah well I do. I want to look out for mum. So, she doesn't need any bastard beating her up anymore."

"Where is your old dear now, she not living here with you?"

"Nah. She's in a hospital."

"What? Is she mental...?" Todd continued with curiosity. "I mean...is she...not well?"

"You ask a lot of questions Todd." Ray eventually replied.

"My old dear died when I was five, me dad soon after." Todd digressed.

"She is in rehab they said. She's been in and out. Here, look at this." Ray diverted again. "It's in New Addington lovely isn't it?"

"It's like country bumkins up there." Todd inspected the brochure.

"Still in Croydon though as far as I know and he won't be able to find us. Its high up, we'll be able to see him coming."

"See who coming?"

"My old man. He's a cunt." They both chuckled at the use of the word.

"It's nice mate, your mum will love it."

"Six weeks she'll be home, they reckon."

"What will your uncle's say about that?" Todd enquired gesturing downstairs.

Ray shrugged vacantly and continued looking down at the brochure, with the daydream he had relived multiple times.

"Look at that garden. Hopefully one day you and any

other mates can come round, we can play football and climb trees."

"I'd like to do that." Todd smiled.

Being a regular on the streets, due to the boredom living with a strict grandmother, he had very few people he could class as a real friend and warmed that he was similar to Ray, having no mother around at this moment. Even though, Ray would be seeing his mother sometime soon.

"How will I get up there?"

"The fucking bus Todd, you know them big red things."

They both fell about laughing again as he placed it back into the box and closed the lid.

"Shall I get us some coke and crisps?"

Todd pondered for a bit but didn't want to keep irking his parental guardian by taking liberties on her curfew rules.

"Nah I better go, my nan always gets the hump when I come home late, but do you fancy going over to Thornton heath rec to play footie with them sound boys?"

"Who are they?"

"You know Paul Chambers and that lot? Derrick Green, Ordel and Errol Williams, from School? Forth years. They are box boys for this mobile disco, a sound system they call it, it's well funny, they always taking the piss, cussing each other. You should come."

"What time?"

"I'll knock for yah about midday."

"Yeah alright, I'm up for that. You gonna be ok getting back home, do you have to go back through the Windmill?"

"Nah, I'll go the long way around and cut through the back of Queens."

Ray lead him back down the stairs as Todd continued to get excited about meeting up for some fun in the park the next day. They appeared together back into the Saloon bar and was confronted by Pete.

"Someone to see you here boy." He announced.

He walked around the bar towards the entrance and was

surprised to see skinhead John and his dad.

"What's this?" Ray enquired as John walked towards him nervously and handed him some bank notes.

"Sorry Sid." John's father interrupted. "When the boy came home with bruises and explained, he told me that he got into a fight with your nephew, I marched him straight around here, the little sod took his little mate's bike and sold it off for thirty quid. Y'know Christine?"

"Why don't you go around there to give it her then?" Ray asked, his voice echoed with insolence.

"Oi. Watch your manners." Pete glared.

"Anyway, no harm done. We didn't want to go around there because her old man may not have been as understanding like yourselves and would have called the filth."

"Hold up a minute. I might call the filth." Sid interrupted with a frown. "What are you insinuating? That we are not law-abiding citizens?"

"Nah nothing like that...I mean err..."

"Do you hear this Peter? I think Mr Stephens here thinks..."

"No. No...I err..."

"Ray! run that round to your mate. Let her know we couldn't recover the bike, but the money should square things up. Thank Mr Stephens for doing the right thing." Pete continued.

The entire pub was all now looking around as the pair stood there nervously. All the while Todd was staring at John with a smirk. John gave a 'help me out here' look, back towards him.

"Ray!" Todd whispered. "Save them." He chuckled, as Mr Stephens continued to squirm out of his slip of words.

"Uncle Sid! John's alright, he wasn't fighting us, he helped me and Todd earlier against N.F Skinheads who were harassing us, threatening to bash us up. I knew about the bike and didn't realise it was hers. We agreed that he'd make it right though, that's all."

"Is that what the bat thing was all about?"

"It was a bit silly really. When I came back from school, I see them hanging about looking at me. Just a misunderstanding that's all. John wasn't with them."

Sid looked at his brother and at Sammy who shook their heads, not believing a word of it.

"Well I'm sure your mate John and his father will be very grateful for your honesty. Just don't let me find out the truth or you'll all be in bother and all. We don't want any thieving around here."

"Well, not from our own eh?" Sammy chuckled.

"Go on son, show your mates out." Pete dismissed, directing his head to all of them towards the door.

Todd was finding it hard to contain himself and nudged at Ray as they walked behind Skinhead John and his Dad who walked straight out towards a brand spanking new Ford Cortina, parked on the corner.

"Ere John?" Todd beckoned. "See! what did I say about him and his uncles? That's gonna cost you."

Mr Stephens stopped and sneered towards them.

"Nice car Mr Stephens." Todd digressed.

"Fiver a week." Ray smiled.

"It's at least a pony Ray, it might get a bit expensive watching your back, people attacking you for no reason."

"A Tenner?" Mr Stephens answered aghast.

"That's a cockle and hen. I said a pony. Twenty-five." Todd corrected. "He saved your bacon in there, they don't like thieves, grasses or nonces Mr Stephens."

"Here you little toe rags. Twenty quid that's it."

"Oh! Flipping heck Todd! It was him you were talking about? With what's her face?" Ray at first hid his confusion and then quickly improvised.

"Yeah. And all he has for us is a score?" They both stared as though privy to whatever facts was of Mr Stephens's concerns.

"Go sit in the car." He shouted to John who was loitering

kerbside. Mr Stephens then shepherded the boys away from earshot.

"Look, that's all I've got."

"A bullseye. Final offer, I know you can afford it." Ray kept up the charade, shrugging himself off from his grasp. If there was a secret, he was definitely willing to pay for their silence.

"Fifty bloody quid? This is Blackmail." He incensed.

"We'll tell me uncles then, see what they think about it." Ray offered confidently. Mr Stephens looked at them with suspicion wondering whether to call their bluff.

"I'll pay you fifty pounds the weekend, I pay you that and that's the end of the matter."

"What are you lot on about?" John asked approaching them as they squared off. Looking confused, when it went from his problem to his father's.

"I thought I told you to wait in the flaming car. You'll get a hiding when you get home for this and say fuck all to your mother."

"Fifty quid this weekend and we'll keep our mouths shut. Or you'll never step inside that boozer again." Todd indicated.

Mr Stephens grabbed his son by the collar and frogmarched him into the car, glaring back at them, who were now in fits of laughter.

"What the bloody hell was you on about Todd?"

"John was…Well we all were, over the youth club in Addiscombe, Sir Philip's. He's had a few double diamonds and let it slip, that his dad fucks his stepsister. She's only a couple years older than us."

"Straight up?"

"I never believed him at first, he tells a lot of porkies does John but the old man looks the type, don't he?"

"Yeah. I suppose." Ray chuckled.

"Boofing a 13-year-old. He needs locking up."

"Boofing?" Ray queried confused.

"Just something them reggae boys use…Boofing." Todd smiled indicating a crude sexual intercourse gesture with his fingers on one hand forming an O and his index pointing into it back and forth.

"If he is…boofing, John's 13 year old stepsister, he'll need more than locking up."

"He was quick to keep us schtum weren't he? And if that's the case, we'll get your mum in that new drum before you know it mate."

"Glad I bumped into you today now."

"Let's go buck up with Christine to give her back her money. You know her dad is minted? We'll get a reward then can buy a draw of weed from the reggae boys."

"Not a bad day's work Todd." Ray laughed as they trundled off towards Christine's flats.

CHAPTER 4

PREPARATION

The 11pm closing time, on a nightly basis, was always extended by one and a half hours until Sid or Pete took it in turns to lose patience with the stragglers, with menacing glares that usually sent most of them home, bar the ones that were too non-coherent.

By habit, a Panda car would always on schedule, roll up outside and hit the blues for a few seconds to enforce the licensing rules. A thumbs up by the landlord at the door, would show the officers they are complying and usually signalled that closing time was adhered to by all patrons.

"Takings are up again tonight. That's just for here and the Mail Coach." Sid confirmed gleefully.

"Sweet." Pete replied, heading straight for the back door to let two indistinguishable burly men into the bar via the kitchen.

"Take a seat, we'll be with you in a minute." Sid gestured with a bottle of Johnny Walker towards the gentlemen, who both politely refused.

"You remember Kenny Arnold?" The one starting the introductions, was their long-time associate Tommy Akehurst. The brothers joined them at a corner table nearest to the bar. Sid pulled out a cigarette and offered to both the guests and accepted a light from Kenny.

"I knew your father Jimmy, good as gold him." Sid recollected.

"So, what do we owe the pleasure Mr Arnold?" Pete asked impatiently.

"Tommy here said you wanted some more information…"

Kenny hesitated, cautious on whether they would be offended by him having any inclines to their line of work.

"It's ok. I explained some of the details, I showed him the landscape." Tommy interjected.

"If that job is something you want to carry out, I'm the inside man." Kenny continued confidently.

"You tell him the target?" Sid queried.

"The target doesn't matter, it's giving you the time to confidently pull the job off, if you accept, I can get you everything you need. Create the perfect situation."

Pete looked curiously towards all the men and poured another half measure of the bottle sat in front of him into the glass.

"You're a phone man by trade, aren't you?" He asked.

"That's right. Yes, in the City of London, that's what will buy you the time."

"Kenny's shown me the apple, we set it all up."

"How much is the take? That's if you've already lined it up." Pete asked.

"They store weekly cash, for Sunday collections. Loose notes, untraceable. It's at least four fifty-five hundred grand, tops. Your young'uns could even walk in there and take it. No problems at all." Tommy confirmed, when it looked as though they were not convinced. Sid got up abruptly with his hand out towards Kenny with a smirk at the understanding that this signalled the green light.

"Meet Sammy at London bridge tomorrow. 10 am and fill him in with the rest of it, make sure you suss it out one hundred percent first, before we all jump."

"Whatever you say Sid." Kenny replied smiling intensely.

Pete winked at Kenny and Tommy, whilst gulping down the fiery liquid, he escorted them back towards the exit and bolted the door behind them.

"Bed! Nose-ache." Pete instructed. He didn't see Ray lurking on the stairs but sensed his presence.

"Night uncle Pete."

"Night. You little sod yah." Pete tutted.

❖ ❖ ❖

The next morning, as instructed, 10.00 am sharp. A smartly dressed Sammy waited patiently beside Telephone house on the approach road to London Bridge station. Observing the long line of yellow vans owned by the ex-Great Post Office Telecommunications company. He wondered, when they ever had time to fix telephone lines. His local was often filled with their workers, almost every afternoon. He was in mid thought when a similar coloured van approached and honked its horn at him with two short blasts.

He climbed into the passenger side as Tommy slid into the middle, to sit on the internal engine compartment cover that was covered with a Shag-pile carpet to make it slightly more comfortable.

"Kenny-Sammy, Sammy-Kenny." Tommy introduced quickly. Sammy acknowledged with a nod.

"My cousin Lenny Sansom drives a taxi same as you Sammy." Kenny informed.

"I know Lenny. He's a good lad." Sammy replied politely.

"Let's go." Tommy commanded impatiently. They drove into the light traffic along the Thames. Sammy surveyed the backdrop of construction sites along the waterway as a new London was beginning to take shape. The scenery of slow development repeated from Southwark Bridge as far up to Greenwich in the South east and beyond. They soon arrived at Tower Bridge police station.

Sammy jumped out first and waited aside for Tommy as he strode around to the side door to the Commer manufactured Spacevan and appeared again with a tool bag and a handheld telephone of sorts. Kenny got out and approached a green street cabinet. With a metal T shaped key, he opened the doors to expose a spaghetti of wires and gave Tommy the thumbs up.

"Follow me." He signaled to Sammy confidently and walked around to a side entrance and buzzed the intercom. The crackly response reverberated back at him.

"British Telecom love." He pushed the gate instantly as the hum released the lock. Into the courtyard they both strode side by side.

"Don't I need the same overall as you?"

"Fuck all that, you're my guvnor if we are stopped but we won't be."

They entered through a second set of doors, they bounced up the stairs two at a time, until they approached what seemed to be a broom cupboard. Tommy sat his tool bag on a counter that was next to a large rack with a mess of wires and removed wires from a yellow testing box out of the jumbled wiring block.

"This sends a little test signal, so we could identify it downstairs." Tommy boasted. "Come on."

He pointed towards the door indicating the exit. They both continued back down the stairs and into a canteen area. Sammy became suddenly nervous, the noisy room was filled with chatter as they were confronted by uniformed and plain clothes personnel sitting at tables drinking coffee, eating sandwiches and reading the daily newspaper. Laughter also consumed the room as some competed on the pool tables.

"Which way is the switchboard." Tommy enquired, his question was replied with a shrug of the shoulders by a couple of the officers, one voice replied, which was a voice Sammy slightly recognised and looked around to see Robbie Collins who was a regular drinker in the Gloucester.

"Switchboard down again?" He smirked winking towards Sammy.

"That's why we are here." Sammy, who was now at ease chuckled back.

"Left out the door straight past the lockers then on your right. You'll hear the commotion." He directed.

They both nodded, thanking him in unison. Sammy

was still none the wiser on what they were attempting to achieve. They arrived at the switchboard and were confronted by a buxom uniformed female officer who was trying to get instructions over on a closed-circuit radio.

"British Telecom love, What's the problem you are having with the board today?"

"Today?" She stormed aghast. "I have bloody called you boys out three times this month. Three bloody times. You do know this is the headquarters for the Flying squad?"

"I do apologize love, my governor is here today, we'll get it sorted for you no problem."

She produced a bunch of keys holding it up by a yellow fob and with a strained smile she indicated to the switch boards distribution cupboard.

"And, you should really address me as Ma'am." She barked.

"Sorry Ma'am. We won't take long." Tommy replied apologetically.

Tommy and Sammy approached the second telephone junction box, which Tommy unscrewed with a screwdriver and handed the cover to Sammy. His eyes lit up with the realisation of the color-coded markings inside. Tommy continued his inspection of the strips of wires in front of him and produced the telephone butt set with the hard-wired connectors, to plug into one of the connections and listened for a tone and then used another tool to push what he identified as loose wires home.

"Go flick the switch on the box upstairs then ask her if it's responding." He whispered to Sammy who looked back at him confused. Sammy disappeared and returned within a few minutes with a smile.

"All back up and working she said."

Tommy used a black marker he produced from his pocket and ticked alongside the coding marked Private Wires kilostream and suffixed it with the letters S T.

"Job done my son." He confirmed once he returned the cover over the distribution box and tightened the screws.

They both walked back to report their finding to the lady who was now all smiles and cheerful towards them both.

"The wiring is a bit suspect. I guess we will need to plan out a complete re-wiring." Tommy spoke fast and with purpose.

"Thank you so much as long as we are back on, I'll put in a call when we can schedule to have it sorted. It's a critical line for us at the moment. We can't afford too much down time." She reported as a matter of fact.

"Just put in a call to the exchange, maybe the schedulers can put the work in for a Saturday. Or Sunday night might be best." Tommy interacted. "We'll grab our tools again from the frame upstairs and my guvnor here will put in the paperwork for you. Good day to you Ma'am."

They left back through the way they came, the break area was less busy now and there were no signs of Robbie, the PC that they had dialogued with thirty or so minutes ago. They climbed back into the van a while later, with Tommy feeling excited and Sammy still a tad confused.

"What the fuck was all that, what's the interest with the switchboard and what is S T?" He questioned.

"Sweeney Todd my old son. The hotline to Jack Reagan and his merry mob. All the phone lines along with their central early alert system to boot." He laughed loudly. "Then tomorrow if Sid & Pete agree, we'll set the young'uns on reconnaissance for the second part of the plan. Then we hit the place a fortnight Saturday." He gestured to Kenny, who chugged the engine into action and drove away.

CHAPTER 5

THE STEPFATHER

He leant against the car door, one-foot crossed the other, his shiny brown shoes almost reflected in the sunlight, the player's number six filter hung precariously off his bottom lip, causing a left eyed squint as the smoke wafted upwards, like the complicated detective on tv, he had the school exit under surveillance. Her eyebrows pinched suspiciously, when she spotted him, she slowed down in an attempt to go unnoticed and hid between the tall fourth form girls and boys in front of her.

"Sarah." He called out.

She cursed under her breath as her heart and nerves swathed in a myriad of emotions. She forced a smile and approached him. He stood up straight to offer her the full view of his smart grey suit with a white shirt. His face etched like an apologetic puppy that had just soiled a brand-new rug. He held the door open for her, while she probed to see if any of her school associates that were milling around, reflected any concerns about him enticing her into his vehicle.

She took cautious steps towards him and the gaping passenger door, his face indicated with a gentle persuasion to get inside onto the warm vinyl seats. The back of her bare legs almost stuck to the soft tacky fabric, the warmth of the heater cuddled her with relief. The green blazer only offered the slightest cover during winter, over the thin white cotton blouse with her neat collar secured by the top button and green and black tie. Her pleated skirt was rebelliously borderline, despite the repeated letters sent to her parents about the standard length all girls should adhere to. She watched him walk around to the driver's side with an excited stride of relief, that at least she hadn't kicked up a fuss.

"How was school darling?"

"Ok I guess. Apart from everyone asking about…" She pointed to the slightly bruised and bloodshot eye, received again over the weekend as his usual temper seared out of control.

"Look I said I was sorry. I don't know what came over me." His hand stroked against her lap as way of remorse, his glances swivelled between her and the oncoming traffic, then pulled away after a British gas van flashed at him to go. He waved his hand out of the window and travelled through the gears heading south onto Wellesley road, continuing straight on towards Purley.

"I thought you was taking me home?"

"I will but not yet. We need to talk, and we can't with everyone else around."

"Everyone else? You mean my mother, your girlfriend?"

"It's complicated, you know that."

"You said you made your mind up. Now it's complicated?"

"It's not as simple as that, I have business I need to take care of first. Then we can move away from this shithole."

"It's not that bad." She giggled and pressed her hand onto his, he caressed his eyes towards her and stroked her face.

"With the money, you won't even have to attend school anymore."

"Promise?" She smiled excitedly.

"I promise." He gestured with a wink trying to keep his eyes on the road and yet prove his sincerity.

"Can I drive?" She quickly changed the subject.

"Not here and definitely not in that." He gestured towards her uniform and stared perversely down at her legs, she crossed them seductively, which made him distract slightly from the road again. He pulled into an industrial unit, abandoned, seemingly for some time, derelict and covered in broken windows. Debris floated across the ground like tumble weeds. She nervously looked at him with suspicion and became desperately taxed at his deception.

"You said we would stop with this?"

"I know but…"

"No more. You promise me of running away and yet here we are sneaking around."

"I just want to prove to you how much I care. We can't be affectionate like this at home, just the pair of us."

"That's your complication, otherwise we'd have left by now. We shouldn't be doing this to her."

"Sarah. You are the one that I love. How many more times?"

"No more Jeff. No! I don't want to do this anymore. You pay no consideration to me about how I feel." She vexed.

"I care plenty."

"Well I'm saying no. I'm tired of being used with promises that you can't keep. All you ever want to do is get off with me. What if I was on? Do you ever consider these things?"

"Yes, I do." He huffed insensitively.

"Well that's a lie. Clean up that mess, was your idea of consideration. Just take me home."

"I thought you wanted to drive?"

"I just want to go home. Please." She pleaded. "I know why you have bought me here. I'm not doing anything with you."

"Jesus fucking Christ. What do you want me to say? I can't just turn it off like a tap, unlike you."

"Well how do you expect me to carry on under the same roof knowing what we know and sitting down for breakfast like a big happy family. Fuck." She yelled almost like a spoilt brat in a tantrum.

He leaned forward to kiss her, she turned away to look outside, towards the weeds and fly tipped refuge scattered over the land. A bewildering moment came over her with shock as her head smacked against the window, his hand choked around the back of her neck.

"You bitch, turning your nose up at me."

She struggled to turn her head as he thumped her into the glass again, she felt his weight on her as he climbed into her side of the car. The vehicle shook as she resisted and fought with him, legs and arms trying to flail in the confined space. He held her down by his forearm into her chest

"NO!" She screamed. "Get off of me. Fucking pig."

He forced his mouth and tongue grossly onto her cheeks as she turned away, left and then right in defiance. Holding her face to forcefully kiss her, until her futile resistance complied. His rough contamination of her mouth, gradually, by his warm breath, she magnetically welcomed the reluctant passion and finally conformed.

A rapid loathing was replaced by harmonious engaging kisses, she had enjoyed for the most part. She still couldn't understand after everything he now knew, why he still wanted her and confusingly why she still wanted him.

His kisses made her forget the pain at the side of her face as her writhing and resistance gradually mellowed to the heat of his zeal, once again subsiding her initial need to reject him, she assisted him to alleviate her panties down her thighs as the fabric cracked by his forcefulness. Her eyes became sedated by his lust as he humped unmorally into her. She mewed to his touches over her blouse. The car rocked in momentum with his aggressive lust, that began to build her up to the brink, teasing her with his rough caressing and made her whisper her love into his ear.

It was over by the time the tingles inside her body built any further towards climax. Without the fear of an interruption, seemed to slow what previously caused tsunami's through her body, but now was suddenly cut dead. His heavy breathing on her remained for a brief while, before he adjusted himself back into his seat and checked his hair in the mirror.

The car ride home was silent. Her emotions racked by guilt and relief, pondering if whether his selfish promises sounded sincerer this time around. Her mind meandered with a multitude of emotions, flung into a mature world that she battled meekly at times, often as today, giving in to her heart strings, determined by so much history. She felt little in common with her peers, the girls of her age in the school netball team, girls who have often spoken on their active sex lives but nothing she could share to compare notes, between who they fancied and had it off with.

Worst of all for her, she was canoodling with her mother's lover, a betrayal of the worst kind. Things could have been, in some ways different, if it were John that she fancied instead, if it were he instead, who crept into her bed in the middle of the night. Regularly caressing her over her nightie, silencing her with his palm in the dark. Although, for two years, before his mother died, the animosity he held towards the people that broke him away from his dying mother was relentless.

John was a rebellious, reckless child that she admired to a point, until he became more extremely right wing. Her mind meandered onto the mutilated dog of that Nigerian family that lived two doors down. The attack was blamed on rural foxes, but it wouldn't surprise her in the least if it was him. She questioned herself at times, whether the same advances by him would be any more a taboo, dating the child of her mum's boyfriend? At times she could have played that hand to see the look on his face. There was always this fight, to justify her predicament. But no one else calls her beautiful or had caressed her the way that he did, that created this bond, made almost instant the minute their eyes met. As a father figure she had no one in her life, he was always there to be kind. He was there all the time.

The paranoia as to why none of the boys at her school gave her the time of day, whether they had whispered her secret. She never felt any malice or disapproving towards her, which would tell the tale if there was a rumour, of her playing lovers behind her mother's back with this man. Tony Brewer, a fifth year, was the only boy to make any sort of contact with her at her school or was it because she made no interest in anyone, even the good looking boys she saw hanging around the Whitehorse estate, when she was receiving a grown man's attention, who owned a house and a car and buys her belcher chains. She stroked around her neck and prided at the heart ring on her index.

Her silent sideways glances, with worshiping eyes, that sometimes conflictedly reflected, what made him so attractive and then, to what did her mother do to deserve the despicable treatment by both of them.

"Listen to me love. I just need time to sort this all out. Just a few weeks I promise."

"I've waited this long. I can manage a few more weeks." She replied as they pulled up outside their home.

"Are you not coming inside?"

"Later. I have to see some people about business. This will cost me a lot of money to relocate us."

"Shall I wait up?"

"No. I might be very late coming back, and you have school in the morning. Let's not risk getting caught when we are so close."

She smiled with more sentiment towards him. She got out of the car, straightening up her skirt as she approached her front door and checked for any of his remnants from earlier. Turning back to wave at the empty space where his car had just been.

CHAPTER 6

THE GODFATHER

Ray was stood at the school gates nattering to Christine Hill and Norma Collins. The girls from his estate would often detour with him to his school in their knee length skirts with pleated fronts and stylish knee-high socks. The light blue blazers matched the striping on their ties and were donned replicating the same as how Ray and the other pupils residing on the Whitehorse estate, who wore their ties as a large untidy knot at the top of their shirts and blouses since the beginning of the 1980 to 1981 school term, almost as an affiliation to their estate. Norma was Christine's best friend, they were two school years above Ray and were like identical twins to a point, inseparable in the way they dressed and hair length, although Norma was a browner colour with matching eyes, in contrast to Christine's deep blue eyes and blonde curly locks. They both twirled their hair or the Hubba bubba chewing gum that they smacked in unison inside of their mouths.

Ray nodded to other boys as they entered to start the school day. He casted off-putting scowls towards those eyeing any interest on his Haling girls. He previously paid little attention to school and was trying to explain to the girls that his uncles were coming down on him heavily, for skipping most of the last school year, due to the continued problems with his mother. This term he would have to go or face the punishment. There was little in the way of resistance, they let him get away with most things over the years, since they had forced joint custody for him to remain living with them, but school, they commanded, was mandatory.

"I'll see yous over the Windmill later." He said absently

just as Todd approached.

"Wotcha Ray." He sang happily. "Hello girls was yous waiting for me, to get off with me before I go in?"

Both girls chuckled as Ray shook his head in embarrassment at his audacious chat up.

"See yah later Ray. We're gonna go and meet Bev." Both girls harmonised as they both walked and then jogged to the bus stop to catch the approaching bus to South Croydon.

"Wished we went to Haling." Todd sighed dejectedly.

"You'd bunk off there as well though, wouldn't yah?" Ray chuckled. They playfully pushed into each other as they both approached the school door heading for house registration.

"Tuck your shirts in, you ruffians." Bellowed the headmaster, Mr Blackman. "You two! Boney M. Don't you have bags for your books?" He continued at Ray and Todd as they approached him. They both removed rolled up textbooks from their pockets giving him a vacant look.

"Your mates keep nicking them off us. My Nan can't afford to keep replacing them." Todd replied cheekily.

Mr Blackman looked at him confused but ignored replying back.

"He's NF, I'm telling you Ray. He always picks on all the blacks and us, haven't you noticed?"

"Just ignore him mate, nothing we can do about it."

"Funny isn't it? His name's Blackman and he's NF." Todd chuckled.

"He's just a cunt." Ray cited laughing.

They entered the noisy corridors with older boys play fighting, then doors slamming as people dispersed once the headmaster appeared into their view. Todd and Ray nodded at each other as they went separate ways down the corridor.

Ray entered the classroom, rowdy behaviour encompassed inside as the usual suspects fired rolled up paper missiles at one another. Ignoring them, he made his way to an empty desk alongside an unusually well-behaved classmate. He looked curiously towards the new face scratching with a compass into the desk. Ray glanced down as he walked past and saw what was etched, the letters, M.i.l.l.w.' An allegiance to South London's notoriously ill-behaved football supporters, he quickly denoted. Ray sat alongside, still staring towards the new kid.

"Wotcha." He greeted.

The boy looked up at him with a slightly solemn glare. His brown hair irritably flicked away from his eyes to meet his and then continued with his head down.

"Alright me 'ole mate." He returned, with somewhat of a thick cockney accent.

"Your new yeah?"

"Yeah. Come dahn from Walworth, me and me ole man. Since me muvvah died, him and his Doris looks after me and me little sister now." His eyes now, were back focused on Ray once he had completed the finishing touches to his art vandalism.

"Sorry about your mother." Ray sympathised.

"Yeah, me and all."

He began to continue again with his etching, as though encountered on scripting the entire club's history, such was his dedication to the wooden desk, even when Miss Goodwin began shouting for everyone's attention. Ray's gaze obediently focused towards the front and the chalkboard at the cute red head, dressed impeccably as she always was. She continued to silence the class, at times sounding like a rattle snake with the continued shushing, chalking up names, asking them in turn to stand up.

"Keith Alsop! stand up please...no tie again?" She sighed and shouted out at four more names before finally returning her focus onto himself.

"Raymond Morgan, how many times do we need to say this? You may have missed all of last term, but the rules of the school have not changed, just because you have decided to come back." She enthused, with a mild sarcastic smile to lessen her confrontational tone. "That goes for all of you. Shirts must be tucked in, ties around your neck, not in your pockets and blaz…"

"I got me blazer on Miss." Ray objected with a cheeky smile, interrupting her mid flow.

"Blazers with collars down, we don't want any Shaking-Stevens impersonations, this is not Top of the Pops."

With that, the new kid belted out the loudest laugh at the comedy which hinted with broad sarcasm.

"Something amuses you Raphael? Which leads me onto Mr White here everyone. This is his first day at Stanley High, I want you all to make him feel welcome."

All the class turned towards him as he shrugged back towards everyone with a broad grin.

"Do you want to share the joke with us all?"

"I'm laughing Miss, cos Shaking Stevens ain't a golliwog, is he?"

"Do what?" Ray jumped up with furious violence, sending his chair falling backwards, diving into Raph with fists and now both wrestling on the floor, tipping the desk over as the classroom erupted.

"Fight! Fight! Fight! Fight!" Was the classroom's jovial chorus.

Miss Goodwin, furiously pushing other pupils aside, wrenched both the boy's arms powerfully, dragging Ray up first, who was visibly showing marks on his face and hands from the brief scuffle. Then she roughly manhandled Raphael, who stealthily loosened his grip from the compass which stuck into the wooden floor with the pointed end.

"Not a great way to start a new school is it Mr White? As for you Morgan, you can't just steam into people and definitely not in my class, to the headmaster with you both. Now!"

Ray shrugged himself away from her grasp, slamming the classroom door behind him.

"Fucking touchy them Nig-Nogs." Raph retorted in a completely matter of fact way. This triggered another attack from Tony Robinson this time, who was sat directly behind him.

"That's enough! You will watch that foul mouth of yours." The teacher screamed. "Both of you out, I will not tolerate this behaviour in my class and you Mr White, you will not last the school term if you carry on with that attitude. GET OUT."

The silence in the classroom was deafening as Raphael scraped his chair around the desk looking for his compass, then made his way to the door. Tony followed close behind.

The three boys were stood outside Mr Blackman's office as Ray and Tony, who had by now, briefly acquainted themselves as allies and stood staring daggers towards an unfazed and defiant Raphael.

"I'll take on the pair of you Sambo's." He boasted. The confidence exuberated from him which in some way, raised some caution with Ray. Tony took a step forward but was restrained by Ray as the headmaster's office door opened abruptly.

"What have we here? The three degrees?" He laughed. "Inside, you scallys." His deep hollow northern voice reverberated the empty corridor.

All three boys trudged in with reluctance, Ray was already prepared for what his fate would aspire to and went straight to the task, assuming the regular position.

"Not even going to explain yourself Morgan?"

"No Sir. It was my fault. I started it." He confessed, looking out towards the window.

"Hmm." He pondered with suspicion. "Mr White. Your reputation as a troublemaker has seen you thrown out of three South London schools already, Roy Castle will be calling you up soon."

His comedy escaped Raphael as he walked towards the filing cabinet and withdrew the long-withered bamboo and began waving it with a menacing swoosh, with a somewhat sickening pride in front of the other two boys. Ray winced at every stroke of the punishment delivered by Blackman and his bamboo, as he received six of the best in quick succession. It was all over relatively quick, but the strength and precision seemed to have tortured his hind for an eternity in his mind, resulting in a frustrated tear that ran down his cheek. Tony stepped up to receive six of the very same. Stroking each lash with the same precision. Suddenly Raphael turned on his heels, midway to the last slash and bolted for the door in a hurry.

The head teacher gave chase, as he fled out of the office, which lightened the final blow as the darting pupil distracted his task, which he perversely was lavishing the prospect of flogging his final insubordinate. Tony and Ray quickly gave chase behind the headmaster as they both chuckled at Raph's audacity.

"What a loon." Tony sniggered.

They both in unison, about turned when Mr Blackman gave up chase abruptly and headed straight back to the office, Raph as quick as lightning was already out of the school gate. They disguised their laughs, keeping an uncomfortable straight face as the out of breath headmaster returned to his desk.

"Return to your classroom and don't let me catch you back here again or you'll receive his share as well. I'll be keeping it on credit for the pair of you." He warned sternly.

"Yes sir." They both replied in unison.

"Go on. Be off the pair of you."

They both went out into the hallway. Tony was surprised by Ray's diversion towards the exit as he went out the school door with purpose.

"Where you going?" Tony enquired.

"I'm going to look for that nutter, ask him what his problem is. You coming?" Ray asked. Continuing down the school path without a care for any consequences.

"We can get him tomorrow." Tony advised with a somewhat hushed voice as not to draw attention, simultaneously surveying the open classroom windows but his voice fell on death ears, especially to an already defiant

Ray who was almost at the gates. He was stood with some hesitance but after some thought he then hastily trotted, looking around with some paranoia, to follow him down the school path towards the street.

Tony caught up with Ray panting and still looking back as he walked at pace towards the high street and stood on the corner surveying up and down the semi busy road. They both looked straight down Portman road and right towards the high street. Looking left and slightly uphill, it took a while for the eyes to adjust and distinguish between delivery workers and the early shoppers, the nonchalant schoolboy was finally detected.

"See him deh." Tony indicated in a Jamaican voice.

Ray quickened his pace across the road, darting in between the traffic. They both together burst straight into the door they had observed him disappear into.

Silence fell over the room, bar the high-pitched sounds from the coin operated machines. The place was scattered with young teenagers in Sta-Prest trousers, some were even in their school blazers. Ray stood stunned, surprised as Raph stood beside a burly skin headed man with the lambchop sideburns in a tight chequered shirt, red braces snapped onto his Levi's and smart tan brogues. Both Tony and Ray jumped as the shop door swung open again, three middle aged men entered in donkey jackets and began working on the newly installed machines at the back corner of the arcade.

"Why aren't you boys in school?" The burly man asked over the sound of the pin ball machines and space invaders which clashed acoustically.

"We all got sent home for not wearing correct uniform." Raph replied innocently "No-ones at their house, so said they can hang out wiv me here, until their parents get home."

Tony and Ray nodded hastily in agreement as the man which they assumed was his dad gestured to them towards the rear door.

"You ain't playing truant in here. Out the back." He

ordered." They both followed Raph in relief, Tony was eyeing some of the rival school teenagers, he didn't recognise the badges but smiled at two of the girls that were dressed in navy Crombie coats and chewed exaggeratedly on their gum. He was surprised as they smiled back with a wink, he nudged Ray, but he was only focused on Raph and whatever situation they were leading themselves into.

They entered into a mid-sized smokey office where a pretty middle-aged peroxide blonde hit aggressively into a calculator.

"Have a seat." Raph invited.

"Can we play outside it's a bit smokey in 'ere" Ray complained. Raph indicated them towards a back door and stole a cigarette from the blonde at the desk.

"Don't let your father catch you smoking Raphael." She said. He ignored her insolently and followed Ray and Tony outside, out of a lean-to and into a grassy area, where four long benches were organised into a square, a weathered summer table separated Raph and his school associates. He sat down relaxing his face into the sun.

"I was gonna ask what your problem was?" Ray sat opposite and stared at him, waiting for an explanation. Raph shrugged as if not understanding the question.

"All that Nig-Nog Sambo business?" Ray confirmed.

He smiled when the penny dropped and puffed confidently on the cigarette.

"Yeah, sorry about all that."

"Sorry?" Ray was bemused. "Are you and your family National Front?"

"No." Raph replied bluntly and carried on looking blasé.

"Come on Ray, let's get back to school." Tony stood up as if bored and not particularly concerned what his motives were for the racial insults.

"Have you ever read The Godfather by Mario Puzo?" Raph digressed.

"Nah why?" They both looked towards one another

confused.

"Wanna watch the film? We got one of them video players upstairs." He offered sincerely, stubbing the cigarette and walked back inside, with Tony and Ray following closely behind.

"Maybe later. We are gonna go back and meet me mate Todd, it'll be break time soon." Ray excused. "PE this afternoon."

Raph nodded to them both and sat in the leather desk chair opposite the blonde that Ray slowly began to assume was his old man's Doris, that he described during that initial conversation in the classroom.

Ray and Tony, after saying goodbye, both stood undecided on the road taking in a deep breath looking back into the arcade.

"He's mental the kid. Surely?" Tony expressed.

"No chance." Ray Disagreed. "He's just un'appy I reckon. Who do you know our age, that sits and reads about a Godfather? Come on, we'll catch up with him after school."

Walking back both he and Tony got more acquainted, although they were leading to their second year at secondary. They only recently have been thrown together since the registration structure switched to house the most difficult children into one group for the mornings, then mixed with the other pupils for Maths, English and PE lessons. Despite being distractive in classes, he was top in his class and was assessed as not applying to his schoolwork to match his intelligence.

Tony wasn't from the Whitehorse estate and was similar to Todd and himself who did not have their fathers around. Tony had lost his to a heart attack when he was very young and an only child that was taken care of by his mother. He lived on the Holmesdale Road by the football ground and surprisingly was an Arsenal fan like himself.

Their affiliations were brought on more by family ties, Sid and Pete, in Ray's case, their family hailed from Woolwich and great grandfather even played for the team during their prewar identity as Dial Square, then becoming a board member of Woolwich Arsenal, before the team upped sticks across the water to Highbury, but the Bryan family remained staunch supporters, passed down to his uncles and then to young Ray. Tony's history went back as far as, he went a couple of times with his cousins when he was about eight years old and now ventured up by himself most weekends. Despite the forced upon loyalty, they still both softened towards their local team.

After school, Todd, Tony and Ray were discussing the punch up with Raphael and how they ended up in the headmaster's office and chuckling with some re-enactment because Tony was convinced.

"He's a nutcase, like that Damian, I bet you a million quid." The laughter continued until a 75-bus drove by, which looked to be filled with school children. Todd eagerly clocked onto two girls staring down at them from the back seats.

"Look! Look Ray! It's them Westwood girls." Todd yapped excitedly. "Come on."

"Leave it out." Ray shouted after him as he sprinted full pelt, followed by Tony, to catch the Croydon bound bus. Ray was stood isolated as they both jumped onto it, almost dragging Tony to a bad fall as he quickly steadied his footing to finally board as it gained speed.

Ray trudged solemnly back towards the arcade, his annoyance for deserting him, was flicking two fingers up towards the bus as it disappeared at the right turn after the traffic lights, which would have escaped them both. He walked alone towards the arcade to see if he could catch up with Raph again before catching the bus home in time for tea.

Entering the arcade, Raph was in deep concentration and barely looked up as he walked over and stood beside him. His verbal commentary boasted about reaching the upper levels of the game as he wiped his last best score and continued the battle. Spinning on the controls with one hand back and forth, while tapping frantically to kill the alien invasion on the computer game with the other. Another frantic minute or so saw him finally banging hard on the side as all his lives were lost.

"Oi. Pack it in." Shouted his father from behind the counter.

"Sorry dad." Raph grinned as he finally focused his attention on his school chum. "Did I miss anything?"

"Nah not much. Doohan, you'll get to meet him if you go back, got involved in the 5-a-side but nothin other than that really.

"Where's your pal the gollyw...?" He quickly retracted. Ray began to look at him again in astonishment, although he managed to divert away from escalating back to the classroom attack when they first met.

"Didn't they have coloured people where you come from?" He asked out of curiosity.

"Yeah but I never been friends with any of 'em. Maybe, apart from me uncle Babs at Millwall but 'e's half caste just like you. Anyway, my dad always said we should stick to our own." He said proudly.

"Well only NF talk like that, are yous all NF?"

"Nah, we are just proud English that's all. You seem decent though cos you are not a grass."

"What planet are you on?" Ray shook his head and began to head towards the door. This boy tested his patience like he had not experienced before, so he was ready now to head home.

"Thought you was coming to watch The Godfather?"

Ray gave him a long stare, confused at what actually drives the shit that comes out of his mouth.

"It's a blinding movie, it's three hours long."

"Three hours?" He deducted with reluctance, what three hours in this boy's company would be like but then politely declined.

"Maybe next time. Uncle Sid and Pete will get the right hump if I came home three hours late after school." Ray excused.

"Have you got a video player?" Raph interrupted.

"Yeah, we got one in our pub." Ray boasted.

"I'll lend it yah, watch it, I've watched it like 100 times." He disappeared into the back before he even had time to accept or refuse the offer, so was now just stood there and noticed his father staring towards him.

"Sid and Pete Bryan are your uncles did you say?"

"Yeah?" He replied. Curious at the questioning.

"Tell 'em Alfred White sends his regards to the pair of 'em. Won't yah?"

"Yeah I'll tell 'em." He responded, looking down towards his shoes. Raphael appeared again with a black plastic case containing the video cassette and handed it to Ray.

"Ta." He thanked him inspecting the box.

"Have a watch of it. I'll see yah in school tomorrow yeah?"

"OK. Cheers. See yah later." Ray trudged out of the arcade and looked back to Raph who stood by the window waving at him and continued towards the bus stop to get home.

CHAPTER 7

EDUCATING RITA

The soft undeniable acoustics of Connie Francis caressed through the beautifully crafted stereo unit, the smart brown four-legged Hi-Fi entertainment system, sat neatly next to the bar, which was in itself, another display of master craftsmanship. The brick-built unit with the glossy oak top complimented the chimney stack with the wood burning heater that glowed like a campfire, soothingly warming the room that reeked with the ambience of an upper-class sophistication.

The secret location was outside of the West end, as far as she could encompass, she spent the journey being swooned by his grace, while the chauffeur and dedicated security officer, sat the other side of the glass partition, concentrated on the road ahead. Driven in a convoy of cars at a cruising pace, she had waved goodbye excitedly, to a less enthusiastic Angela from her Park Lane pick up, to this breath-taking manor house, an eighteenth-century retreat, where she was introduced to the small number of now departed guests at the dinner. Guised by her simpering host as the niece of the humanitarian envoy for West Africa and invited to stay as long as she needed, at this glamourous country house in the middle of nowhere.

She was admired by the dignitaries that attended, who looked her up and down like some auctioning pedigree, some with a coveted wish, that would result in him pulling her from guest to guest, as to not hold enough time for any of them to take her away from him for their own copulation. He knew exactly the type that would try, that gawped with the tell-tale look of a devil's envy.

With her legs crossed bouncing in time to the rhythm, she gazed lovelorn at the charming prince. He poured two whisky and soda's, then turned with the drinks in his hands beckoning to Preston. The personal protection officer was still sat at the kitchen table with the last of the help, smoking one lambert and butler after another, then hearing his name being summoned he extinguished the cigarette into the heavy glass ashtray and putting his jacket on over his shirt, after rolling down his sleeves scruffily, he appeared after a short while ready for his command.

"That will be all Preston. I will not be needing you for the rest of the evening." He dismissed, his voice graced so sophisticatedly, it sent the fairy dust inside her head giddy as she gazed intriguingly towards him, then at one another, in turn they both looked towards Preston as he looked back, with a somewhat disapproving protest about having to break protocol.

"Goodnight sir. Goodnight madam." He replied as the prince's eyes finally huffed with impatience. They watched him leave, closing the large doors quietly behind him. Now he could finally captivate his attention onto his nights companion at last.

"Thank you." She purred as he passed her the expensive vintage. Her broken English lilt exaggerated accentually middle classed.

"You are an absolute delight." He praised as he sat beside her, stroking her smooth shiny dark skin lustfully. Her bosom heaved provocatively, her atypical features exhumed his perverse desire for her, unusual beautiful green eyes that simmered like priceless emeralds sparkling at him with an awed innocence, as the lingering evening became her dream come true, that he was showing so much attention towards her.

"I'm only the concessions girl." She reminded him, speaking with a virtue which elevated her true purity to the nobly gentleman. This motivated his continual lustful pursuit of this beautiful blossom. For months, he had had his eyes roaming eagerly, while she circled the Royal Mayfair aisles.

She was a charismatic beauty, that had many of the well to do gentlemen of the club falling head over heels. His inappropriate impatient advances, she naively repelled by holding his hand.

"I want to dance." She giggled between puckered lips.

Her immaturity amplified that devil's hunger lecherously inside him. His mouth scintillatingly drooled perversely at her, as she swayed Julie Andrews like, in the Sound of Music. She twirled around. Her magnetic smile enhancing her beautiful ebony in front of him.

Forcing him up by his free hand, with reluctance, he rested his glass down to smooch with her under the chandelier lighting, the music faded then introduced the next track, that followed the acoustic crackle over the speakers. He enticed her head upwards to look at him, with an engaging glow that swooned her soul towards the prince as he leant forward gently to kiss her. Butterflies consumed her stomach, with her best friend Angela's nagging voice ringing inside her ears with disapproval. The devil himself diminished any resistance.

She had come a long way since Angela and Lester had rescued her at 1am in Waterloo. She fended off the attacker for as long as she could and could still visualise the stench of cigar and alcohol before that vigilante blonde assisted to prise her from his wicked grasp. With only a trunk full of clothes, they had been side by side forever, under the watchful eye of Sid, the boss, who had also lavished her with sweet kindness. His comparative yearning for her was a possessively devoted one, a few men had the bruises to prove that over the last six or seven months, since she went from homeless and broke, alone in a brand-new land, to being part of a successfully important loving family. Even the brutish looking Lester, Angela's other half protected them both from harm. She was charmed, a beautiful soul with a fairy-tale that continued within her own imagination.

His playful passion as they danced became more intense when he swept her off her feet, she giggled tipsily by the alcohol as he hastened up the wide stairway carrying her towards the master bedroom, this handsome thirty something was strong and boasted athletically, carrying her effortlessly across the threshold. Age did not seem to concern him either, his depravity lusted towards how she wore with elegance that expensive dress, which deliciously prided her femininity.

Her obvious immaturity was camouflaged in the body of a well-developed woman, in contrast to a girl that had witnessed the worst evil than most children in the developed world, a nightmare left behind, a now distant memory since her projection amongst the elite and the powerful. Every night, the captivated engaged her for their Pall Malls and matches.

He had often praised her on her pretty eyes, with every engagement, that she had also discussed after every shift to her friend. The rapport with him and several others that complemented her looks relentlessly.

"Rita, the most fabulous girl in the West end." He often praised, so aloof. Also, curious as to why her name did not match up with the exotic look, of a girl from the African continent. His besotting openly resonated angrily amongst the paid hostesses at the upmarket arena of lust that she worked, that offered discreetly, all what was needed to the deviants of all persuasions.

Sid's protection over her at first disregarded, at any price, any of the offers for her company for a night but the Prince was different, after all, who could ever turn down the future king of this great nation. She was his princess tonight with the palace and all its graces encapsulating her wildest imagination, about the humble subjects swarming to serve her every need.

After alleviating her skilfully from the borrowed Christian Dior and his impatient foreplay, he kissed her below forcefully, igniting fireworks to rapture warmly within her. She felt the loving from his provocative tongue, he basked in the aroma of her arousal, with a heated sensation that drove her eventually to return the pleasure back to him. Tasting his velvet girth increase inside her mouth. Gaging success, when his eyes closed slowly satisfied. The foul taste in her mouth was overcome by her willingness to please, as the late night gained momentum unexpectedly.

His sensitive coaxing and sweetly wooing, for brief moments between the grunts, she began to wonder after some time, why he was trying with endeavour to hurt her so much, with his hateful torment of her lips and breasts. Despite all of her protests, he continued his aggressive breach inside of her, turning her around to sodomise her, then roughly throw her onto her back.

Surrendering to his need, a profound one, seemed to desperately aggravate this treatment of her tonight. With deep breaths exhaling from her lungs, her insides were rushing in confusing waves at intervals, requesting permission with herself to just enjoy the way he pushed his bulky stem into her, almost in a fight between the willpower of desire and her sexual inexperience. It made her shed a silent tear, reflecting back on the start of the evening, from her dear friend wrapping her in a mink coat, to now her naked body sticking to his sweat.

Expecting that he would be a little gentler with a kinder loving, his angered groans did not resemble the lovelorn cooing of passion from Sid, a less sophisticated man with blood on his hands, in comparison was a lot more peaceable and sweeter, who wrapped her in cotton. She worried to a point, that she hadn't loved Sid back the way she had toyed with the prince, although he had groomed the ill behaviour by motioning her body into positions he wanted her to form. The consensual roughness continued to break her spirit, with his determined rigorous clockwork motion.

The repetitive calling of her name, summoning her, demanding and needing for her as he drew closer. Love dissipated in and out as his playful face became contorted. His sovereign looked down at her disapprovingly, she felt the guilt to return the compassion of a loyal subject. She closed her eyes to relocate her mind to a wander into nothingness, until his body finally shook from his sexual manipulation of her and the warmness of her satiny soft insides. She felt his hot semen bursting inside her, he speared deep into her with a deep angry thrust, with a deep bellied growl escaping from his lips as his balls released violently.

His manicured hands squeezed tightly beneath her, while the sweat of him dripped onto her face, his staggered breath bellowing into her neck. She felt slightly suffocated by him, but it was over now, it took a while for his eyes to become warmer towards her, his kisses and cooing returned him back to the charming gentleman again, to her relief.

CHAPTER 8

TOP BOYS

"Christine...Chrissy!" Norma was on her knees on the rain-soaked pavement. The cut on her friend's head trickled red down the side of her face. Norma shielded her to her chest as she tried to get her up off the floor.

"Go and get somebody out of the pub." She screamed. "Wait..." She paused in succession with her last request, once the realisation that Christine began to come around again. She looked dazed and confused and blinked repeatedly as the rain bounced off of her face, she finally got to her feet after gathering her bearings.

"You alright Chris?" Bev came running back from across the road.

"Yeah, I'm fine. what happened, where is Sarah?"

"That fucking bastard took her, he pushed you into that wall and he almost run me and her over. Prick." Norma fumed.

"Dirty fucking cradle snatcher." Bev scathed.

"Did you see him punch her as she got in the car? We should call the police on him." Norma angered.

"What good will that do, she'll just keep telling them what she tells us." Replied Bev.

"We can't tell the police and we can't tell the others. You know what they are like." Christine pleaded, her voice was still laboured and slightly slurred.

"Are you sure you are alright? Bev asked." You really cracked your bonce on that wall."

"I'm fine." Christine nodded still a little weary on her feet.

"He can't bleeding get away with that. He proper shoved yah into that brick wall. We have to tell Ray and that lot, they'll sort him out." Norma said angrily.

"Please Norma." She begged again.

"I'll ask the twins then." Bev suggested. "I'll tell them that he groped me."

"She'll be alright. Won't she?" Christine looked towards her shaking her head as the pain and the distress brought her to tears.

"No! she ain't gonna be alright Chris, she's getting molested by that bloody pervert." Norma began to get teary eyed at the thought of her friend and the hopeless situation she was in. Bev also began to shed tears as they cried unitingly and group hugged under the shelter of the newsagent's doorway.

◆ ◆ ◆

On that same drab early evening Ray and Todd where sitting under the shelter of the bench hut located at the rear of the park. This was the regular hangout for him and most of the young and older teenagers of the Whitehorse & Windmill estates for the most part. At times during the summer holidays the place would resemble a crowded festival, until more recently, forced it exclusively for their own use.

The place they called the camp, was littered with fish and chip wrappers and empty Top Deck shandy cans. They loitered the usual Saturday night away.

"That was a wicked punch up wasn't it?" Todd again reminisced about the earlier events that afternoon.

"Yeah that was blinding. That older lot from school proper steamed into us."

"How's your chin? That was a good dig eh?" Todd laughed.

"That great lump, smacking a pickney like that?" Ray examined, rubbing his chin as they both curled up in fits of laughter.

"Reckon Ian, Sean, Billy Burgess and that'll be coming for us at school come Monday."

"We'll bash em up. Just can't let them catch us on our own." Ray chuckled. The continued laughter echoed under the soaked wooden structure, dim lighting from the streetlights behind the high barbed wired fence, reflected the swaying leaves that dripped with sap and drizzle above them.

"Did you see the Gooners though, they did well against them numbers, I reckon half of Croydon was out for that one. I told you Palace can have it." Todd praised as a matter of fact.

"We still stood. A result in my book. Probably even Stevens."

"Your uncle Sid's face when you picked up that bin?"

"I smacked that reggae geezer on the head with it."

"Pricey?"

"Yeah him." Ray's laugher became uncontrolled as he recollected.

"And then Irish Tommy clumped him. Just to add to his misery."

"It's a good thing Arsenal were outnumbered and backed off. Or else the pub would have got done over, then we'd be in big trouble."

"And you watch when we ask if we can go Villa next week." Todd wondered with disappointment. "About, we are too young. They've seen how game we are, we proved that today and I bashed up at least two of them nifty 50 lot in school."

"That's why we should just go down the Arsenal with Tony, make a name for ourselves down there with him."

"He'll be gutted in school on Monday, that he had to go his cousin's wedding."

"In Tottenham of all places." Ray chuckled.

"We could always go to Millwall with Raph. He says it kicks off down there every week."

"Nah! They're lunatics down there, all that treatment and Harry the dog. Fuck that." Ray emphasised.

"We'll never be top boys at this rate."

"Bollocks to all that Todd. Let it go." Ray interrupted. "We need to think more about plans to earn some readies."

"What about your uncles? Kenny Arnold said there'd be some work for us, whatever came about that?"

"Sweet F.A." Ray huffed. "They want me concentrating on school."

"That's just you. What about me?"

"What goes for me, goes for all of us."

"Fuck school. Should we blackmail John's old man again then? Or rummage his house for dough, he must have piles lying about." Todd plotted. "Or… Get on the steam with Tony, he's making good donzeye pilfering the shops."

"Donzeye?"

"Dosh, readies. What all the reggae lot call it. Maybe we see Errol, for some weed." Todd's mind rattled with ideas none of which sat comfortably with his pal.

"Who the fuck do we know to sell weed to?"

"You know Russel Jackson's mum? She sells weed and all." Todd again digressed. "You should see the tits on her."

Ray drifted silently into deep thought, first adolescently about Russel Jackson's big breasted mother, then more towards Todd's unscrupulous plans, he wasn't going to visit John and Sarah's house under false pretences and steal money. Besides, his uncles would probably cut his hands off. He shook his head in response to Todd and continued to ponder as his friend continued getting wilder in his imagination, with more adolescent digression around Joanne Jackson's whoppers.

The situation with John's stepsister sat worryingly with him in recent times. He had seen her on only one or two occasions, before running into her last week, when she started up a conversation with him and immediately took a young teenage liking to her as they walked down the Windmill road together that day. She attended St Mary's school he learnt, with surprise, he thought she was Haling Manor same as Christine and Norma. She was returning from her Saturday job at Allders department store. Ray had complimented that she wore Farah's and recollecting of her, being one of the first girls he had seen wear them and added accolades that it really suited her. Along with the grey Slazenger jumper she donned, he heaped more praises on her and received a coveted smile back.

The single ended conversation which reminded him that maybe she could help him with some of the items he wished for his wardrobe. His dreamy thoughts remained on the strawberry blond and the peck on his cheek from her, for showing concern. She stopped him at the corner to her road and said goodbye, when he offered that she should come over the park to hang about with him and their little gang more often. Norma and Christine always invited her, but she was put off by the presence of him and his mates and was glad an invite had been offered by him.

"Think we should stay well clear of Mr Stephens. I don't even think them rumours are even true. Plus, I think he is helping with some building permits or something for my uncles, I overheard them in the pub."

"Flipping cradle snatcher." Todd cursed.

"Well we don't really know that, and they definitely don't know about it. They wouldn't be doing business with him. I suppose."

"And because you want to get off with her. Bannercheck." Todd laughed receiving an elbow and a playful punch in the arm.

Their idle conversation waned onto robbing the corner shop for cigarettes and making custom bikes to sell and Sarah's job at the department store became of note again. Until it was broken when they saw the silhouettes of Norma, Christine and Bev trudging across the pathway, they were all linked arms ducking into the driving rain.

"Oi! Oi!" Todd shouted towards the huddle of girls.

Upon hearing their voices surprised them, they wouldn't have thought anyone would be about in the depressing weather. They all in sync, diverted quickly towards the shelter and reached them out of breath and soaked.

"Why yous two sitting out here? It's pissing down." Bev questioned, shivering slightly from the chill.

"Sheltering from the rain." Ray quipped tossing a Wrigley's juicy fruit wrapper onto the ground and the chewing gum stick into his mouth. He offered the pack out to the group.

"What 'append to your 'head Chris?' Todd observed motioning towards the slight swelling, she winced shyly away from him. Ray Stood up and pulled a torch from his coat pocket after he beckoned her towards him.

"That looks quite sore." Ray examined. Norma and Bev looked towards one another awkwardly, while Christine acted with little concern.

"Where's Sharon and Sarah?" Ray asked purposefully, even knowing Sharon was at a family get together.

"Who wants a fag?" Bev diverted.

Christine looked towards Ray with a smile as she continued to disguise the real pain and throbbing she felt inside her head. She adored the way he always fussed over her and knowing how much he cared for her, almost sisterly to an extent, the more it became paramount for her to keep quiet about the truth.

"It's alright Ray. I jumped off the bus at the Whitgift and bashed my head straight into the bus stop." She replied pretty convincingly.

Although the shelter was damp from the rain, the wooden benches had been protected by the sturdy structure. She moved up closer towards him, leaning her sore head onto his shoulder as a subtle way for him to take his suspecting eyes off her, before her own face gave the truth away. He flicked the beam of light off again.

"Why do you carry a torch in your bloody pocket?" Norma quizzed.

"That's not a torch, he's just happy to see yah." Todd guffawed. But his Pinewood studio, Benny Hill comedy drifted over all of their heads.

"Comes in handy. You never know when you're gonna

need it. Give us a light Akehurst." Ray diverted.

She chucked the box of swan vesta towards him, as she continued to pace and shiver to keep herself warm, puffing smoke out like an exhaust. He struck the red headed tip against the sandpaper strip on the side of the box. He coughed with the first drag, then drew it again blowing the smoke out confidently.

"Since when did you start smoking?" Christine quizzed, her face looked at him with a playful disapproving smile. Smoking had become common amongst the boys and the girls at her school and on the estate, when all of a sudden everyone seemed engrossed in becoming adults during their childhood.

"We bunked off one day." Bev replied. "We were with that nutcase from his school. He smoked like a flaming chimney, wasn't long before we were buying three singles out of the paki shop." They were all laughing except for Todd who looked around at Ray confused.

"You bunked off without me?"

"You weren't even in school that day you div."

"Oh yeah, was that the day I went up Oxford street with Tony?"

Ray gestured with confusion, keeping up with Todd and his mad adventures to get out of going to school, so wasn't too concerned about how Todd felt about him hanging out with Raph most afternoons.

"Let me have a drag." Christine saddled closer again beside him as he raised the cigarette tip up to her lips. She puffed the smoke out in a cloud.

"Nah that's not how you do it, you 'ave to take it down. Like this. Look." He explained.

"You n'arf look like your uncle when you smoke. Hard nut." She jested with a cute smile.

"What cha doin' smokin' boy." Ray impersonated in a deep voice laughing, imitating his uncle. He and Christine continued giggling sharing the puffs of the John Player special. Todd was whispering into Norma's ear, leaving Bev feeling left out

"Come sit with us Bev." Ray invited, he put his arms around them both. Christine looked shyly away as Bev snuggled up to him which warmed her immediately as she giggled girlishly, blushing.

"Yous are my favourite birds." He chuckled, tickling them both simultaneously. They shuffled forward sniggering excessively at his touch.

"Do yous two have to snog in front of all of us like that?" Bev diverted to Norma and Todd who were now completely embraced ignoring their spectating friends. Ray spat out the now flavourless chewing gum and stared towards them both despairingly, then turned to kiss Christine, she first evaded his face as she gazed into his eyes in surprise but then moved her head forwards and closed her eyes gently to peck his lips in return. He then turned his attention to Bev, who willingly with starry eyes, fully French kissed him. Christine sunk her head back onto his shoulder as if seeking for his attention, he lingered with Bev until she then turned away abruptly, with a feeling of disloyalty to her friend.

Todd stopped kissing Norma as they were all now sat with their own thoughts, the smokers blowing cigarette smoke outwards. Christine took Ray's cigarette and began to practice, the correct technique.

"How about we go down the pub and nick some Shandy Bass." Todd piped in, fracturing the brief long silence.

"Shandy Bass?" Norma said loudly "At least nick a bottle of Cinzano."

"Ergh." Bev heaved with pretence.

Christine laughed out loud, which made Ray and Todd both look at them. Norma was holding her sides trying to compose herself to start the tale.

"Bev's nicked a bottle out her brothers' car when he dropped us to school one day." She started, as she continued holding her sides trying to explain. "Remember Chris? We were telling her to slow down, when she necked from the bottle before registration, then she threw up all over Mrs Miller during netball."

"That was so funny." Christine began to cry out with laughter at the memory.

"She's in tears this one." Ray's face bore a huge grin towards her.

"Oh, Ray it was so funny."

"And as for you Norma." Bev rang out. "You both helped me back to the changing rooms, Chris says for you to get me a drink and you fill up a cup with more Cin-flippin-zano."

The shelter was erupting with laughter, especially with Norma's innocence on her face as if it was the right thing to do.

"Hair of the dog, my old dear calls it." Came her selfless reply.

"During bloody P.E?" Ray laughed.

"D'yah know what I mean?" Bev agreed shaking her head.

The shelter echoed with their laughter, which then peated out abruptly as they strained their eyes towards some tall figures walking towards them. Ray shone his torch to identify who they were, and noticed there were more following behind, which made him stand up. Todd stood up beside him as they took a few paces forward while the girls sat quietly worried behind them.

"What the fuck are Arsenal still doing here?" Todd said under his breath, as the crew continued marching in their direction, they quickly calculated that they were heading back in the direction of his uncle's pub. The game had ended over three hours ago and Todd and Ray had witnessed several clashes between the rival London clubs, they argued on their way to the park with fish and chips in hand, that in their opinion, Arsenal had been 'run' by Palace, to Ray's disappointment, added to the frustration with the 1 nil defeat.

"Hold up." The leader of the army of thugs commanded as he looked towards where the light had shone from.

"Yous were about earlier weren't yah?"

"Maybe." Todd answered cheekily.

"So why were you running with us when the Palace outnumbered us?" Said another tall lad wearing a leather jacket that seemed to be bulging unnaturally as the torch light illuminated off of the shiny concrete.

"Cos we are Gooners, and that lot are always bashing us up in school. I smacked one in the gob. Me mate slapped one and all." Todd explained.

"That's why we come here, instead of going back to the pub." Ray continued excitedly.

"Smart." The tall lad in the leather smiled.

"So, is that their main boozer?" The leader asked.

"It's my uncle Pete and Sid's pub. They'll be fuming at the damage."

"Palace came at us first. Are they still in there?"

"Doubt they'll be in there now. Usually when a match is on, they use most of the local ones, but it's mainly Whitehorse Estate drink in there, we're a mixture of supporters normally. Some are Palace, Yids, Gooners and a few Chelsea. The landlords are Gooners." Todd responded confidently.

"You's want the Whitehorse on most match days or the Swan and Sugarloaf, that's the main firm's pub, they're always in there, but it's too far to walk."

The leader looked around at the crew, which Ray had now counted up to fifteen and prided at their bravery.

"Fucking waste of time this then?" The leader summed up disappointedly.

"We're here now." One disagreed. "And the station is miles away."

"Selhurst station is only a couple of minutes from the Pub or if you turn right at the top of this road is West Croydon."

Everyone began to look past Ray and Todd at the voice that came from behind them.

"How old are you boys?"

"I'm 12 and 'alf." Todd replied proudly.

"I'm 13 next month. 11th October." Ray responded nervously.

"Fair play to yah. My names Yogi." He introduced. "That came on top for us earlier, but we see yous stood firm."

"We're good heads and well up for it." Todd remarked somewhat desperate for the recognition. Ray winced slightly embarrassed as Yogi and his firm smiled.

"We'll leave yous to your Doris's." He smirked, winking at the pair of them as all the eyes began to adjust to the temporary floodlights from Ray's torch.

"Stoke are at ours next week. We stand in the clock end." He stated and then turned his attention back to his army as they trudged off again as the rain began to ease off.

"Come on, we'll have a quick mooch about at the pub then fuck off."

They all watched their swaggered march through the park and out. Todd was totally awed at the firm and the confidence they exuberated.

"Flippin' Hell Ray. He's one of their top boys. I've heard of that Yogi. You ask Tony." Todd expressed excitedly.

"They come all that bloody way in the rain just to fight?" Christine questioned astonished.

"That's the thing with them. The Twins are the same following Chelsea." Bev reported.

"Can we leave now before we bump into more weirdos?" Norma chuckled.

"Yeah." Christine agreed. "Besides, Bev needs her Cinzano."

They all erupted in laughter as they made their way out. Todd was jumping onto Ray's back excitedly that they had been acknowledged by one of London's hooligan elite. Christine and Norma lagged slightly behind as they exited the park squeezing each other's arm tightly.

"Thanks for not saying nothin' to him about that."

CHAPTER 9

THE SCHOOL ASSEMBLY

The weekend had passed and another Monday morning saw Ray, Todd and Tony gathered outside the school gate embarking on some of the usual mischief. Three older fifth year boys lead by Billy Burgess, approached in their smart uniform, blazer sleeves rolled up, which contrasted against the shirt buttons done up tightly to the top and skinny ties. Ray and his year preferred the loose collar look and thick tie, that barely came past the V of their jumpers.

"Look at these fucking little Gooners over here." They squared up looking down on them.

"Wotcha Billy." Tony greeted.

"Where were you? Did you not hear about your little mates tried to have it with us on Saturday? We had them on their toes." Billy said smugly. Tony looked around confused, Todd was puffing out his chest un-phased. After just arriving at the school gates, Raph was stood unnoticed behind them all.

"Lucky it wasn't us Millwall about then. Jills." He commented with a serious glare towards the older boys. Ray, Todd and Tony all turned around by his voice. Bill and the other older boys named Ian and Stu ignored his comments and walked through the gates just as the bell rang for the start of class.

"Sit on it, wanky scrotums." Todd gestured behind their backs childishly, as the other boys laughed.

They all walked up together while Todd explained to Tony about the weekends exciting events. Ray was engrossed in conversation with Raph.

"How come you weren't about Saturday?"

"I went up to Sheffield with the old man, Plummer and Winkle, fell asleep on the train, I was flipping knackered." Raph replied.

"You missed a good bit of fun outside the pub, Me, Todd and some Gooners, kicked off with Palace. It was reem Raph."

"How did that go down in the Gloucester?"

"Pete give me a clump, for getting involved in it so close to home."

"I make him right." Raph agreed.

"Never let anyone, outside of the family, know what you are thinking." Ray commented, looking towards him then smiled.

"This is business. It's never personal." Raph laughed. They continued with the mafia quotes all the way into class before the teacher shouted at them for their attention.

"O.K class. Today we will be in assembly because we have some exciting news to share about our 2nd year footballers who will be representing this proud school in the Surrey schools cup final a week on Wednesday." She beamed with pride.

"Raphael White, Tony Robinson, Kevin Priddy, John Read and Raymond Morgan. Please go now to the sports hall to Mr Doohan."

The boys exited quickly from registration and rushed excitedly to the sports hall. They were joined by Todd and the rest of the school team including the star goalkeeper Nathan Boyce, who had played all but one of the games without conceding a solitary goal.

"Boycie!" Ray greeted, patting him on the back as they approached him at the entrance to the sports hall. He jostled playfully with the other teammates as they began to congregate into the expansive hall, where they were all directed onto the stage and to sit across the low benches that were laid out, with teacher's chairs either side of them.

Mr Blackman looked unimpressed as he walked in, his disapproving expression radiated to single out some members of the team, who he grudgingly would have to express warm gratitude to, for performing so well for the school. Despite the punch up that was reported back to him after the final whistle.

As the rest of the school began to enter the assembly hall, the disciplinarian headmaster ushered them in patiently while standing at the podium. Ray's English and registration teacher Miss Goodwin sat down beside the head sport teacher Mr Doohan, which always set off gossip amongst the pupils. She was in her late twenties, a pretty, slightly overweight teacher with ginger hair, freckled pale skin and deep blue eyes but without doubt, her sexuality was exhumed by the clothes that she wore. Like the signature v necks that exposed her distractive cleavage and dark silky denier tights, under her figure-hugging skirts that she continually adjusted to cover her upper thighs appropriately from time to time, especially when she sat on her desk in front of the class during discussions, which put her only behind Arts and drama teacher Miss Storey, on the crass adolescent fantasy 'boof list' discussions by some of the pupils, mainly amongst Todd and Tony.

After a moment of suspense, for the nearest seated boys to her, awaiting to see if any brief titillation would be revealed as she made herself comfortable on her seat, Raph nudged Nathan to share a well-known secret.

"e's havin' it off wiv her. Pass it on." He ordered.

"Doohan's 'aving it off with Goodwin. Pass it on" Nathan nudged the next boy along until it reached the end of the line.

"Who's havin' it off?" Todd repeated loudly as the whole bench erupted in laughter.

"Mr Carter...You'll be playing 'Left back on Wednesday afternoon." The headmaster paused to leave room for the boys to all sit obediently. "Left back in the classroom, in detention, if you don't stop misbehaving boy."

Todd glared down the line unimpressed while his teammates bore their eyes towards the gathering in front of them, all with the mischievous look of innocence.

The assembly commenced with the usual preamble about disobedience and damage to school property, both with stern promises of repercussions, before ending with the 2nd year team who had become the first team to represent the school in the district schools football finals, for nearly twenty-five years.

"And finally...Last Friday afternoon, our 2nd year boys played Purley Oaks in the semi-finals of the cup and after a hard game that saw nil-nil at the final whistle. Goals from Ray Morgan and Kevin Priddy, topped by a penalty save from our outstanding goalkeeper Nathan Boyce in extra time, put us through to the finals."

"Hooraaaaayyy." The boys all cheered, as some of the boys pumped the air with their fists.

"OKAY, Pipe down you lot...Next Wednesday afternoon, there will be coaches for first, second and third years to attend the Croydon arena to cheer on the boys in the final."

"What about us?" Shouted a fourth-year boy from the back.

"Yeah?" Shouted another.

"Let me finish." He peered with discern towards the back of the assembly. "Unfortunately, the fourth and fifth years have Mock exams in the afternoon."

He continued to be interrupted when the hall erupted with insolent boos from the older boys.

"But... You can all attend after school, kick of is 4:30 so there'll be plenty of time to get there before the start. So, let's wish our 2nd years and Mr Doohan all the best of luck and a round of applause."

Most of the accolades came from the younger years at the front. Ushered by Doohan, they all stood up to receive the applause and descended from the stage waving and bowing as they past the podium. Raph caught the eyes of Billy and some of the other older boys and saluted an offering to them with his arms out wide as a challenge, which both Tony and Ray noticed and shook their heads.

"He's not all there." Tony chuckled but then they both

directed challenging stares back to them all.

During break time most of the team stuck together for lunch. Ray, Nathan, Raph, Kevin, Todd, Tony, Neil and John all sat eating and discussing general football chit chat, when Billy approached the table and slammed his hands in front of Raph's tray.

"You little boys want to take on the Nifty 50?" He asked rhetorically, as five more boys began to congregate around them.

"Fifty?" Raph queried confused. "There's only six o' yah."

"Leave it out Billy." Tony begged. "We are all mates."

"How about, you shut your rubber lips Sambo." Commanded one of the gang of boys named Sean Hurst. His warning came at Tony's surprise.

"We see yous giving it the biggun on the stage. Let's go outside, see if yous are brave having some fisticuffs." This time Ian Cooper interjected with a taunting smile, flicking at Neil's ear, who along with Nathan had his back towards them.

Raph stood up straight away and was ready with his fist clenched. Ray tugged at his jumper to pull him back down into his seat.

"We'll finish our lunches first if you don't mind. Then we'll see yous outside." He stated confidently as he began to tuck into his chocolate sponge with custard, not even glancing up at any of the boys. They walked off knocking Kevin Priddy's almost empty cup of water onto his already finished dinner plate.

"Ooh! he's hard!" Kevin whispered sarcastically, in fact, more nervously one would assume because he had said it barely audible to anyone else on the table.

"Hurry up and eat that." Raph ushered to Ray and turned back to Tony. "What a fucking liberty, calling you Sambo… Only I can call you that." The table erupted in laughter as Tony playfully grabbed him in a headlock.

"Where are you going?" Ray shouted to Todd, as he quickly stood up after packing his tray, ready to be placed onto the tall tray rack at the back of the dinner hall.

"To the bogs. Buck up with me at the stairs by the sports hall." He whispered between Raph and Tony's ears on his way back past.

After they had finished, only Ray, Tony, Nathan and Raph were stood by the stairs waiting for Todd. Their other team mates sensibly declined the offer of having a fight with the older boys. Todd came along shortly after with a broad smile followed by three fifth year boys in tow.

The fifth formers looked towards Raph with some distrust. Todd beckoned them all to follow him, he produced three wooden mallets and two rounders bats from a plastic bag and handed them out amongst his mates under the stairwell, all of them pivoting their heads around nervously, for any teachers that might have come along.

"Hide them up your back." He chuckled.

"Good stuff." Raph raptured with glee. "Today, we settle all family business."

Ray struggled to stifle his laughter, as the others congregated with confused stares towards him. On many occasions, both Raph and Todd had the strangest habit of finding comedy or blurting out random statements and quotes at inappropriate times. The screenplay script, they had recited over and over again during days when they played truant from school but also whenever they could repeat it under the right context.

"Let's go bash them mouthy fourth year divs up." Todd rallied his friends.

With the weapons concealed, they marched militantly through the school corridors, avoiding eye contact and hoping not to attract any of the usual fight fans that sniffed out many of the past arranged fights to settle old group beefs and personal straighteners. Luckily, the missing boys from their table sensibly did not set off any rumours of the pending lunch time war.

The fifth-year boys talked amongst themselves and paid

little attention to the younger ones. Until, they were outside walking towards Sean, Billy, Ian, Stu and their little gang of eight. Even numbers, with the fifth-year additions in their ranks. Billy immediately looked towards them concerned as they all approached.

"It's got nuffin to do with yous lot." Sean quickly reasoned.

"Nuttin' to do with us." Errol replied calmly in response. They continued past them to stand beside the wall. Errol's mates took up position out of sight, purposefully poised as lookouts towards the schoolyard. Billy's gang were still a bit wary to the uncertainty as to why and what, were the fifth-year boy's motive for joining the second years and even more so, when Ray, Todd, Nathan, Tony and Raph stood to face them all confidently.

"You shouldn't go around calling black people names, like you did my mate Tony." Raph suggested, in a matter of fact way that had Sean looking towards the fifth years, who were all black and Tony and Ray looking at Raph chuckling.

Tony withdrew his mallet first and steamed into Sean, which took them all by surprise when the mallet struck heavily to the side of his head. Ray swung his attack at Ian, who went straight down from the force and then began pursuing his violent interest onto a shell shocked short stocky lad called Gavin Edwards. Meanwhile Raph tore straight into Billy, connecting with a swift combination of bat, fist and two accurate kicks into the midriff, that left his opposition winded and on all fours. Nathan's rounders bat went whizzing past the fracas in the direction of three other boys, who at first backed off, Nathan and Todd began a pursuit that ended in a fair bit of fisticuffs with the three remaining boys, with Raph and Ray joining in to outnumber them.

Taking it in turn to swing and miss and then connecting with one, then for a short while it became unfairly one sided as Nathan and Todd attacked Jimmy Longford on the ground. For protection, he was kicking upwards at them as blows rained against his flailing limb before they left him alone. Turning towards the fourth years who were nursing their injuries, following Todd's and Nathan's, then Raph's and Ray's tag teaming violence on them, they were all pleasantly surprised about the limited amount of comparative collateral damage they received in return.

They walked back to regroup with Tony, passing Sean, Billy, Gavin and Ian who wearily all nodded a respectful acknowledgment back at them. Hobbling with discomfort, wiping at their cut lips and straightening up their uniforms, they appeared to be not in the slightest upset with their performance in the altercation but somewhat awed.

Errol came over from his viewing area of the wall and held open a bag for them to drop the weapons in, also with an approving expression on his face.

"My lickle yout deh. Mash dem like Rambo." Errol acknowledged Tony with a respectful fist pump onto his chest. "Looks like no-one's gonna fuck 'bout with this little posse." He chuckled to his friends and directed them back into the school.

The boys walked back towards the school building with their chests all inflated with pride and with banter all the way, patting each other on the back.

"I got a question for you Tone. It's spinning me nut." Raph contemplated.

"What's spinning your nut Raph?" Replied Tony, almost expectant of something quirky.

"How comes you always go all Jamaican when you're havin a row?"

"Cos me a mash up dem bloodclaart innit?" He replied, with everyone creasing with laughter.

"Mash dem like Rambo." Raph tried to re-enact Tony smashing the mallet into Sean's head, with a hopelessly poor take on the patois.

"Come on boys." Ray grinned. "I've got boring old geography lesson now."

"Yeah. I got maths with Grizzly." Nathan added.

"Who's Grizzly?" Raph questioned.

"Mrs Adams Raphael. Grizzly Adams?" Tony laughed "Haven't you seen that on the Tele?"

"Nah don't watch much tele." He replied in earnest.

"Only the Godfather a million times though Eh?" Ray giggled as they all strode into school towards their classes.

CHAPTER 10

SARAH'S SECRET

"Here you are Sid." Pete was laughing as Ray, Tony and Nathan walked into the Gloucester after school. The three boys looked towards them in a confused way.

"How was school today boys?" Sammy asked with a huge grin on his face. All three boys shrugged nonchalantly, then began looking to each other, half in confusion, the other half wondering whether the knowledge of their petty crime activities have got back to them.

"More to the point. I heard you boys were unlucky during that cup final the other day." He continued.

The realisation hit home with some relief, that at least it wasn't the shoplifting spree in Piccadilly that they were being drilled on.

"Have a butchers, it made the papers." Pete chuckled. "Go on, read 'em it."

SCHOOL'S CUP FINAL ENDS IN VIOLENCE

The final of the county district schoolboys cup final had to be abandoned after fighting broke out between Oakwood High school of Coulsdon and Stanley Heath high School of Croydon. Police were called to attend after the twenty-two-man (boys) brawl with the score even at 1-1. Teachers, coaches and staff at the Croydon Arena intervened to separate the 2nd year boys of the respective schools. The scuffling continued when rival pupils spectating the match became involved, even after the game was abandoned.

As a result, Stanley Heath were disqualified, and officials confirmed that both schools will be investigated about their conduct. In a statement, headmaster Mr Blackman of Stanley

Heath said, there will be serious repercussions for any of the boys involved in bringing our proud school into disrepute.

"I mean, you can't even make this fucking shit up." Sid's face became vexed as he threw the newspaper towards Ray in a temper. The three boys stood in embarrassment in front of the whole pub.

"You two better do one." Sammy directed to Nathan and Tony who were stood as shamed as their mate.

"And I'll be on the blower to your old man Nathan, let's make no mistake about that." Sid added.

Ray looked down towards the floor and patiently ran the incident back again in his head. Cursing again the unfair treatment from his uncle added to the school's decision, to ban Nathan, Todd, Tony, Kevin Priddy, Raph and the substitute that day, Steve Attwood, along with himself, from the school football team indefinitely, who in their opinion, were all unfairly singled out accused of causing the fracas.

"You even made the papers…The fucking papers. Is this how you represent your school?" Sid shouted.

"Let's hear his side of the story Sid." Tommy interrupted. receiving a stone-cold glare from him.

"His story? It says it all in the fucking papers." He hissed.

"What's the fuckin point…" Ray huffed as he threw his bag down aggressively and began to walk out, just as Angie walked in. He tried to barge past her, she sensed the atmosphere and immediately tugged him back by his blazer as he defiantly attempted to evade her grasp.

"Raymond Morgan. Is this a way to carry on, barging past me like that? Come here now."

"What?" He huffed, refraining from any further struggling. The rest of the pub assumed a nothing going on around here demeanour as they looked into their drinks and continued playing darts or whatever they had been previously doing.

"Drop the daggers at your uncle and tell me what's the matter." She soothed. "Sid, not a word." Her no nonsense manner stopped him in his track as he was about to guide her towards the bold headlines on the Croydon Advertiser.

"Yous lot are always preaching about looking after our own. People calling us golliwogs and coons and we're supposed to just swallow this shit and not say nothin?" He stated breathlessly.

"Who's been calling you names?"

"It's not the name calling, its them thinking they can, and we can't do nothing."

"So, what you saying. You caused a brawl because they called you names?" Sammy urged.

"It's not plain name calling Sammy." Angie vexed towards him.

"Yeah! Me, Todd and Tony, any of us. Every time we got near them, they'd start. So, when Tony jumped him, we all steamed in and gave him a kicking. And anyone else that wanted it, we had it with them and all."

"Fair play son." Sammy smiled.

"Sammy...Will you stop!" Angie snapped. Sammy obeyed apologetically with a comforting wink towards the boy.

"Let's go upstairs. I'll prepare tea and you can tell me the whole story. Take these bags up for me, go on love."

He grabbed the Sainsbury's bags from her and retrieved his school bag from Tommy, which was wet after it had toppled a table of drinks due to his frustration.

"Sid. How can you all have a go at him. Didn't you ask him why before digging him out? You know how people used to treat me. Spitting in my face. And he has to go through all that, in this day and age. It's not right."

"I never knew. I just seen the headlines that him and his mates caused a fracas and got disqualified."

"Well if they are calling him or any of his mates them disgusting names, I'll be up that school tomorrow. You mark my words." She warned and strutted past everyone to join Ray upstairs.

Tony and Nathan were spotted trying to sneakily hear

what was going to happen to Ray, peeping through the opaque glass at the shadowy figures inside but then sharply disappeared after Pete snuck up behind them.

"Get out of it…the pair of yah." He yelled as they both took off looking back at him laughing.

Angie sat beside Ray and began to stroke at his back to comfort him. Reviewing the newspaper article with empathy.

"So, is it true, you all caused this big fight?"

He nodded slightly embarrassed, but he was confident that at least she would see his side of the story.

"It was really bad though mum. The names they were digging at us. Sambo, golli, nig-nog, all game and the ref did nothing, our coach did nuffin. In the end Tony drop kicked this one kid, then we all steamed in." He described excitedly.

"And you were the ones disqualified?"

"It doesn't matter, we were better than them, that's why they started all the crap."

"There you go. You should never lose your head in situations like this. This is why they antagonise you."

"Well I ain't standing for any of that. But in truth, we should have held our temper until after."

"Yes my darling. Reacting in that way is never the answer. You should have waited until the game was finished. Always bide your time." She advised with a sympathetic smile. "And then you give 'em a bloody good hiding."

They both chuckled, she stroked comfortingly at his curly hair looking into his eyes adoringly and drew him in closer with a lovingly hug. She had a unique comforting smell of Anais Anais perfume, her trademark odour that always alleviated any problems consuming his young mind.

"Go out and play and make sure you are back in time for tea." She smiled and kissed him on the forehead."

"I love you." Ray proclaimed sincerely.

"I love you too my sweetheart. Go."

Ray passed both his uncles, Sammy, Tommy and the masses in silence and retrieved his bike from the back yard of the pub, navigating past some stockpiled wooden benches and beer barrels, before letting himself out of the back gate. Reaching his arm back over to lock it behind him. Pulling out of the alley he bumped into Raph and Todd, surprised but somewhat guessing they were on their way to the pub to gage how much trouble he might be in.

"We were just coming to look for yah." Raph said with a smirk, disguised as concern, rather than the usual ammunition for the regular mickey taking they were all now becoming accustomed to, a bond of their recently formed camaraderie.

"Yeah, Rambo and Boycie are over the park and said you were getting mannersed. Shame guy." Todd giggled.

"Shut ya trap about mannersed." Ray disagreed. "I actually thought I was gonna get a proper shoeing."

They all laughed as Ray explained that his mum was going to give everyone that's blaming them what for.

"Good old Angie." Todd praised. "Have you seen Ray's mum Raph? She's proper tasty."

He immediately took off at full pelt, laughing, while Ray and then Raph gave pursuit. They all stopped as they reached the wooden shelter where Tony, Nathan, Christine, Sharon, Norma and Sarah were all gathered. Their laughter simmered suddenly when they noticed the girls in tears.

"What's the matter with yous?" Todd worried. They all responded in silence as Tony and Nathan shrugged unanimously. Ray threw his bike down and was huddled around Christine, he then noticed the black eye and bruises on Sarah's face, flushed red with a saddened shame.

"What happened?" He repeated. "Who's bashed Sarah?" He asked angrily.

"That bastard…"

"Shut up Norma. It's no one's fucking business." Sarah screamed and began walking off.

"Sarah!" Ray chased closely behind her. Her hair bounced in anger as she walked hastily, he had to jog a little to keep up with her long stride.

"Sarah wait a sec. Slow down...Wait." He pleaded before she finally came to a halt. With her head down to shield away from his eyes, he guided her head up slowly with honest sentiment and a sympathetic smile towards her.

"We all stick together here and seeing you all bashed up like this. If you tell us and want our help, we'll help."

She looked towards him almost ready to utter the words to end all the pain. He could sense her vulnerability in her sullen hazel eyes, that stared at him forgivingly. She just needed time to feel more comfortable around them, so he wouldn't push her to answer.

"We don't like seeing any of our mates upset. Especially our girls. You're Christine and Norma's mate. Means you're my mate and all." The sentiment spilled genuinely from his mouth, with words that resonated from deep within his heart, that she unwittingly admired, almost swooning.

She smiled as much as her swollen lip would allow. Her auburn hair appeared on fire in the sunsetting backdrop, styled commonly, with a long fringe that laid over her eye and covered most of the purple coloured bruising, masking a much deeper hurt.

A glow of freckles splashed cutely upon her face. He stood for a minute longer, how his mother always did, to take a deep breath, staring at her, with some hesitation. His mind inappropriately wandered about the rumours about her. He eased his hands around her shoulders to lead her back to the group, who by now were all just stood as an audience as Ray charmed her back towards them.

They both walked back over to the shelter and all tried their hardest to talk about other stuff with Todd, the usual comedian, lightening the mood. Returning back to the topic of Ray's mother.

"Ahh she's lovely is Ang." Said Christine with a big smile

"She reminds me of Marylin Monroe." Sharon added. "I remember when she used to sell Avon stuff to my mum."

Sharon was an older lad off the estate named Jimmy Bexley's or Bex to everyone around the estate, younger sister, cutely pretty with wide grey eyes that looked excited every time she was around them all, which many of the boys had fancied at one point or another, but Bex was very protective over her and most of the boys didn't want the grief but they also all saw her more of their little sister, as she was the year below them but always hung around with Christine and Norma who styled her hair and molly coddled her.

"Phwoar, Jilly Johnson she reminds me of." Todd remarked.

"She's page three, you pervert." Norma vexed jokingly.

"Ouch! Why you hitting me for?" He complained as everyone started laughing after he received a thump in the arm from Norma.

"Thanks Norma. Stop perving on me mum." Ray laughed and added another thump into his other arm. "He's never coming around for dinner again."

"Yeah and my mum." Norma laughed. "Yes Mrs Collins. No Mrs Collins. That's him."

"Just being polite. But she's tasty and all, ain't she Ray?" Todd giggled shoving into him.

Raph unwrapped a new box of 10 Rothmans and passed one to Norma.

"Do you want one Sarah?" Norma asked, ignoring Todd's lewdness, snatching the box from Raph.

"You can go twos with her." Raph snatched back the box immediately.

"'ere Ray, remember when Raph stabbed you with a pen knife in class?" As usual, Todd sent the conversation way off topic.

"Pen knife? It was a flipping compass. Div." Ray confirmed a bit bewildered on even mentioning it.

"Sonny flipping Corleone him mate." Tony laughed.

"You're not wrong." Ray chuckled.

"I love that film." Sarah confirmed.

"How come I haven't watched it yet?" Sharon asked.

"That's Norma and Christine's fault Shal. They'd rather have yous watching that soppy West Side love story." Todd dismissed sticking his finger down his throat.

"Shut your trap Todd, It's Love Story, we love that film." Christine huffed.

"Ahh that film makes me cry." Sharon reminisced. "And rebel without a cause. James Dean I'd get off with him."

"Fuck that. Yous wanna get on the godfather Sharon, forget all that soppy nonsense." Raph advised smugly interrupting her swooning.

"Who's your favourite character Ray." Sarah interjected.

"Clemenza. I think. Or the Don Corleone himself." Ray answered.

"I like Luca Brasi." Said Todd.

"But he doesn't even do much." Sarah cross examined.

"Yeah but if you listen, Michael describes him as being a very important person for his father." Todd dissected to Raph's surprise.

"That's a very well thought out observation there Todd." Raph agreed. "But he was strangled to death wearing a bullet proof vest. I mean, how's your luck?"

More laughter and cigarette smoke consumed their camp as the chatter swayed back and forth. Their lingering conversations on movies, music and favourite flavour of crisp passed the time very, very quickly and cheered the somewhat sombre Sarah up and was soon in better spirits. There was also Christine that declared her own reason for needing cheering up, her dad had decided they would be moving off the estate to a place called Keston. As the boy's high jinks made them all forget any woes that betide them.

With the news about Christine moving away, in a fickle response, Ray's, non-too dissimilar magnetic axis towards Sarah, knew, or somehow remembered the signs all too well. Although very young at the time, he almost instinctively understood what someone being bullied looked like. He hadn't paid her much attention, being this was the first real time they had spent in each other's company but as the early evening set in, he found her really eye catching, despite the bruising. There was a cute desire for her from the smiles she returned back at him throughout.

When it was teatime, they all said goodbye to each other, Tony, Raph, Todd and Sharon remained at the shelter along with Bev, who had just turned up after an after-school cleaning job.

Norma, Christine and Sarah walked back towards the estate with Nathan, while Ray rode back at speed towards the Gloucester, pulling wheelies all the way back to the pub.

He screeched his bike to a sudden halt when he caught the sight of Theresa Downey walking past the pub. The teenagers heart throbbed from the lightning bolt at seeing her, beautifully dressed in a tight pair of slacks and high heel shoes with a beige mink fur coat. He could almost smell her mesmerising fragrance even from where he was stood. A similar pleasant aroma that always resonated with the recent pubescent shift that was starting to ascend.

"Wotcha Theresa." He shouted keenly, bumping the bike ungainly up the kerb and then immediately heard the sound of his childish voice repeating back inside his head. She just waved with a sultry silent smile that titillated towards him and then he noticed what had truly captured her attention and the real reason that she had a big smile on her face. She greeted a man who kissed her and swung her around like the romantic hero straight out of a Mills and Boon novel, who then opened the passenger door to a Silver Ford Capri 2.8 injection, as Ray stood looking love struck past the sexy gleaming motor.

He jumped off his bike and watched as the flash looking geezer with the flicked hair and black roll neck under his black leather jacket boastfully speed towards the sunset horizon. He wheeled his own transportation dejectedly, around to the back, his mother looked down from the window as he parked it along the fence.

"I was just about to send out a search party." She said sweetly. Smiling at him starry eyed with love.

◆ ◆ ◆

Just after nine, Ray was sat with his mother watching the TV. She often helped out downstairs but felt she had not shared too much time together, as she kept an eye on Pete and Sid's other enterprises by day, as it was adjudged to be easier getting things done by sending a pretty face than breaking kneecaps. And was more in line to them crossing over into more legitimized ventures.

Their quality time together was short lived when Sid came up with a message from downstairs.

"Your little Doris is downstairs to see yah boy."

"Which one?" Ray boasted, receiving a slap on the leg from her.

"You'll be respectful you."

Ray stomped downstairs eagerly and greeted Norma with a big smile.

"I got something to tell you." She said nervously.

"What's that then?"

"In private. Div." She giggled dragging him by his hand outside. Leaving the pub together, they received childish cheers and raptures from some of the drinkers inside, including his uncles.

"Suppose it's better than him having a punch up." Tommy humoured to the extended laughter from everyone.

He walked with Norma towards the back gate, she then turned to him all serious, when he was expecting, that she wanted to practice some more of the French kissing again after they were all encapsulated with at their camp in recent times.

"That Sarah, she's in so much trouble Ray. We didn't wanna say anything."

"Yeah I could tell." Ray agreed. "Who's bashing her up. Her stepdad?"

"Stepdad? Yeah righto...How did you know?" Norma queried somewhat sarcastic then intrigued.

"Skinhead John told Todd ages ago that he caught his dad getting his end away with her." He said, as a matter of fact.

"How could you know all this and not say nothing?" Norma's face was full of disgust.

"Well we didn't even know if it was true. He gave us some money a while back, I can't remember but I guess he was guilty of something dodgy. Todd wasn't even sure, cos he might have been fibbing. John I mean." Ray shrugged.

"Well for your information, Mr Know-it-all. She's only just turned fifteen and he's her real dad..." She stung, as Ray stood wide eyed aghast.

"No...Step-dad...It's John's step...sister." He paused as the realisation sank in.

"You boys are so thick. Look, she told us they'd been doing stuff for ages. Her mum had been John's dad's bit of fluff, for years. When he left Johns mum, he moved in with Sarah's mum."

"His own daughter? We thought he was just a cradle snatcher, we never knew he was a proper nonce."

"Yeah well me and Christine saw him dragging her into his car after they had a blazing row outside the Mail Coach. We were all coming back from the Whitgift and when we butted in, he shoved Chris's head into a wall...and."

"Hold up. He did what? To Christine?"

"Yeah couple of weeks ago, remember the cut on her head? She said not to tell none of yah."

"Tosser." Ray Cursed. "So, he hurt our Chris and playing that nonsense with his daughter? I'm telling me uncle." He seethed and began hastily towards the pub.

"No Ray Stop." She pleaded.

"Think about it. If he gets wind that we all know, what will happen to Sarah? Or us?"

"Uncle Sid won't let anything happen to yah."

"You can't tell Sid, not yet. We promised Sarah."

"But you told me now."

"I know but…"

"If I tell Sid he'd kill him plain and simple. The dirty…"

"Listen to yourself Ray."

"What?"

"Wanting people killed." She smarted trying to make him see reason.

"So, are we to just let him carry on?"

"The reason she was getting smacked about. Is because he found out she was really his." Norma pulled him away again through the alleyway to the other side and entrance to the main block on the estate. She pulled two cigarettes and a lighter from her jacket as they huddled together to light them.

"That is even more the reason we need to stop him."

"She's in love with him she said. And they were doing it like boyfriend-girlfriend in secret. To be fair he's not a bad looking fella."

"Flipping heck Norma." Ray sat astonished after he jumped up to position himself on the wall. "How are they even carrying on with out the old lady finding out?"

"I have no idea. But she's told us everything. Now she knows he's her dad, she wanted to stop, and he just loses his rag on her."

"There's still no reason not to tell me uncle Sid Norm."

"We can't say anything Ray."

"I can't believe you've disturbed my TV programme to tell me all this for nothing."

"I know, I just wanted to see how you felt. If I'm honest."

"I feel sick Norma."

"Me and all. But she's our mate."

"He deserves to be shot in the 'ead."

"Is that what your uncle would do…?"

"I'm just saying." Ray shook his head, jumping down to stub the cigarette under his feet.

"I better get home." She sighed.

"Come on, I'll walk yah,"

She linked his arm as they walked through past the flats to the cul-de-sac row of twenty or so houses. They passed the Twins and their mates Billy Baker, Si, Theo, Yusef, Bex and Stu as they sat on the wall and leant up against a black Cortina.

"Wotcha Ray." They all echoed.

"Heard you's lot bashed up them dirty Oakwood poofters the other day?" Bex asked.

"Yeah! That's right." Ray Boasted.

"His little lot are game little cunts." Dale reported to his gang.

"Yous should come with us down the shed." Wayne invited.

"Nah! You're alright." He refused. "We might turn up with the Gooners soon though, you never know."

The older boys all laughed at his brashness. Despite the disrespect to their team, he just proved the point.

"Told yah...fearless little fuckers." Bex said proudly.

Ray continued on with a smile on his face which brought a smile onto Norma's.

"Such an 'ard nut." She tickled him under his arm as they came to her house.

"I wish I could invite you in." She smiled. "But Christine would kill me."

"Todd will kill me and all."

"Todd ain't my boyfriend." She defended.

"Not much."

"Whatever." She emphasised flirtingly. "I'll see yah tomorrow."

"Norma?" He called out to her as she approached her front door. "I'll give it one week. OK?"

"OK." She sighed. "Hold up. What?"

"Me uncle Sid. One week." He shouted back confidently.

CHAPTER 11

LANDS OF HOPE AND GLORY

Sid was sat reflecting nostalgically, looking up at the old post-war photos of the grand opening of this building, in-between, from left to right, the patrons and honourable persons that represented the local and district committee. Sat inside Katherine house in Croydon, his mind wandered on reflectance of the past, a somewhat forgotten past, that was lavished in wealth and prosperity but carried too much baggage, essentially, the bestial behaviour that still has him restless, their so-called family member who failed to reveal certain alliances, with syndicates that profited on the sickening dark side of the sex industry, that was associated for some of those entertained at his late father's establishment, that over time, one way or another, smeared that legacy.

Greasing the palms of hooky coppers was a breeze in comparison to keeping up with the politics and the snide back stabbers that had quickly turned their backs at the first smell of trouble. He could never be one of them, part of that social elite that his father carried off so well. Nowadays, the family business comparatively, was a bit more of the lifestyle he preferred, a modest one, with a very small and loyal circle.

He still wasn't used to waiting on anyone either but him and his brother had vowed to keep the lowest of profile's possible, barring the inevitable needs to keep them revered with the highest reckoning in the underworld. He fidgeted with the A4 envelope tapping against his lap. He repeated this, almost subconsciously to battle his impatience, with the odd glance at his watch he confirmed he had waited fifteen minutes past his 11am appointment and toted this up with the inhospitality, that he wasn't even offered a cup of tea.

The perm-haired, middle aged lady with the blue framed glasses that seemed to age her face much older. Dressed in a green and black chequered mohair jacket that matched the above the knee skirt, approached him in a professional manner. With little by way of an apology written across her face, she hesitated slightly by the phone ringing.

His cold glare remarkably made her forget the distraction as she continued to walk over towards him.

"Mr Fairclough is ready to see you now sir." She harmonised. Sid scratched the top of his brow, indicating the disappointment and the tussle with his natural reaction. Simmering the tension inside and slowly getting up from his seat, he draped the trench coat over his arm to follow the receptionist, slash personal assistant, slash call handler, for the Croydon council building regulations, licensing and permits department.

She toddled in front of him, Sid surprised at the size of her sonorous rear, the zipper almost battling to the last, to behold the strained and under-duress teeth together. She stopped abruptly to give a large rapturous knock onto the door.

"Mr Bryan to see you Mr Fairclough." She turned to smile at him, his eyes ignored her as he went inside in front of her.

He tilted his head downwards with his specs, with eyes trained upwards at Sid, like an old school headmaster and now understood his nephew's perspective of being looked down upon, even when not guilty of any wrongdoing.

"Would you like coffee or tea Mr Bryan?"

"No thanks darling. I'm good." Sid replied nonchalantly. "Could you close the door behind you please."

She stood for a moment aghast at his sheer audacity and looked towards her boss.

"That will be all Miss Declan."

She turned and shut the door quietly, then made a quick dash back to her desk when she heard the phone still ringing.

"What can I do for you Mr Bryan?" Sid passed the envelope

towards him as he rocked back in his chair to review the content, application forms and some polaroid's, that made him immediately douse his recently lighted cigarette, set down the paperwork and concentrate more onto the photos. Adjusting his shirt and tie, it took a reflecting moment for his mind to adjust to any relevance.

"What is it that you want?" He questioned with the most worrying of tones.

"Nothing too demanding. First and foremost, 35-year lease on The Gloucester public house and the Swan and Sugarloaf."

"That's the brewery's property, that has nothing to do with the council. I can pass over the license renewals." He generously offered.

"The land registries are council owned, although it's very kind that you can extend our licensing. But we want to own the land that is leased to the brewery, under the 1975 public house development and land registry agreement. I forget which chapter. But it is of no interest to anyone, until someone decides they want to knock it down. It's the land we are interested in, not the property."

"Interesting. I'll have to look into that. Anything else?"

"We are hearing that the government are allowing the purchase of council properties and land, around old derelicts, Croydon Airport and the old power station are prime examples. We want a guarantee. Let's call it a gentleman's agreement for the foreseeable. The registry turned over to us, with a carve up on twenty percent on any sale. I have also these three applications for Latchmere House on Windmill road and 12 Oak House on the Whitehorse Estate."

"And I presume, the guarantees are protected by these?" He indicated with the handful of photos that he began to separate in front of him on his desk. "Who is it?"

"That is our right honourable district counsellor. He received his copies to his office this morning. We understand he is chair to the English Partnership, which we need favourable votes cast to our representative on some industrial waste sites."

"And by representative?"

"All you have to do is get his signature and you won't hear from us again." Sid pointed to the headed paper that displayed the registered company.

"These pictures, they look dated. Why are they only surfacing now?" He diverted with questions meandering.

"Let's just say we're collecting on old debts."

"Will that be all?" Mr Fairclough pondered.

"I don't like being kept waiting Mr Fairclough, so do have our applications looked into post haste." Sid began to put on his trench coat and straightening up his collar in front of Mr Fairclough, who fidgetingly reviewed the photos again and the applications, not really taking in the slightest connection between the two. "And we have several more of you dirty nonces. I'm pretty sure you don't want us going to any of the papers with. Or the Old Bill?"

"I'll take care of it Mr Bryan. Guaranteed."

"Thought so." He smiled and winked confidently and saw himself out, leaving the stunned and bewildered Mr Fairclough, self-loathing, cursing his insatiable perverted hunger that has left him and his associates exposed.

Sid stopped at her desk as she nattered orders into the phone when it took the length of the corridor for him to walk to her, for her to proceed with the appointments and meetings that required urgent coordinating from her boss.

He leant over and scribbled a telephone number onto a pad that he swiped from under her hand as she jotted down notes, she stared daggers towards him with her lips pursed at his audacity. But soon curled a smile that softened her entire face as he gestured a "call me." towards her.

CHAPTER 12

EVERYBODY LOVES RAYMOND

"This is the part wait for it...Have that! Right in the eyeball." Todd laughed incessantly.

They were sitting yet another viewing of the epic Godfather movie and passing around their first ever joint together.

"I don't know why I find this part so funny this time around." Sarah laughed. "And why does the blood look like the syrup from the Mr Whippy van?"

They were all roaring hysterically. She was so in stitches laughing, her hair fell over her face messy, as she passed the self-rolled tatty wrap to Ray. The room bellowed with smoke between the munching of crisps and chocolate that they shared cravingly. Norma was the only one, through the fun and the hysterics, continued to check that the children were still asleep. Despite the raucous, with the repeated exercise, resulted in the same outcome. The five and seven-year-old fast asleep peacefully in their bunk beds.

Todd appeared at the top of the stairs as she shut the door on them and looked suspiciously at his mischievous face.

"What are you doing?"

"I wanted to get hold of you." He said with a romantic grab for her waist. She wriggled with some playful protest to allude his groping hands.

"No. Everyone will know what we are up to."

"Come on Norma you said you was on the pill?"

"Div. I told you I was on my period. Not the pill. And I ain't messing up their sheets. They'll never let us back. We can snog but that's it." She commanded.

"Come here then." He took her hand and forced her willingly into the bedroom.

Back downstairs, Ray and Sarah finished the last puffs of the joint and stared through the haze at the TV with deep concentration on the final scene. Both feeling the fuzzy high from the drug.

"I feel so fucked. I really do." Sarah chuckled.

"Me and all." Ray slurred. "Such a great movie."

"It's so much funnier with the spliff though."

"I like it when you are laughing." Ray declared with his eyes half shut with a broad grin on his face. "I feel like a nice sleep now." His head rested onto her lap as she beckoned him down, she stroked at his curly hair as her eyes also became heavy.

"Thanks for this Ray. Yous lot are such a good laugh."

"Hmm." Ray was struck comfortable and could only purr as she continued to stroke his head and massaging the side of his face, a silence fell in the room before they both suddenly realised that Todd and Norma had remained upstairs, a realisation that awoke him, recognising that he may have wasted a lot of time instead of making the most of the opportunity.

He sat up swiftly and perked his ears towards the horizon at the other side of the door.

"They've been up there for ages haven't they?"

"Yeah they have. And now we are alone." She smiled with the acknowledgment that although he had never said anything to confirm they were seeing each other, circumstances lately had always thrown them into each other's company, but he had never made any other intentions known to her. She leant back into the sofa and invited him with open arms, the combination of the spliff from the £3 draw of weed sprinkled in a betting slip, that Todd had ticked from one of the Steppers sound boys, had lifted any of the inhibitions that without it, would have left her remained in her shell.

"I've always wanted to get off with you." She whispered.

"Me too…" His sentence was cut short as she gently took the lead kissing him. They embraced in an awkward cuddle on the sofa, with a hint of embarrassment, he tried his best to get comfortable on top of her, as they adjusted, until they were more front to front. He tightened his embrace around her, to keep her from falling off the edge, she squeezed tighter as they pecked at each other, her tongue forced onto his, slowing his pace until he matched her tempo.

"You have to close your eyes when you kiss someone." She whispered.

"Is that a rule of kissing?"

"Yeah. It looks freaky otherwise." She giggled. "You are such a nice kisser."

"So are you. Will you…Do you want to go out with me?" He asked politely unassured.

"Ahh. You want to make it official? That's so nice that you even think like that. I thought you just wanted to have it off with me."

"I do." He replied eagerly. "But what if they came back or Todd and Norma burst in? It's not romantic unless we have some privacy… You know, so we are not rushing."

"No wonder all the girls fancy yah."

"No they don't." He argued shyly.

She nodded with a confident confirmation, kissing him again proudly, that she was kissing the most popular boy on the estate. She had sat with most of the girls on the estate and they all talked about him and 'the Gloucester lot' as they were commonly now known. She kissed him some more and allowed his hand to fondle her fully developed breasts, her eyes closed as she began to sense his eagerness, mewing sexually as the kissing became intense, his adolescent impatience began to show as their tongues flicked tepidly against one another.

As he had already feared, suddenly the door burst in with Todd and Norma gleefully surprised by them embraced and taking up the length of the sofa.

"Caught yah." Todd chuckled.

"Bastard." Sarah smiled. "We weren't doing anything. We were just practicing for when we get married."

"I'm allowed to kiss my bird aren't I?" Ray added.

"Oh, boyfriend and girlfriend now?"

"Yeah he asked me out."

"Everyone will be well jealous." Norma giggled. "Especially Christine and Bev."

"What you on about? They're me mates." He dismissed.

Norma budged them both up on the sofa, which left Ray and Sarah, Norma and Todd squashed cosily onto it and continued in the dark, kissing and mickey taking. Norma telling Ray to stop making that humming noise and Ray telling them both to stop smashing their teeth together.

"So where are you gonna take me for our first date?" Sarah questioned softly but loud enough for the room to hear. They were interrupted as the headlights outside signalled the returning parents, she quickly then confirmed with a peep behind her, through the curtains.

"Shit, they're back, tidy up quickly." She commanded, jumping up and switching on the lights, they all began collecting the crisp, chocolate wrappers and empty coke and lemonade cans along with picking out the ripped cigarettes from the ashtray.

Sarah and Norma disappeared into the kitchen and discarded everything into the carrier bag from the earlier Chinese takeaway that Kenny and his wife Jackie had treated them to, for keeping an eye on Jack and Jamie so they could have an evening down the social club. Todd consumed the room with the Potpourri glade air freshener and sat down as innocent as the two boy's asleep upstairs, just as Kenny opened the door and suspiciously surveyed the surprisingly tidy front room. Norma and Sarah reappeared from the kitchen

"Oh, you are back. Did you have a nice evening?" Sarah asked politely

"Yeah lovely thanks." Jackie replied, "Any problems with

the boys?"

"None whatsoever. They were good as gold." Sarah and Norma replied in unison.

"We just watched a movie on the Betamax." Todd chirped in, riddled with a slight conscience as he tried to quickly recollect if any evidence was left upstairs in their bedroom.

"Well thank you for not throwing a party while we were gone." Kenny retorted pulling out a wad of £10 notes, peeling off five. "Here you go, was only gonna give yous a score but seeing that the house is still in one piece."

"No Mr Arnold just give Sarah what she asked you for. A score." Ray interjected. "Call it an introductory offer."

Sarah smiled immensely towards him as he curled back two of the notes and presented it to her. Kenny followed them all to the door to show them out as they all thanked him and said goodbye over his shoulder to his wife.

They coupled up again linking arms as they walked across Windmill Road and past the Gloucester. They separated as Norma and Todd continued over into the Whitehorse Estate. Sarah and Ray walked together continuing up towards the Mail coach in the direction of the main high street. They stalled the journey back to Sarah's by stopping at intermittent shop doorways to embrace and kiss one another. Several cars had past them, the light traffic of taxis and last buses drifted passed on a less than busy Saturday night.

The car hurtling towards them, suddenly appeared from nowhere, they were totally consumed in conversation about the night and stunned Ray to shield her behind him as it came to a sudden stop.

"I've been looking everywhere for you. Where have you been?" Mr Stephens sneered angrily. The smell of alcohol was heavily on his breath, reaching over Ray to grab her by the hair. Ray pushed him with force and received a side clump combination from his fisted palm into the side of the head. Sarah and her father shouted hysterically at each other.

Ray exacted the only reply that he knew and was soon

tag teaming with Sarah as they both attacked him, and both received punches and kicks from him in defence before the difference in age and strength gained him the upper hand. Ray stumbled to the floor from the heavy shove into his back, colliding into a low wall, then onto the cold concrete. He then manhandled Sarah forcefully by her hair into the car, she screamed loud angry expletives at him. He bundled her over to the passenger side and screeched the 2-litre engine down the wrong side of the road and took a sharp right.

Slightly dazed from his head colliding with the pavement, he jumped up from the floor, angered with himself as he shouted loudly towards the disappearing rear lights. He began a hopeless pursuit to the junction to see the car head off into the distance. He felt around the back of his head and the throbbing on his forehead and wiped the blood using his jacket sleeve to mop the wound with irritation, the worst of it being, before being immobilised, it was Sarah inflicting it during the confusing battle with Mr Stephens. The rip in his cherished suede and leather top incensed him even more as he headed back in the direction of home.

He didn't immediately go inside, he sat on the bench that overlooked the four-way junction, angry thoughts repeating in his head wishing on all the worst possible punishment and hopeless fear for what Sarah was currently going through. Todd joined him soon after and immediately saw Ray's face of distress, along with the wound and damage to his attire.

"What the Fuck happened to you?"

"That fucking weirdo cunt dad of hers." He seethed.

"That's it then. He's a dead man. Your uncles will fuck him up for sure."

"Nah." Ray disagreed. "That's too easy mate. He crossed the line now."

"Then what are you saying?" Todd asked looking calmly at him. He'd seen Ray in rows and seen him angry over a bad football result but never like this.

"We'll fucking do him." Ray replied calmly with a

somewhat relaxed demeanour. "Come and knock for me tomorrow."

Without waiting for a reply or comment back, about how ridiculous he had sounded, although the tone in his voice was a million miles away from ridiculous, he banged on the door to the pub and waited. Todd stood almost frozen, as if he'd heard him but had not heard him. The saloon bar door opened after a few minutes and closed immediately behind him. Todd stood watching as he disappeared inside. He then made his way home, plotting with every step, the best way to assist his best friend.

CHAPTER 13

STEPPERS

After a mixed night between sleep and being wide awake. With Sarah and her father running over in his head, his kisses with her had his mind tormented about Mr Stephens and the way he angered over her. What was it that drove a father with so much jealous rage? Burned a sickening feeling in his stomach. There was no way he would let her have anything remotely like a boyfriend. Over his dead body, may be his only stance, his confused head pictured the worst. He wanted to take her to the cinema and to hang out at the Whitgift centre with her. Feeling all the emotions, he pondered on maybe getting the girls to knock for her but erased this thought, after remembering what Norma had told him about him being physical with them.

"You're so quiet this morning baby, are you ok?"

"Yeah. I'm ok." He responded with tired eyes.

"Is it a girl. Did she break your heart?" Sid chuckled.

"Aw leave him alone."

"Actually, it is a girl." Ray finally smiled.

"I might have known. You need to concentrate on your books." Pete discerned.

"We started a babysitting service. Me, Sarah and Norma earnt twenty quid with Kenny Arnold.

"That's a good idea."

"Yeah and we need to get the word about and advertise."

"Ahh my little businessman." Angie prided. "That's you two he takes after."

"Maybe you can print some leaflets for us."

"You don't want to be looking after anyone's chav. Going

into strangers' houses and all that." Pete vexed slightly, bringing his concerns to the table.

"That's why we do it together."

"What are you? The muscle?" Sid ran his inquest.

"Kind of…Well more to walk them home after. We never finished until past midnight."

Angie looked towards Sid and Pete with proud bewilderment flicking crumbs off of her navy sweater.

"I need to get Todd a bike, then we can deliver more leaflets."

"I don't know about that. You need to keep it on the estate. Yous are too young to be travelling in and out of stranger's houses." Pete repeated.

"That's right boy. We can put the word about to people we know." Sid agreed.

"RSTN babysitting service. We are calling ourselves."

"That's a bit of a mouthful." Sid chuckled.

"It's just our initials."

"Well in business it's usually the founding members who's initials you use. And Partners, if you have to." Ray sat interested as always, whenever Sid, Pete or his mother would educate him on the world.

"So, it'd be Sarah Harris and Partners It was her idea." He admitted. Both brothers looked towards Angie, with a playful look on their faces.

"Blimey, we never knew you were that serious about this one boy. Is that why you've been nicking me cologne?" Pete teased with a grin.

"You leave him alone. Teasing him." Angie peered towards them both and then her eyes softened back onto Ray with a roll of her eyes signalling that he ignores them.

"This Sarah, she is not regular on the estate like the other girls?" Sid enquired.

"She's a very pretty girl. Lovely red hair and freckles." She described for the brother's benefit.

"She's in sixth form and all."

"That's why I'm a bit worried about all this babysitting malarkey and you in people's houses alone with her." Angie cemented again, after some thought, to contradict her happiness, weighed in about the pitfalls and disadvantage from a parenting perspective.

It hadn't crossed his mind in that respect, but it was undoubtedly one of the positives of the venture.

"We don't want you getting up to any nonsense boy. You're 14 years old. So, keep that little worm in your pants." Sid alerted half-heartedly.

"Sid…" Angela objected. "Ignore your uncle baby, He doesn't mean to be crude but he's right. Being all alone with a girl, you know?" She hinted.

"I'm not alone with her. Todd and Norma are there too."

"Yes, and that's even worse. You teenagers all put yourself under too much pressure to be irresponsible, trying to act all grown up." Angela frowned.

"Jeff Stephen's daughter?" Pete remembered.

"Step-daughter." Ray corrected.

"I don't like that man." Angie recollected. "Something about him. Didn't he leave his wife, after she was diagnosed with breast cancer and took them kids with him, leaving her all alone?" Angie continued to recall, the things she had heard about him.

Ray was relieved she hadn't heard what Todd had told him many moons ago and what Norma had sworn him to secrecy.

"He is helping us dip our feet…" Pete informed.

"Oh. That makes him alright then?" Angela frowned, with some sarcasm in her voice.

"Anyway, I'm not interested in her family." Ray shrugged. "But I know her brother, Skinhead John."

"Blimey." Angela smiled.

"She never talks much about them, but really knows a lot of stuff. And she works in Allders."

"That's what we worry about, you being so blindingly

handsome and all." Angela pinched at his cheek to his embarrassment as he shrugged himself shyly away.

"Well you make sure you're not doing any playing around with her. Your mum will chop your willy off." Sid laughed.

"Siddy!" Angela warned. "What type of talk is that? You need to sit him down and give him a proper man to boy talk, that's what you need to do."

"Ang?" Sid replied aplomb.

"Well one of yous will have to. His father isn't around, and yous two are who he looks up to." She ordered sternly.

"Nice one Sid." Pete applauded with satire.

"Right it's gone eleven so I'm off to work."

"Make sure you take Irish with you." Sid ordered once he deflected his mind from the parenting task she had delegated.

"And yous make sure you speak with him." She picked up her bag and coat and left kissing Ray on his cheek and giving the no nonsense eye to both Sid and Pete. They both waited until she left and prepared themselves for the uncomfortable discussion.

"It's alright. I know the coo, we have sex ed in school. I know not to go near girls with my willy until I'm 21."

The laughter that filled the room from all three of them had Pete ruffling Ray's hair.

"Well you've saved us from that embarrassment thank fuck." He roared. Sid uncurled him four ten-pound notes with a playful punch to his cheek.

"Take her somewhere nice and make sure you listen to your teachers on this, because Angie will literally cut yours and our bollocks off." He guffawed.

Ray finished his breakfast and continued waiting for Todd for thirty more minutes upstairs and then after retrieving his bike from the back, he waited out the front of the pub. Propping his bike up against the red telephone box, he dialled Todd's number. Which his grandmother answered and informed him, after brief dialogue, preaching that they must keep out of trouble and getting his name wrong for the umpteenth time by calling him Desmond, before concluding that Todd had left an hour ago.

Peering outside, he then witnessed Todd ambling along from the Thornton Heath direction with a satchel dressed like he was going to church.

"Where are you going?" He queried after hanging up the phone and riding over to him.

"To see you off course. Am I late? Half twelve you said."

"You're not late."

"Who were you on the phone to? Sarah?"

"No. Your lovely nan...'Ello Desmond." He mimicked laughing.

"Crazy old bat."

"Anyway, by the way you are dressed, I thought we were taking her to church. Are we going to prayers now?" He tugged at his lapel on the brown tweed jacket then at the satchel.

"Well I thought, I won't get stopped by the gavvers if I dressed like this."

"You look like you're on the fiddle dressed like that what you on about?"

"Are we going to do this or what?" He smiled and proceeded to open the bag to Ray's absolute bewilderment.

"Sweeney what the...What do you think we were going to do? Roll up to his house and massacre him on his doorstep?"

"I'm with you now pop. I'm with you now." He simulated.

Bemused by his blasé Ray grabbed his friend by his jacket and his bike by one end of the handlebar simultaneously and walked towards the alleyway cut through to the estate.

"Flipping heck!" He jangled inside the bag. "You're like that Halloween bloody chainsaw murderer, where the bleeding hell did you get all these from?"

"The Steppers lot."

"What did you say to them to tool you up like this?"

"Nothing. I just asked if we could borrow some weapons."

Ray shook his head and looked at Todd who still had a look of confusion at his disappointment.

"Come on let's go find them." Ray commanded spinning his bike around to face back towards the street.

"So, we are doing this then?" He grinned.

"NO! We are going to give the tools back to Steppers. Unless you fancy going to prison."

"But you said last night we were gonna do it ourselves."

"Yeah but not like this. Come on mate, seriously, what would Vito do and how would he do it?" Ray beamed with mischief. He began to ride out of the alley with Todd following behind after zipping up the bag.

Ray rode his bike in a calm circle while Todd went back to the Green, which was a large grassy area beside the old people's home that had a series of benches where Todd had gone up to a group. They looked older by the way they dressed. The obvious leader had a dark red beaver skin hat and a smart looking cardigan with suede patches. Ray observed this look on the boys in the upper years at school and the estate, between the reggae boys in smart slacks and jumpers and the football lads, like Bex, the Twins and Billy Burgess in the sportswear and Jeans. Ray and his mates adopted a mixture of both styles with Tony, Raph and Nathan already finding light-fingered ways of getting their hands on the popular fashion labels and by Sarah's over the counter discounts.

The discussions surrounding the tools appeared to have become a little heated. At first pretending to be of no interest, he cycled and wheelied closer, while Todd continued to explain that he no longer required the bag of unlimited weapons they had supplied to him and looked as though it was taking some explanation before they eventually took the bag. The leader looked put out, as much as though Todd had insulted his mother and it was only at this point that Ray rode up and joined them.

"This lickle Pussyclaart ah mess I and I about." The leader of the group fumed.

"Come on mate." Ray ushered. "I said we'd be back at the Gloucester in 10 minutes."

All the boys looked evilly towards them both. Ray ignored the looks.

"Alright Ordel. Wotcha Errol." He then greeted as he recognised Ordel Henry and Errol Williams from his school.

Ordel left Stanley heath almost two years ago now, he used to join in with the kick about with the younger years, by Ray's memory he was about the only one who did at the time. Errol had left after expulsion before the end of the Easter term. Since he had left school, he was rumoured to have turned militantly against their perceived racist whites around the borough, exchanging in battles with the skinhead groups that were once the major force but had dwindled by beatings as Errol who had united many of the posse's became the dominant gang of the one-time area skinheads roamed. The other guys bore no recognition.

"Come on Sweeney."

"You pickney ain't going nowhere until you pay me for hiring me tools."

"We didn't need your tools." Ray replied confidently.

He rushed from his perch on the back rest of the bench and grabbed at Ray roughly which made his bike fall to the floor.

"Who's dis, facety lickle half breed pancoote?" The leader growled his rhetorical inquest, his patois stung with menace towards this youngster who unreasonably questioned his authority as his eyebrows furrowed angrily.

"Nah Man. Don't fuck around with this yout' man Stix. Ah dem gangster man's family." Errol immediately stepped in and demanded his release, Ordel also joined in with the protest.

By now the scuffle was Stix holding onto Ray's tracksuit top, manhandling his threads with his face up close aggressively. Errol was tugging at Stix's arm to release him and Ordel reasoning in agreement with Errol. Ray and Todd remained silently worried throughout the ordeal.

"I say fuck dem bruddah's. Me ah de bad man." He prided boastfully gesturing his thumb towards himself for everyone to identify.

"Ok, Ok." Ray surrendered. "We'll pay for them." He pulled two ten-pound notes from his pocket and was immediately released, Stix freed his hand to snatch the money. Ray proceeded in picking his bike back up, slightly shaken but showing his usual bravado, indicating to Todd, who picked up the bag ready to leave.

"Leave de bag." He hissed. Bring I forty extra pounds fe dem. If you want dem or go find tree branch."

Todd dropped the bag back at his feet and followed Ray out of the green and back onto the Whitehorse road. Ray wheeled his bike in stony silence.

"I'll see you get your money back Ray." Todd felt slightly conflicted, that he only got into this situation because of the way he had seen him and the look he gave out the night before.

"Who was that big cunt?" Ray enquired as he mounted his bike once they were back on the main road.

"Stixman. Lloyd something, Fowler… I think, supposed to be psycho with a ratchet knife." Todd detailed.

"I bet that cunt ain't even Jamaican."

"Streatham hill I heard." Todd shrugged innocently. "Don't you remember him?"

"Where the fuck would I remember him from?"

"Don't you remember, when he was rubbing up with that Theresa bird that you fancy at that dance at Lady Edridge. Skinning up one handed at the same time? That was the most gangster thing we'd ever seen."

"Oh shit, yeah. I remember now." Ray chuckled. "I was just about to ask her for a dance and all."

"Yeah you shat yourself." Todd laughed.

"He looked even scarier in the dark."

"I'll get you your money back Ray."

"Don't worry about it." He stopped pedalling to turn and face him. "I was gonna use the money to try and get you a bike for us to get about and promote our business. This is a good lesson for us, that whatever we do. We never do business with people we don't know ever again."

Todd smiled back at him after receiving Ray's confident wink back.

"What about what you said last night. About Sarah's old man and ripping your suede and leather?"

"Forget about it...He can wait."

"Until after the christening?" Todd interrupted childishly. They both chortled as they continued back towards the park.

"Let's go knock for the twins. They both drive now, maybe we can buy one of theirs. I have a different plan that needs skinhead John."

"He's a mod now." Todd corrected slightly befuddled.

"Not sure what's worse." Ray chuckled.

"What are we going to look for him for."

"The Trojan horse Todd. It's no good me knocking for Sarah going by the way she's being treated. We knock about with John and find out more, that's the Trojan horse."

"He's probably down Brighton looking for rockers." He reminded. "And I still don't understand what John's got to do with bloody horses?"

"This is what all them days bunking off and skipping history gets yah." They carried on their journey with Ray walking beside him to educate him on Greek mythology, one of the many lessons they were taught at school that had somehow escaped Ray's best friend and also agreeing with himself when all his summations ran out of road. His mission to help Sarah would require patience and was added along with Stix onto his to do list.

CHAPTER 14

TROJAN HORSE

John Stephens, in his white polo shirt and dark Levi's was a now smarter looking reflection from the yobbish acne riddled skinhead he once was. Since the encounter in the park John had spent the last couple of years intent on never getting turned over like he had been by Ray in the park. The fifteen-year-old had explained over time that the right-wing skinhead adoption, was not even a true reflection of the fashionable movement. Errol who he had befriended after the previous year's racial war in Thornton heath, which had left factions on both sides maimed and one even died after a heavy hammer blow to the head.

The subsequent court cases had some everlasting bonds made after the lucky ones as himself and Errol had been acquitted from the various charges. John now was in appreciation of the sounds of the skinhead and ska movement but had obviously now moved onto a different culture. He invited the boys inside, Nathan was straight over at the record player to turn down the sound which had John irked at the audacity.

"And what do I owe the pleasure?" He began.

Ray smiled looking around again at the neatly arranged house, marvelling at the paintings and ornaments that graced the hallway and the living room. Ray pulled out a furl of five and ten-pound notes and placed on the coffee table in front of John, who began counting.

"We heard you had a job at the camera shop and we need a camera for our school competition." Ray proclaimed.

"Seventy pounds?" John replied in surprise.

"Yeah, we want a decent camera, with a flash and a tripod. Like them Olympus trip ones off the tele."

"David Bailey? Who's he?" Nathan chuckled.

John repeatedly looked impatiently towards Nathan, who was more interested in the record collection beside the stereo.

"I can get you a decent camera for a lot cheaper than that." He smiled.

"Blinding mate nice one, me and Sweeney are doing this project in school you see. We are going over to Canning Town and all the dockyards to capture derelict London."

"I didn't know you was interested in the arts?" He questioned.

"You're joking ain't yah? Have you not seen their AFC Gooners graffiti all over the manor?" Nathan added.

"Don't listen to him. This competition, it's being run by the evening news and the winner gets one thousand pounds." Ray replied excitedly. "One thousand pounds John, that's worth the investment?"

John began to laugh, quietly admiring, from hanging about with them the past months, their dedication to scamming and wheeling and dealing from these youngsters, he deemed really inspiring. The babysitting alone was a masterstroke and even he branched out with the Harris and partners night care services, expanding the babysitting offering amongst the staff at the department store that he worked. It gave them access to places to sit around and have a laugh instead of hanging around at the park all the time.

"Let me turn this up?" Nathan interrupted. "This song by the Jam, it's reem this."

They all listened to the stereo, while John interruptedly boasted to them with a fanboy education about Paul Weller's lyrics and how it applied so deeply to the working class ideal. The way Ray had consumed this, was in John's eyes, Paul Weller and the Jam were gods, but also, John could elude to the magnificence of Joy division with his extended far-fetched tale about meeting Ian Curtis when his mother was a cloak room attendant at the Rainbow theatre. Johnny Rotten, Joe strummer, Roger Daltrey and the two Bob's, Dylan and Marley also set him off on a lyrical tirade that basically just alluded to a 'Fuck the system' mindset.

"You still a Soul head Ray?"

"Not so much. I listen a bit of everything now. Hip – Hop Ska, Reggae and all that."

"Blondie and a bit of Green onions mate." Nathan interrupted continually.

"Booker T and the MG's. Outstanding track. It's so relevant." Mod John expressed. "You sound like a mod yourself Nathan."

Even though his face bore of sarcasm, Ray tried his hardest to keep a straight face, at the pretence that he was in the slightest bit interested on the waffle that was coming from John's mouth. He eventually excused himself to use the toilet

"Is it alright if I use the bog please John?" Ray asked politely.

"Sure mate, you know where it is."

As John continued with his education on popular culture and the artistry of some of the great songwriters in history. Ray detoured into what he had previously discovered was Mr Stephen's study, which sat between the bedrooms and a short flight up from the bathroom. He crept stealthily inside and began to nose around the desk poking his ears towards the downstairs. A repeated search around the large development plan that covered the messy desk, he focussed again on bright glossy brochure that advertised what looked like a futuristic city.

Ray picked it up and quickly fanned the pages, not really gathering any relevance or what he was even looking to achieve, with the added paranoia that he didn't want to get caught. A pull of the drawers and another fanning of pages in a bible sized diary, he surprised this time on two objects falling to the floor, he picked them up and divulged in surprise, pictures of Sarah in underwear, not just any underwear, revealing adult underwear.

She was smiling in both, but her eyes weren't smiling, not the same way that she smiled at him. He stared in shock towards it, her pink lipstick curved provocatively, realising the location of this photo shoot was the very room he stood in. The beautiful skin of her thighs looked so athletically alluring in a white pair of stilettoes, and maturely in the way her breast protruded like a professional. She was stunningly morphed, was this his girlfriend or her mother? He quickly deducted the former, her mother had the deeper red, ringleted hair. With a confused perversion, he put one back and slipped the other one into his back pocket and double checked again, surprised that at the back of the thick diary were four more colour polaroid's of her, which he quickly shut and replaced it back into the bottom drawer and hastily left, doubling back he went to the bathroom, his mind spinning with confusion and lust and then anger.

Returning downstairs, he battled to pay attention to John and also now Nathan, who began to philosophise on the lyrics of the mod band himself. John had somehow educated himself on the entire history and cited word for word the lyrics and reasoning behind them. One song, 'down in the tube station at midnight', he rewound and detailed how the song even hit home about his fascist skin headed views, which he continually apologised to Ray about.

Ray's mind focused for the next hour between the pretence that he was in the slightest interested. The visual of Sarah smiling looking like a page three model. How could she be doing this for someone who punches her in the face. Who gets angry about her hanging about with her friends and could push their friend Christine's face into a brick wall? She should hate his guts as much as he did.

By now he had made several visits between the living room, garden and kitchen, upstairs to Mr Stephens office, to look towards the photo's again sinfully, trying to etch the beautiful picture of her into his memory bank before returning the photo he had stolen. A conflicted fight to keep to the plan, which he really didn't have any idea how any of this could play into an advantage. Blackmail was definitely off the cards, that it might draw more risk or embarrassment towards Sarah, he couldn't take his mind off of her, confused with jealousy for her, excited to soon venture on a lustful road with her. Even being with her and kissing her, the visions of her now was the most rampantly alluring images he had ever seen.

Another piece of information that he strained his waning focus was retaining the name of the multi-million-pound prospectus that her father was preparing to swoon investors with. The temptation from the photos of her, was enough to cloud his judgement, the same evening he repeated the quote in his head.

"This is business, not personal."

"This is business, not personal." The repetition inside his head, continued for days, for weeks, he repeated it over and over again for every bruise that appeared. The calendar would have to coincide with an excuse not to see her, it has to be water-tight, Todd's were becoming too elaborate.

'a gun? 'no guns.'

'a knife? 'too messy, no knives.'

'Well how about poison?'

Todd's insistent cunning struck up the friendship with him in the guise of another door to door venture, during the warm evenings, washing his car every week. An adolescent tactical charade of patience, until a window of opportunity was presented to them.

"Let's just go do that Stixman instead."

CHAPTER 15

TARGET PRACTICE

Another Wednesday early evening after school. The boys gathered at the camp again, with no sign of the girls, the determination on their faces, was shared with the adrenaline and fear for what Ray was planning on leading them into. He hadn't forgotten about the way Stix had handled him that weekend on the green. And seeing him almost too regular, snarling towards them every time, raised the aspirations for revenge. Ray's well laid plan was marked strategically into the dirt like a military general.

"Bikes are to ride onto the opposite side of the road and to watch him from the chip shop, the arcade machine as cover." He pulled out a pile of change for Nathan, Tony and Todd.

"Raph will lure him off of the green and up the alley. Here is where I'll be waiting. As soon as he starts the chase, Boycie, Sweeney, yous'll be the rear guard to ambush 'em, hit em quick and hard. Rambo, you can back them up if needed but get in with us on Stix."

"We better make sure they go down sharpish then." Nathan added after studying the lines.

"Are we clear with the plan boys?" Ray probed.

"Are you sure I can outrun this big black Stix?" Raph queried with concern.

"As long as you chuck a right."

"Oh, that's a relief." He berated sarcastically. "Just make sure you get to him before he gets the chiv out."

"I'll get to him." Ray declared proudly. "And if we get split up, we meet back at the garages."

"Ain't you worried they'll find out it was us?" Todd

worried slightly.

"Nah. Even if they do, we'll hit him so hard, they'll have to think twice about it."

"Blinding mate. Ray is like the Don." Tony grinned.

"Just make sure you smash him before he slices me up."

"Here, stick that down your jeans." Todd passed him a copy of a discarded rustler men's magazine, which had Raph looking confused.

"What's this for? My last wank?"

"In case he jooks you in your bottom." Todd declared innocently, which made Nathan chuckle at the shocked expression on Raph's face

"Right, let's do this cunt." Ray commanded.

They were all pumped up and ready to leave, cycling off on the grifter bikes, their dark leather jackets weirdly had them obscurely resembling a mini version of the Hells Angels. Turning right out of the gates and down towards the Whitehorse roundabout, Ray separated from them as they gathered at the chip shop.

Todd spotted the Steppers crew, but the plan was already going awry when Nathan observed the policemen conducting a stop and search. They looked heated while they were systematically searched. He rode past tentatively, then cycled onto the green, feigning minding his own business, there was a bowler type hat on the floor by the policeman's feet, three out of four of them were tall enough to be Stix. He listened to the names they confirmed to the officers, none of what he heard amounted to identifying their target. He jumped off his bike and buzzed onto the buzzer of the old people's home, hoping they wouldn't turn and arrest him for playing knock down ginger.

"Hello." Came the voice behind the intercom.

"Can you tell Mrs Johnson, she's me nan...that I'll come and visit her tomorrow after school." With a confused silence crackling back from the intercom, he jumped back onto his bike and watched the policemen leave and the owner of the velvet bowler type hat, place the hat back onto his head.

"Dirty Babylon." One of the youths shouted as the panda car drove away. Nathan rode off the green and went into the chip shop to join Tony and Todd and continued with a surveillance of the youths on the green. Stix was seen to hit one of his mates in the chest that sent this so-called friend sprawling backwards.

"Leave him alone yah fucking bully." Raph yelled, appearing right on queue.

"Who y'ah talk to bwoy?" He turned towards Raph, still holding the lad in a tight grip by his jacket, before he let go.

"You. Yah big black cunt!"

There was little time to stand on ceremony, when three of them took flight towards him, he waited until the absolute last, then pedalled frantically away from the green and down the path with them in hot pursuit.

"I gwarn chop up your bloodclaart!" Stix promised, while gaining hot on his heels.

Todd, Tony and Nathan pursued the chasing youths down the dark alley, which meandered by metal railings. Raph navigated around them like a speedway rider, out of the other side, then repeated past the railings at the end, he glimpsed out of his peripheral vision, Ray patiently waiting and dismounted, just as Stix, who must have had a few one hundred meters sprint medals proudly displayed in another life, appeared smiling that his abuser couldn't even out run him on two wheels. He smiled menacingly reaching his hand up towards his hat.

The baseball bat echoed with a crack into his back, with the second strike into his shoulder that sent shock waves of pain, enough for him to fall to his knees, with Raph's running volley connecting viciously into his head. Nathan and Todd flew into the others, who by luck, wasn't as fast as Stix's dash through the alleyway and were now cut off just before the last railings. With Nathan's bike sent hurtling to collide into the stragglers, then with a cascade of strikes combining from a crowbar and knuckle duster immobilised the pair. One hollered after Stix in terror but he was in no position to respond. Todd raised one up by his hair and was surprised and relieved that it was no one he knew and cracked the crowbar onto his knee. The loud scream in pain bounced off the high walls almost like a yodeller shouting from a snowy mountain.

"Now fuck off." Nathan Screamed and watched them run off back the way they came. He followed Tony and Todd to the end of the alleyway.

Stix was under siege, getting an unrelenting tsunami of violence, with Ray and Raph ploughing into him silently, Tony had joined in soon after, only the acoustic of the wooden bats and an extendable cosh made sound and the grunts to generate force could be heard. Stix was cowering in a foetal position, kicked like a ball and battered as the blows rained upon him, as they all now joined in with the savage punishment as the baseball bat crashed onto his back, the crow bar into his legs and arms, his smart velvet hat crushed by their trainers, after comically falling off his head when Ray had first winded him. His deep voice now squealing against the immense pain. Window curtains began to twitch, with no real view of the onslaught that stopped suddenly when Ray lifted his hand as a ceasefire, influenced more due to the time than out of mercy.

"Mr Stephens said hello." Todd shouted, throwing out the surprising red herring at the motionless body, bloodied hands took on a resemblance to red gloves covering his head, shook with a last crack into his lower back with the crowbar. They all looked at each other pleased with their retribution that they inflicted, then jumped onto their bikes. Tony collected up the weapons into a bag and followed the cycle convoy down the adjacent alley and over the railway bridge carrying the bikes over their shoulders.

They stopped at the garages and waited for Tony who unlocked one of the old style wooden green doors, tugging at the big rusty Yale padlock and pulled one of the double doors open for them to place the bikes into and ditched their outer coats into bin bags. They were serious but giggling at the same time.

"Big black cunt." Tony chuckled.

"A leopard never changes his spots." Ray observed in jest.

"How else could I get him to chase me? Threatening to cut up my blood cloth. He was like a fucking cheetah, weren't he?" Raph said with relief, which set them all into a bout of laughter.

Washing their hands and weapons with fairy liquid into a ready filled bucket of water and drying them on towels, which they also threw into another black bin liner.

"How the fuck did the Police not find this on him?" Todd queried, flicking out the ratchet knife with a pencil through the round key ring attached to the weapon.

"Where the fuck did you get that?" Ray said in surprise.

"Out of his hat." Todd confirmed.

"Fucking gavvers are useless." Raph added.

"'ere didn't he carve up that geezer in South Norwood over some Doris?" Tony's mind wandered out loud.

"Yeah. I heard about that. This geezer must n'arf reckon himself. Walking about with the same chiv." Todd replied.

"The kid was in a coma apparently collapsed lung. This cunt must be untouchable."

"Or, no one wants to squeal on him." Nathan suggested. "I'm half tempted to ring Police 5."

"Yeah. Keep em peeled, the cunt." Tony sneered.

"Or. We just feed it to Norma's old man. Make a name for himself." Raph deducted.

"How's your fucking luck. You get a proper bashing then get nicked for attempted murder." Ray laughed.

"Bag it up. You haven't touched it have yah?"

"Nah I had me gloves on remember?"

They left the garages with the knife safely tucked away. They agreed that even in the eventuality he clocked on who it was that had hit him. He could be serving a long time in prison if the knife is tied into the evidence against him.

They all walked down through the garages, eventually circling back onto the main Whitehorse road, breaking off to go their separate ways. Raph and Tony, then Todd, leaving Nathan and Ray to walk past the green. He glanced confidently nudging Nathan, with a simmering pride at the usually busy and noisy congregation that often gathered there at all hours, was now empty.

CHAPTER 16

WHITE HORSES

"Who do you think has the best hair, me or Christine?"

"You of course." He replied absently, slightly yawned by the repetitiveness of the topic.

"Oooh! touched a nerve have I?" She teased with her eyes beguiling at him.

"A bit yeah. Why do you have to keep having me compare you with her, she was just me mate."

"Yeah. But she said she snogged you a couple of times."

"And I snogged Norma and Bev, so what?"

"And Moira." She reminded.

"Who the bloody hell is Moira?"

"She goes to my school, she's from the Whitehorse."

"I've never snogged anyone called Moira." He denied. His mind however cast to him and Todd on a bus journey back from a disco in Purley. But couldn't recall the names of the girls they travelled back with that evening.

"What about these then, out of us three, who has the best?" She prided, protruding her fully curved chest at him, which seemed to be caressed by the cashmere fabric of her jumper.

Ray made an excuse from the interrogation and the hedonism, as though he heard the sound of the child upstairs and went up to check. She followed closely behind, noticing he was asleep and had been for the last few hours. She pinched at his bum playfully for him to turn and face her after they both peered through the door. Taking him by his hand she led him into the parent's bedroom, which was very bourgeois, decorated in Laura Ashley curtains and linen.

"You haven't answered me. Do any of them, have firm nice round tits like mine?" She repeated, perching them at him provocatively, making the visions of the centrefold style polaroid's he fantasised over, replayed guiltily, his adolescent perversion that led to copious late-night autoeroticism with himself.

"You've been very trappy tonight." He observed.

"Trappy? Am I getting on your nerves?" Her taunting gaze was leaving him no room to escape.

"No. Just with the questions."

"Well I need to know."

"Yes, yours are the best. From the outside." He smirked.

He watched with interest as she unbuttoned the side of her skirt and allowed it to fall onto the floor.

"What are you doing?" The nervous hunger was in his voice, shy with an expectancy, that he believed he was ready for.

"I want to have it off with you tonight Ray. Don't you want to be with me?" Her question was based rhetorically, the sparkle in her eyes melted into him, he froze like a deer in a headlight. Her jumper now discarded followed by the tight white T-shirt. Black underwear had his mind drooling, contradicting the voices in his head, about what would happen if he knocked up anyone. The punishment between his mother or his uncles, of which there was no light sentence, whoever the deliverer. She hummed a song nonchalantly that seemed to dissipate his consequential worries.

Laying on the bed unassumingly, yet torturously for him, to want to do this tonight, after many months of teasing their appetites. The song she sang softly completely appeased him, she often broke into songs of flying away, walking on by, songs of empowerment, embodied like a distraction to everything that was blue in her life.

"On white horses let me ride away. To my world of dream so far away..." She sang, studying her nails, almost with pride at the deep red paint that she spent the afternoon dressing them round at Norma's house.

He joined her on the double bed, her sweet lyrics ending abruptly, as they passionately kissed. His nervous lips on her were impatient and anxious. She had to stop to coax him slower and more compassionate, to make this moment special. She rolled onto her back for him to climb on to her. Her heart chimed for him, whispering reassuringly into his ear, the words that made this moment a bit more relaxing. Their warm tongues engaged with long deep kisses as she took command, seducing with her lips, grazing his bottom lip gently with her teeth, arching her body into him. Her panties dry humped into him impatiently.

After his initial stage fright, on how to navigate the intimacy process and her knee jerk dispelling of his slightly abnormal size in her hand, she relieved herself from her panties and parted her legs for him. Looking into his eyes reassuringly, slowly guided him the correct way, with an experience drawn from the ricochet of innocence stolen away from her a long time ago.

She finally coaxed that first feel of tenderness for him, her sexually incited aroma filled his nose narcotically and urged him on, with an awestruck sensation from every stroke inside her, unable to believe that it would feel this good and how beautiful she looked underneath him. She humped her groin gently to meet him, conducting his hands around her body, coordinating the rhythm to savour the moment. Some eager heavenly strokes later, his eyes flickered excitedly as her female wet arousal, transformed him into a young adult. They declared repeatedly, their undying love to one another during the intense delight of them coming together and the excitement of the sensation that devoured him, like an elaborate collection of the best feelings in the whole wide world.

Their breathing was in harmony, she kissed into his neck and purred kitten like from her own new experience in climax. They cuddled under the sheets, their face's a satisfied picture of content.

"You've been humming that song all night." He panted as he gradually regained recovery.

"Didn't you ever used to watch that White horses tv programme, during the summer holidays when you were little?"

"Can't remember the programme but the song sounds familiar. I used to love the Arabian Night's though."

"Siiiize, of an elephant!" She giggled.

"Bez the beast? Sounds like one of Raph's mates down the Millwall." He chuckled.

"They must have had you on their mind when they made that." She laughed with a naughty connotation in her mind.

"What's that?" He replied confused, his mind not on that same level to the innuendo.

She grabbed at him under the covers, crudely stroking it. They both laughed and began to kiss and cuddle again, working up to continue and wishing they had all night. A sensibility took over her sexual urges, regarding the parent who had employed them for the night, at a quarter to one, despite wanting another journey to that experience he had never felt before, they had to stop.

She was eager to dress and continue downstairs, an easier explain if caught in an uncompromising situation, especially in her bed which they had already taken advantage of the trust bestowed to them by partaking their first time together. The obsession over the bed sheets took them a while, forensically making sure it was left exactly the way it had been before they pursued their needs.

As he walked her home after earning their keep and praised once again. Trekking via the back streets and avoiding the main roads, other than crossing the borders of Broad Green, afforded them some secrecy, linking arms, holding hands and his arm around her. They made it to the alleyway that sectioned between two streets, that gave them the cover to say goodnight with long lingering kisses and wishing they could start the night all over again. He emotionally held her tight, love pounding at their young swollen hearts, stirring for each other, not wanting to let her go. Then finally allowing her to do so.

He watched her looking back and waving secretly, he was peeping at her until she approached her front door. To him it was like watching her walk into an abyss, fully knowing the treachery that faced her behind the closed door.

CHAPTER 17

THE GREENWICH PENNINSULAR

"Where are we?" Ray asked out of curiosity.

"This is a place called the Greenwich peninsular." Mr Stephens boasted.

"Well this sure is derelict. We should get some good photographs eh?" Ray looked back, indicating to Todd, who looked distractedly focused as if going through his lines over and over in his head repeatedly.

"Me, your uncles and our business partners are going to redevelop this plot. Your teachers are gonna be well impressed. I'm all too happy to help you boys out with that."

"Yeah? Who'd want to live out here?" Ray peered out and around the baron wasteland unimpressed.

"Ahh, this is the future boys. Condominiums, office blocks and a shopping centre. We have it all planned out."

"Must cost a bob or two?" Ray queried suspiciously.

"It's peanuts, our investments will double, quadruple even. Just imagine restaurants overlooking…"

"We only want to take pictures, save all the spiel for his uncles." Todd interrupted rudely.

"Right you are then. You'll get your pictures." He sighed and continued in silence.

He looked back at Todd nervously. Witnessing the argument in the pub, when Pete had him by his throat late one Sunday evening, with a dispute centred around elevating business costs. Ray continued the battle with himself, on whether he was viewed with any importance to them, and what would be the outcome of consequences, that he drilled into his mind on countless occasions. Todd, with surprising cunning, over the summer holiday period, befriended Mr Stephens enough to offer this opportunity to get on the right side of the Bryans again, through the nephew. Paying over the odds for car washes to begin with. So far, their little ruse was working, Jeff was their friend, set aside from his secret raison d'etre, with his own flesh and blood he falsely shared a more common interest, the love of his Cortina. For a while longer than they had expected, they entertained with the Trojan horse, the days after school and playing truant, number 17 Parkmead close became their camp, the main mission was to mosey about in his office while he travelled on business and Sarah's mother looked after the florist in Sutton.

Sarah's problems with her father were not completely over shadowed and the scars from her early teens would never truly be healed. Saturday night sitting for little Wayne Brooke for his mum Joanne, the babysitting service was a welcome relief for the single mother to go on well-deserved nights out. As the 4-year-old slept, Sarah was desperate to wipe the memories of her incestuous bullying father and warmed to Ray's intimate cuddles.

◆ ◆ ◆

The scuffle began in the car as Todd grappled with the force of Mr Stephen's struggle. Squeezing around his throat from behind the seat with the homemade Garrote wire, his left hand became wedged trying to pull the pressure off from his neck which became cut deep. He drew them up just in time before it could form correctly around it but in turn became pallets of pressure into his neck as he choked. The car swerved dangerously, Ray leant over and grabbed the wheel with one hand, while he began to punch him from the side with rapid violence to the side of his face.

The car struggled for control as the clean plan that they had expected, escalated inside into an unorganised frenzy from the two teenagers. They would both need to use all of their physical might to overcome resistance, their violence became extreme, the punches seemed to mount the adult's struggle to survive.

"I can't hold him, fucking Luca, fucking Brasi." Todd complained hysterically through gritted teeth but held onto his strong grip. Ray continued to hit him repeatedly in the head several times, the victim's eyes bulged insanely under duress from the attack, spittle exited his mouth in spurts as he battled to the last.

The car itself veered when Ray gambled on using both hands to assist smashing fist then elbow into him. The bump shook the bodies inside as it collided into a shallow trench. Todd who was wedged with his knees, forced up in front of him and was leant fully back, choking the wire into Mr Stephen's neck which allowed him to finally finish him off.

The horn beeped loudly over the suffocated last gasp of air. Ray froze watching his face go blue or more purple in colour. Todd relaxed after spending his full weight and effort into the wired choke hold, instantly relieved when he could finally let go. Just as Ray opened his door and heaved a fountain of vomit, when the stench of the violent struggle encapsulated the car.

"Jesus Ray." Todd exasperated.

"What the fuck?" Ray cursed as the reek of death and now vomit overwhelmed him.

"That looked a far lot easier in the film."

"You were supposed to wait until we stopped. You jar."

They both exited and examined the position of the car in the ditch and worryingly began to look around for an answer to get the plan back on track.

"What the fuck are we gonna do?"

"How many fucking times did we go over this?" Ray angered. They both walked frustratingly up and down the layby as dusk began to set, cursing how the well laid plan had gone awry.

"Put it in neutral and see If we can bump it out." With

that, Todd leant in over the dead man and surveyed the lever in the centre console.

"It's an automatic?"

"N! for fuck sake."

"Oh Yeah!" He chuckled. "I told you we need to learn driving."

He joined Ray at the front of the vehicle, avoiding his unimpressed daggered eyes. They pushed front ways and then with their backs pressed up against the bonnet. It bounced a couple times up and down the ditch before it levelled and began to roll backwards unassisted.

Todd gave a short chase and stopped it by yanking aggressively on the hand brake. They assisted each other moving Mr Stephens into the passenger seat. Turning his face away from the lifeless corpse as it stared out beyond the windscreen. Ray jumped in the driver's seat using the front and rear rubber floor mats to cover the sodden seats and stuck the shift into D and let it crawl at its own pace, touching onto the brake, with gentle steering. He guided the car another hundred yards to a suitable place, where the car should have come to a stop, before Todd impatiently strangled him, with the car traveling at 30 mph.

"Right, now grab his legs, I'll grab his arms." Ray commanded.

"Ergh. He stinks of fucking shit."

"Shut up and carry him. Come on."

They struggled with shuffling feet carrying the twelve stone man. Todd made a light-hearted joke about being lucky that it wasn't their head teacher, being that he was at least five stone heavier. They managed to carry, then drag him to the edge of the waterside where they could dump him. Todd ran back to the car and collected the long rusty industrial chain and breeze block from their bags that they had even asked Mr Stephens to assist them with into his car. He hollered out to Ray to assist him to carry the broken off rail sleeper he stumbled across amongst the pile of rubbish that was scattered all over.

"How we gonna get back to London Ray?"

"We're still in London mate."

"Back to the manor then?"

"Well he can't fucking drive us back can he? We'll have to walk."

"We're miles away."

"Let's just get rid of him and worry about that later eh?" He replied impatiently.

They continued with the struggle with the place deserted and now getting dark. Ray surveyed the surroundings and still could not picture the vision of this decrepit dock side land having any value what so ever. He looked over the bank to the U-shaped bend of the Thames, with the cold dark murky water slushing against the stained walls.

"It looks deep enough we just have to make sure we can weigh him down." He surmised.

"The Kiddy-Fiddler sleeps with the fishes." Todd quipped looking down in earnest.

Ray doubled up into a hysterical laughter, which then set Todd off. They tested the water with the car by pushing it several yards away from the body, now wrapped in the remnants of the car boot carpet, tied with chains and a weighty padlock, attached now by a thick rope to the rusty scrap metal sleeper.

"Hold up a sec. We have to wipe off all the handles and everything." Todd began wiping the inside of the car while Ray watched bemused.

"You worry me." Ray chuckled.

"That movie is like a guide to homicide." He sang as he spring-cleaned the car.

Once Todd was satisfied, Ray turned on the ignition to unlock the steering and with a long push for the run up, the car nosedived into the murky water, the crash of the car hitting the river was almost disguised by the rough water crashing against itself, they peered down straining their eyes until when the bubbles stopped and the natural torrent reappeared as if nothing had been entered into the mass. They then turned attention towards the now slightly visible corpse, laying peacefully nearby.

"Do you think if anybody drags him back up, they'd be able to tell who he was?"

"I don't know but they will know someone put him there by the way he is gift wrapped. Let's toss him in the drink and let's go." Ray insisted, now urged to get away from the place.

"Wish we had stuck him in the boot now." Todd realised as they just about managed to manoeuvre him over the edge dangling by a combination of the chain and rope, they rolled the heavy metal that careered the body headfirst down into the mire. Ray's trusted torch shone into the blackened murky water rippling against the light, hoping inside his head at the remaining disturbance to the waterline was the final good riddance. From above the surface as they looked down, nothing was visible to whatever lay beneath.

"We should send Mr Blackman down there next." Ray exhaled calmly.

"And any other dirty noncing low-life ponce." Todd agreed. "We could even start charging people."

"Yeah! Like Jim'll fuckin Fix-It?" Ray looked at him curiously with a sense of bewilderment. "Come on then Sollozzo, no need to hang about like one o'clock half struck, let's fuck off."

He turned away to start the walk home, thinking about his beauty. Todd was still stood there, straining his eyes in the dark towards the water and then quickly jogged to catch up with him.

"Shit! Did you leave the camera in his motor?" Todd asked worryingly stopping dead in his tracks.

"For fuck sake Sweeney. Did we come here to take fucking pictures?"

"Alright mate keep your Alan's on." Todd chuckled as Ray grabbed him playfully in a head lock.

They walked southwards, knowing that as soon as they could get to a bus stop or any part of civilisation they could eventually put a call in to the Gloucester. It wasn't a cold evening, so they walked at a steady pace through some dry grassy land following the riverbank as it meandered from one direction to the next. They used different topics of conversation to pass the time, often circling back after hitting frustrating dead ends, that had them cursing each other on the flawed planning that gave little attention on their actual getaway. The reality hidden with light-hearted humour and some appreciation, that it was not a usual evening exercise most fourteen-year olds participated in.

Distant indicators of loud chugging lorries intermittently, acted like an audio compass that eventually directed them down a long-deserted pathway until they spotted a railway bridge and head towards that direction. A main road became the first bit of civilisation as their eyes adjusted to the first clear site from streetlamps. With only a few cars passing, they continued for another hour or more once the river became camouflaged, there was little in the way of transportation that could get them anywhere closer to home, until Todd became familiar to where he was. The deviations they had taken seemed confusing at this point, that from where they had set out, would lead them of all the places, to here.

"Fuck me, this is Charlton Athletic."

"I never been here." Said Ray in a combination of relief and surprise.

"I come here with Sean and that Nifty Fifty lot. Remember I told you that it kicked right off with them."

"Yeah, I remember. And how come one minute you wanna be Arsenal's top boy. Next you're firmed up with Palace?"

"Millwall with Raph on Saturday."

"Well let's hope no one's about that might recognise yah. Mr Hooligan."

"Alright don't get all lemon, just because you are under

the thumb with your new bird."

Todd was chuckling at their comedy as Ray gimmicked an angry barge into his shoulder. The train station sign beckoned at them like a mirage a few yards up from where the floodlight pylons stood towering unlit. They approached a train guard at the station.

"Are the trains still running?" Ray enquired.

"You just missed the last one." Replied the man. "Why, where are you headed?"

"London Bridge." Ray replied quickly.

"Last train went twenty minutes ago. The one just left was for Gillingham. There's a cab station just up by the shops. It may cost you a fair few." He reported.

"Thanks Mister." Ray echoed with little concern.

They both quickly ran towards the direction of the shops and entered the doorway illuminated by a mini cab sign above. The lone taxi operator was flicking her cigarette into an ash tray, whilst peering into a TV Times magazine, seemingly not that interested.

"Have you got any taxis that can take us to London bridge please lady?" Ray asked and presented four ten-pound notes onto the counter, wary that she may be apprehensive of two mischievous looking lads approaching at this late hour.

"For forty quid. I can drop you there myself." She smiled broadly and punched into a CB radio. "I'm out with customers. London bridge fare. Over and out."

A faint crackled 'Roger' came back over the waves which was in some respects ignored. She grabbed her packet of cigarettes and lighter as she stood up and grabbed at a baggy cardigan to wrap around her, she flicked her curly permed hair out of the collars, ushering them both out politely and locked the white wooden door behind her.

She made very light-hearted conversation with the pair of them, about how long she had run the little cab company for and how it's uncommon to get many fares on a Wednesday night.

"Well my pal in the back come here for a game and bumped into two lovely girls."

"Ahh. Young loves." She purred.

"Well how's our luck? As we've jumped off the last train to anywhere. He remembered that they were actually from Crystal Palace."

The woman laughed heartedly, coughing on the nicotine as she wound down the window to throw out the end.

"You silly sods."

"Tell me about it...Lucky I'm flush at the moment. I'm running a local babysitting service. Been doing it a couple of months and earned nearly two hundred quid." He boasted. "So now I'm gonna do all my wages getting home."

"So where are you going from London bridge?"

"South Norwood." Todd replied quickly.

"You've had a bad enough night. South Norwood is back that way. I'll do you two loves a favour." She smiled.

"If it's not too much bother?"

"None at all."

"You remind me of one of our mate's mum." Todd paid tribute.

"Well, I'll take that as a compliment." She smile, her soft eyes peered at her rear view mirror at him with curiosity.

Ray looked at her, then looked around at Todd confused. She definitely wasn't Angie, or anyone close to them.

"Russel Jackson's mum." Todd grinned.

His cheeky wink had Ray looking inappropriately at her. Her red lipstick rode with smudges above her thin upper lip, her striking silver blonde curls swung back and forth, when she checked for oncoming traffic, as she guided the car across junctions and as she steered, her large chest was touching uncomfortably close to the steering wheel.

Ray smiled secretly as he reviewed the scenery of this part of London, that was very unfamiliar to him, as he began to relax with dreams about his future. Learning to drive being his prime objective, now chuckling to himself at

Todd's observation from earlier, they would have been long ago tucked up in bed if it had been the case today.

Away from the evenings violent encounter, his deviant unremorseful mind, flip-flopped and zig-zagged back onto Sarah, contemplating about her sleeping soundly in her bed, dreaming of white horses galloping in a field. His teenage urges began to familiarise on her perfume in his mind as he closed his eyes in a daydream for her, excited about seeing her again. The babysitting bookings would be in demand, and his reward for tonight will be magnified when he'll be all alone with her again.

Todd and the lady now introduced as Carol, 'Carol the cabbie' Ray mused with a smile, became engrossed, as Todd explained to her, all types of stories about the last time he ventured to Charlton.

CHAPTER 18

SEND FOR THE ZULUS

The room bellowed with the smoker's exhaust, Sid paced up and down with his cigarette cindered down to the filter having the occasional banter with one or two as all his trusted men sat making the most irrelevant conversations. There was Sammy 'The Taxi', Tommy Akehurst, his twins Dale and Wayne and Irish Tommy, they were playing a quiet game of rummy on one of the tables. Robbie Collins was also sat with Pete. Alfred White and Raph sat close by and of course, there was Angela, nervously watching the hands on the clock. Eleven o'clock had passed by quickly to midnight thirty, and still no sign of him.

When he finally walked in, Angie was the first one over to him, his first surprised glance was to Raph and his old man sitting there, he became concerned. The look from Ralph he understood, they had rehearsed private signals, that they had become clones of the cinematic they sat and analysed over a hundred times. Robbie Collins, still in uniform, brought a sweat to his palms and dryness to his throat. Then Sid with that look, the look that meant, 'you will have to try very, very hard to save yourself.'

"Sit down." He eventually commanded.

Ray walked over towards where Raph sat with his dad and knew his dad being there, added a seriousness, cemented by Norma's dad's presence.

Police constable Robbie Collins, now stationed at Norbury nick, was sat there unassuming, enjoying his late pint.

"Now that the guvnor's here, do you want to tell everyone what the plan is?" Pete hissed.

"What plan?" Ray shrugged his shoulders with a bemused look towards everyone in the room. "I never knew we had a family meeting."

"What happened to your hand?" Pete noticed.

"That was Todd messing about." He replied evasively, only now noticing the slight swelling to it.

"Well. It's a quarter to one and you're here now, so seeing that everyone has had to wait around for you. Enlighten us boy." Sid requested, seemingly impatient.

"Me and Todd took a train up to Charlton to meet some birds only…" Ray began to explain the long-winded report of the evening, leaving out the small detail of his girlfriend's father's homicide.

"For fuck sake, shut him up." Tommy shouted as the room filled with laughter.

"Firstly, you should apologise to your friend here for keeping him waiting." Sid continued. "Yeah that's right. Forget about your little Inspector Clouseau aspirations, he has just solved one of the greatest mysteries known to man."

"What are yous on about?" Ray bewildered.

"I know this is a bit over your head so listen up." Pete smiled. "Greenwich peninsula." He waved a brown envelope and frisbee'd it towards him.

Ray began to nervously open it, he read the first ownership of lease, and then a form that read deeds of trust that made little to no sense to him.

"Raph said you overheard us with Stephens and that yous have collected this paperwork from his study."

"He's pinching money off yous, that's why." Ray replied looking at the documents.

"You need to pay more attention in school." Sammy laughed. "Tell us all again Raphael."

"Government grants approved for riverside redevelopment." He read from a pink sheeted newspaper and rustled it folded to make it more manageable to hold, looking like a city toff, only the bowler hat was missing.

"Five hundred million pounds transport and housing funding to regenerate old London dockyards, was given the go ahead today by Parliament, that will see..."

"What's the matter? Cat got your tongue?" Angela giggled.

"So, he wasn't stealing?" Ray enquired nervously.

"Not according to them land ownership, leases and freeholds. Greenwich Peninsular, Albert dock, Shad Thames, Butlers Wharf. That's our names, that's your inheritance."

"You mean all them shitty derelict run-down places, yous are all pleased about that?"

"Sometimes there's money to be made in shit. You'll learn all about that as you get older." Pete toasted.

Ray looked towards Raph who shrugged away his daggered stare. Producing the bank statement from his back pocket and handed it to Sid. He scanned it uninterested, the numbers he totalled inside his head in silence. So, whether this was his stolen money, the total on the initial investment would amount to peanuts in the long term.

"Ok maybe we paid him a little over the odds. And I know you are protecting the family but where was you thinking your little investigation will lead to eh?" He replied.

"I tell you what. He watches too many movies the boy." Sammy laughed out loud.

"Have some R Whites and keep your fucking trap shut." Raph whispered as Ray went and sat beside him. He sat with as much as a smile as he could produce, looking back, in hindsight, all this gives Mr Stephens, is a reprieve but he was not after retribution for alleged stolen money, he had avenged for Sarah and the first thing he would do tomorrow, was to go and knock for her, to take her on the date that she deserved.

He was still replaying the episode over again in his mind, not really concentrating on the people in the room but on the stench, the sound of his choking and bulging eyes, his desperate gasping for oxygen, an episode which will now need to remain as his and Todd's secret, despite Raph's suspicion about their whereabouts, since last seeing the pair of them walk out of school at lunch time.

He watched as Sid and Pete held council, with his mum ensuring everyone was topped up. For the immediate, ownership of these acres of wasteland was still only a pipe dream and there were still more pressing issues at hand. Alfie White was attending tonight to get an understanding of his role to play this coming weekend. It required a team effort to pull off the money plan they had postponed for almost two years.

"Chaos? Is there definitely room for plenty of chaos?" Tommy directed at Alfie for another confirmation.

"Chaos? It's going to be absolute bedlam, they haven't played Millwall for five or six seasons and we run them every time. You'll get your chaos Tommy."

"So Raph are you able to get the main firm gathered In the Barrow?"

"Yes Mr Bryan at least seventy in the Barrow and eighty down in that backstreet boozer." He replied respectfully.

"Bell and Anchor." Ray interjected, looking around at him with a hard stare, to which Raph winked back.

"Rumours have it, the brummies' are bringing two hundred down. All the top boys. We've already fed them." He carried on smugly.

"There are two hundred Zulu's coming against you?" Wayne chuckled. "You must abandon this mission."

The pub erupted in scattered laughter, even Ray forced out a hearted laugh, that it was not only him and his mates influenced by the big screen.

CHAPTER 19

PUBLIC DISORDER

"All units, this is Tango Mike. Concourse London bridge, we have contained a large group of Birmingham city supporters. Tango Mike. Over."

"All units received." Came the voice over the radio.

Riot police and their dogs lined up on the platform in banks of ten, the intel received had them ready to repel the group at all cost, to limit the chance of any major disorder. Accosted and escorted from Euston station, even their evasive plot to land early, catching the 6:10 train from New Street had already been scuppered, following collaboration with West Midlands police. Straight from the outset, the police commander responsible for crowd control, stood pleased that the intel had outfoxed the risk of crowd trouble. But it was still early doors.

Meanwhile, just under a mile away, approximately seventy or so, intent on trouble, die-hard fans, had disembarked at the bank station and were halfway across the bridge, with two fourteen-year olds tailing them like trackers from the other side, trying to look as inconspicuous as possible.

"The Junior business boys in amongst that lot." Ray praised.

"How fucking confident do they look eh? Fucking smart and all." Todd said excitedly. His baggy parka made him look almost impossible and made Ray chuckle.

"More than I can say about you. Where the fuck did you get that coat?" He laughed as they trudged alongside, slightly behind the crowd of men and boys walking purposefully towards the organised meet, ready to surprise.

"Well didn't want any fucker recognising me in me Fila." He remarked as though the ridiculousness of how he looked would not distract any attention. "I was thinking the other day; do you think we should get Gloucester Boy's Firm tattoo's all of us?"

Ray looked towards him without comment, his friend was like this immature sponge of ideas and notions at times had him shaking his head in pity.

Kenny Arnold was sitting in his Telecom van reading the paper then looked at his watch, then agreeing with the voice in his head that it was time. He opened the green roadside cabinet and dialled up his workmate on a similar roadside cabinet just a mile down the road and gave the signal to start the changeover.

A loud roar went up in a surge of volume like a crowded battlefield, being competed on the streets. Missiles began to come down, ricocheting onto the Barrow Boy's windows and doors, which emptied quickly to repel the opposing army, now spread out across the road stopping traffic as horns beeped. The unfortunate joe public caught up in a melee, cowered as they were soaked with full pints of beer, raining upon them like a morning shower. Forty Millwall supporters gave a charge into the lads that Ray and Todd had followed.

"Yessss." Todd cheered excitedly and began to run towards the action. Taking a sharp right before the pub, he jogged down the grey stone steps towards the market. Pulling a flare from his coat, he activated and threw it with all his might into the street as he reached the bottom. Red smoke bellowed and filled the area like a cloud, which set another large gang of men charging out of the Bell and Anchor, they would come down from a narrow alley onto the old Victorian cobbled streets and flank the attackers of the targeted drinking establishment.

Todd ran back up the stairs to meet Ray, who was viewing and resisting the temptation to join in. Another flare was rolled in the direction of the Birmingham hooligans, their haunting chant baying at the opposition before they both jogged away and listened as the noise increased as both sides became excited in battle. No one noticed the alarms going off all around as glass smashing and football hooligan war cries angrily drowned the air.

Sammy and Wayne took their time with torches in the dark, emptying the cabinets of neatly stacked bank notes into large holdalls, stuffing each one to the brim. Two uniformed men approached with bin liners and stuffed them halfway and went in a separate direction from the planned escape route.

The violence continued evenly, as casualties from both sides were dragged up and away as the two opposite gangs of anarchy goaded each other, pausing at times with a hail of insults before trading blows again. News had trickled down to the train platform and the confident police commander was now screaming into his VHF radio again for back up. Traffic over the waves, were dominantly streaming news of the public disorder, when the containment of the main group from leaving the station, became a power struggle between the sheer weight of numbers, versus the batons drawn by the police lines to suppress.

Almost like a breached dam, in a trickle, one or two, then eight and nine escaped. More were set loose as the crowd intent on getting involved became infected like a virus. Gradually there were thirty or so eager individuals began a hasty jog towards wherever the action was, following the echoed sounds from the battle on the bridge and the sirens wailing at them like a beacon.

Four police vans roared up and began to wade in and drag people against the walls as bottles and other missiles rained down the narrow road as the violence began to fan out, with pockets of tens and fifteen skirmishing. Police on the scene began the futile attempt to bring order to the usually quite weekend location. Todd and Ray found themselves being thrown against one of the vans before willingly climbing in, as the two officers grabbed other men and their bags into the back.

"Wait for me." Raph shouted breathlessly. Chasing after it while being tailed by three angry looking black boys in long Burberry coats, scarves and deerstalker hats.

"They must have heard about your reputation Raph." Ray shouted laughing hysterically. Tommy jumped out with his baton drawn looking as though he had served a full career in the Met's riot squad.

"Get back." He warned authoritatively.

Ignoring his warning, Raph continued full pelt towards him laughing. He was flung into the side of the van, which appeared to make his pursuers give up the chase but one of them had already spotted something more tempting to end the pursuit, that would possibly give them, if they weren't so greedy, more chance of getting themselves arrested, than capturing a victim to take out their anger on in front of a lone police officer. An anger borne out of a territorial rivalry, that they stalked every weekend was diverted by a more tempting realisation.

A smashed window, belonging to the Midland bank was obscured by a distorted metal shutter that was bent upwards, laying on the pavement, was an irresistible litter of tens and twenty-pound notes scattered at the entrance. A crowd began to form around the debris, with others closely following behind, some by accident, backing off and becoming isolated down the same road as more missiles smashed against the wall and doorways around them, while the shouting and running battles continued, with ever more police sirens rifling loudly to fill the air.

The police van driven by Tommy, revved its engine violently, the police radio scanner crackled with phonetics, as it took off through the back streets with the blues and twos wailing loudly down the narrow-cobbled streets.

"Tango-whisky, Foxtrot, Spangles, Opal fruits." Todd chuckled childishly. The inside was filled with laughter,

Wayne, Ray, Raph, Dale, and Sammy fell from side to side as they lit cigarettes.

The reinforcement that had caved in the blue line, allowing more supporters out of the train station, saw the once confident commander radioing frantically. The cat and mouse through the streets of London Bridge continued. Mayhem incentivised between the people creating disorder and the law enforcement trying to restore it, the rival factions ignored the police presence as an excuse to cease the fighting. The long battle took another swathe of dog units and riot police to reinstate the peace. Traffic tailed back or U-turned towards the opposite directions, numerous arrests were being made, while ambulance paramedics took care of the wounded.

There was a small group of fifteen or so, mixed between the rival groups, that were receiving special attention as the ill-gotten loot was inspected with high suspicion. All the young men communicated the same excuse, that the vandalism was already done, before they had spotted the opportunity of free money lying around casually during the chaos.

Police inspected the inside of the premise with bewilderment as the central alarm eventually was answered and questions into how these opportunists gained access so easily.

CHAPTER 20

MISSING PERSONS

"We have not located his car either Miss Harris. He'll just be noted as another missing person. Until we get more information, there is not a lot more we can do at this present time." The WPC stood behind the desk combining passion with impatience to move her along.

"It's been nearly two months and I have nothing to say to his kids." She explained in desperation.

"Look, please step aside and wait. I will notify a sergeant to come and speak to you, but he will tell you the same."

"Don't bother. Like I'll just sit around just to get more lip service. I pray you don't find yourself in this position." She huffed and stormed out through the glass doors, which absorbed the small reception area like a green house and adding to the frustration and impatience from the desk officers and visitors alike.

Barging past a couple, who tutted back in response, she stood outside on the steps that lead back down to the street, looking back at the large signage that advertised Croydon police station, she shook her head bewildered at the lack of investigation into her missing partner. Despite the abusiveness he inflicted on her, she still loved him and had wondered every day where he had gone. A proverbial one day he was there, and next thing, vanished. She decided on her next stop to the Gloucester pub to see if they had any further clues to this mystery.

◆ ◆ ◆

"We understand your concern and we've done everything we can to track him down." Sid explained.

"This is a printout of bank statements. We done an autopsy." Pete handed her the three-page document.

"He never had that type of money, have you seen where we live." She replied aghast at the five figure sums.

"Well that raises alarm bells with us as you can imagine. My brother and I paid him a fair sum of money for land and property."

"Jesus Christ." She sighed sinking her face into her hands as she became nerved at the indication that it was not a couple of thousand they were hinting at.

"We have deeds for at least half of what we paid. But we weren't the only investors, so there could be a long line of people all in this same boat." Sid continued.

"This is all too much."

"Can I get you a drink. Tea? A coffee?"

"Can I have something stronger please." She pleaded.

Pete indicated with a bottle of whisky which she declined.

"Vodka please... and Tonic."

"Ice?"

"Please."

He mixed her the drink, with a splash of ice and lemon and placed it on the bar in front of her. She quickly pressed the glass against her lips and gulped half.

"Have you checked indoors for his passport?"

"Passport won't prove a thing Sid." Sammy interjected. "If he's scarpered."

Sid let this settle into his head, false documents once being his forte.

"We all have questions we need answered, so can I send Sammy over to go over his paperwork and see if we can gather any clues, of where he might have gone?" He offered as a narrow gesture.

"But if he done a runner and he owe yous money. Even if he is found. It doesn't shed good prospects for me does it?"

"We all consider him as a dear friend of ours. We don't want to see no harm come to him. Just like you, Miss Harris."

"Please, call me Amanda."

"Of course, Amanda. But we need to know where he has gone. That he is safe at the least, to put your mind…our minds at peace." Sid replied convincingly, walking around to her side of the bar to reassure her that there was no ill will.

She knocked back the drink and gestured if she could have another one. Ray walked in from school with Norma and Sarah, who fell surprised as to why her mother was in the pub.

"Mum…Why are you here?" Sarah queried.

"Looking for your father." She replied.

"Take your friends upstairs please boy." Sid directed.

Ray put his arm around Sarah and led them both past the bar and upstairs. They all sat down while he placed his finger on his lip to indicate that he would go downstairs to eavesdrop on what was being discussed. For a couple of minutes while Sid and Pete explained a next course of action. It seemed after two months no one had any idea.

"They think he did a runner with my uncle's readies." Ray explained when he returned.

"Oh?"

"Yeah. When was the last time you see him?"

Norma looked around at him, she was curious now, after conversations she had with him in the past. Sarah shrugged with a coldness that they both, Ray and Norma could understand. Norma flooded her mind as to whether his uncles had made him disappear or he scarpered out of choice.

"Well, I'll be so bloody happy, if I never saw him again." She raptured. Ray offered her a re-assuring squeeze, so too did Norma from her left.

"What about John? Did he not see him either, I thought they were quite close?"

"John hates him and all. And I don't even know why my mum gives a fuck either." She hissed.

"Well I'm sure my uncles can help find him. They

got connections everywhere." Ray re-assured, more out of consideration than sincerity.

Sammy was eventually tasked to drive Amanda home after four vodka tonics she was not in any real state to drive. Pete offered out of concern that they get her a ride home, with the offer that if she needed anything, their door was always opened for her. She was at a somewhat more comfortable place, they also didn't hide the shared notion, knowing of his liking towards one of the young barmaids at the Mail Coach, which still offered no reference of his whereabouts. They closed with just a simple hint, for her to maybe focus, on what was easier to control in her life. Amanda called out for Sarah if she liked to go back with her, Sarah remained with Ray.

After Norma left to return home, no-one uttered any further concern for her father, as she kissed him with a loving relief. To an extent, Ray battled with his urges, reviewing that being caught in an uncompromising position in the living room, would be a punishment such as the strangulation that had befallen her late father.

"I love getting off with you. I think I'm falling in love." She declared. smouldering into his embrace. A declaration that taunted his myriad fantasia prediction, a white wedding, with Todd, Tony, Nathan and Raph as the best men, Christine, Norma, Sharon and Bev as maids of honour and bridesmaids. The thought unnerved him enough to stop but his heart boiled so much for her without a doubt.

"I love you too Sarah, I couldn't think of being with anyone else. I'd do anything for you." His eyes coveted her as she lathered his lips with hers, squeezing at her breast over her jumper.

"Would you even make him disappear and never come back ever again?" She smiled, curiosity painted her face in hope.

"If only I was Vito Corleone." He smiled nervously.

She drew him back into her to kiss him lovingly, pressing her head into the cushions urging him to caress her, to have sex with her. She humped his thigh, feeling his size increase and her panties dampen, they moaned into each other's mouths until the purposeful thumping up the stairs had them bolted up right on the sofa, pretending to be interested in the six o'clock news.

Pete stood at the doorway behind Angela who was grinning ear to ear at the pretence of innocence.

"Look at these beautiful love birds, acting as though Robert Dougal was interesting." She tittered. "Are you staying for Tea Sarah?"

"Erm…I would love to. If it's not too much trouble." Sarah replied pushing strands of her hair behind her ears.

She got out of the seat to follow Angela into the kitchen while Pete briefly examined Ray about the concerns for Sarah's missing step father.

"Of course, It's no trouble. You are always welcome any time love." Angie smiled.

"Would you like some help?" Sarah offered.

"No thank you my love, you just sit yourself down, you are our guest." She was smiling broadly as she walked her back to the living room then left them alone to prepare tea.

◆ ◆ ◆

Sammy was sat at Mr Stephens's desk, after it alluded that four vodkas was above Amanda's limits, seeing her crashed out on her sofa and snoozing literally as soon as her head hit the cushions. He rummaged through the desk and drawers, scanning through diaries and planners, flicking over the past few weeks with nothing hinting with clues. The itemised phone bills also going back to his last known days displayed with a long list of international calls, the United States and Germany, were the only codes he could positively identify and folded the pages into his pocket.

Opening envelopes some of which contained cheques written out to cash, ranging from a few hundred, up to fifteen thousand pounds. He lifted any documents that mentioned Bryan Brothers and Gloucester Chartered Surveyors and decided after almost forty minutes, when there was not much else he could sleuth, to give up the ghost.

Upon seeing the peacefully sleeping woman on the sofa downstairs, he finally saw himself out.

CHAPTER 21

PROTECT THE MONARCHY

He was sat in the Tabard Inn, located in SE1, at a table peering at the door, supping on his pint of Courage Best bitter. Ironically, it was not because of the bold brand name of the tipple that he drank to settle any nerves, he just enjoyed the taste. With his second starting to disappear as quickly as the first, he settled in for his usual hours, sat here before he ventured home to face the wrath of his wife. He just continued with a volley of thoughts, staring at the door and the people that came through it. He always chose the quiet pub, which was a short walking distance from the hustle and bustle of the City, but not many people sought out this well-hidden public house in the back streets of Borough in the early evening. It was his preferred way to end the day.

His former government assigned job, played against the morality that he had been brought up on and asking for a reassignment didn't bode well for him, in his ambition to clamber his way through the ranks of Royal protection officer, his glamorised babysitting role protecting the future protector of the kingdom, who was nothing more than a perverted glorified playboy. Looking into his pint, reflecting again dissatisfied at his career of working in commodities now, although the salaries was nothing to scoff about, he had envisioned a little bit more than this. Following the great expectations after his recruiting, almost fifteen years to the day, his commander promising him a ladder to the top, if he listened, observed, kept his nose clean and served his country well.

The tall balding man in his black trench coat

acknowledged him as he entered. He listened as the man ordered a pint of stout, and sat with a grin of recognition, with his own mind game that he played with himself regularly, a kind of, guess the agency. He was definitely government and knew as if by telepathy and by the tell tale sign as the man approached, would be another point of dead end and questioning of the old guard and staff, like a bookmarked anniversary.

"Good evening Mr Preston." He greeted and selfishly sat at a stool at his table uninvited.

"Seems like I need to change my routines. You lot tend to always find me wherever I am." He huffed.

"We have the means, as you well know."

"Well if you have come to harass me again, there are empty tables over there."

"That's not very hospitable, is it?"

Preston ignored his response and carried on supping his drink, maybe by pretending he wasn't there, he might just up and leave. He then produced his badge across the short table to make him peer down at the decorated emblem as though to signal a formal introduction.

"Congratulations Superintendent..." Preston offered begrudgingly. "Superintendant Archer."

Appearing around the same age as himself despite his slightly balding crown, he correctly assumed the ladder of success for Superintendant Archer, was at a guess, costly to many unfortunates that crossed the same path, especially those who did not share that secret handshake that catapulted this less than deserved individual ahead of the pecking order, that he himself had learned the hard way.

The superintendent smiled with a degree of gratitude but could sense the impatience as if his crystal ball had already revealed the topic of information he was seeking.

"I'm in line for the commissioner's job. Won't be long now just a few loose ends." He enthused.

"And with that, I take it, you being here, people are still

asking?"

"People are still asking."

"And by my guess, taking a wife with a hostile womb has wobbled the nerves of the powers that be?"

"You sound worse than the tabloids talking like that." The superintendent frowned.

"You know, thinking back on that night. Everyone at that dinner were carrying on politely as though it's a natural thing for a Prince to have an appetite for young females and now all of a sudden, after all he has done…Well, you know where I'm going with this?" He stated pompously.

"Yes and I'm sure there were many, many more, who turned a blind eye…So don't feel too disheartened."

"Oh I can assure you, I don't…For me, when you call a spade a spade you get casted away. That's the problem when you are part of a despicable dictatorship."

"Oh, get off of your high horse Preston. We have a duty to serve, it's not for us to question the rights and wrongs."

"Well if they had listened, instead of acting like a bull in a china shop, you wouldn't be here spoiling my pint."

"The questions still surrounds this person Rita, envoy's niece or whatever she was. The story we had was she was a prostitute, what was your take on that story?"

"She wasn't a prostitute. That much I do know."

"Well what we know, the Humanitarian envoy for West Africa at the time, was an only child and didn't have a niece. According to one of his former aides."

"Listen, with all due respect, whatever his reason for fooling security services and sneaking about with this girl, is anyone's guess, as far as to whether I was witnessed to anything he did with her, I know as much as all of you. But she was very pretty, very well proportioned, shall we say? So I could understand."

"How old…in your opinion?"

"Who knows with them blacks." He crudely responded.

The superintendent shook his head and sank some more

of his stout, he withdrew a pack of cigarettes from his coat pocket and offered it to Preston. They both pointed the cigarette ends into the flame he produced and exhaled from deep lungs. The smoke filled around the table like a mild cloud as they sat silently for a while.

"By your own account, was their anymore encounters publicly that you…"

"He never saw her openly, well at least not with the general public, the only other rendezvous I was privy to, was after the foreign office dinner at number ten. That time, as I told them previously, she came with that clubland gentleman, Francis something. He left on his own after a while."

"Kidbrook. Yes I'm familiar with the name." Archer confirmed. "Can you provide any more details of that night?"

"Yes, he got extremely drunk and then had his hands all over her." He offered sarcastically and rose from his seat after downing the last droplets and offered the superintendent another.

"Please. Just half an ale this time." Archer replied.

Preston took the short walk to the bar to repeat the request for the half pint and a full pint of his favourite dark bitter. The bar lady poured as he waited patiently and surprised in his thoughts again as he counted his money, the change in weather outside.

"The other thing I remember of that period, what she said. This, from the horse's mouth so to speak…" He paused as he looked into the deep-seated memory. "I cannot remember word for word, or the terms in which she used. She appeared to have the belief that her relationship was more than that of fulfilling a perverted prince's needs."

"There is no need to be crass but continue." The superintendent frowned.

"Let's just call a spade a spade…Anyway, maybe he offered her the world. The next queen or a title. Who knows?"

"Brains of a buffoon." He sighed.

"You do buffoons a disservice." Preston chuckled to

himself. "In fairness, not that it's a tea that I'd dip my biscuit, but she had a very womanly figure, hourglass hips, lovely eyes…"

"Lovely eyes? Do me a favour." Superintendent Archer questioned suspiciously.

"Yes, in fact quite stunning, she had very beautiful eyes, could tempt the devil himself." He recalled. "Other than this, that's as much in the way of the story that I remember about her."

"And we assume the relationship was physical?"

"Physical? She could barely walk." He kept that slice of information to himself and put forward the most relevant. "It is not that difficult to workout…but what amazes me, every new command wants to reopen this. My question to them, seeing that someone ordered to throw her into a bonfire, isn't his little secret now laid in ashes, forever?"

"It's not as closed as they would like it to be."

"Maybe they should offer a reward and put a little appeal out with Shaw Taylor." He chuckled.

"Now there is a thought." He brimmed an acute smile about the true nonsense of it all.

"And by the way, I've never told a soul about his escapades or at least nothing that wasn't already common knowledge."

"It is certainly a contradiction, knowing his behaviour. I personally think, why would anyone give a flying fart about where he dipped his toes?" Archer mused.

"No one does, until a scandal rears its ugly head of course. What to me holds more ground, was the fact that he had a very notable thirst for young flesh especially. And not just girls to my understanding, although I never witnessed him fooling around with boys. But who's to tell?"

"This is your beliefs or what you have been privy?"

"There are some things you just can't always turn a blind eye to." Preston huffed.

"Unfortunately that is part of the job."

"Yeah well, In my time, there were always a host of girls.

Five that I can remember. And the only difference with this one, was not only that she was underaged, so the rumour had it, but that she was coloured, that was the only difference... although, I remember Shirley Bassey, he had drinks with her at the Palladium." He pondered scratching his head.

"That has been well publicised, his friendship with Miss Bassey. I doubt that would be any cause for alarm."

"So even now sitting here in 1983, despite many of us being shot down by the liberals about our institutionalised prejudices, that taboo is still etching at the nerves of your superiors?"

"They cannot afford to be blind sighted on this one, that's the concern." The superintendent continued to worry.

"If it mattered that much, truly there should be a greater worry that he could have an army of thes sprogs out there?"

"By a saving grace, none have come forth."

"At least, we have not read of any. He should count himself lucky that he is not a rock star." Preston laughed heartedly as he summed up the embarrassment that could surface at any time for his former employers.

"I shudder at the thought." Archer finished the last of his drink. And pondered for a while looking at Preston as Preston looked more interested into his drink. "Thanks for your time, I can't say this will be the last."

"No. But you will get the same old story."

"And on and on it goes." He managed a creased smile for the first time.

"Funny thing is, going by our celestial past, bastards have been heir to the throne for hundreds of years and executed, for the pure fact that they were bastards." Preston surmised as a somewhat blasé response.

"Well I'm sure you would agree, that is our only hope that no one will be foolish enough to present themselves, if by chance he or she discovers that their alive or dearly departed mother was impregnated by the king of our country." The superintendent concluded.

"To be quite frank about it. It sounds like a pile of bullshit to me?" Preston lifted his glass to that thought and smiled smugly.

"As to us all who no loner seek the seeds of his wrongdoings. However, it's in the interest of national security, unfortunately."

"God save The King of spades and his little sambo sprogs." Preston toasted, partially under his breath, feeling the last of the smooth bitter melt into the back of his throat.

"Thanks for the drink." The superintendent did not join in on the humour, despite his own feelings of the whole subject.

"Imagine if she sprouted twins?" Preston continued chuckling regardless. "Or triplets? Now that would be some story."

He left his stool as Preston approached the bar again his shoulders jumping at his own humour, with the barmaid already halfway into pouring his fourth pint.

"Concessions and cigarettes." Preston suddenly hollered.

"Forgive me. I don't follow?" The superintendent paused as he reached the door.

"The coloured girl, his bit of stuff. She sold concessions, cigarettes matches and what not." He smiled.

The superintendent paused at the thought. She had no more relevance even with this new enlightenment. Facing the facts, he left the pub pulling his coat collar up around his ears. He walked to the end of the road and got into an awaiting car.

CHAPTER 22

RATED EIGHTEEN

He followed Theresa up the short flight of stairs, his lingering eyes followed her curves in front of him to the top. She rattled the keys into the heavy black door, marked number twenty. Flicking on a light switch as she entered inside, she hung her knee length Burberry mac up on the door to an opened closet in the hallway and dropped the keys to her brand spanking new, beaming black convertible SAAB 900 Turbo onto a side table, then continued into a roomy living area and invited him to sit down.

"Can I get you a drink?" She raptured as she disappeared into the kitchen.

"What have you got?"

"I haven't got any beers though." She continued hollering, while inspecting inside the refrigerator.

"I'll just have whatever you are having." Ray replied. The unexpected diversion to her living room had him adjusting himself with that hopeful expectation. He could hear the sound from the kitchen of a bottle opening, before she reappeared.

"Good." She replied as she entered back with two champagne glasses. "It is your birthday after all."

She smiled and cat-walked in the sleek Katherine Hamnette towards him, each step seductive and made the large hooped earrings tap at the side of her face.

"Happy birthday to me eh?" Ray smiled shyly.

Pouring skilfully, she topped up both glasses, they clinked an unofficial toast and began to consume the sharp bubbles. She sipped at her glass and smiled at his nervousness, as he placed his on to the solid glass coffee table, stylishly cluttered with vogue magazines and a remote control to a Bang and Olufsen. Examining the modern décor, Ray's mind wandered with insecurity. She tossed her long deep chestnut brown hair flirtatiously, with her soft and sexy piercing brown eyes staring alluringly at him. She downed her now half empty glass and placed it beside his.

"I hope you didn't make any plans for this evening."

"Well..." Ray quickly distracted away to the arrangement he had made with the boys, to attend a nightclub in Tottenham that Nathan and Tony had organised with Yogi, the top boy hooligan from Arsenal's firm, that they had looked up to since school days. The recently forged alliances in the bars around the City of London, affiliations on neutral territory, endorsed cash making ventures, which trounced the consensus need to bash the fuck out of each other every weekend.

"Nah, not really just a meeting with mates for a drink that's all. Nothing special." He stuttered, his mind was already a long time made up, to blow them all out. "I still feel a bit out of order because..."

"Shut up and kiss me." She caressed, interrupting his nervous chatter. Leaning towards him she kissed him gently. "You are with me tonight. You won't regret it."

Her eyes fluttered seductively towards him with an attraction that magnified a deep and craving need. The lipstick gloss of her sumptuous lips he enjoyed, while his mind meandered inconveniently again, onto the sweetly opulent middle-aged blonde that had taken care of him, a thought which always confusedly conflicted him with guilt, every time he kissed another girl. He shook the thought away to the back of his mind and began to stroke at her breast.

She could feel an increasing yearn for him grow, the heated sensation began to warm her sensually by his touch. She stroked him eagerly down his thighs, which generated searing pounding energy inside her.

"How badly do you want to fuck me." She pined softly.

Straddling onto his lap, she began to writhe sexily against the ever-increasing prominence inside his jeans. She gazed seductively at him while raising her skirt gingerly, then slowly further up, to reveal more of her smooth tanned thighs and the jet-black suspender belts which tugged at the luxurious denier.

Exposing her knicker-less crotch to him, she began to toy between her legs with her finger, staring into his eyes, his eyes then diverted downwards with a fearful excitement. Stirring the wetness from her moist velvet onto her stimulated clit, she panted sexily from the throbbing down below, as the sensation warmed her with an excess of desire. He swallowed hard as she tickled at her pussy making the lush whispered sound from between her legs, echo perversely at him. She submersed her fingers, disappearing gently and stroked tenderly up to her clit again and back, then re-emerged her sticky fingers tantalizingly towards his mouth.

"Taste my pussy." She teased as he lapped hungrily at them, licking his lips sobering the gorgeous taste.

The heat inside her grew desperately, as she slid away to ease herself beside him on the sofa, and parted her legs, begging for him sophisticatedly, which lured him with confidence as she displayed her beautiful pussy before him. Enticing his head instinctively down, tempted by her silky thighs and perfume from her excited cunt, his tongue lavished inside her juicy haven with greed and pleasure from the sweet inhalation and taste. Writhing in time with him, her hands clamped into his wool like hair to pleasure a deeper sensation. Her bosom heaved heavily with her arching back, when she felt his tongue begin to generate a building momentum, which elated her tingling insides. She forced his head away abruptly before she peaked.

"Oh Fuck." She cursed sexily, His compliance was met with appraising kisses at his lips and neck, His excited protuberance was all consuming now as she turned him on, reciprocal were her feelings, heightened more by his gorgeous eyes.

"Let's go upstairs." She whispered softly.

Ray eased himself up to allow her to get up, she offered her hand out to lead him off the sofa, to follow her swiftly through the hallway and up the stairs. She stopped him abruptly again at the entrance to the bedroom.

"Stay there." She commanded, stepping slowly backwards, seductive and captivating, she unzipped the side of her dress, allowing it to fall, then wriggled slowly out from it, onto the carpet. His eyes coveted her spellbinding beauty when she was stood with the black underwear and sexy high heels on display. Turning slowly around to boast her ample round arse, she stepped further out of sight towards her bed.

Mesmerizingly, she beckoned him towards her, he stumbled hastily to join her in front of the bed, the devilish thoughts in her mind, she proceeded to unbutton then unzip his jeans towards the floor. The thought of him had her feeling wet and hot as she sat in front of him, her stockinged legs astride, stroking his erection and gasped with revelation from the contents of his underwear.

"Fuck! It is true?" Her eyes widened with alleviated joy as her memory became engrossed back to the rumours she had overheard from some of the younger girls when she lived on the same estate, she shook away her digression and began to pleasure him with her mouth.

The sensation elated him and drove him ever hungrier for her. As she took him in deep and skilfully to the back of her throat, with precision, she guided her mouth and her tongue, stroking him masterfully, she purred at the taste of him, his hands stroked her hair caressingly, as the succulence almost weakened him prematurely. She retreated back with an almost sixth sense, that broke his thoughts at the suddenness. Her eyes latched onto him and eased herself backwards flat on the bed and began to finger herself with a curious unassured look.

"I'm not sure I need you anymore." She teased erotically, with the sound from her juicy pussy willing him towards her.

"Are you sure about that?" His voice was almost begging

as she teased him with so much expertise, that he grasped his now tortured rigid cock in his hand, that he began to stroke in front of her, back and forth, with the threat of what he wanted to do to her.

"How badly do you want me?" She pined, with a breathless whisper as she fingered her cunt deep. Pointed heels protruded outwards to obstruct his craved advance. While she self-tampered with her clit, now swollen, shimmering wet with desire and anticipation.

"Ahh baby, Look at my pussy. So wet." She gasped heavily. "I'm so, so, horny."

She licked her fingers seductively to heighten his visible desperation. His extended torment continued, when she dispelled her bra to boast her beautiful breasts at him, fondling, biting and pinching both nipples, purring alluringly, she caressed her whole body as her chest heaved heavily as she continually deprived him. She was so tempting, his cock became pumped with jealousy, while she pleasured herself with her fingers lavishly, until finally, her legs came down and positioned for him to fuck her.

"Uhhnnn, Fuck me with your big cock." She swore impatiently, as she slid her soft hands down his shaft and guided it towards her soaking hole, tingling and drenched with expectancy, she rubbed the tip of his huge bulging erection against her sensually slippery folds, until, he was deep inside her, warm, juicy and snug, which forced her sinful eyes shut.

The timely relief manifested with a pleasing outtake of breath for the pair of them as his hardness and her silky passion collided. She clawed with her long nails at his back as he continually shot his thick cock deep and penetrative. Her mind screamed with pleasure and drifted into deep seated matter, to whether she could remember ever having a nicer feeling length as this enter her body, as his grateful aggression pumped inside her.

She pulled him into her as her heels came together

around his back to slow some of the pace and hummed elatedly with the gentler stroking inside, the gradual sensation triggered more creaming and began to shake her body as she panted for more.

"I love the way you fuck me." She moaned filthily into his ear, she wanted him to use and toy with her as the heightened throbbing radiated with an increasing momentum. She screamed in ecstasy to urge him on. The pounding triggered sheer undiluted lust, as her body flexed, and breasts jiggled in time with him, the shock waves combusted up her body climbing into her head and elated into profanity from her mouth.

"OH MY GOD! FUCK ME, YOU FUCK! STRETCH MY WET PUSSY." She cursed loudly, in a sex starved angry tone. "BIG FUCKING COCK."

Torturously he fucked her, deeper and harder. She bucked towards him as she now fully let go and gushed pleasingly from her pussy as it became totally soaked as he unitingly erupted inside. The sheets dampened beneath her, as he slowly pulled out from between her legs, which left her pulsating, she rubbed her hands tenderly between them to examine in surprise, how much she had climaxed and became thirsty at the thought of what he had just achieved. He laid beside her catching his breath, she relievedly kicked off her heels, before she invited him under the sheets to cuddle him.

"Happy birthday gorgeous." She sang sweetly, clinging to his chest lovingly, as his breathing began to simmer.

"Thanks. That was the fucking best." He raptured with a satisfied smirk, reliving the fantasy in his head. The unsophisticated romp with Joanne Jackson aside, this was an unbelievable feeling to be with an older woman, fulfilling a fantasy for her, since he was in his early teens warmed him. He turned to kiss her, almost love struck.

"Make sure you close the door on your way out." She caressed his tongue passionately then rolled over.

His delayed reaction waited for a punchline that never

came. With his face etched with curiosity and surprise, he got out of the bed in a silent huff and got dressed, when she finally sat up to face him.

"I'll be in the same bar next week if you want to see me again. Bring me flowers this time." She smiled cheekily and beckoned him again to kiss her long and hard which embraced them into one another again.

CHAPTER 23

RISKY BUSINESS

"Wanker! Where the fuck were you last night? You missed a right good laugh." Tony chuckled.

"Fucking place was heaving with birds. You'd have loved it." Said Nathan.

"Something came up." Ray said coyly. "Gis' a pint of your finest please Sid."

"Fuck is up with your legs boy?" Sid came back. Lifting up the bar hatch with a fistful of bank notes and a bag full of change from the slot machines.

"Get on this Sid, we organised a night out for the boy's 18th and he don't even have the curtesy to show." Nathan revealed.

"Sounds about right. He's a selfish little fucker." Sid replied sarcastically.

Ray picked up some peanuts from the glass bowl that was laid on the bar in front of him, tossing them in a hail, striking him in the back of the head.

"Stop wasting the fucking nuts." He growled playfully angry at him.

"Calm down lemon, you'll give yourself an 'art attack."

"I'll give you lemon. Saucy little sod." Sid returned, with a light-hearted smile back at him.

"So, what was so important that came up, to blow us all out like that?" Tony interrupted, which made Nathan chuckle cheekily.

"I'll tell you what came up. Tommy Akehurst said he see him leave that bar we met up in, with that Theresa Downey. That good sort that used to live on the estate."

"Fuck off." Tony objected in disbelief. "Haven't seen her for yonks. She's the fittest bird, I'd ever laid me eyes on. She's mint sort."

"You should see her now bredrin." Ray pondered to himself, wide-eyed with a sinful glee.

"Come on Ray, spill?" Nathan taunted. "Did you get the sword wet?"

"Fuck's wrong with yah? What the fuck does Tommy know?" Ray swerved the questioning as he walked around to the other side of the bar to pour himself a drink. Just as Angela entered.

"Oi! What are you doin' behind here?"

He stared towards her with a cheeky grin, then looked her up and down examining her outfit. The tight gold dress hugged over her hour glass figure, which prompted the recycle of that same old sinful desire to re-emerge inside his head.

"Where are you going all dolled up?"

"Working sweetheart." She sang as she approached him to kiss him on his cheek.

"You look beautiful Angela." Tony flirted. Which drew an angry stare back from Ray. Tony raised his hands up in surrender to apologise, while Nathan secretly lavished at her enticing cleavage, which protruded provocatively from the jaw dropping dress. Her long blonde hair bounced and rippled in time as she teetered in the high heels.

"Did I just hear right, you were with that Theresa last night?" Angela enquired, with a matter of fact look over her face. Ray looked away innocently guilt free.

"You wanna stay away from her, she's been around the block you know." She concluded.

"Fuck sake, not you and all?" Ray protested. "We had a drink and a chat that's all."

"Ahh, the innocence." She teased playfully, pinching his bum as he walked away, while his mates fell about laughing at his modest sincerity.

"Yeah! He used to fancy her rotten Angela. Didn't he

Boycie?" Tony declared.

"Like a love-struck puppy." Nathan teased.

"Well if she hurts my little darling, she'll have me to answer to." She playfully cuddled him to kiss him lovingly again. "Have a lovely evening boy's and stay out of trouble."

Irish Tommy appeared in the doorway looking around expectantly in a smart navy suit and a tacky flowered shirt and stood aside to show her outside.

"Tommy, what the fuck are you wearing?" Ray giggled.

"Sid told me to dress smart to drive Angie to work." He answered confusedly in his thick Irish accent.

Tony and Nathan laughed insensitively as they looked him up and down, then stared down into their drinks, their shoulders jumped in tandem as they held in the laughter.

"Leave him alone. Come on." Angie ordered facing up to him to dust the fag ash from off his lapel and to smarten his collar before they left the pub. Just as Sid and Pete appeared again from the back of the building.

"Where's Tommy taking me ole' dear?"

"To work. Didn't she tell you boy?" Pete replied.

Ray shrugged his shoulders, knowing full well, that wherever she was going, was on a need to know basis as the pair carried on serving and organizing the bar.

"So, come on Ray. Did you fuck her or what?"

Ray sat silently aloof, despite the irksome interrogation from them both, looking around as the other regulars in the bar now became inquisitive to the conversation. He finally gave the game away with a broad grin as Tony and Nathan pounced on him playfully.

"You lucky, lucky bastard." Tony applauded.

While the phone was ringing in the background, Pete appeared again as he wiped his hands rigorously to answer it and was looking towards the boys as they continued their high jinks. He gestured with the phone towards Tony.

"It's Todd, said it's urgent."

Tony walked around to the end of the bar and was handed

the phone and listened to an excited Todd who had remained calm when Pete answered, requesting Tony to adopt the same discretion to what he was going to be told.

"Alright mate we'll see you down there." He replied and leant over the counter to place the phone back onto the receiver, then returned back to sip on his drink with a wary patience as Pete whispered his suspicions into Sid's ears discreetly.

"You Ok Rambo? What did Sweeney want? Ray inquired.

"That Wood Green bubble lot with them pills?" He replied calmly, holding his anger down. "They've fucked us."

"Told you." Ray proclaimed. "The old boys said not to do business with them…Boycie is your motor out front?"

"Yeah. Why, where we going?"

"Tell him then."

"Them bubble cunts have done us out of ten grand."

Nathan shook his head in disappointment and downed his beer, Ray followed them out as he necked the last drops.

"Where yous all going?" Sid and Pete questioned in unison, which drew a brittle stare from Ray at the audacity. Their glowered eyes back towards him drew him back respectful.

"Pick Raph up and then over to Jenny's." He smiled back to them. "Don't wait up." He continued cheekily.

Pete & Sid looked to each other not quite convinced by his little lie and indicated to two of the drinkers, who looked towards them understanding their task. They folded up their newspapers and followed the boys out of the pub.

◆ ◆ ◆

The high-rise apartment they congregated at had an expansive view, the Crystal Palace radio towers were prominent as were the floodlights from the sports arena. Jenny's mother offered Ray, Tony, Nathan and Raph cups of tea and biscuits which they all refused politely.

"Just wanted to say sorry about your Bobby, Mrs Temple." Nathan reminded them all of his passing a couple of months ago. Which they all reciprocated their condolences.

"I told Todd to thank all of you for the flowers. They were lovely." She continued as Jenny huffed with impatience as her mother lingered on the chit chat and wanting her to leave the room. Ray purposefully expressed for her to relax, sympathetic that they were not put out to converse with her, especially so soon after her loss.

"He was a diamond Mrs Temple, a true gent who will be sorely missed." Ray took command and stood up to help her with the tray.

He closed the door behind her and walked over to the window where Jenny was stood. She was Todd's girlfriend on and off for the last couple of years, they all met her shortly after they left school, she was one of the receptionist at a car showroom they went to in Wallington, to help the twins collect a fleet of cars for the firm, her dearly departed father was also a well-known man of respect. He was a big face in London named Jimmy Newport's right-hand man and messenger, between many of the London underworld and acquaintance to his uncles. Jenny unintentionally was playing this role tonight for Todd to deliver an urgent message.

"He said he was staying up there to keep an eyeball on them and didn't want to leave the spot. They're driving about in a Gold Porsche…"

Ray gestured her voice lower to keep her calm and to go and get what they came for. She returned with a dark coloured hold all marked with the Head logo and placed the bag beside Nathan's feet. The boys rose in unison and said goodbye to Jenny and then her mother. They left Ray to connect more of the information from her in the calming unrushed way that he does.

"Now listen babe, we are going to leave a Silver VW Golf GTI down in the carpark later tonight. In the morning with these keys drive it down to this address." Ray unfolded an envelope to show her and placed it down her cleavage. "Talk to either Mark or Arthur Naden. They'll be expecting it. Got that?"

"Yeah no worries Ray." She replied removing the paper from between her bosom with an astonished look.

He winked and kissed her on the cheek, then on the lips cheekily.

"Oi! Don't push your luck." She pushed him playfully.

"I don't know what you see in that Todd. You're far too good for him." He chuckled.

"Yeah, Yeah, whatever Ray. Just because I'm not like the rest of your cheerleaders."

"Hark at you." He chuckled back. "You know you love the pants off me."

"Always will babe." She blushed. "You'll look after him?"

"He'll be back in a couple of weeks. Don't worry. And if you need anything, just reach me at the boozer."

"I will do. Thank you." She hinted, with a mischievous sparkle in her eyes.

"I mean it Jenny, anything you need. Even if it's just for a chat." He repeated with a serious look and a wink after he stroked her hair behind her ear.

He left the flat and continued to the elevator, swaggering with a violent excitement as he entered the basement level, retribution, which they had sought after many over the years, was something he sadistically enjoyed and never ventured on journeys of remorse no matter how fatal, Stix personified a barbarous trophy hunter's prime example, their brutality left him with paralysis on one side, and a lengthy prison sentence to boot, added the proverbial insult to the injury and Ray was ravished tonight by his thirst for more.

Entering into the car park, voices echoed where Tony, Nathan and Raph gathered beside a BMW 5 series. Raph was pulling some bags from the boot, which he quickly threw back in and slammed shut as headlights signalled an incoming vehicle which pulled up beside them. Ray felt a sombre despair of acknowledgement as he walked over to the car as the window gently wound down.

"Sid said he needs you back at the pub." Stu Terry ordered from the passenger side. Ray looked in towards the driver, Gary Stanley, who signalled for him to get into the back. With a frustrated huff, he looked back towards Raph who nodded a confident acknowledgement back towards him.

Tony continued to saddle a heavy Kawasaki motorbike and noisily revved the engine as Raph signalled to him to turn it down, so he could confirm that he was clear with what they had planned. Tony patted at the heavy steel underneath the padded leather, then he flipped the dark visor back down and sped out of the carpark heading North.

CHAPTER 24

GREEN LANES

The bike thundered with menace through Finsbury Park heading towards seven sisters and pulled up alongside the gold 944 at the junction of Manor House station. The sound system blaring a melodic four to the floor beat, that the occupants nodded their heads to. Smoke bellowed outwards with that recognizable aroma. The biker and his pillion in their dark helmets nodded in acknowledgement to the beat and sped off from them as the lights changed to green. The Porsche took off steadily and pulled over a few yards on the Green Lanes. Giorgi Konstantin & Derrin Sahil swaggered out towards the kebab eatery which was getting prepared for a busy evening.

"Malaka." Giorgi greeted loudly as he swung open the door.

"You're a malaka." Derrin pushed him in his back to pay more respect.

"Hook me up guy. Small…No…I want a large donner with cheese on the side…What you havin' Sal?"

"Same. No cheese though." Derrin confirmed. They both loitered around the eating booths while waiting for their food.

"Starving man." Derrin announced. He looked down at his pager just as another man walked in who asked the people preparing food, if they do fried chicken.

"Fried Chicken?" Giorgi kissed his teeth. "Come out the shop man. Fool."

The man silently shrugged his shoulders towards his hostility and gazed up at the board trying to decide on his options.

"What the fuck is wrong wiv dem Eedyat! South London

fools. Keep paging me?" Derrin reported with contempt.

"Innit? Same way guy…Jarring." Giorgi replied as he approached the counter to dictate the sides and dressings that he wanted on his food. He was giving the man, who was still undecided gazing up at the menu, a contemptuous look as though he had insulted his mother.

"This dude can't even make his mind up in a frigging kebab shop yah know." He chuckled.

"Come out you chief." Derrin exploded angrily. Shoving the man aside to grab some serviettes.

"Batty man." Giorgi commented in tandem.

"Fuck sake man. Dem fucking idiots man with the paging…Get the message batty holes?" Derrin continued with the frustration as the pagers continued chiming. The man behind the jump shrugged in disappointment.

Doing his best to ignore the tormentors, the man walked back outside and stood by the door on the pavement while he lit a cigarette. He then walked across the road and stood peering down the street, beside a payphone.

A motorbike rumbled near, followed by a BMW that stopped in front of him, that he stepped into and continued to peer back as the motorbike pillion jumped off and walked inside the shop. Several loud bangs could be heard from the street as Giorgi and Derrin received multiple wounds into the chest, stunned by the loudness and the ammunition entering their bodies, they both gasped for air stumbling towards the floor, before each in turn, were terminated by single shots into the head.

The menacing gloved hand in the dark helmet pointed towards the men behind the counter, who had already began cowering in fear when the first shots rattled off into their customers. He then calmly placed the gun into his jacket. People stunned by the noise, jogged away unassured where the bangs were coming from. The man continued calmly out of the shop, both the victim's pager tones shrilling away in tandem as the motorbike revved noisily and then sped off once he received his passenger, who gripped tightly around his waist. Ducking into the speedy horizon, topping seventy mile an hour, they shot past Manor House tube and the BMW 5 series, that had given them a head start. The pillion shook his fist in celebration.

Raph smiled to Nathan as they continued on their journey. The journey taking them back over London bridge into dense traffic, they pulled up on Dover street beside a Telephone exchange in Southwark and pulled up behind the bright yellow van, with the logo glowing as the headlights shone onto it. Nathan flashed his high beams for the occupant to acknowledge him and opened the door and walked over to them.

"How goes it Mr Telephone man." Raph chuckled.

"Fucking piss taker...Worked a fucking treat though them auto diallers." Kenny Arnold smiled proudly as Raph handed him a bundle of notes that he placed into his jacket after a shifty review for witnesses.

"Jarred them to death by the sounds of it." Raph grinned with mischief. "What else you got for us Kenny boy?"

"0908 sex numbers."

"Oh Lovely. Good earner?"

"Looking at a monkey to a grand a day. I'll let you know when it's all ready. Just going back up to run a few jumpers."

"Well crack on. And not a word to his uncles about tonight please Kenny." Raph pleaded slapping a handshake with him.

"I'll keep it schtum don't you worry. I hope you got whatever you had going on sorted?"

"Cooshty mate." Raph replied. "You know what they say? You can go further with a kind word and a gun than just a kind word."

"Yous watch too many movies." Kenny returned a smile shaking his head as they went their separate ways. Nathan pulled over just before another junction as Raph hopped out to make another call from a payphone into the Gloucester.

♦ ♦ ♦

A few people had gathered beside the derelict waterside baron lands of Newham-East London, Todd and Tony were stripped down into their underwear and swiftly swapped the heavy leathers for T shirts and shorts hurriedly in front of the twins, Dale and Wayne, who began stuffing the clothes into metal bins which they topped up with newspapers and lighter fluid, dashing the empty cans into the mix. The heavy steel weapon was wrapped into a navy flannel and shoved into a C&A carrier bag that was placed into the spare tyre well and was traded for two flight tickets to Ibiza. After removing the number plates, Wayne wheeled the bike over the wasteland away from the parked cars, stuffing an old tatty Levi T-shirt into the petrol tank and flicked the lighter several times before the rag ignited. He calmly walked back to the small gathering as they shook hands and departed in separate vehicles, the Akehurst Twins heading away in a Silver VW Golf GTI. The rear-view mirror, Wayne continued to glare at the orange flames before the glow expanded as the tank exploded loudly.

Later that night, Todd and Tony were both sat in the bar at Gatwick Airport waiting for the flight at half past midnight. After a quick change in the waiting lounge toilets, Todd's straw hat and loud shirt in knee length cut down jeans drew inquisitive looks from flirtatious girls on a hen party, destined to the hedonistic sunny Balearic Islands.

"You look like a fucking div." Tony giggled as he lofted his pint up to Todd's.

"Here come the others." Todd signalled and saluted Black Steve, Ricky Garwood, Yogi, Fat Nick and Stevie Betts. "E.I.E." He belted loudly to his fellow Arsenal family as they all affectionately greeted each other.

Tony shook hands with Stevie and quickly began discussing over the business itinerary, while the others flirted around the groups of girls that Todd had already become acquainted with.

"I can't believe Ray and the other boys aren't coming." Stevie sighed.

"They've got a bit going on at the minute, the last thing we could afford is everyone fucking off to party and taking drugs." Tony laughed.

"It is supposed to be the nuts out there Rambo mate." Stevie smiled.

"Never even heard of the gaff until yous lot mentioned it. Black Steve been out three times already?"

"Yeah mate...I'm telling yah, if we can produce the same over here, we'll make a fortune. You just wait until you swallow a Cali mate you'll see. Amnesia brother." Stevie replied rubbing his hands.

"Amnesia? That sounds like a bit of me. We've already been knocked for ten grand might help me forget it." Tony smiled.

"Don't break your heart mon." Stevie's patois rang like a native Jamaican. "I'll get you your fucking ten grand back and then some mate, that's peanuts."

CHAPTER 25

WHITEHORSE REUNION

Ray slammed the door of the Ford Granada after sitting in relative silence for the most part, which irked Gary as he locked the car door and continued across the road to his house, which was located on the road that was adjacent to the main estate. Ray continued into the pub like a spoilt brat shoving the saloon bar door. He sat himself at the bar and was greeted by the barmaid.

"Give us a pint, Bev darling. Please." He commanded. Confidently leaning over to the bar, he grabbed a box of Dunhill's filters, extracting one, flipped and stroked at the gold lighter, exhaling heavily as the smoke bellowed upwards. She placed the lager in front of him, then lit her own cigarette from the box and tried to engage him in conversation, recognising that angry look on his face.

"Are you ok babe?" She said calmingly and placed a comforting hand on him, which in a way broke him away from whatever had been eating at him.

"What?" He snarled.

"Just seeing if you are OK. No need to bite me flaming head off." She smiled.

"Sorry darling, them fucking pricks keep stalking me whenever..." He paused, as she stared back at him with that condescending look that she does.

"Sort it out babe. They're only looking out for you."

He remained silent to whether he agreed or found solace, then immediately perked up when he noticed Christine and Norma entering the pub which surprised him and broke him into a bright smile.

"Hello babe." Said Christine as Ray hugged her tightly and kissed her golden hair.

After she balanced a pile of presents on the stool, he grabbed Norma in towards him to kiss her on the lips.

"What the fuck are yous all doing here?" He said surprised.

"We just popped in, to see if you were here on the off chance." She replied sarcastically.

"Happy birthday for yesterday. We all came down to that do last night and you weren't even there, we were gonna surprise yah." Christine smiled infectiously.

"Ahh. What are you like? These all for me?" He examined the pile of neatly wrapped gifts.

"Yeah you jar. Having us carry them about like fucking father Christmas. Div." Norma laughed.

"Ahh, happy birthday Ray babe." Christine hugged him tightly again, with an elated feeling over not seeing him for so long. Norma barged past her selfish friend's embrace to get a better hug from him, even though, she had seen him more often than her since she moved away. He enjoyed her sweet perfume, she opened her coat in a heated flap that exaggerated getting warm from his embrace, then proceeded to hand him each present to unwrap.

"We would have given you them last night, but you were probably getting your end away. Who was the lucky woman eh?" She responded with a naughty laugh.

"Leave it out." He chuckled back.

Christine looked at him, a slight disappointment crept over her, as if she knew exactly where he would have been.

"I've missed you." She smiled at him and hugged him again really tightly this time. With a little tear that choked her throat. "Go on, open the presents."

He tugged at the larger of the three boxes and pulled out a luxurious brown Italian leather bomber jacket.

"Ralph Lauren? That's ream that." He praised after inspection.

"That's from me and mum." Norma confessed proudly and turned back to Bev apologising for ignoring her and ordered drinks. The second present he opened was an electronic paging device which Ray examined curiously.

"That was from Sharon. She couldn't make it tonight, she was going on a date with some posh geezer she's hooked up with. It was probably him that chose it. What the fuck are you gonna do with that anyway?" Norma's high-pitched voice protested.

"It's a pager. And who's this posh boy, Jimmy Sargent?" He queried confused. Christine nodded with a sarcastic roll of the eyes for him to ignore her.

"I know it's a pager but you ain't a fucking doctor now are yah?" She laughed. "Saying that. A gynaecologist job would be a perfect career for you eh?"

Ray laughed at her futile argument come career advice and gave the thumbs up as Bev placed him a fresh new beer on the bar with Christine's and Norma's beside it and pulled twenty pounds from his pocket.

"Put your money away Norma." He roughly insisted.

"Alright bossy...He ain't changed, has he?" She directed to Bev who replied with a pleasant smile.

"Open my one now." Christine purred. He stared back at her smiling with delight as he revealed the elegant brown box from the wrapping.

"Fuck sake Chris. Come on." He cursed in applause, not in anger by the playfulness in his voice, it was a lovely surprising gesture.

"Here." She snuggled next to him as they sat on the soft benches opposite the bar together and helped it onto his wrist.

"A fucking Rolex. Are you sure?"

"Ray. You are like the best big brother in the world. I love you." She confessed.

"Ahh. I love yah babe." He commanded her into his arms lovingly as Norma and Bev looked towards them beaming. Norma fanned her eyes as she began to well up.

"That is absolutely blinding that...Beautiful." He kissed her once more then prided at the elegant dial. She brushed her hair from her face which exposed her blushed cheeks.

"I'm pleased that you like it."

"You shouldn't be spending that kind of money on a kettle for me. What will your other half say?"

"Don't worry about him. He knows how much I love you." She replied with a Cheshire cat grin. He embraced her almost inappropriately, his hands caressed up and down her back as he nuzzled into her sensitive neck, turned on by her sweet fragrance which sent tingles down her spine.

"Raymond!" Bev hollered gesturing him over to her waving the phone. Christine shook his closeness away, her heart and knees wavering from his touch.

"They should have just paged him." Norma shouted humorously. "Paging Dr Big Cock!"

"Hello." He answered, poking two fingers up at her laughing.

"We're on our way back." Raph's voice echoed with a sense of pride that Ray acknowledged.

"Cool. The girls are all here...See yah soon."

He went back over to Norma and Christine tidying up the rubbish around the table and grabbed the presents to store them in the hallway. He noticed Sid, Sammy and Irish Tommy having a conversation near the doorway to the beer garden and nodded towards them.

"You alright boy?" Sid called out.

"Yeah. I am now." He replied condescendingly.

Sid shook his head gesturing towards them to look in his direction. Ray watched as they all smirked at him, which angered him slightly. He returned back to the bar, pinching another one of Bev's cigarettes.

"It'll stunt your growth you know?" She winked that all-knowing wink at him and savoured on the memories, of them all hanging out at the park, drinking and smoking together, the little reunion she reminisced, about how upset he was when Christine moved off the estate and his heartbreak when Sarah emigrated to America. She was happy that she consoled him during this time, which reflected even more about the two of them getting off with each other at a blues party at a house down Mitcham road.

After a night of dirty dancing to some lover's rock, Christmas eve back in 1984, the kiss they shared on their way home in a shop doorway near the Mayday hospital was her fondest of memories. It was the time she had held his erection in her hand, which at the time terrified her, mindful also at the time of him being on the rebound. Now regrettably, wishing she had gone all the way with him.

"Anybody home?" Norma chuckled to break her from her thoughts.

"Sorry, I was miles away." She confessed and proceeded in getting another round of drinks. Norma was in a deep drunken conversation after a while at the bar later with her, also reminiscing, Norma explaining that she was loved up and didn't get out too much, while Ray and Christine continued catching up.

"Where are all the boys?"

"Raph and Nath are on their way."

"It was such a laugh last night. Pity you missed it."

"Every day is a laugh with my brothers." He smiled.

"Todd and Tony coming?"

"They're flying out to Ibiza." He sighed.

"Oh Lovely...They never said when I spoke with them last night...I could do with a holiday out there, I heard it's really happening over there."

"Yeah you and me both. It's the end of season to be fair and we have business to attend to with my uncles, so the pair of them went with Yogi and the Gooners." He reasoned.

"Weren't Yogi that fella in the park that time?" She remembered.

"How'd you remember that...of all things?" He reminisced laughing heartedly. "I miss our little hang out."

"Ahh, me and all. He makes me laugh so much Todd. And I see he is still with Jenny. She's so funny."

"We were round hers a little while ago."

"She was asking about you a lot last night." Christine nudged into him with a subtle innuendo.

"Leave it out. She's my best friend's woman."

"Hmm...Well, all she did was complain about him, and the sun shone out of your bum." She chuckled widening her eyes indicating her intuition.

"What can I say? I'm a nice guy." He responded with a cheeky smile.

"So why have you not found yourself a girlfriend yet? Or was that who you were with last night, that you didn't even show up to your own eighteenth?"

"Don't you start."

"Come on who was she? I won't tell anyone."

"It wasn't like that...It was business."

"Such a secret squirrel you are. She must be special that's all I can say."

"Nah. I'm just too unlucky when it comes to affairs of the heart...Better off on me jack." He deflected, he knew the name might draw controversy and played it off coyly. For all intent and purpose, it was just a one-night stand, despite how he now, could not get the sex with her off of his mind.

"Ahh do you still ever wonder about Sarah?" She continued like a therapist for him to open up. She was inquisitive in some way to understand where his heart lay.

"I really wish I knew...She just decided to leave."

"But America?"

"I thought I would be her happy ever after." He shrugged as he pondered, the ripple in the pond effect that descended on their relationship after his premeditated revenge, that ensued in that visit to the old derelict dockyard with Todd and the fatal struggle in the car, that still woke him at night.

"Well I think she was mad to leave a handsome boyfriend like you? Crazy..." She smiled flirtatiously, she placed her hand onto his knee as a sympathetic gesture of support.

"I was gutted." He acknowledged. He sought solace in the fact that he could be open and honest with her. Confidentially, he had been secretly heartbroken about his first love, crushed beyond recovery and even worse, having to put on that laddish bravado in front of his mates.

"Maybe she wasn't the one. You will find the one."

"Uncle Sid always says things like that."

"Ahh bless him. He's the same, all butch but a heart of gold. I reckon that's why dad moved us, cos mum had a soft spot. Did I tell you?" She chuckled.

"Leave off. That wasn't the reason." He smiled at her little teasing that always caught him out.

"Do yous still visit the cemetery?" She recollected of the regular ritual his uncle insisted on, that he shared with her when they were younger. Before their visits to Highbury, they attended Rita's grave, like a pre-match superstition, which always brought tears of sadness to their eyes.

"Not in a while, I don't think he goes too much himself." Ray sympathised.

"Do you remember what you once told me about why he takes you there?"

"Not really..." Ray shook his head evasively. He had many theories as a young lad, trying to work out the world, a wild imagination conversed over many hours with her.

"Sarah said you were the one." She digressed again. "Made me jealous in some ways. You two were like the best couple." The topic quickly meandered away from the graveside stories, with the Ray and Sarah love story, had her again fanning her face in an exercise to hold back her emotions.

"Oi! You wanna calm down?" He smiled affectionately.

"I know. I'm sorry. That always sets me off." She returned a nervous laugh and snuggled up to him.

"The one? Not sure if that even exists." Ray laughed. "Besides, how would you actually even know? My heart flips at anything in a skirt."

"Oh Raymond." She giggled. "Of course you'd know. Think about when you just met her and the way you looked at her, how you felt. That's how...When they're the only thing you can think of."

"Hark at you. Dear Deirdre."

"Div." She laughed.

"I know what you are saying. I was besotted, I loved them little freckles on her nose and the way she flicked her hair, the silly little things, like the songs she would burst into. She could rock a pair of Farah's and all. I would have..." He paused with an exaggerated shrug, to restrain himself before spilling too much.

"I remember that summer before we moved. That's all what everyone talked about...Ray and Sarah this...That makes me so sad, especially for you."

"I'm one hundred percent certain that she wasn't all there because of the shit her old man put her through."

"That went on for years, when you think about it. Then his disappearance. That poor girl."

"Poor girl? That's when she changed. I thought she would have been glad that he wasn't around. But I guess..." He grimaced from the clear pain in his heart. He had often wondered and then couldn't understand, whether her feelings for her father, in the weirdest sense, was still a factor.

"Don't let it get to you again babe." She comforted as he shuffled uncomfortably in his seat at the topic and the emotions it reintroduced.

"I'll never forget your words of comfort either." He kissed her affectionately onto her cheek as they hugged.

"I really appreciate that you rang me to get it off your chest and I'll always be there for you."

"I know. That's why I love you and will always love you. But you're a fiancé now." He studied the expensive rock on her finger with a taunting smile.

"Don't let that put you off." She gasped in surprise at herself, that she would reveal it out loud so blatantly, and relieved at the same time as they both laughed it off.

"Maybe I'll ask Norma to marry me. She's another one." He suggested with a chuckle, blowing a kiss towards her at the bar.

She did her usual suggestive jiggle of her breasts underneath her tight-fitting top. Her innuendo miming immaturely of an oral gesture was missed by his eyes as the conversation flipped.

"You know she's with that Trevor Lewin from Pollards Hill now?"

"Who...Norma? Seriously?" Ray surprised. "Blimey I bet he's still in love with us, from when we give him and his boys a slap at your party."

"Do you remember?"

"Yeah...I put a lovely little mark on him."

"Oh my God!" She gasped. "I completely forgot. You used to be a total maniac." She pursed her lips tightly, trying to stifle the laughter from her sarcasm.

"Leave it out. I wasn't that bad was I?" He asked sincerely.

Her eyes widened cutely with pinched eyebrows in surprise at his ridiculous analysis.

"Anyway. What the fuck is she doing with him. He's just a bully cunt. And now I understand what them bruises on her arm are all about." He returned with a more serious concern.

"It's disgusting the way he treats her. She was in hospital last Christmas because of him."

"What the fuck Chris?" He angered.

"Shh...Yes...I know. Don't say nothing to her Ray. Please." She pleaded.

"If he's knocking her about Christine. I'll set me fucking dogs on him...I mean it." He warned.

She could see that usual rush of blood bubble up in his face, eyes darkening, like the gateway to hell itself.

"I haven't said anything." She grabbed his hand upwards to kiss it.

She was nervous about getting that reaction, but in a

nostalgic way, it was the powerful response that cemented that he still wanted to protect them all, it was just her Ray being Ray. Raph and Nathan walked in and were in turn inflicted with long embraces with the girls. Which saved Christine from any further interrogation as she excused herself past him to greet them both. Ray noted the information for a later time as there were more pressing matters at hand.

"Three more pints please Bev." Ray hollered.

"Save one darling. I'll just have a brandy and Babysham." Raph interrupted.

Impatiently waiting for their drinks to be all served, Ray continually stared at Raph eager for the information.

"Did it all go ok?" He questioned at last.

"Well in a couple of hours Sweeney and Rambo will be on a plane. Kenny has a line on some new business for us, the twins have finished the spring cleaning…And the bubbles sleep with the shish." Raph laughed.

"It's all irie bredrin." Nathan interrupted, impersonating Todd. Both Raph and Ray laughed and sipped at their drinks as Pete and Sid walked in with suspicious glares towards the boys, that turned into broad smiles towards the girls waving, which they reciprocated back.

"Hope yous are sticking around to keep these little louts out of trouble." Sid greeted with a kiss on their cheeks.

"I know Sid. Bloody hooligans the lot of them." Norma chuckled.

"How's the old man? Tell him I said hello." He enquired to Christine, which was in his ways, directed to the pair of them.

"Thanks Sid. I will." Christine replied.

"Dad's a Sergeant now." Norma tutted disapprovingly.

No one, especially here, cared that he was Old Bill, he was still considered as one of their own, who until the recent years, was still a regular drinker at the pub. As Sid and Pete did with everyone, no matter what they did, they always encouraged them to do well.

Raph turned back to Ray sipping on his drink wondering

why he was just staring at the girls. Norma was in a tipsy state delighted on securing herself a job as barmaid with Sid and enjoying all the banter, especially with their secret reference about Ray's manhood, to his embarrassment, which always escaped Sid and Pete and made it all the more hilarious because it was their little code. She was soon hinting after the laughter had died down at Christine and Bev about having to leave to meet her boyfriend, which brought a familiar cute glimmer from Christine as she stared towards him, the same sparkle under fluttering eye lashes that he remembered from the first day he became friends with her.

He always surrendered to that look, whether it was to follow her through the Whitgift centre or into Tammy Girl to choose an outfit or a pair of shoes for the next disco, or to go to the chip shop because she hated going and said he'd get there quicker on his bike and even her last days on the estate, when she asked him to make sure that he always looked out for her friends. He vowed that he would.

"We need to pay a little visit to some Pollards Hill cunt tomorrow." Ray boasted quietly, as a matter of fact, his face serene and tranquil despite the gut wrenching feeling towards the outrage. Raph knocked back his drink and smiled eagerly towards him

"I better get an early night then. See you tomorrow. Don Corleone." He pronounced with an extended E that made Ray chuckle. He patted Nathan on the back for his lift home. Embracing the girls, he said goodnight and kissed a lingering kiss on Bev on her way back in through the door as she collected glasses.

CHAPTER 26

POLLARDS HILL

The Pollards Hill estate bordered on Norbury and Mitcham territories, an area not fully governed by The Gloucester, the days of warring or punishing people over certain rights over earnings had been lapsed as they focused on a bigger picture. The respect still carried all across the South from the Whitehorse all the way across to Earlsfield in the west. The large gang on their bikes, scooters and sitting in a Vauxhall Cavalier, with loud music blaring and a strong smell of weed thundering out of the windows, their loud and brash posture purposefully apathetic to the community they disturbed.

By perfect example, was the single mother pushing her toddler in the buggy, navigating with two bags of shopping past the youths as they congregated on the pavement and part of the walkway near her address. Some of them kissing their teeth at her as she tutted towards their chivalry of not even considering moving out of her way. She had to dismount and mount the kerb with difficulty, as the wheels stubbornly misdirected, before she could steady and readjust the bags to continue towards the slightly inclined rampway, up to the entrance door to her block of flats.

The sleek black BMW pulled up gently alongside the congregation of youths and stopped in the middle of the road in front of them all, with two of the occupants alighting.

"Here love. Let me help you up with your shopping." Ray quickly offered and escorted her towards the grey concrete block of flats, paying the rowdy youths no mind. The sudden silence from them, etched with paranoia by his presence, relievedly when he disappeared into the flats. She appreciated his help and offered a warm smile towards him as he assisted her up one flight and dropped the bags of shopping at her door.

"You have very nice neighbours." He said sarcastically.

"They're scum them lot, you see the way they all just stood around. I can see you were raised properly." Her attempt of a smile was sedated by the single mother mundane, but she appreciated that the strapping man in front of her made no ill judgement of her. She warmed to him when he took a quick moment to interact with the toddler cooing inside the pram. Her expectations of a Knight in shining armour evaporated, when she succumbed to the fact, that baring any small miracle, their paths would never meet again. She stroked at her unforgiving ponytail scraped tight with messy straggles falling at her face.

"Manners cost nothing love." He replied jovially.

He assisted her all the way into her doorway with a pleasant wish for her to enjoy the rest of her day. With the hundred and one domestic tasks ahead of her and a needy dependant, enjoyment in any sense was a futile wish.

Making his way back down the stairs and out of the building. Nathan sat in the car idling in the middle of the road, forcing oncoming vehicles to detour around it. Ray approached the pack of youths who all became quiet again with his reappearance. His dark shades obscured the menace in his eyes, as Raph out flanked them and stood as lookout.

"Which one of yous is Trevor?" Ray asked, looking towards the face he already recognised. He looked back at him unable to hide the fear, the scar was long and visible on his face that was introduced to him the last time he saw the two men, now standing on his territory.

"I...I am." He stuttered.

Ray stepped towards him with his hand out in a friendly gesture, to erase his reluctant look of despair.

"I'm Ray. Please to meet yah." He shook his wary hand warmly with a broad welcoming smile. Raph walked over towards the car and opened the rear door. Ray indicated towards the black BMW with a chivalrous gestured command that he followed without protest. The others remained silent, some walked and rode away as if there was nothing of interest for them to be standing about for.

The single mother obscured from his memory forever, peered out at his interaction with them, with a hope he'd teach them all a lesson, then went back to her chores.

"Fucking loyal your mates." Raph chuckled, his arm positioned purposely on the car door, that flashed the provocative glimpse of the weapon tucked into the side waistband of his jeans.

Ray followed closely behind, scooting him up the leather back seats, Raph slammed the door and got into the passenger side as Nathan pulled away with the 3.5 litre engine purring with the menacing sophistication of German engineering.

"I heard a little thing the other day about you Trevor." Ray began.

Trevor remained silent as the car cruised around several corners before hitting the main high street, his mind raced about the unknown and struggled to maintain calmness.

"What have you heard?"

"I heard you can move weight around and have good contacts with Peckham and Wandsworth?"

"Huh?...Oh...yeah." He stammered.

His heart began to beat at a slower pace, after initially being under the impression that he was to come under the firing squad, without even the understanding of what crime he had even committed.

"We have a bit of a proposition for you..." He tapped at Raph's headrest who passed him back a business card.

"We don't want to create animosity stepping on people's toes, so we want Pollards Hill to represent our products." Ray suggested leaving a pause for any questions that he might have.

"Do you know how a franchise works?" Raph added.

Trevor studied the card, advertising Naden autos of Balham, the solid looking card was impressive with letters in bold gold, that jumped out into his eyes.

"Yeah. Like MacDonald's?" He replied sincerely.

Raph surprised at his intelligence and held back on a provoking applause.

"Good." Ray continued. "If you are happy with the terms, this Friday you can go see this fella called Arthur."

"We are talking puff or H?"

"Puff. We don't deal in H and neither should yous. But we have unlimited parcels, so you won't have the need. And we are very strict on that. Is that understood?" Ray commanded.

Trevor nodded in agreement and became a little more confident and fluid in this language of wheeling and dealing in drugs. Once the fear had subsided, he jumped into a negotiating business mode, which was amplified by the change in his posture.

"How much weight are we talking?" He queried.

"How much do you normally handle?"

"Puff, I can move up to half a kilo. Maybe a bit more. Peckham want loads." Came his self-assured reply.

"Half a kilo? nice." Ray replied. Nathan looked towards Raph masking a smirk towards him.

"Pull over." Ray demanded and turned to Trevor with his final instructions. "See our man Arthur, tell him The Gloucester sent you and he'll introduce you to Mr Oxmall, grab a couple of keys, you get a fortnight on bail and we want thirty percent of what you make, on time, every other week."

"Seen, Seen. Nice one Ray. Happy to work for you, it's an honour." He grovelled.

"And let's make this absolutely clear, do not, in anyway, take that little army with you to see him. You and one other that's it. Do not tell anyone who your contact is. And find a place that no other person knows to operate. That's it. Good luck." Ray accented with his finger to punctuate his orders.

Almost blinded by the small printed steps of compliance.

He looked around confused, trying to understand his bearings, as to where he was and noticed he was on Streatham high street.

"One more thing." Raph warned reaching into his inside jacket pocket to pass to him a bag of strong smelling weed as a sample. "Make sure you sort your bait mates out…Tone down the loud music and the anti-socials, the amount of money you'll be earning, you don't need to give anyone an excuse to have yous all pinched."

Trevor smelt the quality and began to see, teasing visions of sitting in expensive leather, similar to the one that was currently caressing him.

"We'll see you soon then." With a malevolent smile towards him, Ray indicated for him to leave the car.

"Can you take me back to where you picked me up from?"

"Sorry mate. No can do. Nathan here has a dentist appointment." Raph held out his hand politely to cement the agreement, Ray turned towards the bustling traffic, ignoring Trevor's offer of a handshake.

"Ta-La." Raph indicated him to the door once more, before he finally exited, with Nathan motioning the car before the door had fully closed.

He stood at the kerbside looking put out as they all peered back at him laughing inside the car.

"Who the fuck is Mr Oxmall?" Nathan queried.

"You never heard of Mr Oxmall. First name Mike?"

"Mike Oxmall?"

"Yeah, one of Todd's jokes. It sounds better over a tannoy."

"Mike Oxmall, Mike…Oxmall. My Cock Small…" Nathan repeated until he realised with laughter.

"You are one evil bastard Raymondo." Raph sniggered.

"Yeah? He'll get his fucking weight down in the Naden's dungeon of torture mate. I can't fucking wait to carve that little cunt."

"I'd be careful if I were you mate. Big bad Trev and his half a kilo empire, they might come after you with their pellet guns."

"He put Norma in hospital that dirty no good cunt. I'll make sure he'll never raise his hand up to another bird."

"Amen brother." Raph agreed. "Where we heading now?"

"Saville row. We need new suits for that meeting next month." He appraised vocally, the importance of the gathering that would outline their future from that day forward.

"Tattaglia's a pimp. He never could have outfought Santino." Raph chuckled as he deviated from the topic.

Tucking his tongue into his bottom lip, Ray simulated Marlon Brando once again, with a whispered American voice.

"But I never knew…until this day, that it was Barzini all along." He enacted, with a long dramatic pause, almost appearing as if his face was in pain, then gestured with his hand scraping under his chin like a native New York Italian American. "Va fangool! Ya stoopid jerk!"

The car rocked with laughter, Nathan was awestruck, by the regular recital of the movie and the childish improvising, that they re-enacted almost daily, over the years they had been together.

CHAPTER 27

THE NEWPORT ALLIANCE

"Mobile Phones. This is the future for us Raymondo." Raph boasted eagerly. He handed the device to Ray who mimicked exaggeratedly at the weight.

"Fuck me. Who'd wanna walk about with this lump of brick in their hand? It weighs a fucking ton."

"This is the Motorola 8500 cell phone son. We'll all have these soon."

"Yeah as a fucking weapon to bash cunts with. Does it even work?"

"Ring the boozer." Nathan suggested, snatching the solid unit from his hand and began to dial. "It'll save us jumping in and out of phone boxes every minute. Hello is Paul MeSkinBack there please?"

The car began to chuckle as he repeated the request down the phone.

"Who answered?" Ray suddenly grabbed the phone from him as he continued laughing.

"Who's this? Oh…Yeah sorry Angie." He answered embarrassed. "That was Nath…Nah don't worry…See yah later. You're a cunt Boycie."

The raucous laughter continued with Ray pretending to bash him on the head with the brick like object, until Raph demanded it back.

They crossed the bridge in three separate cars, two pristine Jaguars, one diamond white, the other jet black and the dark shiny black ford Granada 2.8i with leather Ghia interior. The executive appearing passengers surveyed the emerging skyline of cranes and steel skeletons that was already beginning to transform, along with the empty industrial properties along the east side of the Thames. Still cracking the immature jokes throughout the journey, Ray, Raph, Nathan and Wayne Akehurst at the wheel, blew smoke out of the windows.

Following in convoy, in front of them Pete, Sid, Sammy and Tommy Akehurst rode, where in the very front vehicle Irish Tommy steered, Todd, Tony and Gary Stanley. They approached a main junction and paused to let the trailing vehicles enter the black wrought iron gates as the two other vehicles continued up the dry dusty path, Irish reversed full pelt behind them and swung the car neatly behind stacked containers and ground the smooth engine to a halt. The party rolled up to form a V shape formation with four other cars. All exited slamming the doors, almost semi synchronized, to congregate in front of them.

"Right, I want no one running their mouth off. Especially to Solomon because he can be a cocky little cunt. Do you understand?" Sid directed to them all, but was more singled out to Ray, Nathan and Raph, being that they were the reasons why they were here in the middle of an industrial estate on a Wednesday evening. Ray flicked his cigarette behind him, although appearing a demeanour of non-interest, Pete reminded him of the important lessons they had all taught him for times just like this.

"On my mother uncle Sid." Ray finally replied. Removing his Giorgio Armani shades. He and Raph followed behind his uncles and Sammy into the warehouse as Nathan, Wayne along with his dad Tommy, remained outside with the cars.

"Gentlemen! Come forward." Bellowed an impeccably dressed man in a beige camel coat with an overly sized belcher chain draped around his neck that would have sat proudly around B.A Barakus's. They stood to meet him and six others, equally dressed in suits and camel overcoats. The announcer approached Sid and Pete with a warm handshake and embraced with a familiarized pat on each other's backs.

"This is Michael Swan, Ronnie Martin, Ishmael & Georgie Senior, Aristos Hajimichael and you all know Solomon Maitland." He introduced as some smiled as their names were presented and the odd snarl from the others. Pete and Sid nodded acknowledgment to them all. While Ray, Raph and Sammy stood neutrally aside.

"So now we've been all acquainted, let's keep this meeting short and sweet."

"Short and sweet? What..no explanation on who crossed the water to put holes into my people? I think it might take these a bit longer to explain to them, who the fuck I am around town Jimmy." Solomon angered.

"No disrespect Jimmy my old mate but can you put a muzzle on him with the accusations or we'll just fuck off back to our manor." Pete retorted back, staring into Solomon, taking a couple of steps towards the opposite group.

"Listen. Do you want to make money or carry on just being the big bollocks of Turnpike Lane?" Jimmy Newport interjected.

"That all depends…"

"Here we go…Are you gonna keep up?" Ray interjected, receiving stern stares from his uncles and shrugged his shoulders towards them with innocence.

"Enough!" Newport shouted venomously, eyes peering again into Solomon. "At this moment I don't give a fuck about who did what to who. Now if you will allow me to finish and I swear on the little shit bag grandchildren and I love them dearly…but if you interrupt me again. I'll allow those little South London hooligans to have you for their dinner and all. Are we clear?"

Solomon Maitland looked around at the evasive looks from the other parties, deciding it was best to obey.

"Apologies for the outburst." He meekly bowed.

Ray and Raph adjusted their jackets in synchronisation, their egos bolstered at the accolade. They both kept their eye on Solomon with a menacing glint, that he returned back, his eyes then began to slide away from them, their eyes remained acute.

"These young'uns have a plan on some business that we are all gonna share." He began to pace the floor past each individual, similar to a sergeant major during morning drill. "Seeing that this is not territorial but will need a certain level of control, just so it doesn't become the wild west. Today and this is the important part…Today, any aggs you have with one another ends in this room. I'm sure the end divvy up, will take all your minds off of all the bollocks. Is that understood?"

Everyone around the warehouse looked towards him in acknowledgment.

"Raph when are we expecting this delivery?" His voice simmered.

"Our partners are over there now finishing up. Shipment will land a week on Tuesday." Raph replied confidently. Ray pulled another cigarette from the box and blew out a silent smoke ring up towards the derelict roof.

"So, let me understand the rules again?" Ronnie Martin interrupted. "One hundred and fifty thousand tablets, then what do we do with 'em?"

"That's just week one. Something is about to break over here, our generation are about to let lose all over the country and the market for them little white tablets…" Ray paused to take another confident draw from the Benson and Hedges. "They'll be flying out of our hands the moment they land. No graft involved, except counting your readies."

He walked over towards Ronnie and opened a clear bag containing three tablets.

"Find a club with a nice bird, drop one and I'll bet me brand new Rolex, you'll be ringing me up to tell me about your blinding night." He paraded the little white tablet in front of his eyes with a huge grin.

"Can't the rest of us taste a sample? Why only Ronnie?" Solomon asked.

"I'd…er. I'd give you one, but you'd probably need a lorry

load for yourself, to put a smile on your boat race. Heard you was a right moody cunt?"

The hollow sound of laughter bellowed from all the men as Ray stuck his hand out to shake his hand and with the other produced a clear bag to gift him.

"I'm only kidding."

"Ok then gentlemen. The Gloucester boys will take care of the details and we sit back and reap whatever profits these have projected. It's a new day my friends and I'm glad to form a nice peaceful co-operation."

With his arms astride, Jimmy almost conductor like, oversaw the gathering come to a long-awaited understanding. He shook hands with Sid and Pete gleefully.

"Looks like South London will be left in good hands for the future." He suggested to them.

"They are different to our generation Jim, they are very, very focused. It seemed just like yesterday they were fucking around in the park and causing me grey hair to fallout." Sid chuckled.

"Well enjoy your retirement, you two gentlemen deserve it. And I mean that from the bottom of my heart."

They stood by the entrance to the warehouse, the sunset glinting at their eyes and casting long shadows as they lit cigars and finished off discussions on their retirement plans, happy to be finally stepping away from the politics of running an underworld empire.

Ray and Raph, after taking a while to explain the fascination of the expected contraband to Ismail and Georgie Senior and what the divvy up would be, Sid and Pete watched from the side lines, once they had shaken hands with Jimmy before they all departed.

"Solomon, just to clear up some matters, we are sorry about what happened to your people and we are not the ones looking to tread on anyone's toes. Why don't me Raph and the boys come over to your club tonight and have a drink to celebrate. I heard it was a plush place with very beautiful women. Are you up for that?" Ray's extended hand was offered out.

In return, after a slightly suspicious hesitation, he returned the handshake with a huge smile.

"Come here." He drew Ray in to embrace him with a big hug, which somewhat irked at him and Raph understood the look that came back at him, oblivious to the others amongst them. Who's only focus, was the shining sparkling prospects of becoming richer.

Following the successful meeting, all the factions pulled up outside Vanity Nightclub in the heart of Soho, the unusual façade of black and white marble, stood out and reminded the boys as they pulled up, of club Pascha in Ibiza, they all spent three weeks absorbing all the trappings of the newly discovered Balearic party island, along with the drugs and the women that went with it.

"Fucking not bad in here is it?" Nathan radiated enthusiastically, embracing Ray around his neck as they head straight to the bar. After scoping the venue with impress, he was engaged in conversation with a pretty young brunette, who after a while, began to bore him with her continued talk about herself and money. Solomon snuck up behind him and was a timely interruption.

"Hope you are enjoying yourself. What do you think?"

Ray paused purposefully looking towards him as if not understanding the question.

"The club?" Solomon reminded.

"Absolutely blinding Solomon." Ray smiled back.

"Here, I want to introduce you to my fiancé." He boasted again, which seemed to repeatedly irk at Ray. "Where is she? Over here darling don't keep us all waiting." He gestured excitedly.

Ray began to turn away, bored, almost biting his tongue, having to keep up the pretence that he actually liked him. In truth, he couldn't stand the greasy haired prick, although he knew how dangerous he is as an individual and leader of North

London. And, so it seemed tonight, The West End. But his thoughts were immediately interrupted as he was presented with a beautiful but familiar face.

"Ray Morgan, this is my beautiful fiancé Theresa."

At first, they stood opposite one another as though trying to calculate, whether a revelation that they knew each other would be sensible.

"Nice to meet you Theresa." Ray introduced himself with a polite kiss at both her cheeks. After he had sensed the sheer fear in her eyes that quickly simmered thanks to his quick initiative.

"It's a pleasure." She replied.

"Excuse me a minute Solomon. I'm just gonna find the gents and make sure the boys are behaving." He quickly evaded in order to intercept the guys who were walking over towards him.

"Isn't that fucking what's her face you were knobbing a little while back?" Nathan immediately questioned.

"Listen, make sure everyone keeps schtum. I'm gonna have a piss, we'll have a little drink with him, then we're fucking off."

Ray appeared from the toilet into the plush velvet walled corridor and was surprised again, when she appeared in front of him. She took his hand and lead him into the ladies and straight into an empty cubicle and excitedly began to kiss him. Her smell and recollection of the night they previously shared, he showed little in the form of resistance when she directed his hands onto her knickers, her silky white and gold dress risen way above her thighs by her lifted leg, presenting him the perfect access to feel along her sexy cunt with his fingers.

"Fuck sake Theresa. What the fuck? Fiancé?" He panted.

"I could have fucking died." She giggled. She pecked at his lips as he protested against this backdrop, not quite setting with the mood and came to his business-like spider senses and halted abruptly.

"We are going to go back and have that drink, then I'm

off." He insisted.

"What's the rush babe?" She panted.

"You want to get us both killed?" He whispered despite the surrounding noise of music leaking from the club.

Stealthily, he opened the door and walked out quickly in front of her. She continued out behind him and stood in front of the mirror and painted her lips some more and blew a kiss towards her own reflection, ignoring the curious looks. Her audience tried their hardest not to add the obvious two add two following Ray's departure.

Ray was sat with Raph, who was whispering his concerns and astonishment into his ears after getting the intel from Nathan. Solomon continued with his brash boastfulness, as he introduced one tough looking Greek associate after another, topping up champagne glasses for everyone.

After a while, Theresa returned back to sit next to him, she exaggeratedly paraded her alluring tanned legs at Ray and his crew as they sat opposite, her presence seemed to transfer them all back to young immature teenagers, smitten by her seductive purposeful posture. Their eyes all followed her as she leaned forward with her beautiful cleavage, almost captivating them.

"Drink up boys, we are supposed to be celebrating." He laughed, noticing their envious looks towards his beautiful and sexy possession.

"Salute to you Mr Maitland, A lovely place you have." Nathan appraised.

"Hard work boys that's all it takes and you boys are heading the right way." He saluted back with his glass. "I was already a millionaire by the time I was 20. You've still got a bit to do to catch up with someone like me."

"You're not wrong there Mr Maitland." Raph purposefully grovelled as Ray tipped his glass up to his lips thirstily, his head tilted to an almost right angle, to hide the grin that was about to give Raph's game away.

"Solomon." Ray stood up with his hand out as he was

about to depart. "We are going to head off back to the manor now, we have meetings with some event managers early doors. Thanks for the hospitality. Fantastic place you have here."

He stood up to embrace him again, to Ray's annoyance, his eyes diverted onto Theresa as she purposefully turned completely away to ignore him. She was so devilishly sexy and seemed so skilled in the art of tease and she knew it. Ray walked out with a rage building with every step towards the exit. A rage he gradually began to recognise as overwhelming jealousy.

CHAPTER 28

TEMPLE'S TEMPTATION

The previous months were successful ones as they made good on their word, planned with an almost intuitive instinct, they positioned themselves at the forefront as the news travelled quickly about the underground dance scene that the boys had come heavily involved with. It was not by coincidence, once they approached like-minded people and made the connections through Yogi, Stevie Betts and other keen budding entrepreneurs. Inspired by the clique of associates they partied with, for two fun exhaustive weeks in the clubs and beaches of Ibiza, they imported the feel and the music to these shores, into small back street clubs and fitness centres, to disused warehouses and abandoned arches.

On large wasteland and fields, they planned and mobilised thousands of people during the early hours of the night, undetected by the authorities, to gather and party for twelve, twenty-four and even forty-eight hours in some cases. Revellers danced away to these hypnotic sounds, loved up and energised by the first shipment of euphoria enhancing ecstasy tablets, imported in from Amsterdam, hidden in expansive sound equipment and lighting rigs. It was an instant gold mine, their significant commodity position, held the prices at a premium, so after the organising and partying was over, the small matter of counting up the fruits of their labour took place in quiet unassuming suburban addresses, to divide up between the parties that came together under Jimmy Newport's alliance.

The late Sunday night visit, upstairs in the Vanity club, Nathan and Tony, dropped two holdalls of cash onto the table.

"That's your twenty five percent. Babylon, Energy, World dance and Biology, ticket money and twenty grand on the pills." Nathan confirmed confidently.

"I have to hand it to you boys. These weekend windfalls."

"It's mental. It's getting busier week by week, and some places are still going."

"Acieed!" He screeched. "Who'd have thought it eh?"

"We did." Tony replied insolently.

"We were thinking we could run some nights or daytime events down here for you. Same format?" Nathan interrupted.

"My club is not a warehouse."

"You are missing a trick though Mr Maitland. I'm talking about the VIP's, the party organizers, the DJ's. We have all the brat pack and wild child and people from the music biz, all wanting a chill out venue, it'll be ideal. Look at Spectrum all sorts of posh people are flooding the gaff on a Sunday night dropping pills and all."

"Let me think about it." He replied vacantly.

"It won't even interrupt the Saturday night business. Dress it up and open the doors at 8am. Fifteen hundred people, champagne, 10k all day long." Nathan declared.

"I said, I'll have a think about it but don't build your hopes up. This is a classy establishment."

"Ok then Mr Maitland." Nathan surrendered with a disappointed fury quenching inside him but did not push the issue any further. "Same time next week?"

He indicated to Tony, who grabbed the empty bags after emptying the money onto the large desk. He walked behind Nathan, out of the office door and down the stairs to the empty club, they both surveyed the space, Nathan's visions of backdrops and large speakers, his vain hope shot down in an instant.

◆ ◆ ◆

Ray and Todd sat around Jenny's house in Surbiton over

in the south west of London, with another large pile of money. The four bedroomed property was one of three purchased by the group and offered rent free to the likes of Jenny, Bev, hers was over in Warlingham and Sharon a bit closer to home in South Croydon. Strategically away from the Gloucester, which the proprietorship was handed over to Norma, partly a business decision, primarily out of guilt, after she spent many months of anxiety over her fiancé Trevor Lewin, who had just suddenly disappeared.

What the group had overlooked was the fact that she was deeply in love with him, despite the regular abuse. Owning the Gloucester somewhat provided her with a new focus, confidence and a purpose. He was very mindful in his detest towards anyone that would shatter the confidence with their mental and physical abuse, but at the bottom of all of it, was a desire to be loved and looked after. Which was there for her in abundance from Ray and the rest of the group.

Each of their properties on rotation, were utilized for the sole purpose of hiding weapons, contraband and counting the piles of cash. The influx of income from the lucrative venture flowed like a burst dam as the wave of illegal parties swathed across the UK. With the help of the girls, they had opened Tanning and hair dressing salons, under Tania's Hair and Beauty brand, car repair garages and car dealerships, Sweeney's of Croydon, along with valeting and amusement arcades. A vast cash business empire was formed by connecting with existing, mainly struggling enterprises, to legitimize all the proceeds from the parties, the protection and the drugs.

Jenny, with her curly hair tied up, with sunglasses propped up like a prom queen's tiara counted out the last pile. Of which, every other sunday she would lose two hours listening to their banter and teasing her. Ray watched her from across the sofa, racking up three lines of white powder onto a square mirror.

"Who wants a line?" He chuckled.

"I'll have just the one, then I'm off. Meeting Tony to sort that bit of business out."

Ray's expression of curious confusion etched blatantly on his face and did not escape her qualm reservations, which Todd pre-empted with a wink towards his pal.

"He thinks I'm a fucking idiot." Jenny replied in a vexed tone, she fidgeted with her dress to sit correctly on her shoulders and continued the count. Ray could see that she wasn't buying into Todd's lies.

"Jenny. We have a lot at stake with our business and I always need my top soldiers to take care of things. To make sure no one and I mean no-one, takes liberties. Besides I'm here to keep you company what more do you want?"

"His cock's bigger than mine and all." Todd guffawed inappropriately, to which Jenny threw a brick of bank notes towards him that he caught off of his chest.

"I'm not a fucking bike you lot think you can pass around you wanker." She contested playfully. "And I've heard all about his knob from your little cheer leaders over the Whitehorse."

"Can you and your mates stop talking about my cock." Ray chuckled.

"Look at her, acting like she wouldn't." Todd giggled.

"Fuck off." She smiled.

"Yeah leave off." Ray laughed.

"You are a sort though Ray, I have to admit." She contradicted modestly with tempted eyes.

"Cheers Jenny. Likewise." He saluted.

"OK then. I'll leave yous two to have it off." Todd said and playfully went to kiss her only catching the top of her head as she turned away from him.

"See ya later brother." Ray laughed as Todd grabbed his jacket. "Are you packed?"

Todd sunk his hand into one of the large bags and produced a semi-automatic and stuffed it down into the back of his jeans waistband.

"Make sure you hit me up on the brick when you

are done." Ray requested, fist bumping with Todd. He left throwing a crude signage to Ray obscured from Jenny's vision as he walked out, with Jenny looking slightly solemn.

"You alright girl? He's only playing about with yah."

"Couldn't care less anymore Ray. I've past caring what he gets up to."

"That bad is it?"

"I know you all stick up for each other but I just don't like being treated for a mug." She seethed.

"Calm down babe." He comforted. "Come and have a line. Leave the dough. Come on."

Ray tapped on the leather sofa to invite her to sit and handed her the rolled-up banknote which she placed at the start of the line and made her way across the mirror. The stimulating elation had her tickling her nose. She placed her sunglasses on the table and pulled the hair scrunchy from her hair and allowed it to fall over her shoulders. She turned to him and smiled and sat with her thoughts, allowing for the strong narcotic to hit the back of her throat before she spoke.

"We are already done, you do know that?" She reported as a matter of fact.

"I had no idea babe. He...well, all of us for that matter, we have not been that focused on relationships over the past six months that's for certain."

"Tell me about it."

"Well don't complain too much bird, look at the lovely drum you got."

"You bought this, not him." She corrected. "You're not flash like him, you invest for the future."

"Something Angie and my uncles taught me babe." He stroked at her curly hair, she felt a strong attraction to him but knew it was a line she couldn't cross. She forced down a barrier quickly, diverting to the kitchen.

"Shall we crack a bottle open?" She radiated, offering the bottle of Bollinger from the fridge.

"Crack on sweetheart. Let's get this party started eh?" Ray

went to join her in the kitchen and hoisted himself onto the kitchen unit and lit two cigarettes and offered her one.

She tilted her head as she poured into two glasses to accept the cigarette onto her lips. They both knocked half of the content down quickly.

"What?" Ray queried the expression on her face as she stared with unassured eyes towards him.

"You keep looking at me the way that you do." She voiced with intent, her heart pounded by her longing desire for him.

"How's that?"

"I dunno Ray...Ever since I first met you. I've always wondered about the way you look at me. I never wanted to say anything before...It's in your eyes, like you are stripping me naked all the time."

"I've known you for forever?"

"Must be my imagination then."

"I'm not saying that..." He looked selfishly into his soul while she stared back waiting for his confession. "I've always liked...that way that you carry yourself."

She leant back against the fridge with Ray examining her curly highlighted brown hair, wide eyes, that seemed to always stare with mischief. Although she was petit at 5ft 4, she was fully proportioned and despite this, her breasts looked abnormally huge due to the tight lycra floral dresses she wore, that seemed to compliment the LA Gear ankle length trainers, that clashed between styles of urban and suburbia.

"Is that it? The way that I carry myself?" Her laughter combined with a sharp exhale of cigarette smoke.

"I actually think you are gorgeous...You're fit, I mean look at you stood there. I could totally eat every inch of you."

"Oh my god." She blushed, her heart swelled with butterflies erupting inside with his words, the misbehaviour in his mind was fully transparent.

"Are you surprised that I think like that?"

"No. I'm never surprised, you're all a bunch of Casanovas." She projected. "Anyway, I heard you was seeing someone?"

"Really? Who'd you here that from?"

"Well you must be?" Her question lingered with interest.

"And why's that?"

"Well...You're you. The sexy complicated boss, who acts like he's innocent. Tall, dark...well kinda...and handsome but has a convoy of women all wanting him."

"Pfft. Talking rubbish. I only have eyes for you."

"Now who's talking rubbish? You just want to get off with me and get inside my knickers." Her head tilted with contest, flirtingly overwhelmed. The more she opened her mouth, the more brazen she was becoming and feeling movements inside her silky thong wanting him. The meagre battle line she had drawn since they entered the kitchen was erasing with every word from his lips and look from his scorching eyes on her.

"Well, you're my mate's girl, so you are off limits."

"For some strange reason, even though we are not husband and wife. I don't think that would even stop you."

"It's like the forbidden fruit ain't it?"

"And what fruit is that then Raymond?" She giggled "You're just a cocky little bastard that's all."

She poured more champagne into her glass, he winked back at her cockily, loyalty dissipating by her flirtatious body language. Signals that should have morally switched this topic or should have made him make excuses to go home, but a mutual magnetism continued them down this path with little resistance. She walked over to top up his glass, placing the bottle and her glass on to the side, looking conflicted as she meddled with her hair and then the large gold hooped earrings, almost pondering where this sudden courage appeared from.

"I bet you taste like strawberries. I love strawberries."

"I must be off my head." She doubted herself again with contradiction, when an almost naughty endeavour took over her thoughts as she crept closer towards him.

She stood between his legs and stroked at his thighs. He stroked at her hair and her cheek, the twinkle in her satin grey eyes were alluring and seductive. He leant forward and kissed her. Pausing nervously, she gazed debatably with herself, this was his best friend, that for all intent and purpose, he was showing that long awaited interest that she could not turn away.

They were quickly absorbed, he jumped down from his perch and lifted her petiteness up with her thighs astride, her arms looped around his neck as he caressed her body. They shared passionate kisses that made her murmur with pleasure as he squeezed at her tits, simultaneously fighting with his belt buckle and jeans to urgently unfurl his erection for her.

In one foul swoop, he slid her knickers, drenched with expectancy aside, exposing her tempting opening which had become glistening wet with anticipation for his cock. Swollen with need, he hungrily penetrated her. Manoeuvring onto her kitchen table, tentatively to confirm its sturdiness, he rodded into her greedily, roughly pulling her dress down her shoulders and ravished at her heavy breasts, objects fell around them crudely, as he fucked her and kissed her tits, that she cupped together to tempt more lust from him and enjoyed the sensitivity from his hot sucking and gnawing at her nipples. He went into her deep and hard, she craved at him mercilessly as the long awaited wanting for him finally unleashed.

Clawing at his back as his shirt buttons exploded in different directions around the table. The pain from her sharp nails drove him hungrier into her, with both his hands firmly gripping onto her breasts. Her eyes rolled in ecstasy as the intensity ebbed and flowed, pulling her magnetically closer to a beautiful orgasm with his brutish grip and size.

"Oh my god...That cock. You bastard." She celebrated as the spasms took a hold, reverberating in her voice.

He grunted with gritted teeth as she continued with her demands into his ear, her voice stimulated by the way he felt inside her, which vacated every ounce of guilt. She felt so good, almost arriving in paradise by the rough passion of him drilling her silky wetness, causing magnitudes of waves rushing her entire body. She gripped onto him, aroused to the point that she shuddered from her orgasm and gasped out loud. She could feel the intensity increasing as her pussy gave in to her pleasing orgasm, she screamed with joy and appreciation.

"I want you to cum...I want you to cum in my mouth." She pleaded with sheer lust as he became tensed ready to explode.

Obediently, he pulled out from inside her, rushing towards her face and coaxed his erupting cock into her mouth, she assisted with rapid strokes, her hands cupped his diameter to capture his full force. He leant over to her juicy cunt and began licking her simultaneously. They both groaned loudly at the pleasure as she craved at his big member in her mouth and reared her pelvis to tilt her pussy towards his tongue as he licked energetically between her legs, her pink insides squished as he stirred and lapped at her juicy pussy taste.

Feeling another orgasm shake her body, made her drool over him. He eventually pulled away from her, licking his lips, her pelvis slowly grinding to a satisfied halt.

After taking a few elated seconds to recover, she sat up with a sexy triumphant smile across her face as she adjusted her clothes. Reaching over to a kitchen towel, she wiped any remnants from her face. His face masqueraded with a self-assured confidence that camouflaged his real sentiment.

"You are so naughty, you know that?" She purred.

"I feel...fucking shit about it, if I'm honest."

"I won't tell. But oh my god. You are so hot." She grinned.

"You're actually loving all this?"

"What did you expect? You are such a fucking tease Raymond. Come here."

"Woah...Go brush your teeth girl." He giggled receiving a punch in the arm, before he kissed her sweetly on her lips. Her heart throbbed wildly for him as she purred at his kisses.

Everything about him was just calm and collected, that swagger that always weakened her knees. After a quick organising of the disrupted kitchen, she disappeared upstairs to shower, leaving him sat with himself on the sofa preparing another two lines and then lit another cigarette.

After a while he could hear the front door locking and surprised as she stood at the doorway in a sexy see-through, fully tackled in gloss black hold up tights with red high heels on.

"You gonna fuck me properly this time?" Her voice spilled with deviance and bravado of finally capturing his full attention. With the jaw dropping look that beheld him, the territories of bared skin above the stockings, up to her matching frilly sexy thong captivated him.

Her hair hung sexily over her sultry shy face, lip glossed lips, that oozed provocatively towards him, that set her in a completely new light and made him wish he had approached his craving with more patience. Always aggressively pretty in his eyes with a no-nonsense tone commonly in her voice but as she stood in front of him tonight, visually stimulated more hunger for her.

She straddled on top of him and surprised how keen he was ready to go again, she stroked admiringly at his length before guiding herself onto it and welcomed his lips onto hers as they kissed passionately and worked themselves up into another colliding orgasm.

◆ ◆ ◆

Several more glasses of Bollinger later, Ray was sat at the oak desk at the head of the room, placing the piled-up bricks of money into a bag, with the usual weight of five grand piles his eyes seemed to be counting as he placed each one. Jenny laid on the sofa smoking a cigarette, amusing at his guilt riddled face.

"One hundred and seventy-five thousand Ray, I already counted it." She confirmed.

"Sorry babe my head is all over the place." He confessed as he began to tackle with his guilt again. He was surprised at the quickness, the remorse and uncertainty he felt from her earlier, swept away almost verging like a premeditated plan. Her voice repeating of always wanting him, whispering as they fucked, raised eyebrows with him for certain. The feel of her body however was in total contrast, good enough reason to fulfil that desire. His phone rang from across the room to adjourn his battle with his rationale, he walked over as he checked the time on his gold timepiece and surprised that it was a quarter past midnight. He answered the phone acting as calm as possible.

"Oh…Hello Angie?" He relieved. "I'm sat around Jenny's having a divvy up. You ok?"

His face bore of suspicion as he listened to her figuring out on the other end on his whereabouts for the rest of the evening.

"I'll probably crash here. We've done a couple bottles of Bollinger." He listened cautiously as more information came back to him in the form of the messages received at the pub. He acknowledged that Todd had concluded the business and was currently heading to Spectrum with the Chelsea girls. Taking in the information and recollected, Emma and Amanda who to him, deemed as two high society girls flirting with the unsavoury for the thrills and the status. Another message he received from her, second hand that she read off a notepad, was a message, a cryptic one at that, other than the name, Theresa, which somewhat set more alarm bells inside his head.

The information was a jumbled one of sorts to collect a package from Clapham Common and to call back to a number she would leave on the side for him. He looked towards Jenny again as she eaves dropped on his conversation, before he quickly focused and instructed that he'd be over to collect in the morning and ended the call.

He sat beside her, studying the damage to his shirt and leant forward to inhale another line.

"You've ruined me Armand Basi." He chuckled.

"You've ruined me insides." She laughed back, groping for

a gage to see if he could provide her with more of the same.

"Horny little bitch aren't you?"

"Mmm." She agreed, kissing steps of wanting at his cheek and his lips. He returned the passion back towards her.

"On a more serious note, the next few weeks is gonna be all hands-on deck." He digressed.

"Jesus. I'm already running out of people to trust with all that cash."

"Not only that. Your sister's shop is going to have to ramp up and all, in order to wash all this money."

"Better than what we expected though eh?"

"Without a doubt. You'll get a bigger bonus." He laughed.

"I thought you fucking me was my bonus." She tipsily laughed, slightly staggering over to the stereo, she put some music on, still parading her busty petiteness in the high heels and the sexy see-through, that exposed her peachy round arse.

Ray shook the excitement of her and scooped more cocaine, then popping a third bottle of the champagne. He relaxed back into the sofa as she straddled his lap again, miming to the song with the widest grin.

"This has been the best party I have been to for a while."

CHAPTER 29

TOTAL ECLIPSE OF THE HEART

The number and message left for him at the Gloucester from the weekend had only jolted his memory after traveling with him for two whole days in his wallet. He waited as instructed at the Windmill pub in Clapham Common, patiently since around 3pm. A habit of getting to meetings early, in order to suss any ambush. He was also addedly eager of the thought of seeing her again. He read the scribbled message in his hand 'Windmill four O'clock then call' He dialled the number on the mobile phone, that was already racking up an excessive bill.

The warm summer breeze sang around him, sat in the jet navy 3 series BMW convertible that was given to him by his business partners last Christmas. He had previously preferred a low-profile Vauxhall to shunt him around but some of their legitimized success allowed them to reap some of the finer things in life, like the elegant watch he wore on his wrist, the birthday present from Christine and the Italian designers he donned over his 6-foot physique.

"Hi sexy." Sang the voice, that answered his own question of who he was actually dialling.

"That you Theresa?"

"Yes! How are you darling? You got my message then? Are you on your way, because I'm almost there?"

"Not far away, maybe ten minutes. Lucky, I only really read it the other night...About coming here today." He replied coyly.

"Ok...When you get there, leave your car in the pub car park and walk over to Narbone avenue, number 63."

"That sounds a bit suspect."

"It belongs to my homegirl Natasha and there's only permit parking."

"I don't know Theresa. This could be very dangerous."

"Stop being such a scaredy cat Ray. I've been fantasizing about you ever since I see you all them months ago."

"Well if I'd have known you was engaged to marry one of the nastiest cunts in London I would have steered well clear."

"But you left the comfort of your home to come to Clapham?"

"You got me babe. I can't get you out of my head."

"I'll see you soon then gorgeous." She flirted and cut off the phone.

He began to scan around to Narbone avenue, recognising the street signs from a distance and manoeuvred his car into a position at the left side of the pub, so he could observe the comings and goings. Pulling up the soft top to the car he waited inside patiently. The busy mobile rang a couple of times before he rang into Raph to say he would be M.I.A for a few hours while he took care of some unfinished business. He began again to think about her and the night they shared.

Their business had left little much time for any matters of the heart, even though Jenny was a needed distraction as his only focus was on the cash and building a parallel drug and party organisation that had already seen them successfully promote eleven events, solely and jointly, by force in some cases, of fifteen thousand people or more, the schematics alone taking months of planning in itself. The truth in fact that the true organisers had been threatened, that the only way the parties could go ahead was once they signed the party protection agreement with Gloucester entertainment limited and had the food and drinks and also attractions concessions with Keane, White and Morgan enterprises.

Angela had been a key negotiator for all the events, which had seen the corporation clear a cool £750,000 of untaxed profit in the space of six months. He sat proudly pondering this, although with Raph and Nathan's hunger for expansion, he was forecasting a very busy end of year for 1989.

By the time he spotted the gleaming black SAAB, he hesitated slightly, forcing back his eagerness for her, to see if any other cars were following close behind. Vigilantly sat for ten more minutes, he checked the time at exactly ten past four. He locked the car with the audible and visual security system confirmation and walked calmly across the main road.

Appearing as if he knew where he was going, he scanned with paranoia, the parked cars and house numbers, satisfied as he approached the address that there wasn't any telling surveillance on her, to his relief. Her fiancé emerging as awed and lovestruck enough, that she was seemingly free to move about at will. Theresa had always struck him as a woman that will take what she wanted or needed without hesitation and this is what unnerved him the most.

With the door slightly ajar, he knocked and waited patiently for a response and heard her sultry voice echo back for him to enter inside. She stood by the back door, peering out onto the lawn and turned to face him after a few moments.

"Hello handsome." She purred. His eyes inspected her lustfully, she was dressed as if she was there to chaperone for his interest in the property. The smart navy jacket honoured her cleavage of her heaving bosom inside, the skirt was short and hugged at her slender curves, with a large expensive clustered jewellery decorating her neck. He conflicted with his unloyalty to Jenny, surprised that anyone else would divert his mind away from the sexiness in front of him. He now compared as equally as tempting when she was dressed to seduce. Jenny was unlike Theresa, a fantasy from a long time before, but he still felt the guilt for her all the same.

"Where does your fiancé think you are today." He questioned which rained with an air of jealousy.

"He doesn't need to know my every movements 24 hours a day." She boasted.

Ray pondered on this with a smile, to disguise that her

movement were clearly of no interest. He walked towards her as she stood in front of him expectant. He drew her into him, she gazed lovelorn into his eyes as they kissed in front of the huge patio doors, the overlooking lawn backed onto a large fence, surrounded by tall shrubbery and hedges, that offered privacy from the adjacent properties.

She battled with his jeans to lower them down and immediately set upon his huge erection that had hungered for her. He lifted her up as she kissed him impatiently, the sheer rush of their needful passion exploded. He fucked her at the sink unit before carrying her, stepping tentatively as the jeans cuffed him like a death row prisoner. Hastening the pace, with her long legs wrapped around him. Dropping her onto the sofa, he continued with the loving inside of her moist pussy as she hollered expletives at him and cursed at his very presence.

"Fuck you and your fucking huge cock." She expelled randomly. "You love my wet pussy?"

"Yes…I fucking do." He replied with zealous, that choked his throat as she teared at his back with her nails, which were still tender from the scraping from Jenny's.

"You're so fucking big inside me." She creamed as the pummelling excited her to the heights again, she became conscious of the leather they lay on, distracted for a split second but still erupted her luscious quim over him and the furniture.

His cum exploded inside her as the elation swept in a wave of pleasing groans and moans from the short bout of sex performed in this stranger's house. The ordeal was contrastingly a long way from the socialised gathering of dinner guests that had sat in the same place, discussing arty farty blurbs to impress the householder.

"I love the way you fuck me." She panted.

"Didn't even give me time to take me jacket off." He chuckled back. He sat up to catch his breath, then stood to dress himself. She swiped in-between her legs as he looked down at her so sultry looking as if begging for more. That look of absolute control that she had on him, had him relaxing a little more but wanted the answer that had him nervously checking his watch.

"What time does your mate get back?"

"Friday evening." She purred.

"Why the fuck are we rushing?"

"You were just hungry to fuck me, that's why and I didn't want to stop you." She stood up and indicated to him upstairs, taking his hand to accompany her, looking at her beautiful behind as they climbed, she shook herself out of her jacket to reveal that she had nothing more than her bra underneath.

By the time they entered the main bedroom, she had already unzipped her skirt and discarded it along with her heels. He stripped himself bare and joined her under the luxurious bedding and immediately embraced and kissed like a couple on their honeymoon. The passion radiated romantically as they gazed upon one another, the sex was undeniably intense beyond what they had contemplated.

"Why do I feel so crazy about you?" She declared.

"The fantasy I have had for you from since I was pulling wheelies on me bike."

"Really?" She giggled.

"Yeah, really. I used to always see you about. And you totally ignored me. I fancied you like crazy."

"Ahh. You're so sweet." She cooed into his ear.

"Then I never see you again, you just disappeared. Rumours said you joined the salvation army I even heard.

"Salvation Army?"

"Yeah something like that, your cousin Malc said. I remember thinking I'd still love a view of the tackle under that uniform."

"Anyway. What was wrong with the girls you used to have all over you outside the Gloucester?" She digressed evasively.

"They were all my mates."

"Really? Trust me, they saw you as more than a mate. I used to hear them always talking about you. What's that nickname you had?"

"Nickname?" He queried with a smile.

"Yes, the girls on the estate used to call you some name. What your mates give you. Because of this beast." She playfully grabbed for his dick under the covers.

"Fucked if I know. I thought people had better things to do, than talking about the size of my cock."

"Swordfish or something?"

"Swordfish?" He laughed. "Swordsman…That's Todd that is, he's so immature."

"Oh, let me kneel before your mighty sword my lord." She giggled. She tugged at it some more, then cradled over his legs to begin arousing him again. "I could get slain all day long by your sword if I had my way."

"Your worse than Todd with the comedy." He laughed.

"Lend me your sword, so I can cum once more sir." The laughter continued as they entwined with one another. Tender kisses covered her lips and the ticklish part of her neck.

"Would you leave him for me?" He asked sincerely.

"Raymond, we have a wedding planned for 25th July."

"So why are you with me. If he's the one?" He asked.

"Because he gives me stability and everything a girl could need…" She smiled and kissed him. Straddled on top of him to parade her gorgeous body. "…Except for a big monster sword that you've got."

He looked bemused and taken aback by her statement but melted into her seducing kisses. In all honesty as he told Jenny, there was little time for romantics but once he performed all the oral and animalistic hammering of her insides, that saw her soak the expensive sheets, a jealousy would override his nonchalant acceptance of just being around to fuck her. He wanted her more than ever and goaded himself that Ray Morgan takes what he wants.

CHAPTER 30

A GAME OF MONOPOLY

Raph, Tony and Nathan were South Croydon bound after a full day of collections from Kings Lynne down to the South Coast, as the lucrative weekend trade gathered an unprecedented than expected momentum. But with the money came the relentless punishing as no one had any room for liberties. They pulled up outside their last stop at the Swan and Sugar loaf alongside a Golf convertible.

"Jimmy boy." Raph greeted. "I heard congratulations are in order, you must be well loved up."

"Geezer, She's the love of my life." He replied greeting everyone else in the car with a confident nod of the head.

"She's a good sort our Sharon, one of your own, make sure you treat her like a princess." Raph warned playfully.

"Don't worry mate, she keeps telling me how the sun shines out of all your arses." He chuckled. "Ray good?"

"Yeah mate. Living a king's life and ruining birds with his sword." Raph laughed.

"He's a fucker ain't he?" Jimmy appraised playfully. "I bumped into Todd last night. Rubbing shoulders with them Doris's off of the tele."

"Yeah? Rambo fucked one of them the other night and all, didn't yah Tone?" Raph smiled proudly.

"Amanda Sommers, utter filth." Tony grinned.

"Anyways less chat about my whoring pals. That's the usual amount but we need to start turning it into something else, the pile up is getting ridiculous." Raph interrupted, walking around to retrieve a bag from his boot that he tossed onto the back seat of Jimmy's.

"Listen mate. I spoke to Ray about it before, if we can get it into stock market derivatives, you can move it all over the world. The market is ready for fucking."

"Fuck me, don't tell these lot, they fuck everything." Raph guffawed.

"I'm starting a job in the city next week. You'll get in on the ground floor."

"Hey. We're in, no need for the spiel. You get on the case Jimmy, just set the ball rolling."

"Laters Sarge." Tony and Nathan both saluted.

"On it my son, catches yah later." He grinned widely as he sped away. Raph returned to the car and instructed Tony to head back to the Gloucester.

The pavement outside the pub displayed like a car showroom, with convertible BMW's, Jaguars, a Wrangler Jeep and a gleaming black taxi parked outside. The pub was also undergoing some modernization on the upper floors, which no longer housed Ray and his mother's living facilities, what once was a place of many Sunday dinners and gatherings for The Godfather viewing with his mates, was now fitted to suit. The boys were sat in the transformed expansive office space, with a large executive oval oak table surrounded by six plush black leather office chairs. The refurbishment almost complete, but still awaiting the finishing touches, where all their business efforts had been coordinated over the past months as they all strategized the numerous fronts they had created. Gloucester Boys Entertainment Ltd, Gloucester properties Ltd. Keane, White and Morgan enterprises, Genco, Sweeny's Autos and Todd Carter building Ltd to name a few.

"What's on your mind Ray." Raph started the serious conversation, which halted Tony and Todd's tales of absolute debauchery over the weekend.

"This Newport Alliance."

"Yeah, what's the problem." Raph queried

"Well I'm thinking, sooner or later, this market will get saturated and at the moment we are splitting all our hard work across the four firms across London. We should, at least in the long term, be looking to consolidate."

"Meaning?" Tony asked.

"We stop sharing with them cunts who are not putting in the work." Ray interjected.

"What about your uncles, don't they have a say on any of this?" Tony responded back.

"What's to say? We have fulfilled our obligations up to now, but I can't see how we can continue this on the long-term splitting over four hundred thousand pound a week."

"He's got a point...In Manchester, the price of a pill is going down. People don't want to pay scores for too long. So, fuck 'em, is what I say." Todd agreed.

"Jimmy Newport won't be happy." Raph added.

"For starters, Newport has his fingers in my uncles pies, what he's getting out of this is peanuts."

"Yeah but he won't stand for us crossing the water putting more holes in more people." This time it was Nathan prompting concerns.

"Look, all I'm saying, for now, is suss out their weak points. To be fair, all this, since we started, it was us mainly that put up the risk and Yogi's mob sorting out the muscle, what do the others have to offer apart from counting the readies that we provide."

"He's got a point. And you don't see the Senior's or that Hajimichael mob sharing their income, they're raking in a fortune, the amount of heroin they're offloading. Some alliance." Todd declared.

"Hark at Sweeney. Are you ready to go to war with the Greek Mafia?" Nathan replied. Todd only gestured with his usual, 'game for anything' look, back at them all.

"I think we should at least wait until Sarge gets us in the stock markets. Like you said, once the rave business flattens out." Raph offered.

"People are still gonna wanna dance." Nathan interrupted.

"And do drugs." Tony Added.

"Yeah that's all well and good but it's getting harder and harder getting these events going. Old bill will get on top eventually. It's better now we start thinking ahead, maybe do what you said Nathan and get into the major club business as well...Like that Sunday gaff."

"Spectrum?"

"Yeah. Then it's a weekly steady flow of money, along with the other cash enterprises. And only our people selling the pills." Ray surrendered.

"Anything sounds better than what Sweeney wants." Raph chuckled, noticing Todd's look of disappointment.

"Well Nathan reckons the music in the clubs would be worth millions, in a few years." Tony teased.

"Conquer the world with this shit brother, I'm talking fucking live aid. Stadiums all rammed, you just watch." Nathan boasted confidently.

"Yeah alright. Don't get carried away. But let's get involved. At least to bury all this dough." Ray agreed with a degree of cynicism.

"Solomon didn't even accommodate the club idea I shared with him. He's too far up his own arse when it comes to the Vanity club...The bubble cunt." Nathan seethed.

"Cool mon...When we move, he'll be the first one to fall. And you will get your club." Ray promised. The statement raised eyebrows with all of them except for Todd who just nodded with awe towards him. Sammy entered the room that distracted them away from the unified suspicion of Ray's motives.

"Where'd the Taxi come from boys?" He questioned.

"It's your early Christmas present." Ray said proudly and got out of his seat to embrace him. "You are a taxi driver and we need regular drops, Isle of White, Southend and Cardiff airport. No one will pull a taxi punting his fares anywhere. Besides, Siddy always said you nicked a decent living couriering. We need your services now Sammy Taxi."

"You are aware that the Taxi moniker didn't come about from me doing the knowledge?" He reported.

"No we weren't. But we bought yous a taxi." Raph chuckled.

"Well doesn't seem like I can say no then. Seeing that you all bought me a flaming taxi, does it?" He retorted.

Put out at first, in general Sid and Pete had little in the ways of work for him in more recent times. They played golf and done all the race meetings and little less else as the boys took over. The cigarette vending business was not a lucrative game anymore and Raph had packaged that side of the business and sold it off to an American soda company to add to their portfolio of soft drinks and confectionary vending, for a nice piece of retirement money for them. He stuck his hand out after the room fell silent as he pondered the offer and shook Ray's hands fervently.

"That brings us onto our last topic on the agenda." Ray announced. "Sammy you'll report to Raph along with Tony and Nathan. Todd you'll need to work with Yogi and his teams, pick a couple of good heads that know their way around surveillance."

His directions had Sammy taking notice of what he was averse to, when Sid and Pete were planning a hostile take-over or two and offered a closer solution.

"Ray if it's an MI5 type job you want. And keeping it in house. I know the people you can use. Very professional." Sammy reported.

"Get on it and have Todd shown the ropes. He could do with a bit more subtlety." Ray chuckled.

"So, the plan is we watch and wait?" Tony asked for clarification.

"Yes...We suck up to the bubble like the joey's he takes us for. We gather information, so we can move at the drop of a hat."

The room continued in discussions as Ray slumped back in his chair. Mobile phone's rattled with calls surrounding their headquarters with chatter, laughter and the usual expletives of threats to people not complying to their late payment deadlines. Todd approached him sheepishly with intrigue.

"Thanks for taking care of Jenny." He appraised.

"She's a good girl Todd." Ray looked at him with a guilty embarrassment.

"I know mate. That's why I'd rather you looked out for her...I'm rolling with that Emma now."

"Don't get carried away with all that glitz and glamour, you need to be out of that spotlight. Don't drop her out for them mate."

"Fuck me Ray have you seen her? She's fucking mint."

"Yeah mate and don't get me wrong. I wouldn't kick her out of bed. But, that's all jungle fever with them, always sniffing about."

"Well I'm happy to oblige. Besides, I'm not ready to settle down. Every relationship is just a one-night stand to me. Who wants to be fifteen years in and get janked off because you now both want different journey's?" Todd indicated with air quotes.

"I love how you can sum life up with such a simple analogy. You should be a marriage and relationship councillor you."

"It's the fucking truth mate. You mark my words... Take it from me Ray, fuck 'em and run moosh."

"Unless her name is Emma with big tits eh?"

"She's a good laugh and all Ray. I'm not that shallow."

"Well as long as you're cool mate." Ray sighed with a roll of the eyes.

"I don't mind if anything happened the other night." Todd digressed back to the topic on Jenny.

Ray lit up a cigarette as a means to divert his eyes towards the flame and away from his pal. He knew Jenny would never had said anything, so maybe was just his way of testing the water or giving his blessing.

"Look, I got a lot of time for the girl. She's like family. I'll keep her sweet anyway, take her out. I'm sure she'll appreciate it."

"She will mate. She worships the pants off of you."

"Yeah?" Ray replied airily reflecting on his treachery.

"They all do. Jenny, Sharon and especially Norma and Christine, from when we were at school, you're god in their eyes."

"Leave off." Ray dismissed.

"You are the golden child our fucking swordsman... Fucking love you bruv." He laughed jovially kissing him on the cheek.

"Fuck me! Do you two want a room?" Raph chuckled.

"Who wants a beer?" Todd digressed standing up after his emotional outburst as Raph stepped up to take his place.

"Grab us a bottle mate." He looked towards Ray who nodded an acceptance and the others who all refused politely.

"Grab Ray one and all." He ordered.

"He can be a soppy little sod at times." Ray smiled.

"He'd take a bullet for you Ray, without a doubt."

"100 percent."

"Anyway. Good news, to start off your cunning little plan. Robbie Collins has a link with Soho CID and they have their radars on Solomon. He wasn't saying too much, they don't have much on him, nothing they can stretch and land some bird on. But it's an option."

"What'd he just ring?"

"Nah had a little chat with him the other day."

"That's a good catch. Let's watch that one playout. I can't stand that cunt."

"Yeah! But his fiancé?" He questioned suspiciously.

"Look, I ain't gonna lie to yah. The sex is out of this world, but she knows where her bread is buttered."

"Ok mate, I hear yah. As long as it's business...Your motive I'm on about?"

"Hey. It's always business Sonny. It's never personal."

"Never doubted you Ray. Order and peace are impossible until the number of ruling states has been reduced to a manageable number." Raph quoted intellectually.

"That's a peach of a line consiglieri." He beamed.

Raph aimed a playful punch towards his jaw as he ducked out of the way jabbing back towards him.

CHAPTER 31

THE ROYAL GARDEN

Angela rapped at his door after parking her personalized plate, vintage convertible Mercedes on his drive, another cash present courtesy of the Gloucester Ltd, all the fake executive directors lavishing the trappings gained for being part of the board, mangers and company secretaries generated the fleet of cars parked at the pub and on the estate. Ray's semi new house was another four-bedroom rescued from the recession of 1987, a benefit for the cash rich as prosperity once out of reach for the working class, kindly shone on them. She peered through the glass into the empty hallway and waited patiently before knocking again, humming a usual love song in her head as she stood for five more minutes patiently, she could hear a window pop open above her.

"Are you going to make me stand out here all day?" She smiled, with her hand over her brows to deflect the bright sun.

"Sorry. I didn't realise it was you…One sec."

He appeared quickly after rushing hell for leather down the steps to open the door, his stocky physique was to behold as she stared with a devil's passion towards the strapping man she had raised.

"Go put some clothes on for god sake." She whispered to herself. She strode in with her high heels tap dancing onto his wooden floor as she followed him into the kitchen.

"You look lovely and summery."

"Thank you darling." She smiled.

"Do you want a cuppa?"

"No thank you love. Just popped round to drop these keys." He looked around at her not quite connecting the dots.

"The ones Sammy ordered. The archway?"

"Oh yeah gotcha." He quickly remembered. He placed them on the counter next to the kettle, they weren't required at this moment but was vital in their future plans. She walked around the pile of clothes besides the washing machine and began her motherly task.

"The washing machine won't load itself."

"Yeah I know...That's what I have you for Angie." He smiled cheekily.

She improvised for her greedy eyes, by grabbing a pair of tracksuit bottoms from the pile, shying away to pass them to him.

"Please. Put your bloody bits away." She giggled at him standing in his boxers. He quickly stepped into the pants and stretched a tired yawn as he ambled about. She saw the coffee table was full of remnant evidence of some late-night entertaining.

"Have you had company?"

"Yeah just me, Stella and couple of the girls from the hairdressers. Bev was about for a bit."

"I see her last week. She's doing well, isn't she?"

"Everyone's eating well mother. These are exceptional times." He boasted.

"How comes I never get invited? I can still party." She confessed.

"You ok? I mean, you're more than welcome to hang out with us. Everyone loves my Angie." He praised hugging her. She hugged him back as he embraced her in his muscular arms.

"Jesus, you are like superman all of a sudden. How'd you get so strapping and muscley?"

"It's all that heavy lifting Sid and Pete had me doing." He replied sarcastically.

"My Goodness, you should be a catwalk model for Ralph Lauren." She swooned.

"Me mincing up and down a catwalk? Do me a favour."

"I dunno, the ladies will all be fainting and getting

themselves, all worked up looking at you."

"Pfft, I have enough attention as it is." He remarked cockily, flexing and kissing his biceps and went back towards the kitchen to make his tea. She was swarmed by an illicit daydream. She needed to find someone to take her mind of her loneliness as her hormones were out of control lately and deviating her morally.

"Are you sure you don't want one?"

"I'd prefer a gin and tonic."

He peered back into the living room, she busied herself tidying the messy table. The sunlight shone through the window onto her, in the navy floral short dress. Her sun kissed legs strode back and forth, she appeared to him as her finger tips massaged at her temple to be distracted and somewhat melancholy.

"What's the matter?" He asked once more, as she placed bottles in the bins and placed the glasses into the sink. Looking around to him with her arms folded, watching as he supped at the hot cup as she stood in front of him.

"I'm just worrying about you all the time." She lied, the worrying was more about her unable to remove him from her thoughts and dreams.

"Why are you worried about me for? I'm a big boy now."

"Yes, ain't you just?" She prided with a cheeky smile. "I miss you not being around and all this money you are throwing about. It concerns me that's all."

"We have perfect legitimate money in all kinds of different commerce. And more carrots than bugs bunny, so don't worry." He smiled unperturbed.

"But who's looking after you and feeding you?"

"I eat every day."

"You know what I mean. I…"

"Look if you want something to occupy yourself. Raph's about to open his jewellery shop in Hatton garden. I know you love your diamonds and your tom. You could manage it for us?"

"It's not money hun or that I have nothing to do. I just miss you so much." Tears began to fall down her face which caught him unaware as he looked away to grab the cigarettes.

"What's this all about eh? I'm on the manor every day, come here…What's with the tears?" He caressed her comfortingly again into his arms, she felt the protective safety from his steel biceps as she became more emotional. Her arms snaked around his back as her face pressed into his bare chest. It was the truth that burnt at her and a feeling that she could never get no comfort from. She wiped her eyes with the back of her hand, trying not to upset any of the expensive mascara that dressed her lashes.

"Let me jump in the shower, then we can go grab some lunch. We'll go up to that Chinese gaff that you love."

"The Royal garden?" She gasped excitedly, wiping tears with her tissue swiping under her bottom eyelids. He held her at length to review her mood, until a smile broadened across her face and kissed her, stroking her long hair, her eyes beamed brighter up at him as her beautiful perfume wafted at him enticingly.

"Get a move on then. I'm starving." She giggled.

After he showered, he dressed in an immaculate white Polo T-Shirt and Jeans, checking for scuffs on a line of pristine white trainers under a coat stand by the door, before selecting one, then threw on a brand-new navy jacket and lead her out towards the car.

"Wow." She amazed.

"What this? Lovely ain't it?" He replied proudly.

"Looks like it cost you a bit."

"Seven hundred quid." He boasted. She faced him to straighten his collar correctly and popped the top button he had done up, to offer a more relaxed casual appearance.

"I'll drive." She offered, winking at him, after approving his chosen attire.

"Are you sure? Sounded like you needed a few gin and tonics."

"Yeah I do...but I like my car." She concluded with mischief beaming from her deep hazel eyes.

They motored through the village, Ray currently residing in leafy Warlingham, the drive had her long blonde hair waving gracefully in the wind. He tuned her radio into one of the stations that pumped the underground sounds of the parties that were, without a doubt, setting unprecedented popularity.

Reaching South Croydon, he leant over her to acknowledge associates and friends that he passed. The Swan and Sugarloaf pub was heaving on this bright sunny afternoon, swarming outside with people. There were a couple of individuals that he noted that had swerved him the last couple of weeks, he tipped up his sunglasses to acknowledge that he had seen them, then waved towards them happily as he cruised by. Turning right to enter the last couple of miles to their destination, he called Todd, who was patrolling the pubs and local gatherings, checking up on things, putting his face about and making the weekly rounds.

"Mate, I just clocked the five-gee kid at The Swan." He coded the words purposely in front of her, not wanting to add to any inhibitions about her worries about his day to day.

"Same message?" Todd came back.

"I'll let you decide on the recipe. I'm sure you'll be creative." He clicked from the call and lit a cigarette. Angie looked towards him, he acknowledged that she enjoyed the occasional smoke and passed her the cigarette after a few puffs.

They pulled up to the restaurant and was greeted by the owner Martin Yan, who went a little overboard with his demand like orders, making his staff scamper around as he ushered them both inside. The slightly busy restaurant had some heads turning in recognition of him. They both greeted a middle-aged couple, bearing interest on their well-being and general social chit chat.

After refusing politely to join them at their table, he

guided her to the best table selected by the owner. Ray ordered her a gin and tonic and himself a tiger lager. He reached out towards her hand and stroked it comfortingly.

"Make sure you fill your boots with this lovely grub."

"I love this place." She aired excitedly. "Do you bring any of your dates here?"

"Leave off…This is our special place. I remember bringing you here on your birthday."

"I remember, that's so sweet."

"And you in that dress today. Absolutely stunning. You always remind me of a movie star."

"Really." She beamed slightly blushed. "Which one?"

"Marylin of course. If she had longer hair." Ray smiled.

Angela broke into the broadest simpering smile, that twinkled at him with undeniable love and a comparable heartbreak.

"Well you often remind me of that singer, the strapping handsome lad with the dreadlocks and a guitar…" She tickled her chin trying to remember the name of the heartthrob she had seen on MTV and reminded herself to seek out the song that he sang that caught her attention, along with the talented man that made her fall into a fantasy about him and uncharacteristically, in the middle of the afternoon, playing between her legs after working her panties down, the thought she shook away quickly, when the name suddenly spilled from her lips.

"Lenny Kravis…Krevis…is it?" She pronounced incorrectly, smiling and confirming with herself that they definitely shared similar good-looking qualities for sure, captivating many a lonely heart with his voice or in Ray's case the jovial radiance that burnt so deeply and tormented so frequently, that she could love him in all the wrong ways.

"Nutter. It's Kravitz not Krevis." He chuckled.

"Oh, you know who I mean." She tapped at his hand, playfully lingering on it as it rested on the table in front of her. His eyes so catching, so identical as her late beauteous best friend.

"Todd used to reckon you looked like Jilly Johnson." He reflected back to the banter in the park and the trips to football.

"Who? I never heard of her. What did she star in?"

"Page 3 of the Sun."

"That cheeky little sod. I'll slap him when I see him next."

◆ ◆ ◆

Todd pulled up outside the Swan and greeted some of his old nemesis from school. Everyone was best buddies now, since the summer of love gripped everyone known to them that were under the age of 25.

"What are you having Sweeney?" Billy Burgess rang out.

"Half a lager will do. I'm not stopping." He went over to greet Ian, Theo, Si, Bex, Keith, Andy, Chunky, Sean and Mickey Hurst, with a mixture of the Whitehorse estate's Chelsea and Palace top boys that had always socialized and drank together. The females accompanying them all flirted their hello's and kisses onto his cheek.

"Yous all sorted for tickets for next week?"

"Yeah most of us." Bex replied.

"Alright, cool. Let me know if yous need any more. I'll get them dropped round."

"Nice one mate…Me and Billy are in here most evenings after work. Thursday and Friday's definitely."

"Bev'll have some last-minute ones and all, so I'll send her up on Friday night."

"Oh, blinding mate. We can't wait, the last one was fucking top mate, should have seen the convoy that left from here, it was alight." They all agreed.

The discussions began to reminisce about the mega parties and the quality of the rushes that enhanced the nights. He purposefully ignored the intended target, who in turn, purposefully pretended like nothing was afoot, once it appeared he was only on a social visit.

Unfortunately, Todd was the last person he should have been worried about, with most of the drinkers outside, Danny, The Gloucester Boy's new enforcer, had been waiting patiently inside for the right opportunity. Tony turned up soon after, with music blaring from a monster sound system installed in his Wrangler Jeep that had everyone distracted. People began to dance to the mobile party. The bass shook to the dance anthem called French kiss, to which no one noticed Danny beating on one guy and manhandling him into a waiting van. His mate stood frozen, with a fresh pint in his hand, without a tad of inspiration to intervene, especially with the gun holstered in Danny's waistband removing any of that doubt. The barmaids and the landlord also conveniently turned away.

The party continued outside regardless, until Todd signalled to Tony once the van was set in motion, rocking slightly from side to side as their enforcer delivered the groups message.

CHAPTER 32

THE SOCIAL GATHERING

She slammed up the curb in the smart Mercedes pulling back up to his house. They had returned after four hours of eating and drinking at their favourite restaurant.

"Jesus, that was like the scene out of Bullitt that driving. I'm gonna need a big line after all that."

"Shut up. I thought I done quite well on five gin and tonics. Darling." She giggled playfully.

"Five? It was more like ten. Darling." He corrected.

Stepping out of the car she was awkwardly tentative in her high heels. She tipped the keys into her clutch bag, pulling out a tube of lipstick, twirling the base to expose the Fuchsia gloss tip and painted her lips pouting towards him.

"What's with the lippy? We ain't going out on the town love, just me front room." Ray laughed back.

Keying the door, he invited her inside with a chivalrous gesture for her to enter before him, shutting the pleasant evening breeze behind them and entered the living room. Reaching straight up to a shelf to retrieve a tin box with a secret compartment that he opened up with an intricate tap on the side that contained several wraps of cocaine.

"Rack em up then party girl." He insisted.

The phone rang again, this time interrupting her protest about him being a terrible host. He paced the room speaking into the phone, commanding with a cocky swagger. From the restaurant to home he'd answered an influx of calls. At this point he reminded her of how Sid and Pete had the same presence, that identical brash confidence when they were growing into the strong leaders that they became or was it the inevitable strong genes of his father. She idolised at him the same way she did his uncles when she was 13 years old and learning the ways of the underworld with them.

He entered into some banter that she joined in with, as Todd with his usual comedy irked him, with his insistence on taking her out on a date. He offered him some gentle expletives before he hung up on him abruptly.

"He's such a div." Ray laughed.

"You always get so wound up with him. He's only playing about with you. I'd never go out with him." She reassured.

"Yeah I know." He laughed sarcastically. "Imagine him as me step dad?"

He made her laugh at the ridiculousness of it as she stroked the powder back and forth trying to measure up an identical amount.

"Was everything ok?"

"Yeah just the usual. He's off to that new Subteranea club in Kensington again. With his TV star."

"Don't you wanna party with your mates?"

"I'm partying with my mate ain't I?" He chuckled.

He nudged her over across the sofa and took over the lining up of the narcotics onto his glass table, smoothing a bigger evenly measured line and passed her the 18 carat gold custom made device, for her to inhale her share of the strong white powder.

"Mmm." She approved as the spike hit the back of her throat. She relaxed back in the settee, adjusting the tightness of her dress as it rose up her thighs, her crossed leg danced with the expectancy of the adrenaline from the narcotic and watched him take his share. She watched him spark up a cigarette, taking a moment for his own hit to blend in slowly with the earlier alcohol.

"Don't you feel weird doing this with me?" She rasped feeling herself blush awkwardly.

"Nah! Not at all. You know the crack anyway. It's just a social thing…Music." He announced, hyped up by the drug.

Her eyes followed him as he went to the tall stereo stack and attempted to tune the radio in to listen to what she had criticised earlier as crazy music. A highlight from one of the legal stations had her demanding that he stopped the dial.

"Wait…Oh my goodness, Ray, this song. Leave it on please." She said excitedly, she hummed at the introduction and stood up smiling joyously.

"This was my Rita's favourite. I used to play this song to you when you were just a little baby." Her eyes twinkled at the recollection.

"Doubt I'd remember it then."

"Come on. Come have a dance with me." She made a reach for his evasive hands playfully and swayed from side to side, eventually all by herself after he refused to take up the offer, he stared towards her, not really feeling the vibe but happy that she found joy in the song. Her eyes closed completely as though transporting herself to the home of Tamla Motown.

He poured them each a drink and then found himself beginning to enjoy the soulful song and joined in with the last part of the catchy chorus.

"It's too late, to turn back now, I believe, I believe, I believe, I'm falling in love."

His sinful eyes looked worshiping upon her, she swung around looking radiant the way her hair fell over her face. He prided that she had enough of the drop-dead gorgeous appeal for someone to want to sweep her off her feet, but the inappropriate conflicting feeling refused for that option, his head beholding her beauty once again. His thoughts were exonerated by the fact everyone laid compliments about her, she had an air of absolute radiance and kindness but her unadulterated sex appeal circulated like a virus inside his mind.

She tugged at his hand jarringly again, then finally had him succumbed enough by the song to playfully dance and twirl her around as the ambient room drew her back to the Mayfair club and the parties from a bygone era. Her eyes stared up at the strapping man, her mind also conflicted. The phone rang again suddenly to break the mood.

"Alright Jen...you ok babe? Who yous with?" He queried in succession and listened to the long explanation.

"Yeah sweet. Me? I'm in me drum. Nah, I'm on me jacks here with Angie. Yeah ok, see yous in a bit."

"Who was that?" Her inquest was met with slight insolence in her voice.

"Jenny and Tania."

"Do you want me to go?"

"Shut up. Stay and have a party. They are grabbing Nathan from the Gloucester and coming over. You said you wanted to party, now's your chance." He laughed.

She smiled masking her initial disappointment, with the understanding that her enjoyable evening spending the time alone with him was about to end but somewhat relieved.

◆ ◆ ◆

It was several hours and a plethora of booze carried in by Nathan and the girls. The cocaine and alcohol created a very chatty and humorous atmosphere that was centred around the spacey kitchen area. Morphing at times into a dance floor, whenever a popular tune came over the pirate radio, the volume increased with disregard for any neighbour of his detached house.

"I love your dress Angela." Tania praised after her long introduction, on when and how she met Jenny and all the gang.

"Ahh, thank you love. This is John Galliano." She replied twirling around in a girly tipsy manner.

"It's so lovely. And you look so beautiful. I know women shouldn't do the age thing, but you look like you are in your twenties."

"Blimey, she'll love you Tan." Ray chuckled, although, he agreed again, the alluring thoughts that she was a looker for sure.

"She's such a sort Ray." She continued heaping the compliments."

"I really like this one Nathan...Darling, according to my driver's licence, I should be in my late fifties by now." Angela smiled elatedly.

"Shut up! You are not that old?" Tania amazed.

"That's a long story, to when I was a young girl trying to nick a living and had to lie that I was older." She lapped at the relentless praise. Although in her head, she felt a bitchiness to suspect that she was trying too hard to please but at least she was genuine.

Ray and Nathan had an excessive amount of interruptions on their cell phones on business and also refraining from inviting more people to turn the gathering into a full-blown rave. She spent the night chatting with an envious inquest of Jenny and her intentions. Jenny had to explain continually awkwardly, that she used to be Todd's girlfriend until they fell for one another, ironically, explaining that she was at the mercy of cupids' arrow when it came to her adorable. She became exceedingly protective as she became increasingly drunk. The conversations repeated over a wide range of topics, that digressed back and forth to give anyone what for, if they hurt him or broke his heart, and the added apologies if she was speaking out of turn, as the alcohol and drugs took effect, not just on his covetous guardian but on all of them.

After Angie's approval, Nathan was now intimately escalating his pursue on the good-looking Tania. Her dark hair with the tinted golden-brown ends bounced onto her shoulders as she flirted with him and laughed at his jokes. Working his way confidently with her, stripping down the flimsy barrier of general friendship.

Angela was feeling giddy from the night, trying to keep up but she was not the party animal she once was, especially compared to these. She was already semi succumbed to the drunken tiredness that was beginning to overpower her. Jenny relievedly drew Ray's attention to her for him to assist her, intoxicated and unstable, up to one of the three spare rooms of the large house, with some difficulty as his own intoxication sapped his usual steady self a little. At least in as much he could barely carry her.

Staggering ungainly into the room, he helped her onto the bed. The awkward fall, had him almost on top of her, as she looked up at his eyes. She drew her lips up close to him, with an equally strong embrace around his neck, possibly, with the excessive consummation, brought to her a strong urge to kiss him.

"Thank you for a wonderful evening baby." She slurred, her eyelids were already at half-mast, slowly giving up on the fun evening. Her roving hands tried with defiance to make him stay. Jenny had already gone back down to resume the party, feeling slightly awkward at seeing him having to deal with her in the state that she was in. Her earlier sophistication now a distant memory of the night.

"Help me with my zip." She forced herself upright, suddenly shaking herself awake with futility, indicating behind her back for his urgent assist. He adjusted himself away from her to guide the zip down to the small of her back. Kicking her shoes with a flick of her feet, catapulted one shoe to hit one side of the wall, the other flopped off her foot to bounce off the bed and onto the floor. With heightened concentration, she wriggled out of the tight dress, leaning her back into the bed and raising her legs to free herself as he looked sheepishly away.

Revealing to his licentious eyes her body in the tidy white underwear, exploded his mind with the most inappropriate thoughts, peaking to confirm she was finally ready to be tucked in for the night. She laid on the bed exposed, her long hair covering her face untidily and trying to be cohesive in a conversation with herself, apologising again about him having to see her in this state.

"Shut up and go to sleep. I Love you." He sniggered at her sweet voice fading, destination nap land.

He quickly managed to help her under the sheets and kissed gently against her forehead and the tip of her nose. Watching her peacefully unconscious for a moment, then at the big grin on her snoozing face before closing the door behind him. He was about to return downstairs, when he laughed at the sound of Nathan and Tania going at it like a porn movie, she groaned loudly enough for him to walk the hallway and close the door to its fullest.

"Don't want yous waking Angie." He shouted but was ignored as they continued fucking.

Jenny was holding the gold snorting device out for him after waiting patiently downstairs. Disappearing the line, his mind brimming with lust, he drew his attention to her and hungrily began to kiss her. The air of sex was already doing battle inside his jeans. They groped at each other as their urges grappled them with seduction.

"Why do we always seem to fuck a lot in kitchens?" She smiled as she coaxed his erection inside her. They fucked briefly as the occasion encapsulated them before they paused halfway as she demanded to continue in the bedroom. He grabbed the half drunken bottle of champagne and necked it, holding her outstretched hand as they travelled the stairs and into his room. Lifting her onto the bed, ignoring the airs and graces, he proceeded to hungrily eat her pussy, her personal aroma scented her horniness, she encouraged her clit harder towards his eager tongue.

When she came in an eruption from his short instrumental toying between her legs, he climbed on top to fuck her, sliding inside, just the way she liked him, deep and hard, she yearned for him loudly, undeterred about whether anyone could hear her pleasure. Her body quivered feverishly from his narcotically charged intense fucking until he pulled out to spill his hot cum onto her naked breasts, she cupped to position them to capture his full load, milking the last droplets into her mouth, her eyes magnetised onto his, appraising with gratitude.

He rolled over satisfied, tossing the box of tissues from his night stand onto Jenny as she wiped his love from between her breasts. Reaching for the champagne bottle, he pitched some into his mouth that over spilled onto his panting chest and passed it over to her before lighting a cigarette that they both shared. Tania appeared at the doorway and startled them both, she had a devilish grin on her face, her long curly hair caressing her shoulders like a waterfall, he coveted in surprise at her flawless body when it came into view, the third mouth-watering sight that night.

"I can't sleep and he's snoring away like a goodun." She smiled. She walked over bare chested without a care in the world and bundled onto Jenny then laid spooning with her as they giggled with innuendo towards him.

"She thinks her luck is in Ray, can you believe her?"

"Huh...Blimey." He replied shyly.

"Bloody hell. I never would have had you as the shy type."

"Me shy? I'm just worried about ruining yah." He echoed confidently. Jenny's eyes widened thirstily as she flung open the covers for Tania to cast her eyes on his monstrous beauty. He covered back up quickly in protest.

"Oh wow, Jenny, no wonder you are always smiling so much whenever you speak about him. He's huge."

"Here, unless you want to help her clean her girly cum off of me, shut up and have some more gear." He offered off of a membership card, for her and then for Jenny as they sat up.

Jenny leant over to kiss him once the line slid to the back of her throat, between the sips of the champagne bottle that they all shared. After a while of banter, the girls were jabbering away about who had the best boobs and the chances of them sharing him. Ray's reluctance to commit to the engagement was largely due to Angela in the adjacent room, as hard as he wanted to entertain the idea. He telexed the excuse that the code already violated with his intimacy with Jenny, wouldn't flaunt very well, especially with Nathan just down the hallway as they both snuggled up to him with roving hands.

They laid silently, his mind raced as the cocaine battled with the alcohol that he had consumed and integrity. Jenny continued to stroke and massage at his smooth caramel skin, purring with her excessive sexual desire for him, continued to possessively coax another arousal. Tania with the approaching reality that he was warming to the idea, from Jenny's continual antagonising. He went as far as turning towards her with a filthy digression to meet her hesitant lips. Her recent bravado vacated as his tongue stroked at hers with Jenny's devilish encouragement contaminating her to see it through. Her hands stroked against his giant erection until an equally crashing sensibility paused them in the moment. She quickly excused herself, consciously deciding to wake Nathan up to tend to her encroaching hunger instead, inspired by the heated after-thought of sharing that huge cock with her friend.

After Tania's hasty retreat, Ray's mind relievedly raced away from that sexual discrepancy for a little while longer, before Jenny, after a brief reflection on the disappointment, finally ascended into a selfish celebration, when she could successfully regain the rigid rod for her own to embrace deep inside her again. The early hours inside his home echoed with unified panting moans of pleasure. Nathan had discovered a second wind after Tania's unexpected ravish for him. Jenny's body was being treated again, to the rigour that seemed to multiply the orgasms that his masterful cock delivered in droves.

Meanwhile, awoken by the sexual commotion, Angela returned from the en suite after relieving her bladder and capturing a long guzzle from the cold water tap. She tossed and turned, disturbed by her head pounding and the audible groans and creaks, from both ends of the hallway.

Behind closed doors, her imagination wavered into an unwanted envious visual, that made her dehydration and insomnia increase. Her hand wandered with a guilt-ridden reluctance, caressing with strokes between her thighs, her knickers eased down her legs and cast aside to create more freedom, with a need forcing butterflies inside. She began circling her clit dipping a finger inside then another, increasing momentum gradually, the tips of her fingers rubbing against the spot that made her eyes close again, mewing to herself and harmonising with the squishing sound of the self-caressing below, increasing in time with the volume from the adjacent room. Her free hand reached up to squeeze her full bosom that heaved in elation as she drew herself close. The ache in her body surged as the finale was met by the manly roar of satisfaction next door.

She stifled herself to a whimper as the fierce sensation was released over her whole being, collapsing into the thick duvet that her legs clamped against, her face planted deep into one of the duck feather filled pillows that suffocated her scream.

CHAPTER 33

STIFF LITTLE FINGERS

Is an Alternative Ulster,
Grab it and change it, it's yours,
Get an Alternative Ulster,
Ignore the bores and their laws.

The Music blared excessively loud. His eyes draped in darkness to cement the torturous fear they intended to inflict.

"Stiff little fingers. This song is by." Tony circled the victim menacingly. The butterfly knife continual click as he spun it with precision, terrified and unnerved him in his seat. Bound by the rope across his torso, his hands secured with cable ties, purposefully tightened to cut off the circulation, he already could not feel his fingers or the pain from the already severed pinkie that his capturer had already operated on.

They say they're a part of you,
But that's not true you know.
They Say they got control of you,
And that's a lie you know.
They say you will never be free
Free, freeee.

He continued singing the punk song, air guitaring up close, he pogoed and bullied him with cuffs around the head and poking him with the sharp blade.

Todd was sat on the cellar steps reading the sun newspaper and supping on his cup of coffee, not even distracted from the words. The headlines, large font for sensationalised outrage, was reporting on the parties they had jointly organised, which had him chuckling at some of the outrageous comments.

"Ere Rambo. Have you seen this? Frenzied teenagers bite heads of pigeons." He shouted over the music. "SPACED OUT? We're fucking loved up. Silly cunts."

Tony glanced briefly over towards the big headlines but only acknowledged with a thumbs up.

Several hours earlier. Tony had been partying with Todd over at Subteranea with Micaela, Amanda and Emma. The trendy club was popular with the affluent 'It' crowd of the West End and the popular party scene. There was a drug trade rife inside but the Gloucester pair where strictly only there for socialising and not for business. This individual's reckless chatter to people that identified themselves as Soho C.I.D, accidently exposed the main dealer who was blatantly networking to get amongst the VIP's that were associated with Todd, Tony, Ray and their organisation.

Entry level infiltration, beginning with this now captured individual was to befriend Anton, the World Party promotion organiser who was already seventy thousand pound deep in debt with them. Todd's quick thinking, following another trip, rather than the regular queues for toilet cubicles, in the back-stage entrance, there was an unused gangway through a broom cupboard type door, that allowed on the last occasions, access to his own private sex room that he enjoyed with Emma. He climbed the sectioned timber framed wall to peer out at a commotion and witnessed Soho C.I.D, heavy handling of their now unlucky victim.

"Get us the intelligence or you do 15 years for possession with intent." The tall C.I.D dressed all in denim had demanded.

Despite Christopher's protest and confident stance that they had nothing on him. The Mets finest seemed desperate to get some results and Anton Haywood was deemed to be Public Enemy number one. That came as no surprise, West End was off limits as far as the drugs went. The big raves were more or less under strict management, which protected any shut downs and were pretty much policed by the four main firms. Recent headlines however, Police were now drawing a heavy line and Anton being the most outspoken and provocative as the self-adopted King of the Raves, unknowingly offered himself up as the lightning rod.

The remit was to use this captured Christopher to work his way into the Party organisers circle and see where it leads. A lucky touch for them, Robbie Collins had warned that some departments were looking into intelligence around the whole party scene, prodding for weak points, Anton and Christopher being that weak point. A phone call to Raph and the crew were again rubbing their hands at another gift, having identified this Christopher, was one of Solomon's trusted gofers for pick-ups and drop offs. The question Todd and Tony wanted to know, how can they use him to their advantage. Ray, Raph and Sammy entered after a few hours of bullying which signalled Tony to hit the stop button on the portable music centre.

"What the fuck do you know about Stiff Little Fingers Tony? That's white man's music." Raph chuckled.

"I had X-ray Specs lined up next." He replied.

"Christopher Bamford-Gray." What brings you to this neck of the woods." Ray laughed menacingly, interrupting the banter.

"Does Solomon even know he's out and about with the riff raff?" Raph interjected.

Ray looked closer under the light and saw some of the damage that Tony had inflicted and looked towards him and Todd in disapproval.

"Shall I prep him for the Naden's?" Tony smiled, wide eyed, like a sinister psycho deviant.

"Heel Rambo, I think you done enough with the music. Clean him up and bring him upstairs." Ray commanded.

Raph signalled in agreement, to Tony's despair and followed Ray back up the stairs. Raph had already poured out drinks, Nathan, turned up to join the gathering of abductors after thirty or so minutes returning from an intel catch up with Robbie Collins. Nathan never spilled any intricate details about his heated words, he demanded that the reluctant Collins, remembers who it was that kept him and his family in a nice home and the ability to afford lavish holidays.

"He's defo grassing for Soho C.I.D. Subteranea and Vanity are under obs, they're not even looking at us."

The news pretty much summed up what they already knew and points to where their prisoner can now be assigned as their little Trojan horse. He was assisted into the plain room, his eyes squinted as the daylight pierced the big airy unfurnished lounge, a kitchen cloth bandaged his wounded hand. The empty house was another recent purchase which would be under renovation after its use, the basement was the unique selling point Raph had identified.

"Have a drink." Ray commanded.

He downed the large Teachers from a plastic cup, the only crockery available in the house, the bare kitchen providing the choice of refreshments left over from some kind of gathering when the house was laid vacant. Christopher ravished the fiery liquid with a thirsty fear as to how this would end for him. Seven hours he had estimated, that he was unconscious and in the boot of a car and may have passed out several times during his sadistic ordeal.

Ray placed a large bag of white pills on a table in front of him. The look on his face almost pictured with relief that his fate would not be ending in death, at least not in the short term.

"Take this to Anton as the bait."

Christopher looked towards the bag trying to understand the quantity in his head.

"There's 20,000 in there and you need to get him to bring it to Solomon, need him to agree to buy the parcel and Anton can serve it up for him on the side."

"But won't that put him in conflict with you?"

"There is no conflict with us, but according to our sources

there is some serious heat on you, so you can either cooperate and feed that to the Old Bill…." Ray explained.

"Or you can come back downstairs with me." Tony grinned

"But why would Solomon back him, he's a stranger?" Christopher protested almost apologetically.

"Well that's down to you, sunshine. Anyway, you should know, otherwise you wouldn't have been pinched yourself. How did you get yourself captured with two thousand pills unless yous were branching out?" Raph continued.

"Ahh did you see his face Ray, they get near on seventy grand a week from us and it still ain't enough." Nathan observed.

"Solomon didn't know about my little side venture." Christopher pleaded innocently.

"Let's assume that you are telling the truth. I'm sure you can work things out with him and Anton. Solomon's a greedy cunt." Raph again interjected.

"That's the only way you live." Ray surmised. "You go to Anton and offer him a way out from what he owes us, that he offers Solomon the package. Use your imagination."

"I'll do my best." He agreed, gulping more of the drink leaning his cup outward for more.

"There's profit that makes 130 to 150k, if you dangle that carrot to Anton, 40k taking off what he owes us. It's a win-win for him. And a road to redemption for you." Ray terminated the conversation. "Whichever way you do it, you talk him around."

CHAPTER 34

FOR AULD LANG SYNE

It was New Year's Eve and the firm had all gathered with Solomon to see in another year of prosperity, the new decade seamlessly transitioned from the last, their alliance sharing the fountain of wealth, which was in itself cause for celebration. The Vanity club was heaving and Solomon was looking down smugly at Ray. His sexy fiancé danced flirtatiously alongside him and seven scantily dressed women, all vying for the rich men's attention, that flaunted with champagne and snorted cocaine openly in plain sight. Solomon contradicted against his stifling rules of getting high on own supply, he was fed two dove marked tablets and now unable to control the elated feeling of pride in his club, the music and the women around him.

Theresa openly kissed him, the visual did not escape Ray who watched his roving hands caress all over her gorgeous curves. Raph noted the look on Ray's face, despite his protests that he was not in the slightest envious, but it was obvious it was subduing his will to party. He supped on a water bottle seething under his breath, that they had all been invited down by him but treated as Joe public by their so-called business partner.

This to him was a show of the disrespect, a purposeful one at the least. It was no secret that he was the dominant force in the west end. Which in itself, alluded that despite the tons of money they delivered, the adulation was kept to a belittling gratitude that they were allowed to operate because of him and not because of who they viewed themselves to be.

"You wanna cheer up son." Nathan interrupted his

thoughts.

"I'm good Nath." Ray replied embracing him with a kiss on his cheek.

"Look at him. The bubble cunt." Nathan scathed

"Who? Solomon?"

"Yeah. Treating us like Joe public."

"Well he can count himself lucky that this is neutral ground eh?" Ray smiled, once he realised that his smugness and disrespect would only be short lived. He summoned to Raph who was already getting in the party mood with two blondes that had not stopped looking over at them.

"This is my best pal Raymond." He introduced Tina and Chloe. Tina keenly set her mark with an amorous embrace.

"Alright sweetheart." Ray spoke loudly over the music into her ear.

"Me and my friend Chloe was just saying that we recognised yous from that big World party in Kent."

"Yeah? That was a wicked party." Ray agreeed proudly.

"That was the best. You looked like you had the best time."

"Them doves are the bollocks." Ray conversed with her. "Where yous from?"

"The Blue." She announced proudly.

"Bermondsey girl eh?" He smiled, she seemed a nice girl, her long hair flicked and tickled his nose as he spoke up close with her. Her hands touched at him flirtingly with a glint that he was by now well accustomed to. Todd and Tony, both stood close by and unusually, were not seeking any female attention. They checked back for a minute or two and then circled the surrounding dance floor and bar. They surveyed the placement of security, stopping to talk to men with mean faces and scars, with orders that they at least act as though they were enjoying themselves.

Yogi was there firmed up with a group of his mates, a mixture of football thugs and violent enforcers, all sat in the sumptuous leather booths, champagne and women flooded his corner. Ray excused himself from the girl he was in conversation with, to join Yogi for a quick toast ahead of the clock striking midnight. He seated himself beside him after shaking the hands with the few who paid respect to him, with Tony stood guard at the bottom of the steps that elevated from the busy dance floor.

"Your boys all get the brief?" Ray asked smiling.
Yogi patted at the heavy steel inside his suit jacket. He seemed over dressed for the occasion when Ray himself chose a simple Polo Shirt with jeans and a gleaming white pair of trainers.

"He's got most of his firm at the bottom of the stairs. Two guard the top."

"How many?"

"Sweeney reckoned about 15 in total. We can still get to all of them."

"Good!" He prided. "And you took care of the grass?"

"The grass is cut." He hinted sinisterly.

"Alright sweet." Ray acknowledged. "I'm going back to that Doris to see in the new year."

"Be lucky my son."

"See yous on the other side." Ray grinned and made his way back to Raph, Nathan and the girls, Chloe, Tina and a dark-skinned brunette named Tracey after being acquainted. He nodded towards Raph who had a big smile, checking his watch as his arm perched on Chloe's shoulder. Nathan's champagne cork exploded into the air as the group cheered.

Solomon elatedly looked down on them from his V.I.P perch up above. Theresa also looked down towards the edge of the dancefloor. She was now scathing at the pretty girl with the heaving bosom with her hands all over Ray. Solomon had his attention now diverted onto the entrance to his area that his security guarded like Buckingham Palace, peaceably explaining to Todd that it was a V.I.P only area.

"I just wanted to say happy new year to Mr Maitland." He explained feigning desperation in his voice. Solomon indicated him inside with a wave of the hand towards the heavy-set men, who acknowledged and then allowed Todd beyond the partitioning that was cordoned off with velvet rope attached to gleaming gold-plated poles.

"Just wanted to wish you happy new year Mr Maitland and that Ray sends his regards." He said joyfully.

Solomon resisted the urge from the pill he had taken, to protest as to why it was only he who took the need to pay homage. He was joined by Theresa, who was inquisitive inside her own mind as to why Ray had not shown any willingness to enter the upstairs all night and was seemingly satisfied, to just send an errand boy.

"Happy new year Mrs Maitland." Todd smiled and took her hand, slightly forcefully, to place a kiss against the impressively expensive rock on her finger. She returned the pleasantries, peering unnoticeably behind her back to look down at Ray again. The pair of them kissing brought a feeling of sorrowful fury as she watched Solomon slur into Todd's ear, about how great his club was and equally as proud, of the prosperous income their organisation was bringing in.

"You boys are genius. The parties, the pills."

"Well happy to do business with you Mr Maitland. Long live the monopoly." Todd laughed.

"And I totally understand now why they are so popular." He quickly changed the topic onto the recreational benefits of the contraband.

"Did you pop one Mr Maitland? Fucking blinding." Todd laughed out loud. "Anyway, I'm going back downstairs to Ray and the boys. Happy new year." He again expressed to them both.

"Happy new year. Tell Ray to come up and say hello what's the matter with him?" He requested, then turned to beckon to Ray downstairs, but he wasn't looking, he was deep under Tina's charm and purposefully ignored his gesturing until he was satisfied that he had acted uninterested enough. He toasted his half empty glass up towards the sky at him and gestured that he was too much engrossed. Indicating towards the beautiful woman in his arms as she looked up with a smile. He indicated at his watch that it was five minutes to midnight, Solomon continued to gesture him upstairs. Raph and Nathan both noticed and smiled towards each other and simultaneously walked towards the red and black carpeted stairs.

"I've just got to go say hello upstairs." Ray excused, realising the time was approaching.

"Oh! But it's almost time." Tina huffed with disappointment.

"I know. But you see that important looking man upstairs? He owns this gaff, he'll get the hump if we don't go up and kiss his arse. It was lovely meeting you darling."

He pecked her on the cheek and proceeded upstairs behind Nathan and Raph. She stood aghast with her friends, she was totally under the impression that she would end the night fucking him, after confessing her true intentions just a little while ago. Despite her alluring curves, the tantalising scent of her perfume and the tell-tale twinkle of her eyes, would never had been enough.

Ray's moral compass was already aligned towards his conquering thirst for violence and never gave her a second thought, as of that moment. Tony met them at the stairs and lead in front of them as the countdown began to see in the year 1992. The music stopped while the crowd all in unison rang at the top of their voices…

"Eight, Seven, Six, five, four, three, two. One…HAPPY NEW YEAR."

The crowd cheered, when an intro to a bass driven track dropped from the DJ booth, which caused an eruption of elation from the crowd.

Suddenly, gun shots exploded into the ceiling from downstairs around the area where Yogi and his mean looking associates from Broadwater farm, Holloway road and Summertown estates were sitting, just as Ray approached Solomon to embrace him.

Chaos ensued downstairs as five, then six more loud

bangs echoed over the music. Bedlam conveyed when hysterical people, went from enjoyment, to absolute fear when two large bodies fell with a thud at the dancefloor perimeter. Tony's long blade stuck into a huge bearded man's back, after he ushered everyone out from the V.I.P towards the stairs. Ray immediately grabbed Solomon, Raph grabbed Theresa with Nathan leading all them towards the exit. Pushing women and men out of the way. Todd remained in the empty V.I.P area with his gun cocked, the kick back reeled up into his arm muscles as the man who had his back turned inspecting the melee, fell to his knees and forward onto his face.

Tony withdrew a double barrel and turned towards the large man who he had already stabbed, as he reached in vain to retrieve the razor-sharp weapon from his back, he blasted two rounds into the chest and prided as the flesh caved him in with force, driving his victim into the wall. Todd wiped his gun and grasped the dead man's hand, to force the gun into it and pulled the trigger again aiming with precision upwards into the roof of the already dead victim's mouth. He stood up and looked around hurriedly for any witnesses. The upper floor they were stood, was calm compared with complete pandemonium downstairs, gunshots and CS gas creating panicked hysteria as everyone fled.

Tony waited at the top of the stairs before concealing the sawed off, then sprinting together in the direction of another set of stairs. They grabbed three cowering girls, hiding behind the rear bar and told them to follow. Tony kicked out at an emergency exit door exploding through it with ease, into a corridor and ushered them quickly through.

"What the fuck is going on." One of the terrified girls screamed.

"Fuck knows." Todd hollered. "We're just getting the fuck out of here."

Entering the busy street, while ducking Solomon's head down low, to resemble a fleeing president escaping an assassination attempt, he led him into a side street full pelt.

They continued running at pace, scanning behind them to analyse any impending danger. Cars screeched away in droves, congesting at the junction as people in a mass of confusion took flight. Sirens wailed from all around but still seemed in response, nowhere near the scene, as new year revellers filled the busy streets and tail backs began to form.

Ray froze abruptly when a brief tug of war had Solomon flung head first into a waiting van by three large men in dark overalls. He put his hands up in a confident surrender.

"Do you know who you're fucking with?"

Solomon could hear Ray enquire into the gun barrel pointing at his face. The gun clicked as a response to call his bluff, with an empty bullet chamber as the man retreated into the vehicle. The van reversed carelessly, clipping wing mirrors that showered the tarmac with glass. Ray followed its trail down the road to the next junction in vain, then jumped into the black Mercedes as it screeched alongside him.

Raph forced Theresa into an awaiting black taxi that just happened to appear and purposefully waited with the door ajar. Looking anxiously into the hysterical crowd, he spotted Ray take a right diversion as gunshots could still be heard ringing out from inside.

"Shit…Drive…Just go, get her out of here." Raph ordered to the driver and threw a wad of cash down onto the seat beside her then sprinted to follow his friend.

"What about Ray?" She shouted in a frenzy as the door slammed and the taxi shuddered away. The driver continued in silence until he was passed by a stream of police cars and vans hurtling in the direction of the club.

"What happened in there?" He enquired.

"I have no idea. One minute I was seeing in the new year. And the next, it was absolute chaos." She replied looking back nervously as blue lights flashed and sirens wailed in response to the confusing incident that she had been rushed away from.

"Stop at a phone box for me please I need to make a call." She requested, biting at her nails nervously.

After several pauses, the white van sped away from a side road having earlier circled the club several times, anticipating the people they were there to collect. As it head northbound, Solomon was for the last fifteen minutes swiftly sobered up as the nightmare ascended, from the loving elated feeling he had inside his club and celebrating the new year with his wife and friends, to one of this absolute terror as two masked men trained shotgun barrels towards him. Confusedly, with the timeline now askew, what he had thought was light headiness from the drug, was actually the steady draining of blood, he now realised puddled around him, congealing into the corrugated metal floor, triggering the sensation of pain coming from his thigh area, he stroked at it to confirm with clarity, on the open wound inflicting his discomfort.

Now he visualised one of the abductors wiping a long blade onto his overalls and placing it into his pocket, a purposeful targeting of his femoral artery or there about, the blood he was losing was not at an alarming rate, but he was not expecting the ride to end with the aid of medical staff, this was meant as a slow torture, the knife man knew his anatomy, it was his forte, to immobilise the victim.

As the confusing situation settled. His head rocked back with a lack of control, the hooded men observed him with a violent perversion, head tilted almost with a portrayed empathy.

The voice from behind him, in his shaken state, came like a calling from god himself, the spiritual dialogue he centred his petering attention on.

"In this world, there comes a time when the humblest of men, that if he keeps his eyes open, can take his revenge on the most powerful." The voice quoted loudly over the engine noise, an excerpt from Mario Puzo's novel.

A sharp swing left and then another one to the right almost shook him up from what felt like a dream and now riddled with fear, when realisation drew him towards his final breath. He fought for every last one as the van now shuddered

THE GLOUCESTER BOYS

to a halt. His eyes could barely open as the strange aura of blood exiting his body and pounding head laboured him, still sat upright. The doors flew wide open, with the masked men disappearing with their weapons now concealed into their leather jackets. Removing their cover and overalls that they tossed back into the van. They proceeded unremorsefully into back seats of waiting cars, with engines humming idly. The headlights beamed into his eyes before the shadowy figures faces, illuminated into recognition and jolted him half awake.

"Why have you done this to me? We are supposed to be partners, aren't we?"

"That partnership has run its course. It was only a matter of time and the old bill would have had you. This way will be quicker."

"I don't understand." His voice became more laboured.

Raph clambered into the van with a short-nosed pistol by his side.

"Time is up for the flash greedy litte cunts like you." Raph declared. "But it's all in good hands."

"I underestimated you Gloucester boys. Fucking South London." He slurred with a somewhat pitiful smile, his mind became lucid.

"It wasn't personal Mr Maitland." Ray comforted.

"It's just business." Raph concluded pulling the trigger.

The loud bang echoed inside and also the industrial waste ground they had driven to. He tossed the gun beside him and jumped out with Ray still peering in. Apart from the jolt to the head the portly corpse remained upright, he continued to gaze in as the petrol-soaked projectile was ignited. Raph tossed it beside the lifeless body and retreated towards the waiting cars.

The two vehicles circled quickly to face the exit kicking up dirt as the v12 engines purred away. No-one looked back towards the glow behind them. They were out onto the main road before the explosion sparked the night sky briefly, like a makeshift firework display introducing a new year. Raph looked back towards Ray's cold powered stare in a silent homage. Nathan also sat in silence watching the scenery outside the window. The driver, Billy 'The Face' Benham kept his eyes on the road, checking his rear view for Irish Tommy, Luis -The Scouser, Arthur Naden and Danny following in convoy. Chain smoking onto his second Rothmans, he offered his pack to his passengers. Raph picked up the phone from the dash board to check with Tony and Todd, who were almost safely back at the Gloucester.

"Do you want me to call Sammy…See if the girl is ok?"

"Nah, leave it. I'll check on her in the morning." Ray replied coldly.

CHAPTER 35

GOLDERS GREEN AND GLOUCESTER

He smiled intoxicated by the alluring figure standing in the bright shiny room, swaggering of extravagant wealth and style. He stood arms folded with his eyes trained between her and the news on the TV. The repeated headline report outside the Soho nightclub, surrounded by a gaggle of officers and news cameras, that had camped outside literally since the initial police response. Questions centred on the severity of the incident, firearms were still a rarity on these shores with concerns that all the gunmen were still at large. Irrespective to Theresa, there was little she could draw from the reports, as to whether any details could assist or would have been some comforting relief, as to what had happened to her husband.

The smart inspector detailed, in front of the lens and boom microphones huddled around him, what to him seemed like an underworld power struggle was played out in front of hundreds of people. The vague information only named two fatalities and three severely injured, with little or no witnesses and also a hint that they had no contact with any of the organisers or the proprietor unavailable for any comment.

They would appeal for witnesses from the nine hundred or so that would have attended the New Year's Eve party. Ray surprised on this, he had initially figured that there was, at an estimate, a two to three thousand capacity at the least.

"Have you tried him again?" He deflected.

"He left his phone here last night." Theresa replied, the concern in her voice, somewhat flittered with guilt, that she had called upon him as the only means for comfort.

"What about the people he worked with?"

"Well there was only really Christopher that new the ins and outs."

"Hmm." He pondered purposefully.

A knock at the door had her eagerly rushing towards it as Ray composed himself with hindsight.

"Good morning! Are you Mrs Theresa Maitland?" He heard from an official sounding voice. She took a long pause as she looked towards the faces with a nervous worry across her face.

"Yes I am…Please come inside." She eventually invited.

"Do you want me to stick around?" Ray offered, stood with a lit cigarette by the kitchen doorway acting with a disguised concern at the face he had just noted from the report on the tele, looking suspiciously at him, with a cute looking uniformed female officer standing beside Theresa.

"And you are?" The inspector queried.

"A friend." He reported innocently.

"We are looking for Solomon, we need to ask him a few questions. Do you know of your husband's whereabouts?" He turned away from the evasive guest and back to who he had initially come to see.

"He never came home, and I'm worried about what happened at the club last night."

"Well we are happy to report that he was not any of the victims of the club shooting, but we need to know if he was aware of anyone that might have wanted to wage war inside his club?"

"We were all seeing in the new year and all ran for the door when we heard the shooting. We were all together but then he got left behind in the crowd."

"Do you know any of the people with him last night. Who did you leave with?"

"I was forced into a taxi by one of his business associates. They told me not to worry, so I came home and waited."

The inspector paced nosily around the large living room,

his eager eye reviewed the framed pictures and the domicile for any clues. Ray looked at him with hidden contempt.

"Did you come home with anyone or speak to anyone to ask about his whereabouts?"

"Yes. I called his driver but got no answer…"

"Listen." Ray interrupted. "We were all at the club last night and as Mrs Maitland said, we all ran to the exit, like everyone else. Until we got to the exit everyone was together it was a scramble for safety to get outside. It was close to a stampede."

"And where did you go following all this?"

"Me and my lot head to our motors and fucked off, to put it quiet bluntly, seeing that the whole night had been ruined."

"And there are people that can vouch for that?"

"Pardon my ignorance…" Ray shrugged his shoulder in vagueness. "But I'm only here to offer support to my friend here. Mr Maitland is probably wondering who would start shooting up his club, on New Year's Eve. We have been there on untold occasions with no agg. So, you need to stop looking into who can vouch for me and find the people who took such a liberty."

"We are doing all that we can. But we need as much information as we can get." Raptured the female officer, diffusing the situation with a compassionate arm on Theresa.

"Please call us when he comes home. Its paramount that we speak to him." She continued.

"If I hear anything I will call you." She led them to the door as an unsociable hint. The inspector stood stubbornly with a distrusting stare towards Ray. He nonchalantly puffed on a cigarette with a condescending look back at him.

"Can I pinch a smoke?"

"Sure. Help yourself." Ray invited and sparked his lighter towards his waiting lips, after removing one from the packet and drew the smoke in heavily.

"Thanks…If you hear of anything that can help us out with this investigation, it will be greatly appreciated." He offered sincerely.

Ray nodded in acknowledgement as he walked towards the door. Theresa looked worryingly back at the inspector and at Ray who stood with a careless arrogance.

"I'm really worried now Ray." She walked over towards him for him to embrace her. With the menacing attraction attacking him relentlessly, he squeezed her body tightly to him. She backed her head away to kiss him, conflicted with more guilt by her actions under the dismal circumstances.

"Look, I'll head back to the manor. I'll speak with Raph and we'll put some feelers out. Ok? I don't know who his enemies are, but we can ask about. We'll need to pull back on our usual business if the gavvers are sniffing about though. But don't worry I'll take care of you." He proposed. She smiled gratefully with understanding.

"Bell me as soon as you get any word." He re-emphasised as he stood on the huge drive.

The illustrious mansion was all the reason that saw to his downfall, his excessive flaunt of wealth. The domicile was a jaw dropping three million pounds, he evaluated and made him wonder prematurely, if she would inherit everything that he owned. Including the Vanity club. He grasped his thick coat against the cold as he started the sporty VW and waved at her as she stood at her doorway.

He cruised down the wintery leafy affluent streets of Golders Green with his phone to his ear as he spoke to Raph.

"Ere how's my luck being there...Old bill came to see her."

"Fuck me." Raph surprised. "How did that go down?"

"Still on the missing list as far as they can gather."

"Good. How is she?"

"A bit worried as you can imagine."

"Well at least you showed your face...And whatever else." He laughed to himself.

"Leave off! I'm not that callous." Ray appraised. "You should see this manor though mate. Fucking Yid country. This is what diamonds and drugs buys you, we need to get involved."

"You wanna slow down. It's hard enough washing what we have."

"Well that's what you are employed to do me old china. Get the laundry done sharpish." He chuckled.

"Cheeky fucker. I'll see you back at the plot and don't forget the old boys will be about this evening."

"Fuck me. Here we go."

"Easy Beefy. I'm sure it's just social." He reassured.

"Do you reckon Sammy said anything?"

"They won't know nothing. Stop worrying."

"You'll be surprised at what they know. They're like Columbo the way they suss us."

"Yeah, well, keep your cool and try not to cave in to them."

He clicked off the call and continued his journey back over to South London.

◆ ◆ ◆

He parked at the Gloucester pub, which was busy with the Palace fans after the New year day fixture against Brighton and Hove Albion. Several drinkers, formed of the usual suspects, stood outside the doorway scanning desperately for opposition. Some of the faces from the congregation acknowledged him, as he navigated around them to get to the entrance. Norma and the new barmaid both vied to get to him his usual tipple from the cold fridge. Norma authoritatively, placed the German bottled lager onto the bar as he propped himself onto a stool to engage them.

"Happy new year darling." He kissed towards Norma, she tip-toed against the bar in her tight black dress to meet him with a smacker, that she always seemed to enjoy. "Has Angie been about?"

"She was earlier, before kick-off helping out." She excused herself to serve the customers patiently waiting, after seeing Mandy was already serving the far side.

Ray knocked back at the beer raising it towards the Akehurst twins, sitting at the large table with some local faces, Danny Blades, Nostrils Pete, Ade, Terry Toes, Robbie Two sides, Fraser, Sommie, Mickey and Clive as they laughed hysterically at whatever story was being told and was about to go over to join them, when he quickly spotted Norma's mother Janet, appear through the crowd of bodies, parting like the waves, with a stack of empties in her hand.

She teetered in leopard print high heels with a low-cut dress that clung to her every curve, her Napier faux pearl necklace transcended her resemblance to a Sean Connery Bond girl, oozing with confidence as she flirted with the riff raff who wolf whistled and made inappropriate comments about her as she past.

"You're old lady here?" Ray smiled towards Norma.

"Yeah she was bored at home. Dad got called out on some shooting in London last night."

"Hello Raymond." She purred.

Ray admired her, in her navy figure hugging micro mini dress that was identical to her daughter's. They embraced when she finally relieved her hands of the empty glasses, easing herself between his legs with a lingering kiss, the charm of her perfume, attested to stir his perversion about her. Her jewellery on her wrist chimed like maracas behind him before she released her welcoming grasp. Ray spun her around for his final seal of approval.

"Mrs Collins! You look fucking great." He cemented.

"Stop with the Mrs Collins." She flirted.

"'Ere Norm. You need to tell the old man he might have some competition."

"Oi! You cheeky sod." Norma laughed. "Will you put him down mum…We need help."

"It's lovely to see you Ray. You are looking well handsome as ever. And my Norma said you are all doing really well."

"Can't complain." He replied confidently. "I'll have a drink with yous later. I'm just waiting for Raph and the rest."

"Aren't they all upstairs?" She quizzed.

"Only Todd and Tony up there at the minute." Norma interrupted.

"I'd much rather ogle at yous pair in your lovely dresses." Ray flirted. Both women laughed, Janet kissed him on the lips again, in his mind, signalled that he could have her if he wanted. She went back around to help behind the bar, as more customers began to pour in. He watched them both sinfully with an imaginary vision of whom to choose, given the option and pointed for another beer. After receiving his refill, he left with his devilish fantasy in his head.

Climbing the stairs to the GBE offices, he found Todd and Tony tag teaming on an unidentified woman, not recognising the only part that he could identify her from, which was her arse, with the scene resembling a dirty movie, he killed the loud music abruptly.

"For fuck sake yous two." He laughed.

"Do you wanna go? She's well game." Todd offered, his face obscene with lust looking back at him, while he pummelled the girl from behind, her moans of pleasure warbled comically, with both returning proud stares at him as they carried on shamelessly. He offered them five more minutes and turned back to make a couple of phone calls.

The tartly clad woman, he recognised as the owner from the Wallington tanning salon, appeared after a few more minutes. Her initial intention was delivering ticket money for one of the South Coast parties and as it now seemed, proving she was open to do whatever was required for GBE. He said hello in surprise at her as she winked a flirtatious greeting back at him.

"I was hoping you would join in. I've heard about that big cock of yours." She teased, as he watched her, a little taken aback, tootle off down the stairs.

"Fuck me. I never would have put her down as that type of lady." He reintroduced entering back into the room.

"It's always the quiet one's Ray. You could have had a slice.

Give her a proper stretching." Tony laughed back.

"Yeah! She told me." Ray chuckled. "And I don't mind yous bending filthy birds over in here. As long as yous wipe your fucking stains up and me Angie doesn't walk in...You slags."

The room aired with laughter. Ray observed the bagged up piles of money on the floor beside the large screen TV.

"What's this doing here?"

"Solomon's drop. We still carry it out yeah?" Tony enquired. "Boycie said he'll ring around, see if there are any of his crew left."

Ray acknowledged proudly, once the penny dropped, that they were covering all the angles to throw off any scent, which to him, will be shy of one hundred grand well spent.

"Get him to bell from phone boxes. Police are still looking for him."

"Good luck with that." Todd sniggered.

By the time Raph and Nathan had joined them followed by Sammy Taxi. It was eight thirty and sounded as if the party downstairs was in full flow. Fifteen minutes or so later Sid, Pete and Tommy Akehurst turned up all looking dapper as per usual looking like Saville row point of sales.

"Fucking gun fight at the O.K Corral." Pete discerned looking around the group suspiciously. "Your subtle ways of doing business eh?"

Ray was up and out of his chair to embrace his uncles in turn and shake Tommy's hand. The unified look they all reflected stood with innocent confusion. Sid sat down in the seat Ray had vacated and lit one of the cigarettes from the pack on the desk.

"What's the crack then boys?" Sid tested.

"Well to me, it looks as though North London are at war again, that's as much as we know." Raph replied confidently.

"Really? During these prosperous times?"

"Well not everyone is included Sid, so maybe people are beginning to take exception. We also got word that he was branching out...Don't know who with." Raph concluded as his best possible explanation.

"We all bolted for the exit and protected him and his Mrs when we saw none of his boys were about, but he insisted in sticking around. It's his club after all. He loves that club." Ray explained.

His uncle's glare burned into him to submission, he stood positive with confidence. They both sat in silence, glaring around at them all for the weakest link, before having to concede by recoiling their suspicion.

"Anyway. Until we know what happened to that flash Greek prick, make sure you take his cut up to whoever the fuck is left in charge over there."

"And then explain yous'll be backing off, until his issues are resolved." Pete relayed in turn.

"100k on the floor right there, we'll make the drop tomorrow night." Ray confirmed.

"Put it in the safe, for fuck sake." Pete ordered after unzipping the bag to see the neat pile of notes. Todd immediately went over and pulled away at the secret wall compartment, behind what appeared to be a fully plumbed in fireplace.

"So, are we going downstairs to have this party or what?" Sid smiled, stubbing the cigarette into the ashtray.

"Let's 'ave it." Todd saluted with a champagne bottle ready for opening. All the men followed them downstairs, Pete still had some business he wanted to discuss as he held back.

"So, what's the news?" He queried.

"News?" They both continued the same air of ignorance.

"Essex. What's the news?"

"Oh yeah...We met with them yesterday morning, but I don't think we share the same interests." Raph declared.

"More to the point, we should stay well clear of them fucking lunatics." Ray confirmed spinning his finger close to his head. Pete looked at them both with some scepticism, then became overcome with pride. Without a word, he turned to make his way downstairs, leaving Raph and Ray behind to secure the door to the office, which was marked with a gold coloured private sign.

"Fuck me. I thought they had sussed us." Ray relieved in laughter as they eventually joined the party downstairs.

CHAPTER 36

JULIET CHARLIE FOXTROT ROMEO

Angie entered the Whitehorse estate's annual New Year bash a little after eleven o'clock. Ray's loving eyes immediately greeted her from his position at the bar, which then turned suspiciously to the dapper looking stranger beside her. He was tall, in a smart navy suit that flaunted his affluence, his lusting hands around her waist. She immediately diverted from saying hello to Janet, Norma and everyone else and rushed over towards him, he was already immorally inspecting the high heeled knee length boots before she even removed her fur coat, to display her beautiful but revealing silk dress, that irked at him like a baseball bat to the head.

"Darling. Happy new year. This is Richard...Richard this is my handsome Raymond." She giggled, kissing him consecutively at his cheek, leaving visible lipstick glowing on his skin. Richard stood with his hand awkwardly outward for what appeared an eternity and immediately felt the hostility. Angie gave Ray that same no-nonsense stern look, with her hands on her hips that demanded compliance, before he returned the gesture with a firm handshake.

"That's better. Now why don't you two get acquainted." She then turned with a smile towards Sid and Pete who embraced her and also directed the same suspicion towards her date. Richard was now beginning to feel totally out of his comfort zone, in a South London pub which was a million miles away from the exclusivity of the Knightsbridge dining institution that he had wined and dined her.

"What's your trade Richard? That's a lovely whistle you have on. I'm guessing..." Ray pondered while he necked some more of his lager. "You are a merchant banker?"

"Not quite. I am an investment banker, with Nomura international. The suit is Armani...Bespoke." He boasted nervously.

"Can I get you a drink?" Ray offered.

Richard strained his ear through the chaos of volumes, from the juke box, clashing with the late arrival disc jockey lining up for his first track. The mix of Showaddywaddy and Salt-N-Pepper mashed with confusion into his auditory.

"A cognac please." He smiled with a pained squint.

"A cognac?" Ray insinuated provokingly with an insolent snobbish tone.

"I understand your reservations about me. Your mother is a wonderful lady and I will respect her honourably, if that's what you are worried about."

"I'm not worried about my Angie. She can look after herself." He pushed the brandy that he ordered across the bar swiftly, with the liquor staining upwards in the glass from the momentum when it came to a sudden stop, on the sticky surface in front of him. Ray, then excused himself, leaving Raph and Nathan continuing politely with idle chit chat to try and make him feel at home after uncharacteristically feeling some pity towards him.

"A word please..." Ray ordered with a jealous grip onto her arm. Sid noticed and looked around the table frustratingly at his brother, Tommy and Sammy.

"This kid won't let go of how that cunt Lester treated her."

"Well he can't keep scaring them off. I'm beginning to lose count." Pete worried.

"I wonder where he is now?" Tommy pondered, reflecting back to when they took him on a transit van ride to the middle of nowhere and left him deserted, after a good shoeing during the journey.

Meanwhile, Ray and Angela were outside, with her trying to appease his concerns, explaining that it was only their second date and no plans on taking it any more serious than dinner and drinks.

"Baby, he's a gentleman and I'm not saying that you have to like him, but you will be polite."

"And then when he fucks off like the rest of them, what then?"

"It's only you that scares them away. Can you at least let me have some fun tonight, instead of you getting angry? Please?"

He looked towards her playful glint in her eyes as she looked up at him, until he slowly simmered his initial temper.

"Come here darling. I know you only want what's best for me." She kissed his lips and embraced him warmly, her long hair sweeping his hands as they caressed against her bare back. They lingered for a while before she let go to return back inside.

Sid called him over, after he diverted to greet other guests that he hadn't seen in a while, to sit with them and persuaded him to drop the evil daggers that he continually sent towards her date, who continually failed to hold any gaze back towards anyone.

"She's a big girl and you're not a baby anymore. Let her have some fun." He commanded.

Norma came over with more drinks for their large table and stroked at Ray's back, already knowing how he felt about Angie having boyfriends.

"I'll have my break in a bit for a chat babe if you want?" She whispered her offer with a compassionate embrace against him as she bent to meet his cuddle.

"Shall we go over the windmill?" He chuckled.

"Does that shelter even still exist?" She giggled back.

With his anger now dispersed and finally concluded, once Nathan and Raph both confirmed, that he was ok by all accounts. Sid and Pete engaged everyone about stories of the nightclubs they once ran, which was a repeated tale they always shared once they had consumed a large amount of whisky. The party flowed with laughter and banter between the younger Gloucester boys and their elder predecessors.

As they consumed more alcohol, they descended into the adolescent antics, with the constant boast to any woman in close proximity, about Ray's Viking sword lodged inside his jeans and which woman had the fittest arse or which one looked like they had the best lips for blow jobs, then regressed onto plans for a boy's only holiday, with the count up of twenty-five to thirty possible takers flying off to the beaches of the Costa del Sol or Ibiza.

Todd, Nathan and Tony sharing details similar to timeshare sales people of past hedonistic travels they had experienced on the Balearics. The wild stories gained momentum as they downed an excess of drinks.

With the night drawing to a close, Angie had made a quiet exit, choosing not to disturb the large group and make Richard any more uncomfortable than necessary, which had not escaped Ray's eyes. Many more had departed to get the beckoning sleep, as a result of the demanding consummation or to head off to all night parties, pairing off with the plethora of pretty females that had constantly flirted throughout the night.

Norma left with Todd after his whispered offer, that she obviously couldn't refuse. It left Mandy and Janet to the task of clearing up. Irish Tommy and Sammy helped with assisting the incapacitated drunks into a fleet of taxis before departing themselves.

Ray was sat on the stairway, having called Theresa who confirmed that she still had no news and was on her way back from seeing Solomon's family in Wood green. She detailed that above the compassion for being the wife of their beloved, they were more reserved with an unwelcoming hostile response about him as though they were not so much concerned, but more in surprise that he had survived his lifestyle that long.

He echoed some sympathy on her, although being drunk and in need of a good fucking with her again, he didn't want to invite a backlash about the inappropriate timing. Surprisingly, there was a point to contemplate, that she had still invited him over. She had to huff a silent disappointment, that he was of no real state to entertain that possibility, on a journey that would take the best part of an hour. Returning to the now empty bar, his only assist, to his best ability, was to help Janet bolt the final locks, seeing off Mandy, after she waited for her boyfriend to pick her up.

"Shall we have that drink?" She purred invitingly, with an enigmatic smile, which he pondered on briefly, with the battle alert from his loins guiding him to see where this could lead.

"I don't know if I should." He replied unassured as she extinguished the main lighting, leaving the soft fluorescent of the bar, shining upon her full-bodied size twelve figure in the tight micro dress. Her legs looked athletically strong from weekly aerobics, pounding thighs holding up a thick round arse, he continued with the constant examination of her enticing physique while her back was turned. She poured herself a G&T and placed a Southern comfort and lemonade on the bar for his consummation, he stared at her like a gallery exhibition. She toasted her glass towards his, her glossy lips pursed provocatively at him, confidence bolstered by the compliments she had received all night and flattered by this situation, when it was clear that there had been an obvious flock of women vying for the chance to spend the rest of the night with him, yet here he stood, with his smitten roving eyes upon her.

"I better have this one and go before…"

"Are you worried about me seducing you Raymond?" She interrupted, with her voice sounding sexily husky from the loud night, as his intentions collided between the good and the bad.

"Worried no. Guilty yes and I have to admit, you look fucking amazing." His saluted compliment was met with her twirling and exhibiting everything for him to admire, returning to look deep into his eyes, she surmised that there was no time for beating around the bush.

"If you must know, because I am sure you must be wondering, a woman like me and an insatiable appetite, with a husband so busy chasing a detective inspector career? One can get very lonely at night." She confessed with a cheeky wink, pausing for him to fill the gap. She leant over teasingly, with her sumptuous breasts almost propped on display on the bar.

Their eyes simmered with contest in the dim lighting, both seemingly debating whether to stick or twist. Her poker face was an easy give away, it wasn't love that she was after, that was a definite. Meanwhile, he struggled in the tug of war with himself as to why he shouldn't oblige.

◆ ◆ ◆

They rode in the hired taxi towards his house, the driver with his eyes trained keenly towards the illuminated streets, while her sexy perfume teased his erection, which multiplied from her tenderly lusting kisses that almost made him explode immaturely inside his pants from the expectant urgency.

The twenty-five-minute ride finally concluded on his drive, with a tenner thrown towards the driver as they disembarked in a haste. He continued to kiss her while he battled to get the keys from out of his pocket, her hand also deep inside his jeans by the time the door was ajar. They accidently toppled backwards by their controlling hungerful groping of each other, resulted in her back crashing the door shut.

Without losing any time, he had her upstairs with a trail of his jacket and her coat, then flopping onto the bed, with her forcefully getting him onto his back and fighting with his jeans to expose the offering she was yearning for all night. In fact, not just the night, for as long as her unquenchable appetite could endure, following lonely rampant nights having her finger herself aggressively for an orgasm.

Her eyes widened hungrily at the sheer size of his throbbing girth and slowly lunged it into her wanting mouth, with a warm scintillating fellatio that curled his toes as he kicked his trainers, then his jeans and pants hurriedly away from his feet.

He squeezed at her firm bosom heaving under her dress as her hot mouth coaxed at his cock majestically, he journeyed his fingers to tangle into her hair, his cheeks puffed from the electrifying sucking she performed. To the point that he could wait no longer, he summoned her away in need of her wet pussy to sit on top of it. Pulling her top down to reveal her fantastic breasts in front of him, he marvelled at how this woman, at the tail end of forty something, had this angelic body of a swimwear model.

"You're fucking so sexy." He panted eagerly.

With her full upper body on parade, her dress was nothing more than a waistband, her eyes closed as she began to ride his erection up and down and became wetter and wetter with his penetration and the way he molested her curvy arse, pushing her downward until he was so deep inside her. She moaned with content, by his impetus fucking of her soaking cunt, his enormous satisfying rod impaling up and down to meet her grinding thrust.

"Squeeze my tits harder." She demanded as he grappled them like a beast. She bounced up and down on him, her hands forcing down onto his chest, her shadowed face almost celestial against the lighting from the hallway, her heavenly lips spilled with filth and curses begging for him to fuck her, repeatedly urging his hardness deeper, never wanting it to stop.

He fucked her front ways and from behind as sweat streamed down as he pumped her with constant velocity, pulling her hair like a forceful insult and uttering dirty words into her ears.

"You love this? Don't yah? Slut." He growled aggressively.

"Oh Yeah." She bemoaned. Her eyes swimming in desire. "Fuck me. You bastard. Fuck my pussy. Fuck me like a dirty whore."

Her spontaneous cursing was like a rhetorical appraising for every motion of his stiff cock, sliding and pounding her, battering her insides with no compassion that she again pleaded for more.

Parting at the silky wetness, his tongue devoured into her after he forced her onto her back again, lapping at her pink swollen clit like a feast. The stimulating passion enveloped her emotionally and made her eyes flicker by his vivacious toying of her pussy, it made her lips tremble from the intensity, feeling like a masterful interlude from the unapologetic roughness from him.

By the time her eyes opened again, his eyes were again looking down at her. She glided her hands along his huge cock, the touch of the sheer size made her dry mouth drool in anticipation, roughly prodding it against her clit that made her pussy gush from the sensation of him guided back inside. Wrapping her legs to clasp around his back championed the pummelling, deep throbbing piston like thrusts, with his hands brutally massaging her breasts. Rigorously moulding them so hard with praise, they would surely be bruised come the morning, such was the ravenous way in which he treated them, her plump nipples were sore from his teeth as he bit them both in turn that sent her mind wild with passion.

Her legs widened to the extent, leopard patterned high heels digging into the fabric of the covers beneath and her nails clawing his back like an angry wildcat. Until finally, his thundering ejaculation blasted inside her with excruciating exhilaration, his face shivered, and his calves contracted mercilessly cramped with fatigue.

Kissing him with appreciation, her simultaneous orgasm felt like a crippling of her insides and shook her scintillatingly all the way to her toes, she nibbled at his soft lips, worshiping from the ecstasy that consumed her as the final stages of their eagerly awaited conclusion had them canoodling with a commentary of heavy breathing. They were now both laid out on their backs gasping for breath, she finally removed the high heels and alleviated from the tight dress over her head to assist her body cooling, which was now burning like a furnace.

Her naked elegance with faux pearls sticking to her neck from the sweat, laid glistening and bare. The orgasm pounding her head elatedly as she kissed his muscular body thanking him for a fuck she would never forget. His cheeks puffed in a somewhat guilty relief, he turned to face her with a drunken grin that combined with the exertion to spin the room.

"Is it okay if I stay for a bit?" She whispered towards him, he studied her face which radiated an unadulterated mature beauty that he pondered on. He could only reply with a nod of his head as he caressed and cradled her, now amazed by how young and soft her body felt. They stroked at each other with comforting touches, that drifted him into a dream, of which, would remain undisturbed, at a contrast to the usual insomnia with his mind racing at a hundred miles an hour, with plots to expand his already expansive empire.

While he snoozed as the alcohol slowly sedated him, she dressed in silence and checked her gold watch at the time and began to plot her excuses, for in case when she arrived home, her husband would interrogate her. Surprised that it was only half past three and timed that she was sure that the way that he had fucked her and the brief time they laid together that it was almost sunrise. She kissed him while he slept and took one last perverted look at his big beastly anatomy and pondered whether to wake him with it in her mouth. She licked her lips provocatively and wished that she had no one to answer to, so she could have another encounter with him battering her while pulling her hair.

The thoughts continued as she went to the hallway and called the mini cab number on the card wedged into the mirror frame on the wall and whispered her address into the phone and the location of her pick-up, which after some hesitation, she finally deciphered from the pile of letters beside the phone.

Peering out of the window with some reluctance about leaving him, wanting to be awoken by his stiff erection inside her again and then making him breakfast after. She shuddered the immature thoughts that clouded sensibility. As the headlights pulled in, she stubbed the cigarette into the ashtray and buttoned her coat with one last pause with confliction, she closed the door behind her to enter the awaiting car.

CHAPTER 37

NOMURA INTERNATIONAL

The job interview although a foregone formality, was clearly out of his comfort zone with the questions being asked of him. With a corporate dialogue prepared for him, he sat up projecting an enthusiasm and kept eye contact with confidence, while he absorbed their voices which might as well had been Japanese. Coincidently, that he was being interviewed for the entry level vacancy at the Japanese bank.

"In five years. I see myself as part of a successful trading team in derivatives. It has been an ambition of mine to understand the workings of the stock market. Ever since the history lesson at my school, about the wall street crash of 1929 and the depression. It truly inspired me about the whole industry. It's the markets that affect the world. This isn't a job for me it is a passion." He applauded himself on the line he had recited, which was one of many sent to him from his mate Jimmy Sargent, from what he remembered at least.

The looks on his assessors appeared less equally as impressed. Alistair Maxwell, a tall lanky individual, possibly Oxford or Eton educated, with a ton of initials after his name, looking pompously disapproving towards him, for no apparent reason. Kelly Rose from human resources seemed to be the assigned spokesperson, conducting the interview discussions and putting forward the questions that bordered the Spanish inquisition, about his strengths, his weaknesses and also the scenario re-enactments, of which, the true answers, outside and away from office etiquette, would result in someone being introduced to a Chelsea smile at the end of his Stanley knife or beaten to a pulp. His mind wandered psychotically to Trevor Lewin's disfigured face, screaming in agony and bawling for his mercy, a smug smile crept across his face, as though relieved after an excruciating hour and thirty minutes, when the interview concluded.

"Thank you for coming along Mr Morgan, we will be in touch with you on whether you have been successful."

They all unitingly stood up and offered handshakes. Escorting him out as though they could not wait to get rid. Ray took no offence, it was lip service after all, so would not take it to heart, in fairness you needed to be exceptionally bright with an economics degree or know very powerful people to land a job like this, even at a basic level.

"Ray Morgan." Came the voice from the bank's senior derivatives analyst James Sargent, walking alongside and immediately introducing him, to the Head of derivatives and commodities, Dellas Edminston.

"What in the earth are you doing here?" He smiled broadly.

The warm embrace had the interviewing staff stood in awe, with surprised looks all over their faces, waiting patiently to continue showing him out.

"I just finished being interviewed for Commodities trader. I was just leaving but it was nice bumping into you." Ray replied.

"Like wise. I've not seen you since…" He pondered.

"God knows…87 Pascha? It's been that long. Look I have to run now. Give us your number and I'll bell you for a catch up and a beer." Ray rushed to speed the conversation on, apologising for taking up their busy day while they waited to see him out.

"Make sure you do. Be lucky." James shouted, after handing him his business card and watched from the top of the stairs as he continued being escorted.

"You know James Sargent?"

"Yes, me and Sarge go way back." His taunting smile painted smugly on his face again at the new implication.

"He is our lead trader at Nomura." Kelly Rose declared, now deciding on polite small talk, worried now that the golden boy of the bank was a friend to the candidate and how it would now be viewed if his application was an unsuccessful one. Apart from his spiel on the history that led to the great depression, it was by far the worst ever interview she had ever conducted.

"Thank you again Mr Morgan. We will be in touch." She smiled and shook his hand again more warmingly this time around. For Ray it was a justifiable exercise to get in on the ground floor and to work his way up, they already had the small investors waiting to piss away the inheritance and life savings to their trusted stock brokers, Keane and White investments, another limited company subsidiary made up by Raph, which listed the umbrella's that totalled around seventeen at the last count. For true authenticity they required a badge and the ugly coloured coat to stand on the trading floor.

Dressed in his expensively smart Paul Smith suit, he flagged the taxi to get to his next appointment. Once inside Sammy passed him his cell phone to check in with James, for a laugh about the look on their faces and to confirm that Kelly from HR, on his recommendation, will be confirming via Nomura headed letter that he had the job by next week, which was music to his ears as he relayed the good news to Sammy.

"See! that's why your uncles wanted you in them books and getting a decent education." He lectured.

"Shut up, you silly cunt." Ray replied, which had them both laughing.

Arriving at New Bond street slightly late, he pressed on the button at One Hundred and eighty-two for Mitchell, Weeks and Holding solicitors and was buzzed in and hit the lift to ascend to the fourth floor.

"Mr Morgan thank you for coming." Greeted Katrina Weeks, one of the senior partners at the law firm. He also greeted Theresa Maitland who was with her late husband's solicitor, Emile Rosenberg from Duncan Lewis and Rosenberg of Golders Green.

"OK...can I get anyone a coffee or a tea before we start?" She offered from the head of the shiny glass conference sized table that they all sat at. Everyone echoed a polite 'no' in the room and went straight into the order of business. Emile had a couple of motions that had little or no interest to Ray regarding Mr Maitland's estate.

The Vanity club of 158 Wardour street had not been reopened since the night of the shooting and the 25-year lease allowed to lapse, to Ray's surprise, Mr Maitland's picture was painted very differently on paper. The details being thrashed out by the two practices over whichever laws or rules that satisfied both parties amicably. Or it be sold to redevelopers who have earmarked the listed property over the last five years, which really gave no value to Maitland's estate and argued by Miss Weeks as a futile fight of ownership, to which, Duncan Lewis and Rosenberg agreed for company director, Mr Nathan Richard Boyce of Gloucester Entertainment Limited, offering to extend the lease ownership for the foreseeable future.

"Company secretary signature for Gloucester Entertainment could you sign your name please here. And here please Mr Morgan. Perfect." She harmonised.

Theresa shot him back with a filthy look of disgust, the way she had leant over him and watched him pause to smell her fragrance before he even lifted his hand to the paper.

"This is the best way forward Mrs Maitland and lifts some of the burden from you. One less thing to worry about." Emile smiled, to which she remained vacantly uninterested with her eyes trained with jealousy at the way she swarmed around him with the paperwork, standing at the desk flaunting her legs.

"Slut." She screamed but it was all inside her head as he purposefully didn't even acknowledge that she was about to leave.

"Thank you for your time. Thank you very much Mr Rosenberg. I'll get the confirmation copy of the agreement to you first thing." She shook both their hands, slightly aghast at the obvious hostility from Theresa before returning back to her client.

"So that's it then?" He smiled standing up to shake her hand that lingered somewhat inappropriately.

"Congratulations." She smiled, with her eyes bright with satisfaction on closing yet another deal. Ignoring what she had inoculated more times than she could remember, from her rich alpha male clients. The hourly rate was worth the while.

"So?" He flirted with almost a natural habitual need with any woman to do so. And laughed when she acknowledged his trademark and regular innuendoes.

"If you had breasts you might stand a chance."

"I know...so you keep saying. I still reckon I could turn your persuasion."

"Good day Mr Morgan." She again empathised with an uncontrolled smile. He shook her hand again and returned to the street. Sammy had spun around after ignoring several hand waved requests even though his amber light was off. Ray jumped into the back seat and admired the gorgeous legs already inside.

"Head to the Park Lane Hilton." He ordered before he greeted her with a kiss.

"I thought you were gonna wait around to fuck her. Drooling over her the way you did. You pig."

"You'd have more of a chance than me." Ray smiled with a cheeky wink. It took a while for her to get the hint.

"Noooo?" She surprised.

"Oh yeah. She's a lesbo, carpet muncher."

"Hmm. You should have invited her. I always fancied a threesome with another woman."

"Mmm. Me and all."

Theresa straddled on top of him and began to grind herself in anticipation.

"Well Mr club owner. Maybe tonight but I have to choose her." She purred sexily into his ear.

"Make sure you dress to kill then and we'll see. I can't wait to ravish you again."

"You'll get a hard on the minute you see me."

"Can't I just fuck you now?"

"No, I have some very important people to meet first. You will have to wait." She whispered alluringly, stroking at his bulging front.

"Make sure you check me in for the Penthouse, for the afterparty." He placed a big wad of notes into her hand to secure the reservation

"If you think I'm sharing you with one hundred other people tonight, you may as well drop me off here." She teased offering the cash back to him, her order non-negotiable.

"Ok...Just for us then, to get down and nasty yeah? Champagne on ice and all that?"

"I'm going to fuck you senseless." She surrendered.

"I can't fucking wait to plate you." He slid his finger into her wetness and tasted the already heated moisture from her.

Sammy was distracted by the sensual performance, watching Ray's hand caressing her bottom, bewildered at the morality. As the taxi waited at the red light, she stood up while he assisted holding her. She lifted her skirt to remove her knickers, ignoring the shock from other road users, who just about managed to glimpse inside. She climbed back on top of him, holding up her amorously scented underwear to dangle in front of his nose, that he took a deep perverted inhale of. They played this sexual tease with one another until they pulled up to the destination. She stepped out with them both watching her sexy walk into the late afternoon crowd.

CHAPTER 38

THE VANITY

The club was all dressed up and resembled a lavish looking ballroom or as exclusive as the private members club owned by the Bryans during their heyday and a far cry from the working-class tack of their local. Suited and booted, everyone associated with GBE and all the subsidiaries, done them all proud, as they entered to a round of applause.

"You all look a million dollars." Ray beamed towards them, Nathan looking overly emotional with his name on the dream he yearned for over the last year.

The Vanity club's re-opening night was far removed from the dance party scene, at least for the first night, this was an invite only R.S.V.P black tie and cocktail dress event, with no expenses spared. Sid, Pete, Sammy all the Akehurst's, Tommy, Jackie, Bev and the twins. Robbie, Janet and Norma Collins. Nathan, Todd and Tony, Irish Tommy and many faces of the South London underworld. Sharon, Tania and Jenny along with the majority of the Whitehorse estate. With many of the representatives of the Acid house party organisations, made up a who's who of the dance music industry, celebrities in their own right. All the staff from the salons, arcades, public houses, car showrooms attended, with praise for their bosses, their employers, The Gloucester boys. Camera flashes exploded for most of the night to capture memories for all involved. Champagne and exotic cocktails were aplenty for everybody who wanted to have a good time and take advantage of the open bar.

"I'm so proud of you Raymond." Angela beamed, her stunning red dress forced lusting and envious eyes from the mixed crowd. Ray spun her around with compliments, in agreement with the men and women in attendance.

"I didn't do all this alone, this is all Raph and the boys. Without them I'd have nothing." He reflected grabbing Todd who just happened to walk by. "This man especially."

They both embraced rocking each other from side to side, a teary-eyed Angela joined in with a heartened kiss at both of them. Todd's kiss lingered as an inappropriate laugh at his friend's expense. Tony, Nathan and Raph were also over as they group hugged with cheers and laughter as more champagne was handed around.

"Listen up. Listen up. Boys! Ladies, gentlemen and horrible bastards." Raph began. "I don't know what to say, other than, I fucking love all yous with all my heart. We've been through and I will continue to go through a hail of bullets for any one of yah. I'd die for you all. And Raymondo...Our moody Swordsman. Who'd have thought, we'd still be friends after I kicked shit out of you the first day we met?"

Everyone fell about laughing, while he dodged a playful lunge at him. The area downstairs had everyone looking upwards at them, while Raph gave his speech after Sid had repeatedly hushed at everyone for Raph to continue.

"Raise your glasses to The Gloucester, all the boys, Sid and Pete. Sammy Taxi, Tommy. The Naden Brothers, Angie, The Whitehorse and everyone here tonight. It's been a massive team effort. Here's to us all. Here is to the Vanity club which I can proudly announce as ours."

The room erupted in cheers. Raph, Ray and everyone hugging again, Angela fanning tears of pride as she clung to him as more cameras illuminated the upstairs and downstairs before the lights went down and the music began with Fabio & Grooverider introducing a smooth rare groove classic.

Ray spotted her as their eyes met and adorned her from afar, in the breath-taking, mouth drooling, little black number. The dress covered her like a vogue model. He followed her graceful stride feeling the urge inside for her, he excused himself through a crowd to greet her, with her sumptuous kiss raising a bit of a concern for people who knew who her late husband was.

"Aren't you going to introduce me." Angela asked sarcastically.

"This is Theresa. I'm surprised you didn't recognise her. She's from the manor." Ray replied.

"It's me Angela, Betty's daughter. I lived on the Whitehorse...A few years ago." Theresa interjected.

"Oh my god. Yes, I do remember now. I didn't realise you was the same Theresa my Ray used to talk about."

"And you are still looking beautiful. You always were." She complimented, kissing her on the cheek. "I love that dress."

"Thank you darling...Yours is absolutely stunning." She replied. The low back and revealing front of her Paul Gautier dress left little to the imagination. Raph pulled Ray away for a word while the women nattered away.

"Look mate...I'm not wanting to stamp on your heart strings. Sammy told me all about your little performance with her earlier, but it's a bit strong, her being all over you like that. In here of all places."

"Who the fuck care's eh?" He laughed. "It's not like I'm bending her over in full view...I was just happy to see her."

"You may as well raise the flag pole, nicking the club and all. It's so blatant. Just be...you know. Just hold it down a bit, before people start talking."

"I will..." Ray reassured. "But at the end of the day. Fuck 'em all. We are the fucking Gloucester. Top boys, everyone knows that." He boasted kissing him flush on his lips to Raph's playful protest.

After seeing Theresa and Angela having a good time, getting on like a house on fire, he decided on seeing this as a good opportunity to mingle, and went around greeting everyone else, including Jenny, who was far from impressed about the lack of attention he had given to her. Following a few words in her ear, reduced her to force back tears at his insensitivity, that more or less amounted to keeping her mouth shut or leave, he went over to Sid and Pete and the rest of the guys.

"Fucking loud in here ain't it?" Sid discerned giving him a big hug.

"What's the matter with yah. Didn't yous used to run clubs?"

"We never had all this mad jungle music smashing our heads in though. Plus we just sat upstairs away from it all." Pete laughed.

"Yeah? Well Nathan will get the offices sorted and an extended closed off V.I.P area and a green room behind the DJ stage. A little freshen up here and there, this place will look the bollocks." Ray prided but between the loud music and the information, neither Pete nor Sid were too interested in at this present time, most of it went over their heads, Sid was also distracted by the approaching Jimmy Newport.

"You remember Jimmy Newport." Sid interrupted.

"How can I forget. How are you Mr Newport." Ray greeted respectfully.

"Marvellous turnout." He appraised half-heartedly shaking his hand. "Is there somewhere quiet where we can have a talk."

"Certainly Mr Newport, follow me." Ray beckoned him down and across the dancefloor. Followed by scorching looks of resentment from Jenny and contrasting worry from Sid and Pete.

They walked towards the back of the club, to a stairway leading up to the old offices and storage spaces on the upper floors. Raph watched worryingly from the upstairs V.I.P with Nathan.

"Excuse the mess in here. Nathan is having some changes made. Utilise more to accommodate more." Ray explained.

"Ok let me start by saying well done, for how you boys have risen and established yourselves as excellent businessmen."

"Thanks Mr Newport. That means a lot."

"Just between you and me. I spoke to your uncles and they said they have me blessing to ask. Because as you know, I have to ask. From the horse's mouth."

"What do you need to know?"

"Solomon Maitland, he didn't have many friends but the ones that he did have aren't very happy."

"Well I'm hoping myself, Raph and the boys are considered in that same vein."

"Of course, but this thing with you and his widow?"

"Widow? I don't know what you mean."

"Ok let me be blunt. Solomon goes on the missing list, I assume dead, seeing that most of his firm have been wiped out by gun shots or electrocution or by bolts of lightning."

"Such a bad run of fortune over there." Ray sympathised.

Jimmy Newport paused to light himself a cigarette and offered the silver cigarette case towards him, which he declined.

"And now you have the club. You see...tonight must have taken some planning. People are putting two and two together."

"Firstly, we came to the rescue, because otherwise they would have turned this place into some arty farty theatre. We've kept it under the same vein. Mr Maitland had very successful nights and this is just a good bit of business." Ray explained.

"I'm talking about you and her. People know, and people are asking questions."

"Ok! I understand where you are going with this. And I hold my hand on my heart..." Ray gestured with hand on his chest. "Despite how it looks, please, tell everyone asking the questions. To stand on me, if they have any concerns over matters that are of no concern to them...I'll happily stick a gun in their mouth and tell them what's what." He gave a broad smile of no compromise that had Jimmy looking at him dumfounded.

"Ok Son...Just letting you know."

"And I'd appreciate, as a favour to my uncles. If you can provide me with the names on all the misinformed and I'll happily put them straight."

Jimmy gave him a long stare back and began to walk back downstairs and back into the main club. Ray followed close behind and went back to the VIP, with Raph and Nathan looking towards him with concern. Ray went past them all to Theresa who gazed forlornly towards him, breaking her concentration away from Angela, with a fuck the world assuredness, he embraced her with roving hands and kissed her full and lovingly onto her lips to everyone's surprise. Sid with his usual glare made his way towards the upstairs after shaking hands with Jimmy, who then quickly departed.

"Fuck are you playing at Ray?" Raph protested. Grabbing him away with a disguised embrace.

"Stop fucking worrying will you. It's a party." Ray smiled above his annoyance, then turned back to Theresa. Raph turned to Angela to have a word, maybe she would talk sense into him.

However, she was also acting a little out of character and appeared to be spreading peace and love to everyone that she became engaged with. He looked over towards anyone who he could share all his concerns with, one appeared in the form of Sid, whose frown did not replicate that he was having a good time. Looking none too pleased.

"You ok Sid?"

"I'm ecstatic boy. Can't you tell?" He stormed sarcastically. "Your little mate just basically told Mr Newport to go fuck himself."

"About her?" Raph indicated towards them.

"Speak to him Raph. You have his ear, I don't want to keep giving him the speech. The reason you can operate at this level is because of Newport."

"Don't worry, I will. Let him enjoy the night and I'll speak to him."

Downstairs Jenny after shrugging away her disappointment was on the dancefloor with Bev and Sharon, feeding off of the nice vibe from the new doves. The provocative music had everyone in the crowd uplifted, she danced with a sexy rushed feeling on her face that Bev and Sharon noticed her feeling inspired by the heartfelt music coming from the speakers.

"You alright there Jen?" Bev enquired.

"Yeah…fuck him and that whore. I feel fucking amazing. Have you tried one of them new pills? Oh Mate." She purred and continued to dance with her chest heaving and her body exhilarated from the exstacy.

It soon became apparent that the pill was being introduced by Todd as the party took on the feeling of a full-blown rave. Sid, Pete and most of the older Gloucester gentlemen had already left, leaving the young loved up generation behind to party. Angela remained embraced by hugs and emotional whispers from Theresa, dancing together in the upstairs V.I.P. Ray and Raph were sat on the luxurious leather seating, looking upon them as if at a strip club. Ray had several rushes from his ecstasy tablet that first Todd and then Theresa had force fed him and left him blowing out labouredly as the drug took effect on him.

"These pills Raph. Fucking blinding mate." He smiled. "I fucking love all yous."

"I'm fucking off me nut here boy." Raph confirmed in reply. His eyes rolled insanely as was Tony's sat beside him, who after a while, could no longer hold back from the way the bassline and melodies forced him onto his feet, with his hands in the air praising the almighty. Theresa and Angela danced together provocatively under the club lighting shimmering off of their dresses, that rose upwards with seduction from their hands on each other's sun kissed legs, alluringly tempting and now joined by a host of scantily clad females, that were led upstairs by Todd and Nathan into the middle of them, all gyrating to the music.

"Me and Theresa are going for some air are you coming?" Angela purred to him after a while, stumbling slightly which made Ray catch her onto his lap. His embrace formed around her waist.

"Woah. Steady on Angie." Raph laughed.

"How are you feeling?" Ray whispered, his hand stroking against her soft skin.

"I feel fucking amazing…I should never have got on this. That Theresa is a really bad influence."

Taking her seat next to him, Theresa began to stroke at his leg and kissed him seductively. And kissed at Angela's shoulder as she formed her arms around both of them.

"Let's go." Ray commanded into Theresa's ear.

"Angie's coming." Theresa purred and grabbed her by the hand and led her to follow him down the stairs. The music got louder with more bass, as the dancing crowd whooped at every new drop that the DJ's played. He ignored having the good manners to say goodbye to everyone, with his mind only focussed on fresh air and respite from the pounding speakers.

They entered the night air with some relief as the cool night stroked kindly at them. In a hail of giggles, the two women linked arms in a staggering tipsy stupor, they flagged down an approaching taxi which rushed towards them in a desperate claim for the fair. They all fell into it, onto one another as their unsteady state had them tottering like toddlers.

"Park Lane hotel." He just about managed to remember where they were going, grabbing at the door handle steadying himself to slam it shut before it shuddered away.

"You are with us tonight." Theresa smiled suggestively.

Ray withdrew a large packet of cocaine and shared a scoop with the women, their already heaving bosoms radiated with the charged-up elation that encapsulated them.

The taxi driver professionally focused on the road and navigated through the traffic, which sped rapidly past their eyes, the west end scenery flashed by like a film on fast forward. They reached their destination in what seemed like seconds and entered the hotel, Ray, with a woman on each arm, they appeared to be holding each other up, as they staggered through the lobby.

CHAPTER 39

PENTHOUSE PASSION

Entering the elevator with the cocktail of champagne and narcotics sloshing inside them, lusting for him, Theresa began to kiss at his lips, she pressed up against him. Angela's hazy eyes stared hungrily at the couple embraced and felt Theresa's hand run inappropriately up her inner thigh which brought on a wave of desire, she then paused to accept Theresa's lusting lips onto hers. She openly welcomed with her warm tongue between giggles as he complimented them on how great they both looked.

The lift came to a relieving halt at the penthouse suite level. They all exited together, the women hanging off of each other. Theresa's hand stroking at Angela's bottom, lifting up her hem line to feel her soft skin as he swayed in front of the door searching for the key. He tapped with a gold V.I.P card onto the reader that opened them up to a splendid layout of red velvet, draped around black leather furniture, and silk satin sheets.

Awaiting champagne bottles in branded buckets, filled with ice, had corks immediately released up to the ceiling without further ado. He captured the overflowing bubbles at the bottle neck with a quick slurp, then began to pour. The evening's excess had him lurching drunkenly back and forth towards the glasses on the table. Sudden fully charged violins began to bellow ambiently, to introduce Lenny Kravitz's 'It ain't over.' flowing through two pillar-like speakers, that she clicked on from the remote control on a wall panel beside the super king-sized bed. The rhythm of her hormones had her sassing to the sultry tones, with sheer lust in her eyes. She climbed onto the midnight black satin sheets, designed for romantic anniversaries or unscrupulous affairs. He rocked in time to the music, their private extended party began to take its course.

'So many tears I've cried...So much pain inside...' he followed the chorus, rocking over exaggeratedly from the pill to the tempo, he turned to see them both embraced like lovers on the bed. His conflicted mind had him gulping the glass in one quick guzzle and sat down on the red velvet chaise longue, situated at the right-hand corner of the bed, almost positioned with purposeful foresight to spectate at the iniquitous performance. The thoughts in their spine-tingling heads as they now openly desired on one another, whispering words inaudibly, hands began caressing breasts, turning each other on. Like a debate between their souls, between their kisses, a tactful conclusion to comply to her needs that hungered so desperately for him, Angela declared her well-kept secret about him into her ear.

Nothing had prepared him for this, although the devil inside his head began to lust at their beautiful bodies cavorting in his full view. They caressed in front of him in a haze, from what he saw as a friendly exchange between the two of them, had become a fantastical dream from an X rated movie. His head shook with a bewildered aura as the loud music thumped into his ears. He puffed breathing heavily, watching them, his cock bulging unethically at the pernicious sequence he viewed.

Theresa began by commanding Angela's damp folds with her tongue, lifting up her dress as her legs parted to welcome her. She made good on her wish to do it with another female, with this sexy mature, now writhing under her masterful tongue, manipulating her clit, sending Angela's hands tangling in her hair. Theresa's eyes peeped seductively at Ray, sat watching perversely, demanding him to review how she could seduce and have anyone yearning for her touch. Angela played with her breast and sucked at and squeezed her nipples, the hedonistic pill and the lavishing licking navigating between her thighs, made her body tense and her mouth moaning with pleasure, Theresa's tongue was teasing, north to south, purring with pleasure from her feminine essence.

The room was spinning faster as his head filled with ambivalence as he watched them and slurped at the Courvoisier and champagne cocktail he had now concocted, met with the sharp line of cocaine that hit and tickled the back of his throat, with his bulging eyes locked onto the passionate bodies cavorting on the bed. She beckoned him invitingly to come closer, which he obeyed hypnotically when she began her ascension up Angela's curvaceous body.

Elevating their dresses, both women's hair fell erotically messy and wild, pearls and diamonds dressed their sexy necks. Their alluring eyes colluding to entice his soul to follow them to a heavenly hell. Theresa was on her knees in front of him on the bed and began his slow undress as he wobbled ungainly, he shrugged his shoulder to release one sleeve and the next. With a power surging down to his cock as she forced down his shirt and pulled at his trousers.

He assisted himself with the rest as both women seduced him with selfish kisses between themselves again, like a mouth-watering recipe on this huge sized bed. The £2000 a night penthouse was descending towards a venue for an unimaginable sin. She yanked at his underwear to pull him forward, bracing himself from crashing into them with strong arms over their entwined bodies, he kissed at the bare skins beneath him. An incestuous inhibition berated inside his head, begging that she came to her senses first, at a stage when narcotically, sensibility and morals vacated him. She was lost from any integrity by her love starved tingling. A devious wanting of her tantalising body threw him into a similar vein, with an undeniable desire that imprisoned his mind as it craved for her.

There had been a sex hungry devil inside Theresa that wanted to see this little experiment through, as he snuggled in between them invitingly, descending his underpants, unfurling his fierce erection baiting for intimacy. Angela was so turned on by his body with a drunken incest that was urgently awed by his length and began her point of no return as she stroked at his stiffness.

"I want to share his big cock with you." Theresa declared her risqué fantasy to all, kissing at his mouth, to his chest and all the way down. Gaping deep into Angela's eyes, with his mouth-watering bulging girth inviting their attention. Angela bit her lip at the tempting wish, watching Theresa as she licked at it willingly as it twitched in expectation, then into her mouth yearnfully, then offered some to Angela who moaned with joy at his taste.

His eyes closed from the eroticism of the forbidden anticipation. Another rush from the drugs, coaxed his manhood to throb as the humid saliva of their beautiful mouths in turn coaxed him rigid with lust. Angela's lips vibrated with appreciation, taking him deep into her throat.

His own combination to pleasure, had him guiding his desperate hands onto their breasts, each nipple in turn pinching them, Angela knelt upright to lean her cups into him, arching her back, flicking her hair as the eroticism bayed her on. The room echoed with sexual tension and perversion as their voices goaded with sin above the bass tracks that pumped with a sexy R&B rhythm.

At a point of the expectant twinges as they suckled their mouths up and down his length. They turned attention up his body as it ached from the masterful foreplay. Now both vying for his tenderness, Theresa masturbated him, his girth expanding inside her palm, urged hungry kisses onto Angela that was passionate and warm. Their tongues danced with sexual delight, she mewed in need for him.

The evening was totally out of control now, a filthy lusting took over when the bolt of passion had him guiding her onto her back with Theresa spurring them on like an influencing, all controlling, serpent of desire, she helped guide him into her and began to masturbate herself with a perverse craving and wanting, while watching Angela's eyes roll with horniness, her face became washed with heavenly pleasure to the sensation as he fucked her. Feeling the fierce size of him stretch her to send the most illicit shivers down her spine. Her legs widened, welcoming as her pleasure multiplied with every stroke.

"Fuck her baby. She feels good, doesn't she?"

"She feels so fucking good." He groaned as the soaking wet arousal wrapped warmly around his cock.

"Oh yes…Like that…just like that." Angela cooed softly, pouting O's of pleasure with simmering eyes. Theresa leant over to kiss her amorously. Angela's breathing strayed erratically, her lips stroking at Theresa's then magnetised onto his as they entwined with the most wicked passion. His muscular body hammered between her legs in a drunken cloud of hot-blooded compulsion.

"Kiss her gorgeous lips. She is so fucking gorgeous." Theresa leered at them feverishly.

He obliged willingly, continuing the kissing of her luscious mouth passionately and fucking her warm wet pussy as hands stroked tenderly at his back between the clawing.

"She wants you so bad. Fuck her deep." Theresa continued her fiendish coveting commentary.

"Suck my tits." Angela begged for his teasing mouth, sucking and biting her plump nipples, as the pressure built inside her. She reached down to plunge at her wetness, at the pooling from his tremendous fucking, then tasted her sticky fingers, sharing onto his tongue, kissing more hungrily at his beautiful lips.

"Fuck her harder. Make her cum all over your big fat dick." Theresa wished under her breath as the turn on choked inside her throat.

Angela felt him spearing inside of her with rigour, spurred on by the filthy lustful look on her face, so sexy.

His hulk like rod seem to expand with the deep

penetration that made a heatwave of desire beat inside her heart, the scintillating fucking emasculated her completely, like she had never felt before, the sound of their bodies colliding reverberated with her juices caressing his pounding, her arse left the bed when she arched upwards to meet him, now ready to cum in an instant. Theresa sang to it like an aficionado, cheerleading from the sides, stroking tenderly at her own wet folds with her fingers. Her body began to shake beneath him as her orgasm drew close.

Biting her lip, she clenched against him like a hot wet vice, the powerful orgasm lingered with force, her body shivered, like an imploding ricochet sent through it by his jack hammer thrusting, that she yelled at with a satisfied scream. The ecstasy pill hit him with another strong wave, his glistening rigid rod eagerly attested now for Theresa, shining with the slick from Angela's cum, she leant back, kissing her, then kissing him, with a unified pleasure. She began to play with her own pussy supremely with a wanting patience for him, as he broke away from Angela to sink his cock hungrily inside Theresa and began to pump with a marathon stamina into her soaking wet cunt that devoured him, his thickness now sending Theresa's head spinning and cursing his brutal cock inside.

Angela turned to admire the erotic vision of the sex in front of her, bodies sparkling from sweat, she teased at her beautiful nipples, with his hands diverting onto her sumptuous breasts with tentative strokes as she purred alluringly as the room bayed in a chorus of perversion, applauding a beauteous immorality.

"Fuck my wet pussy." Theresa rudely begged.

"Oh Yeah, she's soaking for you baby. Look at you." Angela's copycat goading was filthy with desire, inspired by the sexy brunette that he pummelled and began toying with her pussy in time, as the fuel of alcohol and drugs inside her berated hedonistically, she stroked his face with loving passion, shivering with jealousy, recovering from his onslaught and thirsty for more.

The sound of their vulgarity triggered his fully loaded balls, his eyes rolled, intoxicated by her silky quim, he pulled from inside her, her soft hands assisted his throbbing girth to spurt hot white semen violently onto her breasts as she leant into him, priding them to soak in his cum. The joint combination of the concoctions inside him, sent a rasping croak of pleasure out of his mouth from the most ecstatic he had felt as she drained every lasting drop, his arse cheeks clenched, and cock shook with electricity from her tongue, licking him and flicking at his slit. All erupting in synchronous, rapturous, loud and joyous, chorus of groans ululating from them.

Angela assisted alternately onto hers and then Theresa's to extend and for her to climax again. Theresa squirted a volcanic burst from her pussy perversely, drenching Angela's fingers and the expensive sheets, from the turn on of his ejaculation that covered her, that she used to lubricate her fingers to share onto her tender clit. His tongue lapped at the silky soaking nectar that had gushed from her hole, like a dehydrated journeyman, she also stroked at the hot sticky wetness for her own thirsty mouth. Angela began to kiss her, to share the extraction that glistened on her lips and breast like an exotic trail, while he watched appraisingly on his knees.

The sinful orgy was over, he collapsed in-between them as they held hands almost covenant, locking their fingers and spaghetti of legs together, sapped with exhaustion, the women either side of him, they all laid strewn naked in bed, deluded of consequence or guilt, as the night had come to an end under the sheets.

CHAPTER 40

THE MORNING AFTER

Her head pounded for a split second as she adjusted her eyes to focus and regain her bearings. The view of just an expansive room computed without recognition, her head slowly levelled unable to recollect, to figure out where she was and why she can't remember even getting into this bed. Fear encapsulated her, if she had been taken advantage of. Previous horror stories began to grip her as she gradually peered sheepishly behind her after checking her bared body, more fear crept at her in slow motion, first to where she was last night and then to who she was with. It became all a confusing combination, why the fuck was she naked in their bed? This was enough for her to slip gently out of the covers, her body weak through the unknowing, the hangover or whatever it was he had done to her. Anger frustration and guilt battered into her in one gaping swoop.

"Please don't wake up." She repeated as she hunted for clothes. Her dress and her shoes were scooped up, her bra laid on the floor at the side where Theresa slept, her face snoozed with a peaceful beauty almost angelic, retrieving the separated underwear, she began the hunt for her clutch bag that was somehow covered by his underpants on the table, which had also disturbed the unused lines of coke. She seethed at the powder, blaming it for this predicament she now found herself in.

More confusion elevated she couldn't even remember, whether she wore a coat, cursing under her breath, the feeling of death warmed up doubled the anxiety of having to escape now into the public. Scantily dressed always looked distasteful in the morning, the perception of the misdemeanour that had brought her to this point and now having to parade shamefully for the whole world to judge. Being dressed so inappropriately, never alluded to a person that bore any thought to the consequence, that presented you there at a moment in time like this. She couldn't care less of her appearance, this was a deeper shame, way past the tell tale signs of the messy hair and stale mascara.

The exact time was evasive, daylight was slowly creeping in, but the twilight could be introducing dusk or dawn as she nervously sought out her possessions. She shot a glance back towards the bed with more relief and disbelief, unable to fathom how in the world she has awoken naked in bed with them, she could only surmise of a worst scenario. The large door closed with a sophisticated pump into the frame that shook him awake, in his own confusion, gathering his bearings and the flock of hair beside him was enough comfort to send him back to sleep.

Alighting from the lift, the thirty second ride ended with food for thought that spilled with chapters comparable to the doomsday book, flooding her with consternation and denial, how could she even had considered that. An inevitable must have played out in that room, it was like a confetto of emotions that immersed her head. She was weak enough to succumb and she knew it, days and nights with her inappropriate yearn for him, his jealousy of her being with anyone, his eyes, the way they captivated on her...

The accent calling out her name escaped her at first. She stood outside catching her breath as the crisp air attacked the light skimpy fabric, her face and bare legs.

"Angela." He called out again, she turned towards him like a bolt out of the blue.

"Lester? Oh my god." She surprised and really didn't know what else to say at this point to the tall dreadlocked man.

"Long time?" He was dressed smart in a black roll neck with grey slacks, his hair dangled over his shoulders like thick vines but the bizarreness of him standing there had her dumfounded.

"What are you doing here?"

"I and I was just here pon som business, nutting special." His voice instantly triggered forgotten memories, unwittingly that voice was always soft during conversation, harmonically even, it was his tone and spiel that drew her towards him many moons ago. His stare burned towards her almost seeking the truth in her eyes.

"Don't ask." She replied before dismissing him hurriedly. "Look...It's lovely to see you... I have to go."

"Wait...Wait nah?" He pleaded, following behind her. "Let me give you a ride home."

He pulled at her arm as she continued walking away from the rank of taxis that were available but nothing at this time could settle her into a rational thinking, where exactly was she walking to at god knows what time in the morning.

"My car right dere so. Come Angela." He begged again persuasively, leading her by force, blocking her path like a sheepdog. She was soon sunk into the leather as he purred his car away with a secret smile, reminiscent of the good times. With an almost auto pilot, he navigated towards Victoria bridge.

"You look well." She finally broke her silence after absorbing the metal Mercedes badge prominent at the front like a scope on a sniper's rifle. A big gold bracelet hung on his wrist and clattered against leather and metal as he changed up and down through the gears.

"Me can't complain y'know Angie...You look good as well."

"Still the man of mystery I see...What have you been up to...I haven't seen you near on fifteen years and that's all you can tell me?" She shed away her concerns that kept her quiet for half the journey, partly looking for reasons, had he changed or was this the same toxic and abusive Lester Morgan that she had dated for three and lived with for five years respectively, he seemed unrecognisable or maybe she was, because of how she felt, digging for a new reaction, an apology maybe but nothing was forth coming.

"You forget? How's Sid and dem man?" His question rattled with cynicism. It was not his decision to leave and wasn't a topic he was willing to entertain.

"I'm sorry." She conceded.

"If you must know. A Tufnell Park I live?"

"That's nice..." She replied.

"Big house me have... I just do some wheeling and dealing and keeping low profile." Lester confessed boastfully, he left his comment up in the air for her to ponder. Despite the way he was treated, he proved at least to himself that he could still make it on his own, without being bossed about, leaving that environment all them years ago had done him the world of good, with good fortune along with it.

"I'm glad everything worked out for you."

The next forty minutes was just the polite conversation about nothing in particular, he wasn't conversing as though he wanted to reveal what he had done for the past years, following his escort out of the flat they once shared all them years ago. She remained coy about her situation, the lack of forthcoming was not as a tit for tat, it was more to a point about how she hated herself, for what she couldn't remember about the night before.

More lingering thoughts consumed her about the lad she claimed was his and reflecting on that fact, the miscarriage caused by one of his beatings, the softened blow was Rita's providing the perfect cover after her death, that only her and Sid and so it seems Pete knew about and now also the coincidental anxiety of getting this lift home from him made the journey the longest car ride she could ever have imagined.

"Pull over here please. Yes, right here." She insisted, indicating a few doors down from her address purposefully. "You better go before anyone sees you. Thanks for the lift."

"Hold up deh woman..." He grabbed her hand before she could exit.

"You had that whole journey to say what you wanted to say. I have to go now."

"It's just…Me haven't seen you fe a long time and you look so good."

"That's so bloody typical Lester Morgan. I look so good that you haven't even asked me anything about your son?"

She paused with the reality of her conniving contradiction immediately as it left her mouth. She shook away his hand and slammed the door to partially run down the street, slamming the gate and feeling now like an absolute out of control wreck. He watched her with a hopeless bewilderment.

"Nice Yard." He smirked to himself with the door number that confirmed her address, he will give her some time, she was obviously in a high emotional state, like the fifteen years they had been apart had not changed her, still reckless and he could sense it was still due to drugs or drink or both. This was a stroke of absolute luck, as he pressed the on button on his phone with red LED's flashing five missed calls. He returned them, ringing back a very irate companion, he was missing the best part of an hour and left her still waiting in a room at the Park Lane hotel, four floors below the penthouse that was again beginning to stir as daylight battered its way through the curtains.

Recovery from these heavy nights were never previously this painful following the semi overdose of Courvoisier, Dom Perignon, cocaine and two of them dove marked tablets had thrown his cohesion and emotional state into something similar to 9.9 on the Richter scale. His eye blurred into vision onto Theresa, fully dressed looking less of a sophisticated sex kitten of the previous night.

"My fucking head." He complained.

His awakening changed her complexion from fire to one of mischief, her own thoughts now worried as to Angie's clandestine departure, more overtly what kind of reaction there would be after the fallout. She walked and sat at this side of the bed stroking his hair.

"Do you remember much of last night?"

"Huh..?" He replied totally confused. "I can't remember a fucking thing."

She kissed him caressingly, looking at him, he was unable to focus for too long, squinting his eyes. She pondered on the acts they performed last night which was also a matching blur. However, with some conflict surrounding the threesome, if he didn't remember getting it on so illicitly with his mother or whether the secret she let on to her, was to help exonerate her from the passion she felt to partake in a taboo. If it was a true secret that she shared, would this be the best time to console him whatever the true perspective, how would you deliver either way, that punching blow that he had or had not fucked his own mother. Both thoughts turned in her stomach like an aftertaste.

"I have to go." She stressed disappointedly.

"Wait! I'll drop you home..." He began to get himself up with a struggle. She restrained him, reminding him where he was and that he did not have a car to drop her.

"Silly...We're at Park Lane darling. I'll get a taxi."

There still appeared to be a complete blackout, that she wondered whether this was down to a realisation of his actions or he truly forgot. She remembered and replayed the hot sexual scene back inside her head of how strong his desire was to fuck them both. That fiendish addictive desire and utterly exotic turn on of his incestuous frolic, made her stir with wetness that battled whether to strip and fuck him again. The result of that taboo was to her, the best ever sexual experience.

"I'll call you later." She whispered. Within the time it took for her to reach to the door and look back at him once again, he was fast asleep without a damning care in the world.

CHAPTER 41

THE HANGOVER

"Where the fuck are yah?" Raph shouted into his earpiece, after he slowly gathered who was calling him when the sharp telephone ringing was eventually answered.

"In bed mate. What the fuck is up with you?"

"Oh, nothing...I've been ringing you forever."

"Don't. I just woke up and me battery is dead. I'm still at Park Lane hotel."

"I know where you are. How do you think I got the number? Div...I'll send Rambo up to get you." Raph gestured to Tony who departed immediately.

They had all gathered at the GBE offices minus Ray, after they had all agreed on the 12:30 meet.

"Sid is fuming with us and wants to see us at the office."

"Fuck is up with them now?"

"Fuck knows mate. He never said, he just sent Tommy."

"Ok mate. Tell him I'm in the penthouse."

"Don't fucking fall asleep again."

"Alright fuck. You wanna calm down beefy." Ray stressed against the noise in his head from the conversation.

It took several tosses and turns before finally having the inspiration to get up. Pottering about for forty odd minutes, he took a shower and dressed in the complimentary robe and slippers provided and began to tidy up the remnants of an evidently wild night. The spare packets of cocaine tempted him to do a line to liven him up but with the pending meeting with his uncles, refuted the idea. His head pounding and shortness of breath, battled with any motivation to leave the room, let alone face them.

He drifted to Angela with a sudden bout of confusion and worry as to where she ended up after he left the Vanity. Leaning over to the phone again to dial her number, he took a few moments to recollect it off by heart and listened to it ringing out. This unknowing, sparked him into some sense of urgency, to dress quickly and make his way to reception, counting out the big wad of money from his jacket was enough to cover the expenses. The grey-haired receptionist smiled upon receiving it and took her some time to divide up the itinerary and the complimentary to print out the final bill that totalled, minus deposit, sixteen hundred pounds, seventy-five pence. The wad he counted at seventeen hundred was recounted reasonably quickly, he held back on asking for her assistance for one of their regular sunday evening counts and waited for the receipt.

The voice behind him in argument with a female voice turned his attention away, not in recognition, it was just the hostile tone. The man's eyes stared at him with a meagre acknowledgment of the visible compassion shared in witness to the nagging. Ray had a slight snigger in his mind that he disguised with a sympathetic expression, going by the speed of the lady's mouth as she berated him, he wouldn't wish that kind of punishment upon any man, especially if he was in a similar delicate state as his own. Upon which, Jenny wafted briefly into his thoughts, still feeling a bit light headed, he turned back to receive his receipt and signalled for her to keep the change. He sparked up a cigarette and coughed as the nicotine hit him at the back of his throat, he took a few puffs before casting it into the ashtray on a table beside the door.

Following the arguing couple outside, the lady sure had a lot to say towards the dreadlocked man, now walking in silence alongside her. Ray continued to laugh to himself at the comedy and continued looking for Tony. The breeze struck him in relay to the previous hot bellowing shower to awaken him a little more. The woman was now faced up to the man confronting him with aggression, who's expression pictured someone who was fed up and almost ready to react.

He kept on staring towards the couple with distinction, with the man in particular, trying to place a finger on his resemblance but the high-pitched noise from the woman was enough to distract and drive anyone crazy. He then turned his interest towards the excessive beeping.

Tony's wrangler pulled up just in time, he needed to sit down, his body feeling the strain, dehydrated, fatigued and his head offering some little snippets, flashbacks to why he felt the way that he did.

"Fuck me Ray...Looks like you had a good night. Where's the bird?" He queried laughing.

"She left but I barely even remember her leaving, or even fucking her for that matter."

"Jesus...If you can't even remember dipping your sword, you must be in a bad way boss." He laughed.

"Don't mate, I feel fucked. Lend us your phone, need to see if Angie got home alright." He picked up the phone to dial and received no reply again.

"I thought she went back with yous." Tony noted.

"Did she? Nah...not with me and the bird."

"Pretty sure you went out with both of them. Jenny was well fucked off."

"What the fuck is her problem?"

"Are you fucking sure?" Tony laughed."With that little show? Mate, it didn't go unnoticed. She loves you I guess, or so she was telling everyone...She was in a right old pickle. First it was Todd, now it's you blowing her out. Everyone's screwing mate. What's the deal man?"

"What the fuck has me fucking this bird have to do with anyone. I fucking dreamt about her since I could cum in a sock."

"Well your uncles ain't happy that's for certain. Did you fuck em off last night or something?"

"Fucked if I know." He surrendered. "Them fucking pills."

"They're fucking lively mate." Tony replied.

"Fuck me are they." Ray sympathised.

"But you shouldn't mix 'em. All you need is that rush my son." He advised, chuckling at the state of his friend.

In fairness, they, Tony especially, had binged on many occasions with a plethora of drinks, drugs and debauchery and can expertly, with confidence, cement that public service announcement. They continued the journey in relative silence, with a dead battery on his phone, he refused to speak with Jenny, who called Tony wanting some air time, Ray signalled his intent not wanting any kind of confrontation. If she's ringing around, she's either on the warpath or to reconcile, he had no interest in gambling on either possibility. The couple outside the hotel was enough for him to draw his conclusion.

◆ ◆ ◆

They pulled up to the Gloucester, when all Ray really wanted was a nice hot bath and his bed. He greeted some of the regulars with a feeble wave and Norma behind the bar with an affectionate kiss, with some banter, she took the piss out of his demeanour. Her mother was met halfway down the stairs, he had not seen her for the obvious reasons, since their New Year's night encounter, he smiled at her with a dismissive hint as she passed. Her eyes glinted with a sly secrecy as the memories of him came flooding back. Ray's mind could think of nothing more than what was facing him at the top of the stairs and other than a polite hello, left her somewhat deflated.

"Do you two need me to bring you some drinks," She purred from the bottom step.

"No thanks Mrs Collins." Tony replied politely.

"I'm good thanks." Ray replied, with the wound resonating in his voice.

They both entered into the smokey room, Sid, Pete, Tommy Akehurst, Sammy Taxi and Raph sat at one end with Todd, Nathan, Billy 'The Face' and Luis Scouser occupying the other seats that left two vacant.

"Sit down." Sid instructed to him sharply, which he happily welcomed the invite. Tony walked around to the window standing behind Sid and his brother.

"Are you proud of yourself then?" Sid rhetorised.

"Look uncle Sid. Whatever you are mad at, I totally understand. Please can you just get to the point of whatever it is and I'll agree to it.

"I'm afraid the damage has already been done...Telling Mr Newport to go fuck himself and playing your nonsense with Solomon's Mrs? And you see that little gun play at that club, do you really think everyone is that stupid?"

"Not this again?" He sighed. "Look...ok...So me and Theresa have been fooling about but that's it...She was lonely because he's shat himself and fucked off..."

"Listen to yourself...All the fanny yous lot have flying in and out of here and you shack up with the lonely widow?"

"What is the point in all this? If you want me to drop her, I'll drop her. If you want me to apologise and grovel to Mr Newport, I will and all." Ray surrendered.

Raph and the rest of the guys remained silent, glancing at each other, not quite sure where this will lead. The one thing Raph had already surmised, was that Luis being here, meant the old boys were expecting some kind of retaliation.

"Do we need to get our heads down?" Raph interrupted.

"Well I guess that's down to whoever is wanting to question how come our Swordsman here is knobbing Maitland's supposed to be grieving widow? And, South London nicking his nightclub. All of a sudden?" Tommy interjected.

This brought a stifled chuckle from Todd, it wasn't often they heard the older gent's reference him like that.

"Exactly that Tommy. That's what we have, maybe some mystery vigilante Greek cunt from North London, sneaking onto the manor, tooled up wanting the answers for himself." Pete agreed.

Ray remained silent to their theories, looking towards Tony and Todd who both shook their heads with a silent and an absolute 'who gives a fuck?' demeanour, in agreement with his open readiness to bring on all comers. Nausea and a pounding head relieved him from any inspiration for impertinent protests, at this instance, grief, bother and to a point any of the career aspirations that had brought him to this, can have a breather. Tonight, he just wanted peace and quiet.

"I'm sorry alright…Just make the calls or whatever you have to do for a sit down and we'll straighten it all out. And I'll fuck the bird off."

"Good." Sid replied, somewhat taken aback by the lack of insolence, when he had prepared himself for a battle of words, following his stubborn nephew's fuck the world attitude from the previous night.

CHAPTER 42

THE BILL HAVE EYES

Sid's face was etched hard with worry, it seemed bad news and lack of sensibility or whatever the contributing factors had now bought to him, another escalation of exertion, looking sullenly towards the weeping Angela.

First and foremost, she could not face the shame of last night's memories as details crept into her head. The confusion from what even elated her to carry through the act. She repeated again her torment of not being able to explain why, or even how, she would reveal a closely guarded secret that they had held onto for so long, that it could spill from her lips so easily and now, how she could even face him ever again, after the perceived incest. Avoiding his calls was one thing but there was still no resolution for Theresa knowing the truth and repeating it to him or anyone else for that matter, how would he take it? It rained with a hapless precariousness swallowing her wholeheartedly.

"I still can't get my nut around any of this. Fucking drugs Again…drugs have come back to fuck things up…Again." He repeated of the barometer that always tested his blood pressure.

"I don't even remember what happened or even why I would blurt out such nonsense to a complete stranger."

"If you even did or you imagined you did. And believe me, I still can't for the life of me, figure out what is fucking worse."

"Please Sid. I'm in enough turmoil. Not that I can remember conclusively but I'm considering, now, with the way I feel. I know…I must have…I'm the lowest of the low."

Her hair fell over her face and hands as she covered

up cowering into her tears. Sid continued to pace the room, unsympathetic to how she felt at this current time.

"Well, with some consolation, if we can find one in this complete cluster fuck…going by the state he was looking when I see him earlier…I doubt if he'd even remember."

"He knows. He must do…If it's all coming back to me like this. I can't believe this nightmare. What are we going to do?"

"You want the truth? Other than feeling sick to my stomach. There's only one action in my mind. This woman…" He brushed back at his hair in an uncharacteristic despair. His eyes burned into her in disgust.

"Maybe I can go and see her and speak with her?"

"You've done enough talking for a life time." He rejected.

"We can't just do nothing."

"I'll take care of it and I'm hoping she'll just believe, that was an excuse and you are living with the fucking shame. You left them there. In the bed. So let's wait and see, there is not much else we can go on, whoever remembers what and… Fuck." He cursed loudly, then quickly calmed.

His fist formed as a restraint against his face as he sat down at her table to review his temper, when it appeared that he was getting as bad as her in the losing control stakes.

"We'll gage the situation. Worst outcome, everyone will think like you just said, that yous are the lowest of the low. If it gets out. I'm hoping that it's been long enough that no one would even give a flying fuck anymore."

The embarrassment on her face was enough not to extend it out, especially with what was about to spill, about Rita doing summersaults in her grave. Under the current circumstances, the aftermath still had the one and only conclusion in his head.

"Well I don't care what people think about me…It's him I want to protect. I'll happily take her out of the picture, if she talks any shit about us."

"And that would be a great help, seeing that everyone is pointing a finger down here about her fucking husband. No

Ang...The only person you need to see right now is him." He deduced, setting himself ready to leave. "And you need to keep your fucking clothes on this time."

The door slammed loudly as he left, tears flooded her face as she sunk into the cushions and remained there inconsolable, for near on forty-five minutes. The phone rang to break her from her miserly self-pity. It must have been the umpteenth time it had rung. Mustering the little bravado that she could gather up, compounded by Sid's voice replaying inside her head, that she had to speak with him, subconsciously confirming that it could only be him ringing, she nervously composed herself.

"For fuck sake...Finally. I've been worried sick wondering what happened to you...Are you ok?"

"I'm fine baby. Been passed out the whole day..." She paused again nervously, gaging his tone and direction of the conversation. She knew him enough that he was not feeling any anger for certain or hints of guilt at this moment.

"Do you want me to bring you anything?"

"A time machine to when I never ever drank so much would be nice." She sighed.

"Wow...You must be in a bad way."

"I feel like death warmed up."

"Well just bell me...I'm gonna get me nut down. I'll probably take the week off. Sid's got the right needle with me again..."

"About what?"

"Theresa of course and everyone having a problem with it."

"He just wants what's best for you darling. We all do...I just hope we haven't messed it up..." She paused again, stifling back the tears as she became emotional again.

"Hey. You can stop that and all."

"I'm sorry."

"I know he means well...I'm 100 percent sure yous have not messed anything up. If anything, it's me. I need to stop being selfish, after all yous have done for me."

"Do you mean that?"

"Of course I do. I need to consider what's best for everyone around us, not just me...And you need to stop getting so bloody emotional."

"I know my love."

"Shall we go for dinner tomorrow?"

"Dinner? Just us?"

"Yeah. Royal Garden. Just the two of us...and just food. Don't think I'm getting smashed for a long while, after how I felt earlier." He laughed.

"I'm with you on that..." She became overwhelmed by the innocent conversation, hearing his voice, erased all that had consumed her for the majority of that day.

"That's a date then. Half seven I'll pick you up."

"I'll see you tomorrow then."

"Yeah get your head down, think I'll be finally sleeping like a baby tonight."

"Sweet dreams then my love."

"Night."

After the call, she felt surprisingly a lot more relaxed and wished she maybe had that conversation, before she even surrendered it to Sid...But there was still the hard realisation now, which lay upon how or what Theresa would respond with, there was nothing that alluded to any hint of guilt that she could gage from him. Could there have been a wishful barometer, that a possibility exists, that he knows the truth and just doesn't care?

The careless wish wouldn't be such a bad thing, although, knowing the truth, would only lead to questions and the danger that entails, that they had shielded him from for all them years. She went upstairs to let the hot vibrant shower clear her head but her heart couldn't clear from her inappropriate love.

◆ ◆ ◆

Raph's phone ringing at 2 am startled him awake, after the speech from Sid and the disappointment echoing from their mentors, he worried fearing the worse. Scrambling for his senses to press the answer button, his left hand felt numb after laying awkwardly.

"It's me...I need to talk to you urgently, something has come to my attention. It's not good."

"Where are yah?"

"Round Tommy's."

"What the fuck Nath. What's the coo?"

"It's not what you think. You crank. And I'm not discussing it on the blower either."

"Come to me then."

"You're a paranoid fucker yah know that?"

"I love you Boyce. But calling me at two in the morning asking me to come to Tommy Akehurst's house? Behind the Naden's, I'm not walking in there at the drop of the hat. I can assure you that."

"For fuck sake Fredo" He chuckled loudly. "I was having a drink with him and Bev...Div."

"Yeah well chop fucking chop. I need some shut eye."

It was another half an hour, as Raph paced his front room eager for the news. He debated on giving Ray a call to give him the heads up, which he negated. Although he agreed to remove himself around any simmering debate surrounding Ray's questionable moral alignment.

Putting the husband out to pasture, just so he could get his end away, was most of the firm's understanding...Ray never gave love up that easily. So, decided that he would be on a need to know basis for now, until he could get a better understanding of where all the cards will fall. And concluded from the look he gave him earlier, he was not going to take the easiest of routes.

"You ok hun?" Whispered her voice. Raph turned to see his well-kept secret.

"Go back to sleep Bel." He ordered. "Nathan's coming

around about some business…go on."

"Ok babe…Don't worry, I wouldn't want to give your little secret away." She replied, with a playful shush by putting her finger on her lips.

"It's not that I don't want them knowing about you. It's just, that world and my world…I want to keep separate, that's all."

"I'll leave you in peace then." She rubbed her naked breasts up against him to remind him not to have Nathan outstay his welcome, just as the distinctive knock interrupted his wish on a quickie before he arrived. He watched her creep upstairs before answering the door.

"This better be good Boycie…" He warned, inviting him in with a paranoid glance over his shoulder, brought on by an insecurity that he might not have come alone. A feeling elated relatively quickly before joining him in the living room.

"Good? This is a fucking blockbuster moosh." Nathan replied gleefully. "Although this is third hand."

"Third hand? Fucking wake me up at two in the morning on a Chinese fucking whisper?"

"Fuck that Raph, just listen." He vocalised excitedly. "Bev is with Jenny last night, Jenny's buzzing and half with the bollock ache about Ray, his hands all over Theresa, right?"

Raph sat himself down seeing that it might take some time to get to the point.

"So, at the end of the night, Bev is half dragging Jenny out to get home, they're all looking fit remember, despite being off their nuts. Bev first noticed him looking lost, staring over their shoulders for whoever was coming out of the club. Bev thinks he's a taxi driver and says they need a cab. She knows he's not a cabbie, she's clued up. Fuck knows how she has but she smells he's old bill, posh old bill…"

"It's quarter past three Nathan, can we speed this up?"

"Ok…long story short…he was posh old bill, very snobby in tone she said, sussing his accent or something, looking about for someone. Bev snags him with questions, going by his description of her, without mentioning her name, he's obviously looking for Theresa. He said he was her ride home. Bev knows full well she's already fucked off with Ray. So how comes this unlucky sod is none the wiser? So, pleading with him, that he taxis them home, she's quick to point out to him that she may have left with their mate, possibly back to the manor, there's an after-party, blah de blah. This sets Jenny off, on the sheer mention of her name. Bev excuses that her friend ain't well and all that and in the end he agrees. This is what she's half inched from the back of the motor, when he's stopped to fill up at the Elephant and Castle."

He handed over the black leather wallet with the silver Met badge. Raph took a while for the picture to focus recognition of her face, although slightly younger and with less of a smile.

"Bumbaclaart!" Raph's response was one of confusion and translated into patois.

"New Scotland yard brother or that other main mob. Spooks. I reckon."

"She can't be…What..married to Maitland and heir to his estate and all that?"

"Fuck knows Raph, whichever way this plays out, she's still old bill. Fuck knows what division."

"That don't even make sense. If she came to the club undercover, sniffing gear, doing pills and fucking our Swordsman, how the fuck does that help out any investigation?"

"And why leave that lying about?"

"Well I doubt she had the pockets, going by what she was wearing last night." Raph pointed out. "Could be though, if she went rogue. It could have been a reminder?"

"That would make more sense, you can tell she likes the lifestyle. It's mad, knowing that she's from the manor. We'd have known. Surely?" Nathan concluded, unassured about it all.

"And that's the problem right there. Ray's been in her

before the alliance?"

"Do you want me to look more into that?"

"Nah. Maybe it was Maitland they wanted. To be his fiancé. No! married even. That takes time, planning, patience." Raph shook his head as he stood up and began to pace the room, rapid fire questions entered and left his thoughts.

"Who the fuck knows Raph, whoever planted her are obviously sneaky little fucks." Nathan continually debated.

"What did Bev say about it all?"

"Well...Other than, the questionable attention about her hands being all over Angie. She just tried to recount if she ever let on about any business around her. They got very chatty at one point during the night. Then she had a right old barney with Jenny for talking to her." Nathan digressed.

"No, about the geezer...What does she reckon?"

"She doesn't know what to make of it, once they were in the car, he didn't really give much away, didn't ask about anything in particular."

"This is like a fucking Twilight zone...How we're careful and The Swordsman ends up poking some undercover fucker..."

"I really don't think it's us."

"And how did you work that one out?"

"Other than him banging her and last night at the club, when has she ever been around us?" Nathan reasoned.

"That's a good point, but also, that's how they work, chipping away. We just have to hope that he hasn't been singing our business into her ears after he's bolted his load." Raph paused with his scepticism.

"Ray ain't no chatterbox, that much we do know." Nathan confidently reassured.

"So where did Bev get dropped off at in the end?" Raph digressed again in agreement to that notion.

"Dropped them at the Newton Arms on the pretence that's where the afterparty was. He left them there, after a nose about. When he fucked off, she called her old man to get them both. That's pretty much it."

"Alright Boyce...let's keep a lid on it for now. Let me sleep on it."

"What about Ray?"

"Not yet. We'll get more info from Bev, then we'll see. Maybe Collins can help."

"Thing is, Collins gave us intel on that Christopher ponce and that Soho had Maitland on their radar. So, if he's not wise on this old cunt sniffing around us. What does that imply?"

"And if she is that deep. It has to be a higher level."

"Well lucky we are above board. Apart from the bags of cash. I guess."

"Not completely, we have some exposure still with the Amsterdam connections. That's why as of now, it has to be me and you at the top, then everyone else."

"Don't know what Ray will have to say about that, but the old boys keep wrangling him anyway."

"Yes, and I guess that was the point of the meeting earlier, Ray knows he's being reigned in, so he'll live with whatever we tell him."

"Yeah he's better off counting his riches and ruining birds." Nathan laughed, which Raph deflected from getting into any comedy.

"Alright, tomorrow, give the Gloucester the once over, then get everyone to scrub all the houses. Tools, money, everything. Separate us all from any of the little touches we have going on. If Todd or Tony want to take charge let them. But...and make this absolutely clear, other than the muscle, I want no one else carrying, then keep them, Todd especially, in check. I'll make sure they know this is coming from Sid and not us, just so he doesn't go all wild west on us. And eyes open on dodgy looking vans parked up for hours on end. I'm going to bed. Is there anything else?"

"Yeah. Who's the bird you got upstairs?"

"Goodnight mate." Raph ignored. "See yah self out."

He did have a slight chuckle to himself. With everything

that they just discussed, there was no panic in them. Come what may, it finally dawned, the enormity of their success and that it shouldn't be about the chase or the show of muscle anymore like it had been what drew them ambitiously. They were smarter than that and would open the door to where their ultimate focus should be. Nathan watched him disappear upstairs.

"A cup of tea would have been nice." Nathan muttered under his breath and chuckled at Raph's rude two worded response, then left closing the door quietly.

CHAPTER 43

RED ALERT

Raph's first port of call the next morning was to meet Sid. Following his early morning phone call to him, he was already happy on the decision that there has to be a new hierarchy in contact and discussing any business, illegal or otherwise. Sid was wary enough about how things worked, retirement or not, with all things considered, a war time state with due diligence is now required and praised Raph, for the proactive thinking ahead with contingencies already introduced. This need for due diligence was heightened by him producing the badge identification of what they can undoubtedly recognise as Theresa.

After Raph's initial shock, as they both stood in his kitchen, the revelation of the bikini clad, curvaceous black woman, with the short red dressing gown parading inside his house almost had Raph choking his lines. Offering them coffee, Sid took a moment for his attention to settle after politely declining. Dallying, Sid laughed at the way his jaw gaped in awe and gave him a couple of gentle taps under his chin to snap him back into the here and now.

Questions then raised to whether she had targeted Ray, if that was the case, the damage could be limitless. Sid's immediate concern was that in the likelihood that Ray was the target, was it criminal or closing the loop on the secret they hid about his origins, which by the knowledge shared by Angela, she had already personally helped compromise. Either way, the threat was present.

"Ok just make sure everything is squeaky on your side, have Todd and Tony run the operation with Sammy, to change the routines, but they must have eyes in the back of their heads. Ray has to keep his nut down, and luckily for him, landing that stock market job helps us out, no more distractions...And don't crack on about that sneaky little cunt either, but if he keeps seeing her and she doesn't throw him any caution not to, then say nothing."

"You sure Sid...I'm sure if he gets a whiff he'll do something about it."

"No...This puts me in a position for only one outcome. I know he's your mate but he's only thinking about his cock as far as she's concerned. Say nothing."

"He's me pal Sid."

"You silly sod...what?" He grinned somewhat mischievously. "You boys watch too many of them flaming gangster movies. Look, the fallout of this, especially after his treatment of Newport, me brother already decided to put a track on her, to figure out her routines. Because other than this mountainous headache, we also need to be wary if one of Maitland's people have a radar on her to get to Ray. So, don't matter whether he's been spilling more than his bodily fluids into her, we've already set the action."

"Fuck me." Raph relieved. "I thought..."

"For now, don't think anything. Keep him occupied on the main goals and leave the criminality to us. Got it?"

"Loud and clear Sid. How about Angie...they got very friendly with each other the other night."

"Why? What'd you hear?" Sid questioned, almost uncharacteristically revealing his hand about his main apprehensions.

"Nothing, but you know what women are like?"

"Don't worry about Ang, she's been around us long enough to know better about blabbing her mouth off. But I'll have a word to be one hundred percent." He deflected.

Raph surrendered in agreement, trying to work out if Sid was as ruthless as he was rumoured to be, to pull the trigger on anyone that put them in jeopardy.

"I still can't understand that someone from the manor is some double agent. I always thought she was in marketing."

"Could be the reason why they used her...if it was someone that wasn't our own, we would have sniffed them a mile off."

"Ray was at hers when old bill interviewed her when Maitland went missing, according to him, the drum they lived in was a palace."

"Well let's not waste any more time figuring out the when's and the where's." Sid surrendered. "That was a bold move yous pulled off. But you've now left yourselves wide open."

Raph stood silent and fidgeted slightly to check his phone as an incoming call, saved him by the bell. He rejected the call to look Sid openly eye to eye.

"It's only Nathan." He excused innocently.

"Some bollocks on yous, I give you that."

"I don't know what you mean Sid...What move?" Raph deflected.

"The possibility is not lost here that Maitland himself as well could be..."

"Undercover old bill?"

"Yeah! You allow that to sink in for a moment."

"With that mouth of his? Nah...No way." Raph reassured.

"Anyway, fuck all that. Get with Sammy and leave no stone unturned and I mean that, sweeten anyone that might have a reason to turn state's witness, you should have more than enough spare bags of money lying about to keep them onside.

"We don't have to worry about anyone like that, especially our lot, they're adhesive." Raph validated.

"Ok. Well, you go with your instincts on that. But I can assure you of one thing that will get us all nicked, is that drug trade in your own club. Squash it and I mean immediately, every time I get a major pain in the arse it's always to do with drugs."

"Well we are where we are Sid. We shouldn't knock it." Raph replied.

"If people have to work it...you just make sure Soho C.I.D and Collins has a body or two to keep 'em sweet." Sid paused for a moment to see if Raph had any objections. He restrained from debating the same old argument.

"We hear you Sid. We'll be careful."

Sid then began to ponder on the forever trail of bodies in rivers and basements, that his nephew and crew have had him, and his brother, left to dredge and cover up to protect them over the years and decided on the spot to reintroduce the old chain of command.

"And my last gripe with yous. I don't want to hear of anyone or anything else being dragged over the Naden's. As far as yous are concerned, they're officially retired as of today. Clear?" The end comment he left up in the air, with the smug looking glare on his face towards Raph.

"Whatever you say." He huffed slightly and could now understand what Ray meant about them.

There was no point in even gambling on an excuse with a poker face holding a royal flush. He never for once considered, what they would do in situations like this and ultimately, counting themselves lucky from another perspective about these men who have seen it and done it and so it appears, way ahead as far as knowing everything that they did. The young men still had a lot to learn.

CHAPTER 44

WHAT HEART'S DESIRE

He pulled up outside her house, beeping unceremoniously at her. She was already by the kerbside, expectant and startled from the noise. Entering the car with his eyes burning towards her gloomy appearance and the way she had dressed, didn't escape his intrigue.

"Blimey! I've not seen you in a pair of strides for years."

"Yes, I know love. It's just reflecting my mood."

"Tell me about it, you're always sounding so emotional, especially last night."

"I've not felt myself since that party."

"Well you need to liven yourself up, bloody stride's on and all that. I need my old sexy Angie back." He smiled.

"Ray do you reckon…?" She paused. His words again triggering that harmonious rhythm inside her.

"What?" Reckon what?" He stared worryingly towards her.

"Oh, Nothing…" She sighed with deep melancholy.

"No come on, get it off your chest."

"I mean, just us, and the way we are, do you think people look bad on us?"

"They wouldn't dare…Besides, why can't we be affectionate and have a laugh with each other and hang out? Nothing wrong in that. Personally, I think we're kinda cool, symbolic even."

"Really?" She smiled. "Do you mean that?"

"Course I do. Now buckle up for fuck sake, let's go have that dinner. I'm starving."

She concentrated on her seatbelt as he pulled away, her

mind still conflicted by his words as she stroked her hair fidgetingly and wiped her palms on her lap in a constant deliberate restraint, even more so of the fact that it appeared that he had no recollection. This confused her more than anything and it began to show in the lack of conversation coming back from her.

He mused on the silence from what used to be a flurry of unreserved chatter between them, her natural ability to act towards him had changed and she couldn't find words to deflect from that fact and increasingly paranoid that he had already noticed the difference.

Relief fell upon her once he pulled into the parking area to the restaurant, she also had the influx of calls to his cell phone to thank as the timely conversations had him distracted for the most part of the journey but also changed the smile on his face to frowns of concern.

"Blimey…Everyone acting like their holding hot potatoes at the minute."

"Why…what's going on?" Her questions presented more relief that echoed in her voice, for a less shameful subject to turn their attention to.

"Raph, he's having a meltdown that eyes might be on us, so now demanding that I focus all my energy on that bank job with Jimmy Sarge that I'm starting next week."

"He's probably right you know and that's more likely coming from your uncles…You need some normality."

"Normality? Have you seen what goes on in the city? It's a lot more civil being a hooligan or a gangster." He laughed.

Greeted by Mr Yan's wife Gretchen this time as they entered, they were shown to their usual table after they waited with drinks and had polite conversation at the bar, while the patrons finished up at the table, paid their bill and left. The staff cleared everything efficiently to make it presentable for them before they were seated and introduced to their waiter for the night. After the usual preamble for more drinks and todays specials, Ray still had questions about her attire and all the motherly conversation she seemed over occupied with.

His phone rang again and surprised him, he eventually answered, Theresa had finally called him after several unsuccessful calls that day. She stared at him with some trepidation and fear preparing itself inside her head, then praying that he wouldn't make a public scene. The phone call in retrospect was short and to the point.

"Who was that?"

"Theresa...Sounded like she was crying."

"Really?"

"Yeah, she said she had some bad news or something. Money related." He evaded the real details of her call. "I'm not quite sure why she would ring me for that, considering..."

"That's what people do who care for each other."

"She's only with me for sex." He parried to her surprise.

"I thought it was a bit more serious than that, she still called you wanting to share her problem?"

"What am I? Her agony aunt now? She'll be ok. Anyway, enough about other people's problems. What do you want to drink?"

"Oh." She recollected her thoughts quickly, with an adjustment to her mood. "I think I'll have a G and T."

"Good choice you need to liven up."

"I'm so sorry, I just feel a bit funny today, not myself."

"I'm here for you Angie, get it off your chest whatever's eating at you. I'm all ears."

The drinks soon arrived. She took a large swig of hers while she confirmed what she wanted on the menu, usually she could stuff herself with everything listed, but all of a sudden, had a lesser appetite because of the butterflies flip flopping inside and just ordered the shared hors d'oeuvres and beef in black bean sauce, he ordered his modest Peking duck and vermicelli and returned the menu to the waiter who then left them alone.

He stroked at her hand, which she took his in return affectionately staring towards him.

"Why do you never call me mum anymore?"

"Seriously? This is what's getting you down?"

"No, it's just..."

"I thought you were my Angie now that's all."

"I know love, I love that so much, but I know this sounds silly, especially...I know I'll hate myself for saying this...but sometimes...I get a really bad feeling about us. I mean not bad but weird."

"That's nuts, we've always been this way. Haven't we?"

"And that doesn't make...I mean...you don't think of me... You know?" She stumbled awkwardly over her words, she nervously wanted to hint about their indiscretion, something to jog his memory, but purposely unable to find the words. Taking a larger swig of her gin, she lofted her glass up to wave at and attract the waiter's attention again.

"Blimey, you really are thirsty."

"I just don't know how to put it in words. What do you feel when you look at me?"

"That's an odd question...what do I feel? I don't know... You are my Angie...And...What's brought this all on?"

"Nothing...I mean, it's just when you get the hump over the boyfriends I have, it makes me feel warm and loved and everything else. I just think...why you do it? And when I get all giddy when you compliment me. I'll shut up. I'm talking so much nonsense."

"No, it's not. And I have to admit, truthfully, I don't know why I do. Part of me just wants you to be with someone that deserves you and then selfishly...believing that no one does. Not the ones I've seen." He gulped his lager racking his brain at the conversation and couldn't help looking deep into her eyes, almost struck with awe about her as she smiled sweetly back at him.

"And that and just being with you is why I continually feel as if it's..." She procrastinated with more alcohol as if the glass contained the lubricant to her vocabulary to detour towards what went on in that penthouse suite.

"I love you that's all. Nothing wrong in wanting to protect you. I don't know what else to say." He stroked her soft gentle hand gently from across the table, the affection ricocheted deeper than just way of empathy, those eyes of his told her all that she wanted to know.

"What if I took your father back?" She offered randomly in reflectance away from the sin they commited on those sexy black satin sheets. Maybe it was the fact she hasn't felt the way about anyone, since the way he had captured her heart, and feeling that same silly teenage buzz, like ginger ale on the brain.

He paused with knitted eyebrows, while he pondered the random topic, with his mind see-sawing, looking for that trigger to whenever he could even remember what his dad was all about, other than a nasty and malicious bullying cunt.

"I'll get less of the hump if you were dating Todd."

They laughed together at his response as he watched her, then made a serious thought to remove any doubt.

"And...seriously...I'd kill em both." He leered with confident sincerity.

"I'm gonna die an old spinster at this rate." She smiled regarding his explanation but still couldn't erase the way she felt and embarrassed by the nervous mumbling at him. It somewhat cemented, that through his eyes, there would be no one worthy and that wanted her to just lay it on him. This was a hopeless situation and she had no right to feel how she felt.

They ate and then drank a few more alcoholic glasses, despite their earlier promise, including a last-minute cocktail, as a toast and a promise that he would be more sensitive to her needs and that it wasn't his place to judge anymore. His mind wandered reflectively as her tipsy smile warmed at him, which sent an awkward incredible rush of thought about her, like a recognition of an ingrained confusing affection, which hammered into him like an arrow.

"Here's to me finding someone as loving and as handsome as you darling." She sang tipsily as her clouds of anxiety were completely absolved.

With a check of his watch, triggered by the pile up of glasses on the table, he hollered at the waiter for the bill and counted out the £170 including the tip, then escorted her out, she linked his arm as they walked towards the door together. A couple of ladies who were eyeing him for most of the evening, looked at the pair of them with some envy, which caught his eyes.

"You ok girls?" His voice was purposefully passive aggressive, not quite sure what it was that interested them.

"We were just admiring what a lovely couple yous are." One smiled innocently.

They both laughed out loud and thanked them as they left. All though it was a somewhat ridiculous observation coming from strangers, an awakening had hit home, what they had both evaded from their whole discussions they had since picking her up that evening.

They stopped at the car, he gentlemanly opened the door for her, offering the fine cowhide interior, an expensive odour of luxury greeted their return. This courtliness, after he stared for a while longingly upon her, triggered every inappropriate feeling flooding overwhelmingly inside of her again. Almost like a last ditched attempt to sympathise to the pressure from her heart strings. She battled for a split second but failed as his irresistible lips beckoned, she wrapped her arms lovingly around his neck to kiss him, their mouths collided softly which he returned, unreluctantly with undiluted passion. The sensual feeling of warmth as they softly stroked at each other's lips was so wanting his hands stroked her irresistible curves, that appeared to suddenly frighten them both to stop, with a slow, 'who would cave in first at the outrage' demeanour, that never came in any form of escalation, from either of them, only curious uncertainty.

"I'm so sorry, what the hell am I doing?" She cursed apologetically.

"No. It's me...that was me. I should be apologising, that

was fucked up." His eyes dipped downwards at his feet.

Totally disorientated by it all, they were both blushing with confusion, his head now battling with clarity, what he had excused to have been the most inappropriate erotic wishful dream about her, now he understood and now this terrified him, begging himself for forgiveness.

He drove the car with a soft R&B song, detailing the singer's heartbreak of a failed romance and needing for no one else, inconsolable, ready to do everything to win back that heart, that had escaped without reason. They both peered speechless out of the windscreen to the song, not knowing the best appropriate words to say to one another. The journey ending relatively quickly but felt like the longest journey home, when he pulled up outside of her house.

Sat in a continued silence together, surprisingly and almost in sync, they both left the car and were walking up the pathway, her walk had a purposeful high heeled sashay, that flounced at his desire, watching her turn towards him with her unadulterated beauty, under the night lamps that radiated back at him, he was a moth to a flame as she rattled the keys to the door. He stroked his palm at her enticing long hair that continued down to the small of her back, magnetically, as though his hands where guided by the devil or an out of body force.

"I can't help myself from thinking, that I just want to be naughty with you." She declared as she turned towards him with a soft whisper into his ear, which struck him dumbfounded.

Continuing in silence she climbed the stairs, her earlier feelings now stripped bare of atonement. With his terrified thoughts now inside his head, offering no escape from his mind, was merely a dissipating inner sense pleading for him to leave. She stopped at the top stair to look back at the apprehension in him, her unbearable addictive lust could only offer a cry me a river, as to the rights and the wrongs, then she never looked back.

He climbed the stairs to follow her, unrushed, unsure but unable to stop himself. He entered her dimly lit room, her jacket discarded onto the bed frame, her hair pulled ravishingly to flop with beauty over one shoulder of her sleeveless silk top, that presented the perfect glimpse of her soft skin, her curves jutting out insatiably from beneath the fabric. Not a word was uttered as he stood there motionless. She stared up at his eyes that returned covetingly back at her. Irresistible, like a force majeure colliding them together, had them embraced with their hearts pounding for one another.

Long lingering kisses of passion that was impatiently fuelled with excitement and uncertainty, only their attraction drove them and the will that justified. Tugging at each other's clothes, the consuming craving for one another had them eventually panting lovingly between the sheets. Her heart was a flame as his mouth explored her body, her legs wrapped around him encasing him in between her thighs, his hands gripping tightly against her buttocks. The blood gorged vessels in his shaft, were eagerly ready to deliver his passion into her. Their bodies chimed explicitly and together whisked them away from all that was real, like the dreams they once succumbed to alone.

The car parked across the street was oblivious to them, blinded by a universe under her sheets, where no one else existed, no rules to break or ethics to adhere to, just their inexplicable and unexplainable desire. Whoever this was that witnessed with interest, the shadows of the couple madly in love, momentarily silhouetted at the window. It was bad news watching, with a selfish goading at the people of interest and a flagrant ambition that would now set out to completely shatter their whole world.

Epilogue

The operations briefing room chatter simmered of last-minute details as he entered with a frown. Smokers extinguished their remains and all turned to meet him at the head of the table. This was not the usual impromptu meeting to discuss any success or failure in any given operation, recent revelations necessitated the need to plot out contingencies.

The door opened again with a late arrival which finally signalled that the meeting could commence. Chairing the meeting was Chief Superintendent Donaldson, coughing into his fist to attract all their attention, along with the deep authoritative ahem that fully hushed the room. He flopped three copies of the daily tabloids onto the desk. The large font sensational headlines painted a crass kiss and reveal on the country's ruler...

THE SUN - THRONE INTO CHAOS.

THE EXPRESS - ILLIGITMATE TO THE THRONE?

THE DAILY MAIL - ANDREW: I DID NOT HAVE SEX WITH THAT GIRL.

"As you may all now be aware, these irresponsible headlines have been created to and will cause complete embarrassment to the UK. And it's another addition to the already annus horribilis to his majesty. How they got to this source and report so irresponsibly is still beyond me."

"Sir, if I may intercede?" One officer offered himself to get his matter out of the way. The eyes all surrounded him with impatience.

"Special officer Ford Sir. We believe the claimant, one Andrew Croft 21-years-old, from Clitheroe, Lancashire. From our understanding, the subject, after his grandmother deceased, stumbled upon a series of letters and other keepsake from his majesty out of a box in the deceased's loft."

"Grandmother? So that makes…?"

"If I can continue sir? He was abandoned by his birth mother and raised by the deceased, one Mrs Eileen Croft until he was about seventeen. Sir."

"What are the snippets from these letters?"

"The content of the letters hasn't been established. But the gist of it is, his majesty offering to take care of mother and baby."

"And remarkably, the first thing he does…he goes straight to the papers?" The Chief superintendent fumed.

"Sir, what was also uncovered was a birth certificate, so the dates do match and these photos." He cast an envelope towards the head of the table which reached the nearest officer, who handed it to Donaldson.

Retrieving the photos from the envelope, he studied at length the royal prince posing for the camera with unidentified individuals. As innocent as the picture appeared, there were scantily clad women clearly identifiable in the back grounds and two clearly recognisable underworld figures that were currently serving thirty years for their well-publicised crimes.

"In these photos taken at…" He paused to recollect the name of the establishment. "The Royal Mayfair, circa 1967."

The chief superintendent strained from one photo to the next, ashamed at the fact he was frequenting the same establishment as convicted psychopaths. It was the way he was posing openly for photos, looking seemingly unconcerned, especially with the selfish Prince's cheesy smile, that had supposedly made some of the unscrupulous women from the places he frequented, lose their minds and their dignity to him.

The photos were passed around the table for viewing, with raised eyebrows in surprise that someone of that magnitude was openly frequenting sex clubs with notorious gangsters.

"The swinging sixties eh?" Another younger officer remarked in disbelief.

"The gold dress is an envoy's niece Sir. The lady with the pinstripe is this Andrew Croft's mother. Sally Jenkins." Ford continued after the murmurs died down.

"And has the story been validated by anyone?"

"Well the only formal validation has come from a former protection officer, in an interview conducted in April 1970…Where it was confirmed in little detail the relationship Miss Jenkins and with another young woman, Rita Keyne, that's all sir."

"And it would be safe to assume he was not close enough to confirm conception?"

"No Sir…I mean…We can quite safely assume that he didn't."

"Sir, can I make a suggestion?" offered one of the ranking officers present, chief inspector Oliver. "Has he considered renouncing?"

"You must be joking; would you like to put that forward. People have lost their whole livelihoods going against his ego."

"Then maybe, we can speak to this envoy's niece and the Keyne lady. As well as, reaching out to both of their families?" The chief inspector retracted.

"Sorry to interrupt again Sir. The envoy's niece and the Keyne lady are the same person?"

"Well excuse my cynicism on most of what you have told me, can I assume that piece of information has been verified?"

"From the information provided on Miss Keyne, was that she was killed in a car accident shortly after. The Jenkins lady is reported to be an Alzheimer's patient at a facility in Cheshire."

"This is turning into an enormous shit show of dead ends." The Chief superintendent remarked. "So, what are the facts that we have. From the former R.P.O?"

"Only to confirm that during his time, code name Purple four-one definitely had relationships with one or maybe both of those women, but we believe it was this Keyne lady in the gold dress."

"So to date, we have no intel if she had a child and the perceived child that we do know about, spills his all to the press?"

"At present, we have yet to explore that avenue."

"Please, can we make that our top priority?" He commanded and began to scratch his full head of grey hair.

"Yes Sir."

"Also, can we get him or anyone back in for more information?"

"Unfortunately, the former RPO...er...Preston is also now deceased. Suicide sir."

"Marvellous. Thank you officer Ford."

"One more thing sir, may not hold much, we have from a report in our files that he gifted a Fabergé egg to one, a maternity present. Which ties in with the newspaper. Although we are unsure if reported treasure was discovered in the old lady's belongings."

"Well, let us get to these editors of all these so-called newspapers and retrieve everything they have. This is not just a threat to national security but making us the laughing stock of the entire free world. Arrest them for conspiracy to blackmail if you get any resistance or breaching official secrets act...Let's shake them up. We need everything from them."

"We have officers over there now."

"Good. And when you have finished with them, start the search again for anyone and everyone connected to this Mayfair place. Before anymore scandal resurfaces."

"Sir. Permission to speak openly?"

"Go ahead."

"Trident...Sir

"I'm not familiar?"

"Unofficially, the unit had been set up to tackle the influx of Jamaican yardie criminals and on a wider scale, have been looking at some low-level gang activity, broadly around Tuffnell Park, Broadwater Farm and Stockwell, we have reason to believe one of our targets..." The detective inspector named

Almey peered downwards at his notes. "Lester Morgan, he has recently been the main suspect on a double murder, from interviews conducted with him March 21,1992, he mentioned several times of his connection with Royal Mayfair club when asking for representation. So far, he has only named a Francis Kidbrook, an 85-year-old, no previous records on file, only that he resides in the Algarve. Morgan's claims were that he was the main muscle for the club, a real piece of low life and Kidbrook provided girls by order. I believe Ford will hear his name crop up from his enquiries."

"I'll dig more into it." Ford agreed.

"Is this Morgan a reliable source?" Asked the Chief Superintendent impatiently.

"We could dangle him a carrot or two. Sir." Almey offered.

The Chief superintendent leant to his left, towards the chief commander that whispered into his ear and began nodding at the information.

"Go ahead, use whatever means."

"Certainly Sir. Thank you."

"Anything else that I need to report upstairs?"

The youngest at the gathering at forty-nine years old was Scotland yard Chief Inspector Moran, dressed in civilian clothing for an appearance at the old bailey. He was usually the focus of the meetings, to brief on the top priority met investigations on anything from counter terrorism to white collar crime.

"Not on this particular case. We had an undercover that has gone AWOL. She was four years into the Greek-Cypriot mafia investigation, and it's been four and a half months now of no contact."

"Greek mafia? Why on earth does an investigation warrant four years? Can we not prosecute on what information we already have at hand? That's a huge drain on financial resources."

"It's O.C Sir. Part of operation Pear tree."

"Ok. We will have to bookmark it for another time. Have

the summary on my desk by the morning, I'll have to brief the Chief constable. That will be all."

THE END

PETE NICE

Next in this series.

CITY OF NO ANGELS

Printed in Great Britain
by Amazon